About the Author

USA Today bestsell... penned more than fif... She's married to her... active girls, and is a... found on Twitter, Facebook (Fan Page), and ... julesbennett.com. She holds contests via these three outlets with each release and loves to hear from readers!

Kimberly Lang is a Southern belle with a trouble-making streak and a great love of strong heroes and even stronger heroines. A former ballet dancer and English teacher, she now does yoga and writes the kind of books she always loved to read. She's married to her college sweetheart, is mum to the most amazing child on the planet, and shares her office space with a dog named Cupid. Visit her website at www.BooksByKimberly.com

The summer she turned eleven **Aimee Carson** left the children's section of the library, entered an aisle full of Mills & Boon, and pulled out a book. That story started a love affair that has followed her from her childhood in Florida to Alaska, Seattle, and finally South Dakota. She now counts herself lucky to be a part of Mills & Boon's family of authors. www.aimeecarson.com

American Affairs

COLLECTION

American Affairs: Florida Secrets

JULES BENNETT

KIMBERLY LANG

AIMEE CARSON

MILLS & BOON

First Published in Great Britain 2020
By Mills & Boon, an imprint of HarperCollins*Publishers*
1 London Bridge Street, London, SE1 9GF

AMERICAN AFFAIRS: FLORIDA SECRETS © 2020
Harlequin Books S.A.

Her Innocence, His Conquest © 2011 Jules Bennett
The Million-Dollar Question © 2014 Kimberly Lang
Dare She Kiss & Tell? © 2012 Aimee Carson

ISBN: 978-0-263-28197-2

MIX
Paper from
responsible sources
FSC™ C007454

FSC
www.fsc.org

This book is produced from independently certified FSC™ paper to ensure responsible forest management.

For more information visit: www.harpercollins.co.uk/green

Printed and bound in Spain
by CPI, Barcelona

HER INNOCENCE,
HIS CONQUEST

JULES BENNETT

To my sister, Angel, and best bud, Erin.
Thanks for the laughs, the brainstorming, the
movie nights, but most of all . . . CAKE!
I wouldn't make it through this without you
crazy guys. :)

Huge thanks to my editor, Charles Griemsman, for
the insightful book on Miami life.
I'm ready to move!

And lastly, big thanks to Roxanne St. Claire for
setting me straight on the seasonal weather in
Miami when she said they only have two seasons:
hot and hell. Thanks, Rocki!

One

"That's what I like to see. The foreman watching over her crew."

"Forewoman." Anastasia Clark concentrated on the swift work of her men and tried to keep her eyes off the broad-shouldered man who'd sidled right up against her. "You seem to keep making that blunder."

"So I do."

Risking a glance, Ana darted her gaze to the side. Zach Marcum was just as rugged and, dammit, sexy as he had been the last time she'd seen him in Victor Lawson's office nearly two years ago. Why did she have to find him so attractive?

"Let's step into your office," he told her, peering at her through his dark sunglasses. "We need to discuss some things."

Ana clutched her clipboard to her chest as she turned fully to face him. "We can't talk here?"

Who knew what went on behind those mirrored aviator shades he wore, but she was thankful she didn't have to look at him eye to eye. Those dark, exotic eyes could cause a woman to go utterly speechless. Any other woman, not her.

God help her. They didn't raise men this sexy where she was from in the Midwest.

Zach's mouth quirked up. "No, it's hot."

He turned on his work-booted heel and headed in the direction of her small trailer as if she were just supposed to fall in line simply because he said so. He was just like her father. Just because she found him one of the sexiest men she'd ever seen, didn't mean she thought his cocky attitude was acceptable.

Never in all of her life had she ever dealt with a project manager with such arrogance…or sex appeal. She had to omit that last thought from her mind or she'd have more to worry about on this job than Miami's daily afternoon rain.

If Victor Lawson hadn't been the world-renowned billionaire hotelier building this resort, Ana would've declined without hesitation.

She had plenty of work and more than a steady income, especially since she didn't spend on frivolous things. Every bit she made after bills—and her father's gambling counted as a bill—went into stocks, savings or to her mother.

But the meeting with Victor and The Marcum Agency forced her to face reality. This project would boost her reputation into amazing territory. Zach's twin, Cole, and his fiancée, Tamera, were the designing architects and wonderful people. And, from what Ana had heard, the couple had been reunited thanks to Victor Lawson hiring both The Marcum Agency and the architectural agency Tamera previously owned.

Ana hadn't met the Marcum twins' younger sister, Kayla, but she'd only heard amazing things about her as well.

Which left Zach. There was one in every family. One person who just had to be the star of every show, the flashy one, the one with all the attention, deserved or not.

Zach was a complete replica of her father—or at least the man her father used to be before he gambled away everything they owned. A handsome man who had more money than he knew what to do with so he flaunted everything he could, including and especially his charms, knowing the women would simply flock to his side.

Well, if Zach thought that's how she worked, he had another think coming. She was and always had been a professional. And she'd be damned if she'd let Zach and his architectural ego mess with her mind or the most important project she'd ever had the opportunity to contract.

She didn't have just herself to think of. She had a crew of men and women with families who depended on her. Not to mention her father, who had already called her seeking another ten thousand. If Ana's mother would just leave the man, Ana would pay for anything for her. All the money going to front her father's habit could be used to put her mother in the house of her dreams. And her father could fend for himself. He was long past due to stand up and act like the man he claimed to be.

Turning in her dusty boots, she followed Zach into her on-site office.

He'd already entered, making himself at home by taking a seat in an old yellow vinyl chair opposite her desk.

"What's up?" she asked, closing the door behind her to keep in the refreshing air-conditioning.

He slid those sexy sunglasses off his face, tossed them onto the drafted plans on her desk. He then had the gall to rake that heavy-lidded bedroom gaze over her face as if he expected her to get turned on and swoon.

The hellish Miami heat must be getting to her. She nearly did swoon.

"Did I do something to you?"

Stunned at his blunt question, Ana jerked back a bit. "Excuse me?"

Zach's hands rested on his narrow, denim-clad hips. "I've always been a good people reader. Comes from being the quiet one in the family, always sitting back and observing. What I'm getting from you is that you don't care much for me."

Nearly choking on her laughter, Ana propped a hip on the corner of her desk. No way was she going to sit completely down. She had to keep the upper hand here, on her turf. Instead of smacking him in the head with her clipboard, she professionally and calmly laid it on her desk.

"Zach, I hardly know you. I have no problem with you or our working relationship."

He stepped closer, his brows drawn together as if assessing her. "No, the issue isn't our working relationship. You're one of the most professional companies I've worked with, thus far. It's you. There's something about the way your back straightens, that defiant tilt of your chin when I come around. It's subtle, but your attitude is a bit forced professionally which makes me wonder what you're compensating for."

"Attitude?" she repeated. "Let's not get into attitudes or personal assessments. Is that all you came here for?"

"Where is the rest of your crew?"

Ana didn't fidget with her hands like she wanted to. No way would she let Zach know she was nervous or edgy.

"My crew will be here within the week." She looked him dead in the eye, even though it cost her heart extra beats. "We are finishing up another project in Seattle and the rain up there has put us behind by a month. Mother Nature doesn't care about deadlines."

Zach closed the gap between them, rested his hands on the edge of her desk, right next to her hip. "You are putting a multimillion-dollar deal on the line because you can't work through the weather?"

Now she rose to her full height, which still came in a good

three inches below his. "I can work through anything, Mr. Marcum, and remain within budget and deadline."

A smile broke through the ruggedness of his stubbled face. "There's that slight attitude switch again. You're getting all worked up and you called me Mr. Marcum. It was Zach just a few minutes ago."

Millionaire or not, Zach had a bad-boy side that made her want to scream. Why did he have to have so much sex appeal? And most importantly, why did he have to know it?

No, the most important point, she argued with herself, was why did she find him so damn attractive and infuriating at the same time?

"May as well call me Zach," he continued with that cocky grin. "We'll be seeing so much of each other until this project is complete that we'll practically be married."

Ana smoothed stray hairs off her sweaty forehead and gave him her sweetest, sarcastic smile. "Lucky me."

"I knew you'd come around," he mocked. "The concrete will be delivered on Monday. Your crew will be available then, I assume?"

Ana nodded, keeping her mouth shut. Even though he was professional in every aspect, his personality grated on her nerves. Even so, she couldn't let it show, but she would make him choke on his charm. She refused, *refused* to let him see just how he affected her feminine, non-businesswoman side.

She wondered if any woman ever threw what he offered back in his face. Probably not. And not that he was offering her anything by any means. God knew she was just one of the guys, always had been. She'd grown up on construction sites and always seemed to blend in.

But how easy it would be to fall for the sexy, bad-boy image he portrayed—and portrayed well—knowing all the while beneath the well-worn jeans and black fitted T-shirt a millionaire businessman lurked. Ana bet he lived up to the total bad-boy persona and rode a Harley and had at least one tattoo. Oh, what she wouldn't give to explore his body to find that ink.

"You're overheating."

She jerked her attention back to him. "What?"

His hand came up to her cheek. "You're too hot. Get some water."

Get some… What? God, she couldn't think. Not when his thumb caressed her heated skin. If he didn't stop, a little flush would be the least of her worries.

How in the world could her body betray her like that? She couldn't, wouldn't, fall in line with what she was sure was a long trail of busty bimbos tripping over each other to fall at Zach's feet.

"I'm fine," she insisted, swatting his hand away. "I need to get back out there."

"You'll get a drink of water before you fall over in this heat." He moved to the small fridge beside her desk and pulled out a bottle of water. "Drink. I can't have my forewoman out of commission before the first beam is raised."

Taking the bottle from his hands, she twisted the cap, knowing he was right. "Thanks."

The cold, refreshing water was what she needed, but no way would she admit that to Mr. Overinflated Ego. And she certainly wouldn't admit that his touch had affected her in ways the heat of the scorching Miami sun in June couldn't.

Mercy, the man was potent. And she'd thought his looks were sinful. Maybe he deserved that cocky attitude he sported.

"Better," he commented, still studying her face. "You need to keep water with you in this weather."

"I have a cooler out there for me and my crew. This isn't my first job, you know."

His breathtaking smile widened. "Yes, I know your reputation."

What in the world did that mean? The sultry tone, the way he cocked his head to the side made his words take on a whole new meaning. He acted as if he knew who she'd been intimate with. Surely he wasn't going to get personal with her...was he?

Tingles shot through her body from the top of her overheated head to the soles of her feet. She didn't want these uninvited emotions. Didn't have time for such nonsense. She worked with sexy, cocky men on a daily basis, but for some reason Zach's heavy-lidded gaze, his shadowed jaw and all that alpha attitude made her tingle in spots she didn't know could tingle.

"Mr. Marcum—"

"Zach," he interrupted.

"Zach. As much as I'd love to sit in here and sip water in front of that air conditioner, I really need to get back out there. Was there anything else you desire?"

The arrogant smile disappeared, replaced by a slight shrug of his shoulder. "My desires are endless, but we'll start with keeping you hydrated."

She'd seriously have to watch her wording around this man, but she had a terrible feeling anything around him could be a double entendre.

Ana capped the water bottle and led the way to the door. She opened it, gesturing for Zach to pass through.

"See you tomorrow," he called as he strode to his flashy motorcycle that no doubt cost more than some of her crew's yearly wages. Perhaps she should load up on the cold water. Between watching that man saunter away and the unbearable heat, she'd need all the hydration she could get.

But she quickly reminded herself that her father had all the charm in the world. He'd once been at the top of his game, too, in his own construction career. But his gambling habit and his love of numerous women shattered any hero status Ana had given him.

A psychiatrist would have so much fun in her head. But she didn't need to pay some stranger to tell her she had commitment issues because her father had shattered her world by destroying her faith. Nor did she need them to tell her she lived a simple life, even though she had money to be extravagant, because she didn't want to get pulled into a world she couldn't control.

She turned back to the site, but her body tingled all over again at the sound of the roaring engine as Zach sped away on his bike. Mercy, that man made an impact even when he wasn't in sight.

Sexual harassment. That's precisely the lawsuit he was going to get slapped with if he didn't quit antagonizing Ana. His flirtations had been subtle, especially for him, but he just couldn't separate business and pleasure when it came to Miss Anastasia Clark.

But how could he keep his distance? He was architectural project manager, after all. Granted, he was finding mundane reasons to stop by and the project was only in the second week of construction.

And if the rest of her crew didn't show by the week's end, she'd be seeing a whole lot more of him. Personal aspect aside, this project had to be flawless, within budget and on time.

Today, though, he was glad he'd stopped by on his way into the office. Damn fool woman was on the verge of heatstroke.

A distressed damsel…his favorite kind. Women like that appreciated all his assistance and in turn, fell for his charms.

Zach nearly laughed. He had a feeling Ana didn't fall as easily as most women, nor would she appreciate his help. No, from what little he'd been around her, he knew she was independent, stubborn and private. That was the type of woman from whom he should duck for cover, but he found himself wanting to dig deeper, to uncover her secrets.

She had a vulnerability about her, something that reminded him of his baby sister. Both women wanted to be so strong, call all the shots, but they still had a gentleness about them.

Ana wouldn't like that he'd zeroed in on that trait so quickly after meeting her, but he understood her kind.... He was a master of hiding feelings himself. Wasn't he still confused and intrigued by his ex-wife? A woman who slid out of his life as easily as she had slid in and had recently returned wanting him back? How pathetic was that whole situation? She may want him back, but Zach refused to put himself on the line like that again. Sometimes in life second chances were necessary, but his ex-wife would not get another chance to hold his heart. Not after she left town with a guy Zach at one time considered a friend, leaving behind only a pathetic note.

Turning to much more pleasing matters, Zach didn't miss the fact that Ana damn near combusted when he'd caressed her flushed cheek. Her moment of silence wasn't only due to her being overworked and overheated.

And that was just one more thing about her that intrigued him. He'd worked with women before, but skinny white tanks and well-worn jeans never looked so good on any of them. Maybe it was all that deep crimson hair Ana had piled in a curly mess atop her head. Maybe it was the way she silently challenged him both professionally and personally.

Yeah, he was in for it. Anastasia was definitely a what-you-see-is-what-you-get girl even though she tried to hide her private and personal life.

The flashy socialites he was used to were shallow, no digging deep there. And that was the best kind. They always knew the rules up front. He didn't do relationships, didn't do marriage. Fun times were all he wanted in his future.

But something about peeling away Ana's intriguing layers

had him smiling. The passion she no doubt buried deep would be amazing if he could just get to it. She would be another perfect distraction—and there had been plenty of distractions lately—to get his mind off his ex, Melanie.

Zach pulled into his designated parking slot at The Marcum Agency, noting Cole's empty spot. Now that his twin brother was engaged to his college sweetheart, Tamera Stevens, Zach was seeing less and less of him.

Good for them, so long as the lovebirds didn't try to play matchmaker. Every time someone found love, they assumed every single person in their life was looking, too. Quite the opposite, in fact, for Zach. He wanted to remain single. Actually he loved every minute of being a bachelor—that way he could nurse his heart privately, put it back together piece by shattered piece and never give it out again.

Zach made his way up to his office, nodding to his assistant, Becky. As usual she was on the phone making appointments, taking new client questions and scheduling meetings with contractors.

He closed the door to his office, which might not have been the smartest move considering he was now alone with his thoughts and, once again, his thoughts circled back to Miss Clark and her dark red curls. She certainly had the proverbial temper that went along with the hair, but he had a feeling calling her on that stereotypical assessment would be detrimental to their working relationship, not to mention any personal involvement he wished to have.

Ana's quick temper and attitude rivaled that of his ex-wife. Perhaps that's why his mind kept going back to Ana, and why he both had an issue with her and was attracted to her from the get-go.

Was it her fault she reminded him of the woman who'd left before the ink on their marriage license dried? No, but it was her fault that he couldn't get her off his mind. If she weren't so damned intriguing, there wouldn't be a problem.

That irked him. What irked him even more was how one person could remind him of both his sister whom he loved with his whole heart and the woman who had shattered him to pieces.

But Ana had the best reputation in the business and had never had even one complaint about her work ethic or the finished product. Ana's construction company was one of the top in the nation and he knew he'd made the right choice in accepting her bid—even though this was the biggest project she'd ever tackled, he and Cole had faith she would work that much harder. He knew she'd started her company from scratch and built it up herself, one beam at a time. He couldn't help but admire that, considering he, Cole and Kayla had built their own firm on nothing but hopes and prayers as well.

But the woman had his thoughts all jumbled together. He didn't know if he wanted to pursue her or avoid her like the plague. Oh, well, he had a year or more to figure that out. Not that he'd ever taken that much time getting to know a woman. The chemistry was either there or it wasn't. In this case, the chemistry was most definitely there.

Zach sat down at his desk, pulled up the spreadsheet on his computer and checked to see where they were on the schedule.

If Ana's crew came even a week late, they would still be ahead of schedule, but he wouldn't let up. If he slacked now, the whole project could fall behind. On time or early was the only way he would work. Especially with Victor Lawson.

The man had the capabilities to launch The Marcum Agency and Ana's company, Clark Construction, into a whole new stratum of clientele. Just another reason to remain close to Ana's side.

"Zach."

His assistant's voice cut through his thoughts. He pressed the intercom button. "Yes, Becky?"

"Miss Clark is on line one."

Did the woman have a sixth sense where he was concerned? Here he was thinking about her at the precise time she decided to call and interrupt the beginning of what was sure to have been a wonderful daydream.

"Put her through."

He picked up the receiver, pressed the button. "Anastasia."

"Zach, we've got trouble."

Two

He sat straight up in his chair. "What is it?"

"There's a tropical storm moving toward Miami."

"I hadn't heard about it," Zach stated, fingers moving swiftly over his keyboard to look at a weather map. "How far out is it?"

"We've got a few days before it reaches us," she explained. "There's still a chance it'll turn or break up, but I wanted your opinion. To be honest, I'm not that experienced in tropical storms seeing as how I'm originally from the Midwest."

Zach blew out a breath, not too worried once he saw the green blob on the radar map. "They are pretty common, but we certainly can't afford to lose time. The good news is we don't have any actual structure up, so if it does reach land, there should be little damage, if any."

"Hopefully this will be the worst of Mother Nature's fury and any storms will miss us when we actually start on the construction," Ana added.

He closed the screen. "We'll keep an eye on it. For now, though, continue as planned."

She hesitated and Zach wasn't sure if she'd heard him until she said, "Um…sounds good. Thanks."

The pause she gave, as well as the shaky response, intrigued him. Gone was the firm, confident Ana. Interesting, he thought. Unchartered territory unsettled the hard-as-steel forewoman.

He disconnected the call just as his brother strode into his office.

Zach smiled, leaned back in his seat and crossed his ankle over his knee. "Well, good to see you in the office."

Cole's wide grin obviously couldn't be contained. "Sorry I've left this project in your hands, but Tam needed a break after her father's passing."

Cole's wife, Tamera, had lost her father to lung cancer a month ago. Because Cole and Tamera had recently been reunited, they took a much-needed vacation to Aruba after working on the design for the Miami resort.

"I understand. How's she doing?"

On a sigh, Cole eased himself into the leather club chair across from Zach's desk. "She's holding up. I honestly think the discovery that her father was behind me breaking off our engagement eleven years ago was almost as much of a blow to her as Walter's death."

Tamera's late father had nearly altered her and Cole's future by coming between them when they were college sweethearts. But fate's gentle hand guided them back together after eleven years of separation. Walter hadn't wanted Cole to marry his daughter, hadn't wanted a man who couldn't financially provide when he was too busy caring for his siblings after his parents' death.

Zach knew the two had loved each other and the breakup nearly caused Cole to have a nervous breakdown. But the man had just worked harder as he and Zach finished college and started their own firm.

Cole had never been the same since calling off the engagement years ago, but now that he had Tamera back in his life, Zach's twin was in a much better place.

Okay, so maybe love was meant for some people. But very few.

"You're good together," Zach observed. "She's strong and you're there for her. She'll get through this."

Cole nodded and motioned toward the blueprints spread across Zach's desk. "How's everything coming at the site?"

"No glitches yet." Zach gazed down to the design. "I feel like a kid waiting on Christmas. I just can't wait to see this completed."

"We all feel that way." Cole lifted a brow. "Want to tell me what's bothering you?"

Damn. He hated this whole "twin intuition" thing they had always shared. Some people rolled their eyes or laughed at the idea that twins could actually share a bond that deep, but Cole and Zach knew it was possible.

"She shouldn't be so fascinating," Zach blurted out. "Why does she have to get under my skin? And, more importantly, why do I let her?"

Cole chuckled. "We're talking about the forewoman? Anastasia?"

Zach blew out a breath. "Yeah."

"She is attractive," Cole agreed. "But not your typical choice. What's got you so riled up all of a sudden?"

"I can't put my finger on it."

God knew he'd spent countless moments trying to pinpoint exactly what it was about Ana that made her the subject of every blasted thought lately.

"Perhaps she's immune to your charms and that's what's gotten you so bothered." Cole smirked at Zach's scowl. "Just a suggestion. Or maybe you're drawn because she's strong-willed. Like Melanie."

Cole rarely mentioned Melanie's name. And even though he wasn't far from the truth, Zach refused to respond. Silence spoke volumes, though.

"Seriously." Cole leaned forward, his elbows on his knees. "Maybe she is the one who will finally push you over that last hurdle to get over your ex-wife. I doubt Ana is like the typical giggly gold diggers you've been seeing."

True, Ana had been matching Zach instead of allowing him to keep control of their conversations. She'd been an equal. With her take-charge attitude, Ana wasn't about to let her guard slip, especially where a man was concerned.

Something about her almost seemed hard in that aspect. Had something happened in her past? Perhaps just working for so many years around manly men had put that hard edge to her personality.

Who knows? More importantly, why the hell was he spending so much time trying to dissect someone who technically worked for him? All he wanted was a little one-on-one contact.

"I won't deny she's sexy as hell," Zach told his brother. "But she's controlling and all business."

"And you have a problem with all business, don't you?"

"Only when that stiff side comes from a stunning, frustrating female I'm going to be working with for the next year." Zach stared at his brother across the desk. "I just need to consider Ana one of the guys and forget that she looks like a woman who should be wearing diamonds and dresses instead of a hard hat and a tool belt."

Cole leaned forward, his hands flat on the glass-topped desk. "Why forget about it? Why not present an opportunity for her to be that diamonds-and-dress woman? I mean, if you can't get that image out of your head, maybe there's a reason."

Zach nearly laughed at the thought. "You're in love and it's hindering your thought process. Ana would spit in my eye if I suggested I take her out."

"Sounds like you're scared of the possibility."

Zach glared. "I'm not scared of anything."

"Prove it. Take her to the party Victor is throwing next weekend. Call it business, if that makes you feel better."

Zach laughed. "Why the hell are we even talking about this? She's not my type, so it shouldn't matter what she looks like in a formal atmosphere. I'm more concerned about what she looks like in a much more intimate setting."

Cole eyed him, the smirk still in place. "We're talking about it because you can't get her off your mind. If you think you can't get her to be your date, then don't worry about it. She's probably not interested anyway. And we both know that's exactly what this all boils down to."

Not interested? That wasn't possible. He'd seen the way her pulse kicked up, her breath hitched when he'd rubbed her cheek. No, Ana was most definitely interested.

So what did he intend to do about it?

Pathetic. Utterly and completely pathetic.

Zach found himself, for the second time today, heading toward the mysterious redhead surveying the construction site as she stood between two of her crew members. Two men who towered over her and stood just a bit too close.

Okay, so jealousy wasn't pretty. He wasn't admitting to that severe emotion. But he didn't like that she considered herself "one of the guys." She was anything but.

And so what if Cole's mocking words fueled his already raging fire? He refused to believe he was here because his twin planted a seed of doubt in his head about being able to get Ana to date him. Why did he care what she thought of him?

Because for some reason she already showed disdain toward him and he hadn't done a damn thing to her. Obviously she'd had a bitter experience, probably with some jackass on the job site, and now he'd stepped in, ready to charm her into spending some intimate time together for the next several months of the project. Perfect timing. Was she worth the trouble of proving himself?

Dammit. He'd never felt the need to prove himself to anyone before.

"Zach."

Breaking through his thoughts, and halting his steps toward Ana, Zach turned his attention from the sexy forewoman's sweet denim-clad backside. His sister, Kayla, stepped from her pearl-colored four-door sedan looking beautiful as always with her dark hair smoothed back from her delicate face. With her bright pink suit and shiny silver heels, she certainly didn't belong on the dusty, filthy construction site. Good thing she was more the decorator for their firm. She certainly added beauty to everything around her simply by being there.

"I just missed you at the office." Kayla closed the gap between them and smiled. Then she turned her attention over Zach's shoulder toward Ana. "Hi, we haven't formally met yet. I'm Kayla Marcum. You must be Anastasia Clark."

Zach hadn't even heard Ana approach. He turned his body so he could see both women.

"You can call me Ana."

The two women smiled at each other and Zach couldn't help but notice they were both so different, yet equally as striking and vibrant. Even though Kayla was polished to a shine and never anything less than perfect, Ana's fit body and well-toned arms proved she cared just as much about how she looked and that she was polished herself—in a whole other way. And he certainly didn't think any "sisterly" thoughts about Miss Clark.

"What did you need?" Zach asked his sister.

Off in the distance one of the men whistled, and not a

"whistle while you work" kind. This was the stereotypical wolf whistle.

Zach didn't turn to see what unprofessional jerk had made the tacky gesture, but he did notice Ana excuse herself and march over to a group of men setting up barriers and preparing the perimeter of the structure for the concrete.

"Sorry," Zach said.

Kayla shrugged. "No need for you to apologize."

"I'm apologizing for mankind in general. That's rude."

His baby sister rolled her eyes and smiled. "Like you've never whistled at a woman before?"

"Guilty, but I haven't for a long time because I realized how disrespectful it was."

Kayla peered over Zach's shoulder. "Looks like Ana has the situation under control."

Zach turned, surprised to see Ana off to the side with a young, twentysomething man, her hands on her hips, shoulders back. He couldn't hear the words, but from the look on the employee's face, he was not on the receiving end of a pleasant conversation.

Oh, what Zach wouldn't give to be able to listen in on that tongue-lashing. Women in power were nothing short of sexy, he thought, so long as he remained in control.

Zach focused his attention back on Kayla. "What did you need me for?"

"Oh, I wanted to let you know I had to go out of town for another buying trip. I'm leaving now. The jet is waiting for me."

She eyed him with those wide, rich eyes, grinned, and Zach's stomach clinched in a most uncomfortable knot. She always got that look before she asked an unfavorable favor. He didn't even want to know what put that evil sparkle in her eye, but he had a feeling he was about to find out.

"No," he said before she could even ask whatever question she had swirling around in her pretty little head.

A smile spread across her face as she cocked her head to the side. "I'll email you a detailed list of everything you need to know."

"No."

"Please?"

"No."

"Cole would do it for you," she insisted with just enough of a pout to be cute and impossible to say no to.

Zach laughed. "First of all, I'm never getting married. Second of all, Cole would never, *ever* coordinate a wedding shower."

Kayla sighed in frustration. "I didn't ask you to coordinate it. I just need you to work on a few details for me while I'm gone. It won't be anything major."

Zach gave her his best bored look, crossed his arms over his chest and waited. For what, he wasn't sure. But he certainly knew he did not want any part of planning any kind of shower. Not wedding, not baby. Nothing. He designed and oversaw steel structures. He did not assemble froufrou place cards with little bells.

"Fine." The squeal of delight as Kayla jumped and wrapped her arms around him made him smile. "You knew I'd cave," he muttered.

"You always do with me." She eased back. "I'll forward you my spreadsheet once I'm in the air."

As she teetered away on spiky heels, her words registered. "Wait," he called after her. "Spreadsheet?"

"See you in a week," she yelled over her shoulder as she slid behind the wheel of her sleek luxury car.

"God, Zach, I'm so sorry." He turned to Ana's frustrated tone. "I hope she didn't leave because of Nate."

"Nate?"

"My ex-employee."

Zach shook his head. "Oh, no. She's on her way to the airport. Wait. *Ex*-employee?"

"I fired him."

Dumbfounded, Zach stared at Ana.

"Don't look at me like that," she insisted, turning to walk toward her office. "I won't accept anything less than professional behavior on the job."

Zach fell into step beside her. "Considering this is my site, too, I have some say. He whistled, Ana. Kayla wasn't offended and if she wasn't then there shouldn't be a problem."

She climbed up the rickety, wrought-iron steps, placed her hand on the knob and looked over her shoulder. "That I would've tolerated. Maybe. But as I got closer, his back was to me and he said some derogatory things about her *and* me that I'd rather not repeat. I won't accept demeaning comments toward women from my workers and neither should you."

Stunned at her matter-of-fact tone, Zach followed her into the air-conditioned office. "I don't accept anything less than professional behavior. But I would appreciate being brought in on such dealings that have any implication on this site."

With her back to him, she pulled open the top drawer of a file cabinet and began shuffling through papers before pulling one out and reading, still with her back to him. Not that he didn't appreciate the view.

"Hello? Are you listening?"

She peered over her shoulder. "I'll apologize for acting without consulting you, Zach, but I did what I thought was best."

"Your instincts were right. Just remember we're married to this project and like any good marriage, we should discuss major decisions."

"That's the second time you've mentioned this project being a marriage," she told him, her brow lifted in curiosity. "Being a world-famous bachelor, I'm surprised you know about marriages."

Damn. "Don't stereotype me, Ana. People aren't always what they seem or what the media make them out to be."

"You're right. Sometimes people are worse." She dropped the file on the edge of the desk and stepped toward him. "You haven't even thanked me for standing up for your sister, a woman whom I just met, by the way."

Zach took in her flushed face and the passion in her eyes. He didn't know what he wanted to do more, applaud her for standing up for his sister, kiss her senseless or throttle her for making him so damn confused lately.

Any woman who could match him in conversation and passion would surely match him in other, more fascinating areas. Perhaps that's why he couldn't get her off his mind. Beneath her cool exterior lurked an ember he wanted to fan to life.

"I'm just surprised you fired him without hesitation," Zach stated.

"That's because you know nothing about me, Zach." She looked back down at the papers on her desk. "If you did, you would know that I don't tolerate men showcasing their testosterone."

And that statement just solidified his previous assessment. Some jerk in her past had given her every reason in the world to be bitter toward the entire male gender, at least on a personal level.

"Anastasia, since we're going to be together on an almost daily basis for months, I think we better clear some things up real fast." Zach paused, waiting for her wounded eyes to come back up and meet his. "That chip on your shoulder has got to go. There's no way to work this long together and not have personal involvement on some level. If you have something to say to me, stop dancing around the topic and just say it. I know you've had a bad experience. You've got distressed damsel written all over your face."

He waited for her to correct him or defend herself. But damn if the spunky woman didn't break into a smile. The pointer just clicked upward a notch on the Ana Admiration Chart.

"Are you finished analyzing me?" she asked with a tilt of her head. "You may be used to flaunting your million-dollar smile at women and having them swoon at your feet, but don't look for me to get involved with you on anything other than a professional level. I have no secret past that you need to worry yourself with, nor am I a— What did you call me? A distressed damsel? Do you need an excuse to ride to a lady's rescue, Zach? Well, ride on. I'm not interested."

She advanced even closer. Zach refused to step back. He wanted to see those amber flecks in her green eyes. He wanted to breathe in that hint of floral fragrance that probably came from the shampoo she had used in all that hair—he didn't see her as a perfume spritzer. He wanted to watch her mouth as she matched him in this interesting conversation.

These sensations he was feeling and the head games he was playing with himself were certainly nothing he'd ever experienced on a job site before.

Damn, she was the sexiest little thing. He couldn't recall a woman getting in his face, demanding attention from him that was in no way a sexual come-on.

Purposeful or not, he was beyond turned on.

He had a feeling that the more he hung around Miss Anastasia Clark, the more fascinated he'd be.

"I've worked with men my whole life," she continued, "so I'm immune to charm. There's no come-on line you could throw my way that I haven't repelled before. So if your intention is to try your playboy style on me, you're wasting energy that would be put to better use on some busty socialite."

Yup. She was definitely going to be fascinating.

"Feel better?" he asked, not even bothering to hold back a smile.

Her brows drew together. "What?"

"Do you feel better since you put me in my place?"

Rolling her eyes, Ana laughed. "I doubt anyone has put you in your place, but I did want to let you know not to waste your smiles and flirtations on me. It wasn't professional, but you asked and I don't lie."

Zach rested his hip against her desk, in absolutely no hurry to leave. "What if I don't consider flirting with you a waste?"

She started to walk around her desk, but froze. "You're kidding, right? Can we get through this project without embarrassing ourselves?"

"Sure. On one condition." He waited until she turned fully to face him once again, and for some reason he opened his mouth without thinking the demand through. "I need your help planning my brother and soon-to-be sister-in-law's bridal shower."

Ana shook her head as if she hadn't heard him correctly. "Excuse me? Bridal shower? You starting a moonlighting career?"

He should've known she wouldn't make this easy for him. Perhaps, though, she would think he had a softer side and find him impossibly irresistible.

Yeah, right. With the smirk on her face, she was happy to have ammunition with which to make fun of him.

Yes, Ana was the perfect distraction to keep Melanie out of his mind.

"My sister is in charge, but she had to leave suddenly." And why was he explaining all of this to her? Since when did he ask to be mocked? "She asked me to help."

With a quirk of her arched brow, Ana eyed him. "So why are you sucking me into this? I've never been married."

He laughed. "You're a woman."

"So glad you noticed," she said dryly.

"Oh, I noticed." His eyes traveled down her fit body, unable to stay in one specific spot because she was just so…amazing. "I've noticed a lot about you."

She didn't cross her arms over her chest like most women would've. Ana kept her hands to her sides and actually tilted her head and rolled her eyes as if he was boring the life out of her. God, she had a strong backbone. How could he not find that attractive?

"Should I be flattered you're lumping me in with the other lucky ladies in your life?" she asked.

Zach chuckled. "Oh, Anastasia, you're definitely nothing like the ladies in my life, I assure you. You stand out all on your own."

Her eyes widened, her nostrils flared. "Can we get back to when you were begging for my help? My heart can't take all these romantic lines."

Begging? If he wasn't careful, she *would* have him begging.

Zach stared into her eyes, which wasn't hard considering she was nearly as tall as he was. What had made her so hard, so bitter? This wasn't about the project.

Even though he told himself it wasn't his problem, he couldn't help but wonder what it would take to make her warm up to him. He didn't want to be her shrink; he wanted to be her lover.

"Kayla's emailing me a to-do list," Zach explained. "What do you say we meet for dinner later and discuss the shower plans and the project?"

"You've got to be kidding me!" Ana exclaimed with a laugh. "You expect me to go on a date with you to help with a bridal shower to which I know neither party getting married? Is this how you normally get women?"

"Forget it." He wasn't going to beg or show weakness, no matter how much he needed help with this shower. He had no doubt Kayla's list would be detailed and lengthy, but he'd do it on his own. "And don't flatter yourself. I wasn't asking you for a date. It was business."

Let her stew on that.

"Business?" Ana seemed to think about her options. "Fine. I'll meet you at Hancock's at six. It's the only restaurant I've tried since I've been here and I know the food's good. If you're one minute late, I'm leaving."

He stepped closer, so close she tipped her head back to look into his eyes. "I'll pick you up at the condo you're renting. My assistant will have your address. I'll make reservations and tonight, Ana, you'll try something different."

"I'm not looking for different," she insisted.

Zach took her bare, slender shoulders in his hands and hauled her against his chest. "Neither was I."

Her eyes dropped to his lips. "You wouldn't."

"Timing's wrong," he muttered, hating himself for being a gentleman. "Just consider this your warning for when it's right."

The pulse beneath the sun-kissed skin on her neck pounded almost as hard as his own. Her tongue darted out to moisten her lips and he knew she was aroused. Welcome to the club.

The chirp of a cell attached to Ana's hip startled him. He stepped back, giving her a chance to answer.

Her hand shook as she jerked the phone from the holder. "Hello."

In a split second, her face went from passionate and curious to pale and stiff. "I'm busy right now."

Interesting. Zach was just grateful he wasn't on the receiving end of that icy voice. No, he was just fine being on her steamy side.

Which just went to prove his point. She wasn't immune to his charms like she insisted. The brittle, professional tone she used on him was nothing like now. At least when she spoke to him, there was heat in her voice. There was passion in her arguments.

"I will get back with you when I can. I'm working."

She disconnected the call, clipped the phone back on her hip, keeping her eyes averted from him for a minute.

Zach wondered who could get her so upset with a thirty-second call, but someone had and in the process had taken away the meager progress he'd made in chiseling away at her secure walls.

"Everything okay?" he asked, growing uncomfortable with her silence.

She glanced up at him, still void of any emotion he'd just seen in her eyes moments ago. "Fine," she snapped. "Now, as I told my father, I need to get to work."

Her father. He obviously didn't hold a special place in his little girl's heart. A pang of hurt settled in his chest at the ever-present memories of his own father.

Zach shook off the morose thought, not wanting to delve into his own past when he had the present and the future to concentrate on. All he wanted was to make this project run on schedule, within budget and be the most brilliant structure Victor Lawson had ever laid eyes, and money, on.

Getting the fiery Miss Anastasia Clark into his bed would be an added perk. And she would be there.

Unable to resist touching her smooth, heated skin once more, and because he wanted to replace that icy glaze in her eyes with anything else, Zach ran a fingertip down her cheek until her eyes locked on his.

He offered her a grin, holding her chin until the corners of her mouth eased up just a notch. "See you at six." Zach released her and headed for the door. "Oh, and don't wear your tool belt, Anastasia."

Three

Dressed and ready, Ana stood on the balcony of her condo overlooking the ocean. She loved the coast. Too bad all her jobs weren't in a sunny climate with the smell of the ocean to accompany her to work every day.

Most of her work took her from her Midwest home either farther west or north. Florida was certainly a place she could get used to. Building lavish, multimillion-dollar resorts was another thing she could get used to. Her company normally dealt with businesses or hotels and some smaller-scaled resorts, but no job compared to what she had going on now.

There was the day spa in Colorado that had left an impact because she had built it for post-cancer patients to not only receive treatments, but to get some much-needed pampering during their recovery time. That had left a special place in her heart.

And now Victor's resort would also leave an emotional impact.

She checked her watch once again. Zach had two minutes

before he was late. Typical chauvinist. Men like him thrived on the fact that women waited on them. And they expected their women to gasp with delight when they showed up at the door with an elaborate bouquet or expensive bottle of wine. As if that's all it took to get *her* into bed.

No, thanks. She wasn't the type to sigh, nor was she that easy to get into bed. Considering she'd never gone to bed with a man, she certainly wasn't going to start with Zach Marcum. He'd probably think being a virgin at twenty-eight was unheard of, but she was living proof. If her skirt-chasing father hadn't turned her off to intimacy, the gossip and stories she'd heard from her own mostly male crew over the years would surely have done the trick.

Besides, Zach was already getting more than he deserved. He was so used to women jumping through hoops for him at a moment's notice, and here she was following orders like a good little puppy. That was it. She would not, she vowed as she watched the whitecaps roll onto the beach, follow him into the bedroom. Handsome, sexy, impossibly charming. Yes, he was all that and so much more, but she had willpower. She'd survived this long in a workforce full of good-looking men. Surely she could work a few months with one drop-dead gorgeous playboy.

The heavy knock on her door jarred her from her thoughts. Cursing the jittery nerves deep in her belly, Ana smoothed a hand down her bright blue dress. She'd packed several dresses for this trip, certainly not with the hopes of going on a date, business or otherwise, but because she knew Victor Lawson liked to throw parties and show off his Star Island home and she would be expected to attend. But the dress she wore tonight wasn't fancy. Just a simple, fitted cotton tank. Though the dress showed off her slender, fit body, it did little to give her any of the feminine curves she wished she had. She was and always had been plain, simple…boring.

She strode through her condo and opened the door before she changed her mind.

Zach's swift intake of breath sent shivers through her. Zach Marcum shocked over a woman? Interesting. Maybe he didn't expect his women to do all the ogling.

"You look amazing."

Ana laughed. "You sound surprised. You did tell me to leave off my tool belt. Right?"

She didn't want to be affected by his heated gaze as it traveled from her freshly painted pale pink toes, up her bare legs to the rounded neckline of her dress.

"I just didn't expect…this," he said, bringing those dark chocolate eyes up to meet hers.

"It's just a plain dress, Zach." She had to lighten this tension. "I'm sure you've seen women in much fancier things."

"I have," he agreed, "but none of them could pull off simplicity like you can."

She felt a bit uneasy that this playboy was first speechless and then complimentary. Still she laughed, grabbed her key and slid it into her purse. "If you want me to put my sweaty tank and holey jeans back on, I can, but it comes with a hard hat and tool belt."

The smirk she'd come to know spread across his face. "While I admit you do look amazing in your work attire, I much prefer this sexy look."

Oh, dear. She may just sigh after all. Sexy? Now she saw why women fell so easily into his trap.

"If you're not too stunned at the fact that I do actually look like a woman off duty, shouldn't we go? You did make reservations, right?"

Zach brushed an auburn curl from her face, tucked it behind her ear. "Damn if I don't lose my head around you."

She didn't want to react to him, but her body couldn't help it. She tingled everywhere his eyes roamed. He might as well have caressed her with his big, strong hands. But that was all physical. There was no emotion deeper than that, which was fine. Ana could handle sexual attraction, but she sure as hell didn't intend to act on it.

Before this situation got even more uncomfortable, she ushered him out the door and headed toward the elevator.

When they slid into the elevator, Zach reached over and hit the Lobby button, then turned to her. "I have to say, not much makes me lose my train of thought. But that dress... It's like second skin."

"Did you think I'd actually show up wearing only sweat and my hammer?"

He closed his eyes. "Hold on. I'm getting a fantasy."

Ana couldn't help it; she laughed. "You're pathetic."

"Guilty." Zach shrugged. "Seriously, I owe you a nice dinner for standing up for my sister today."

Shocked, Ana smiled. "Is that all this is about?"

The elevator opened and Zach took hold of her elbow to usher her out.

"That and I need your help with planning this shower."

"You could've just given me the list of things Kayla wants you to do. There was no need for you to use up a free evening with me."

Now Zach laughed, forcing her attention back to the rich, soothing tone. He jerked her to a stop and forced her to face him.

"What's so funny?" she demanded.

"I never took you for a coward."

Ana wanted to wipe that knowing smirk off his face, but he was right. She was a coward on so many levels. He had no idea. She'd seen his playboy confidence, but when he'd conversed with his sister, his ego took a backseat to brotherly love and compassion. She didn't know what side of Zach she'd see next and the thought that she might just find every side attractive frightened her. She liked to be in control and around him, she wasn't.

"Call me what you want, but we both know you're so used to getting what you want that you made up this excuse to get me on a date." She tried her best to control her growing attraction to his bad-boy persona and heavy-lidded bedroom eyes. "I know your company has an impeccable reputation, but crossing the line into anything personal would be a mistake for both of us."

His smiling eyes grew dark, sexy. "You know as well as I do that that statement was just wasted breath. Deny all you want, but this mutual attraction is only going to cause more and more tension throughout the project if we ignore it."

She crossed her arms, lifted her chin and refused to get into such a personal discussion in a hotel lobby. She tugged free of his grasp on her arm and walked through the automatic doors and out onto the covered breezeway.

Thankfully the valet was absent, so Ana continued. "I'm not denying anything. I'm stating a fact that this project is my number one priority. I don't have time for a personal life, Zach."

Zach reached out, curled his hands around her bare shoulders and looked straight into her eyes. "This project is my number one priority, too, but I won't let it consume my downtime. And what we—yes, we—do together in our personal time has nothing to do with our working relationship."

This was an argument she knew she couldn't win, but once he found out she wasn't experienced, would he be as interested?

Zach led her toward a car she'd never seen the likes of before. The emblem read Bugatti, whatever that meant. Probably another word for "my car costs more than your yearly salary." Whatever the type, it was parked in a no-parking zone. Of course, the valets wouldn't dare move the superexpensive vehicle.

After assisting her into the lavish car, Ana settled into the soft leather seats as Zach slid in behind the wheel. When he didn't start the car immediately, Ana glanced over.

"Something wrong?" she asked.

He stared out the windshield, squinting against the sharp sunlight. "I'm beginning to think so."

Confused, she waited for him to elaborate, but the silence continued for several long moments.

"This is going to get complicated." He turned to her. "Whether we ignore the sexual tension or not. You and I are going to get complicated."

Ana didn't know how to respond. This level of sexual tension wasn't something she knew much about, but she had a gut-wrenching feeling she was about to find out sooner rather than later.

Blowing out a breath, Zach reached out and brushed her hair over her shoulders, his palm settled on the curve of her shoulder. "I'm up for the challenge. Are you?"

Could he hear the thumping in her chest? Honesty. She had to remain honest with him…and herself. This may be going faster and further than she'd intended, but she couldn't rein in her betraying emotions.

"Do I have a choice?"

He stroked a fingertip down her cheek. "No more than I do." Then he turned to start the car.

Mercy, how could she try to form immunity to this man when his touch was so gentle, his words so powerful? No wonder he had all the confidence in the world. There was no way any woman could resist his charm.

Was there anything sexier than a powerful, self-reliant man who made no qualms about the fact that he wanted you? And the man was so wrapped up in his family; that had to say something about character, didn't it? Oh, and let's not forget the way he looked on his big, black motorcycle. Not to mention the heavy-lidded bedroom eyes and dark stubble outlining a strong jaw.

For the duration of this project, they would be spending nearly every day together. Lord help her, this was going to be a very long year.

Four

The restaurant Zach took her to was certainly nowhere she'd ever choose to go herself. And though it was perfect, she'd never admit it to Mr. Overinflated Ego.

As the maître d' showed them to their reserved table, Ana took in the decor. Lush tropical plants in earthenware pots separated the dining tables, providing a cozy atmosphere. Low, soft lighting and one entire wall with a trickling waterfall made for a relaxing, intimate experience—just what she needed.

Ana slid into the curved booth in the corner beside the waterfall. Zach, too, slid in…right up to her side.

She eyed him with a quirk of her brow. "Do you plan on staying this close while we're eating?"

Beneath dark lashes and heavy lids, Zach returned her gaze. "At the first opportunity, I plan to get a lot closer."

Ana stared back into those deep, molasses-colored eyes. "Do you have a physical attraction to every woman you encounter?" she mocked.

"Not at all. I won't lie and say I've been a saint, but I also won't apologize for being honest and letting you know where I stand."

"Honesty is something I certainly appreciate, but I have to say, I don't trust easily."

He nodded. "You'll trust me. Maybe not now, but when it counts."

Oh, Lord. Did he mean…? Flirting was one thing, but his tone was so serious, so final. Sex was obviously something that came easily to Zach—or so the tabloids hinted at—so this conversation was probably only uncomfortable for her.

How had she lost control of this situation? Losing control of anything at all around Zach Marcum was not a smart move. She should be a pro at dealing with playboys considering all the self-proclaimed Casanovas on the job site. Unfortunately she'd never been on the receiving end of one's affections.

She turned in the booth, facing him fully. "Zach, we are nothing more than business associates and I'm helping you plan a wedding shower. That's just about as personal as I've gotten with anyone. Ever. Trust is an issue with me, but not one I care to fix."

Zach leaned down to her ear and whispered, "You don't have to do anything. I'll take care of fixing your trust issues."

His warm breath sent shivers throughout her body. Oh, man. This guy was good.

Too good. Too…rehearsed, like he'd said this before.

The waiter—thank you, God—chose that moment to come over. Ana ordered her dinner, but whatever Zach ordered was lost on her. She was too busy trying to figure out how to get ahold of this conversation, this man.

Once they were alone again, Ana shut out the romantic ambiance of the upscale restaurant, and the sexy, powerful man sitting within touching distance, and cut to the point.

"Why are you trying so hard?" she demanded. "You could surely have any woman you want."

Those bedroom eyes sparkled. "Not every woman."

The heat in his tone said more than his words.

Okay, so this wasn't a safe path to travel down.

"What list did Kayla give you for the shower?"

Zach grinned at her complete change of subject. "I need to form a seating chart and figure out the menu."

Much safer ground. "Sounds easy enough."

He eyed her. "You haven't seen the list of guests. There are specifics beside each name. Certain people can't be seated with each other, and the women with the children should be seated closest to the door for bathroom breaks."

Ana couldn't help but laugh at this high-profile mogul discussing wedding showers, seating charts and toddler potty rituals.

"It will be fine. I promise," she assured him, patting his arm. "But first, let's start with something less scary. The menu."

Zach nodded. "That I can handle. Steak and chicken are always basics."

"This is a bridal shower with women," she reminded him. "We like something less…masculine."

"You just ordered steak," he reminded her.

Ana shrugged. "I always have a huge appetite."

His eyes traveled down to her waist and back up. "You don't look like it. So what should we have? Carrot sticks and dip?"

His mocking tone and the little glint in his eye kept her smiling. Joking she could handle. It was the bedroom talk that gave her a problem.

"What time of the day is Kayla having the shower?" she asked.

The waiter came back, dropping off their drinks and

complimentary bread. Ana took a sip of her water and relaxed into the buttery leather booth.

"She said mid-afternoon. Two or three."

"Okay, so let's make this fun." Ana plotted quickly in her head. "What about a spin-off of an ice cream social? The shower will be after the guests have already eaten lunch, so various desserts would be perfect for women, and ice cream will be a hit with the kids that have to come along."

Zach turned a bit more in the seat, slid his arm along the back of the booth and offered her one of his killer smiles. "Keep going."

Pride flooded through her. Why she wanted to impress this man with plans for his sister-in-law-to-be's wedding shower was beyond her. Actually she just wanted to help out because he'd looked so completely lost when Kayla had dumped this on him.

And it was a good thing she'd stepped in when she did. Steak and chicken? She simply couldn't envision wealthy, beautiful socialites in vibrant sundresses, probably with floppy hats, gnawing on a T-bone.

"We should have this outside." Ana shook her head as the ideas swirled around. "No, make it somewhere that could be inside and out. We want them to mingle, chat and enjoy the celebration. Plus the ice cream would need to be out of all this blistering heat."

Zach held up a hand. "Isn't this a shower? Aren't the women supposed to sit around, sigh over the rock on Tamera's hand and play silly games?"

Ana shrugged. "I suppose if she wants a traditional, boring shower. Is your brother marrying someone boring?"

He chuckled. "Not at all. And knowing her and my sister, they will love this idea."

"Feel free to take the credit for it and be a hero," Ana said, reaching for a piece of warm, buttery bread.

"Why? It wasn't my idea."

She tore off the end piece and shoved it into her mouth. "They don't need to know a virtual stranger came up with plans for something so intimate and personal."

He eased a bit closer. Close enough now she could see the black slivers in his dark chocolate eyes.

"You're not a stranger, Ana."

The piece of bread she was holding slid from her grasp and fell onto the stark white linen tablecloth. She wanted to blame her slippery hands on the glazing from the bread, but honestly, Zach's warm breath combined with his intense stare had her all but trembling.

"Zach, you're not getting me into bed."

One corner of that sultry mouth kicked up. "Is that what I'm trying to do?"

"Aren't you? We can pretend you're flirting or just being yourself and I can giggle and bat my eyelashes at you like a good little tease…or we can skip all that nonsense and get to the heart of this tension between us."

He lifted one of her escaped auburn curls and tucked it behind her ear. "It's called chemistry. Not tension. Tension makes people uncomfortable. I'm perfectly fine."

"That's because you're used to throwing your charm out and having women latch on to it so you can drag them back to your lair."

Zach threw his head back and laughed. Ana waited, with very little patience, to see just what was so funny. If he even attempted to deny that he was a playboy, she feared she'd stab him with her salad fork.

"Ana, I'm not a Neanderthal," he said in a low, still chuckling voice. "I don't drag women anywhere they aren't willing to be. Don't get your back all up because you're angry over your attraction to me."

Maybe she'd have to use that salad fork after all.

"Your ego and your comments are out of control," she hissed. "I won't deny I'm attracted to you, but I also don't need to act on every urge I have. And I don't have time for games."

Ana tried to scoot over into her own personal space. Zach must've thought she was making a dramatic exit because he grabbed her arm and whispered in her ear, "I'll apologize for my comments, but you know I'm right."

Ana kept her gaze on the roll she'd dropped onto the table, trying her hardest to avoid turning her head and looking him in the eye. He was so close that if she turned even the slightest, their faces would touch.

The devil on her shoulder wanted to know if that would be so bad. The angel on the other shoulder must be asleep because she didn't say a word. Or maybe she was just stunned speechless because Zach's large hand encircled her entire bicep in a warm, gentle hold.

Ana closed her eyes. "I can't do this. Seriously, Zach. I can't even pretend that we'll be more than business associates because I won't play a tease and I won't lie to you. Please stop pushing me into giving you something I can't."

His thumb stroked over the curve of her shoulder. "That was never my intent, Anastasia."

Now she did turn to meet his gaze, leaving their lips barely a whisper apart. "What was your intent?" she whispered.

Other than his lips settling over hers in a possessive, yet tender way, Zach didn't touch her. Ana didn't want to respond to those lips, but how could she not? Why did she have to deny what her body so desperately craved, ached for?

It was so easy to give into the gentleness. She'd never known such a delicate manner could be possessed by a man like Zach.

Ana wasn't one for PDA, but they were well hidden by the strategically placed potted palms. Even though kissing in public was never something she would've done before meeting Zach, she was discovering there were a lot of things she hadn't considered before meeting Zach.

With a sigh and a tingle streaming through her body, Ana leaned in just slightly. Enough to let Zach know she wanted this. Still, he didn't touch any more than her lips and Ana knew, without a doubt, he was letting her decide how far and how intense this kiss would be.

He tilted his mouth just a bit, easing her lips open. She'd given him the go-ahead with that little sigh and by leaning into him. A light, feathery touch slid across her jawline. His fingertips.

Chills popped up over her entire body. And before she could comprehend another thought, Zach eased back.

"My intent is to show you how desirable you are and that not every man takes advantage of women."

Ana opened her eyes, swallowed hard. "Maybe not, but not every man has good intentions."

His fingertips continued to stroke her jawline. "There's nothing wrong with giving in to your needs, your passion. I'm a patient man, Anastasia, and I believe you're well worth the wait."

Great, now her chills had chills. At his declaration—or was it a threat—Ana knew she was fighting a losing battle.

Did he have a clue about her inexperience? Did she bring it up? And how did one start the ball rolling with a topic like this?

Though she didn't want to admit it, Ana knew she'd long since lost control. And much to her surprise, she didn't care.

Five

Zach sped through the palm-lined Miami streets. When darkness had fallen over the party town, Zach had taken off on one of his favorite motorcycles to clear his head, taste a bit of freedom he refused to let go of and work through whatever problems were plaguing his mind.

And right now all three of those scenarios revolved around one sexy, stubborn forewoman.

Zach eased his Harley to a stop on the beach side of the street. The full moon beamed right onto the whitecaps of the waves rolling into shore.

After he'd dropped Ana off at her hotel, he'd needed to do some major regrouping. There had been almost an innocence, a naïveté about her tonight. He hadn't missed the way her hands shook when he'd scooted closer, the quivering in her voice when he'd stroked her bare shoulder.

The hitch in her breath when he'd finally kissed her. He'd never taken so much time before kissing a woman before.

Never had to rein in his emotions when all he wanted to do was act on them.

And to say she had a hidden passion would be a drastic understatement. Ana had leaned into him; she'd given up control and handed it over to him in the span of one audible sigh.

There wasn't a doubt in his mind she would be just as passionate in a private, intimate setting. A woman with such fire and determination for everything that she came across in life would surely match his own desires.

Ana may be powerful, controlling and in charge in her business, but he intended to pull all of that from her when he got her into bed. He'd already had a glimpse of how easily Ana gave into her urges.

One part of him wished he could pinpoint the exact reason he wanted Ana so much; the other part didn't give a damn about the reason. She was beautiful and unattainable—a challenge tailor-made for him.

Zach's cell vibrated in his pocket. He reached in, checked the ID and sighed as he thumbed the green button.

"Melanie."

"Can I come over?"

Zach felt the immediate tightening in his chest. Here was the woman he'd married, the one he thought he'd love forever. The one who'd left without a backward glance…until now, when she realized her mistake.

"Mel, you left me. I don't give second chances."

"I made a mistake. Can't we just talk?"

As much as Zach wanted to, he couldn't, wouldn't give her the opportunity to destroy him again. He wouldn't give that to any woman.

"I have to go."

Zach disconnected the call and shoved his cell back in his pocket before staring out onto the whitecaps ebbing and flowing along the beach. He couldn't help but think of his wedding day and the brief months of wedded bliss…followed by the whole nightmarish moment that he'd just as soon forget. And he would, just as soon as Melanie quit calling and texting him.

Yes, his ex had done something to him that damaged him, but he also took some blame for the disaster. If he hadn't left himself so vulnerable, so open, he wouldn't have been so hurt when she left him for one of his so-called friends.

Cliché, yes. But Zach was moving forward, getting on with his life and making the most of every moment of his freedom and bachelorhood.

He refused to be analyzed, or to even admit to himself that he'd thrown himself in the path of every single woman he could since his divorce. So what if he wanted to enjoy the company of a woman without the baggage of a relationship?

And if he wanted to spend the next few months entertaining Ana, then that's what he would damn well do.

But if he didn't curtail his desire for Ana, the entire crew would know. This physical pull he felt toward the forewoman had to remain under wraps…preferably under covers.

Working with such a juxtaposed woman every day for months wouldn't be a hardship, but it would be trying on his patience. Patience was certainly not something he'd ever had, but he knew if he wanted to be with Ana, and he did, he'd have to dig deep to find that most elusive quality.

He also figured he'd have to take this seduction plan slower than he would've liked. Ana was hesitant to give into her desires. He couldn't quite pinpoint why, but whatever secrets she hid in her past were her business. All he wanted was her now, in the present.

Forget the past, don't think about the future—his mantra for the past couple years. He'd lived any way he'd wanted, saw whom he pleased. On some insane level he should be happy his ex-wife had left him for another man because he could do whatever the hell he wanted.

But he found himself wanting Ana on a physical level that was starting to consume each and every thought.

Would Ana be willing to step around that wall of defense she'd built around herself? If not, was he really willing to risk the possibility of another rejection? For intimate time with Ana, absolutely. Hadn't he steeled his heart? He could certainly handle an intimate relationship with Ana.

Relationship? No, he didn't do those. Flings? Certainly. But he had a gut feeling Miss Ana was not a fling-type girl.

So he was back to asking himself the relationship question. Would he—?

Zach cursed as he looked skyward and saw the dark clouds closing in over the full moon. He started his engine back up and headed for home as the first raindrop landed on his forearm.

He didn't consider it a coincidence that the rain interrupted his thoughts just as they were about to venture into a territory he wasn't quite ready for. Fate was telling him something.

No way was he at a point in his life when he wanted to explore deeper feelings. And honestly, he didn't know if he'd ever be ready to give any woman, even Ana, something more than his body. And that was just fine with him.

A week had passed since Zach had made a pass at her in any way. Oh, they'd worked throughout the day at the site, but he was all business, all the time.

As she stood in front of the bathroom mirror in her condo suite wearing only a fluffy towel and light makeup, Ana felt the nerves flutter in her stomach. Tonight was anything but work.

Victor Lawson was hosting a party, so of course she was not only invited, she was expected to attend. Zach would be there which made Ana take special care while fixing her dark auburn curls. The South Florida humidity made her hair unruly, so she pulled the large-barreled curling iron through it to smooth the ends under and pulled it back into a low, loopy bun.

She gave her hair and makeup one final check before she made her way to the closet to choose between the few dresses she'd brought to Miami. She fingered the hangers, eyeing the ice-blue cocktail dress, the short emerald halter-style or maybe the bold, purple strapless.

The emerald halter won. It was comfortable, light and flirty. Plus the color really accented her eyes which would be great because she didn't wear that much eye makeup.

Ana chose her undergarments with care, but not because she planned on anyone else seeing them. Quite the contrary. Having sexy, feminine, lacy lingerie gave her an extra boost of confidence. And she knew attending a high-class party with numerous Alpha male types—Victor, Cole, Zach—she'd need all the confidence she could get.

Considering she had a meager bust, she decided to forgo the bra and donned a pair of black lace panties cut high on the hip. She slid the dress over her head and tied the chiffon straps around her neck.

Then she stepped into a pair of gold strappy heels.

Turning from side to side in front of the closet mirrors, Ana smiled. No way did she look like a construction worker now. If Zach thought he wanted the dirty, plain tank and jeans girl, wait until he caught sight of her inner vixen.

Make that the virginal vixen. Ana chuckled. Oxymoron, anyone?

After touching up her lip gloss, she slid the slender tube into her small, gold clutch at the same time a heavy knock sounded at her door.

She glanced through the peephole, not surprised to see Zach, looking as gorgeous and sexy as ever, on the other side. Of course, she wasn't going to tell him he looked gorgeous or sexy. Those were details that he already knew about himself.

Besides, she had a feeling he'd had enough women to stroke his ego.

But she would make him just a bit miserable tonight. After all, she'd been miserable since he'd laid that talented mouth on hers.

She smoothed a shaky hand down the front of her short, flowing dress and opened the door. Zach's wide eyes raked over her from head to toe, twice, before settling on her glossy lips. The look on his face made her grin and do a little happy dance inside because she'd chosen the right outfit for the impact she wanted.

"I'm glad I came to give you a ride," he said in a raspy, sexy voice. "If you walked into that party alone, you'd be eaten alive by every eligible bachelor there. And probably some married men, too."

Ana conjured up that inner vixen and cocked a hip to the side as she slid a hand up the door. "What makes you think I want to ride with you? Maybe I wanted to walk into Victor's party alone."

Those chocolate eyes grew darker as he looked at her. "You keep taunting me, sweetheart, you'll have to face the consequences."

A flicker of arousal mixed with fear crept through her, but she kept her stance, refusing to let him get one up on her just because she was inexperienced. And why was she purposely antagonizing this tiger? Was she finally done being one of the guys? Did she really want to take a chance on letting Zach have his way with her?

Good Lord, she had come so far. She was actually enjoying this banter with Zach.

"If you don't want to be taunted," she said, smiling, "keep your distance."

In one swift step, he closed the gap between them, snaked an arm around her waist and brought his face within an inch of hers. "I've tried. Even when you're not with me, you're filling my thoughts. What do you suppose we do about that?"

Suddenly not feeling so confident, Ana placed her hands on the hard planes of his broad chest. "I say we get to the party before Victor wonders why we're late."

Zach's eyes roamed down the V of her halter. "Once he sees you, he'll not only know why we were late, he'll completely understand."

Ana gave him a not-so-gentle shove, pushing Zach away. "Simmer down, lover boy. Let me grab my key and purse. I hope you don't think I'm straddling one of your flashy bikes for this."

Zach cocked his head and grinned. "I'm pure class tonight, Anastasia. I brought my new Camaro."

"Camaro? I thought all you flashy playboys liked expensive, foreign cars."

He shrugged. "We like all kinds of toys and I have my fair share of foreign models, but I always wanted a Camaro when I was in high school and we couldn't even afford a beat-up car, much less something flashy. The second I laid my eyes on this new model, black of course, with a sharp set of rims, I knew it was mine."

Ana studied him. "Are you telling me you didn't have a car as a teenager?"

Zach stepped a bit farther into her bedroom as she gathered her things. "No. Cole and I shared the car our mom drove before she and my father passed away, but we didn't have our own. Poor Kayla, she never had one until she got her first job in college and bought one."

Ana wanted to know more about this surprising childhood of Zach's. How had the three siblings gone from one car and no money to numerous lavish homes and a multimillion-dollar business?

"I appreciate having a Camaro now, though," he said with a

menacing smile. "I wouldn't have been man enough to handle all that engine when I was younger."

She laughed and stepped toward him in a silent gesture to leave. "And you think you're man enough now to handle it?"

His smile slipped and his heavy-lidded eyes held her in place. "I'm man enough to handle anything."

Unsure of how to respond, Ana retrieved her clutch and key from the dresser. After sliding the key into her purse, she turned, ready to face the den full of lions. Please God, she prayed, don't let me be the only woman at this party. Then again, with a man like Victor Lawson, there were probably dozens of women to dangle off his arms.

"Who's that?" Zach asked, nodding to the picture on the dresser.

"My grandfather and my mother." She didn't want him to come any farther into her room. Her pictures were personal, just like her life. "Ready?"

He nodded and extended his elbow out to escort her. Looping her arm around his crisp, black dress shirt, she immediately felt the heat permeating from him. Heaven help her, the night had just begun.

As they approached the elevator, he straightened his arm and laced their fingers together. The gesture was intimate for her, probably not so much for someone like famous ladies' man Zach Marcum.

They rode down in silence and made their way across the marbled floor of the lobby and out into the balmy Miami night. Onlookers wouldn't think twice about the dressy couple, hand in hand, getting into a flashy car for a date.

Looks could be deceiving. That was something she knew firsthand.

Zach opened the passenger-side door of his Camaro and assisted her in before closing the door. As if she needed another one of her senses honing in on him, the masculine, crisp scent from his cologne, which somehow mixed perfectly with the new-car scent, completely enveloped her just as the plush leather seat did. The man himself may as well wrap those big, strong arms around her. The impact of her current surroundings was just as effective.

Before she could analyze her cozy ride, Zach slid in beside her and brought the engine to life.

"I was going to bring the 'Vette, but I only keep the top down and I figured you wouldn't appreciate your hair getting blown everywhere."

Ana crossed her legs and laughed. "For something like this, that was a safe assumption. Normally, though, I'd love it. I'm not too worried if my hair is perfect or if my lipstick is always in place. With me, what you see is what you get."

Oops, bad choice of words. She knew it even in that split second before Zach's eyes darted to the side to give her a visual caress.

"I haven't got anything yet, have I?"

His words may have been teasing; his tone was anything but. This man wasn't known for his somewhat wild lifestyle for nothing. He knew what he wanted and he never let anything get in his way.

And right now, he had his eye on the prize. She may as well parade around wearing nothing but a shiny red bow.

Six

The second they entered Victor Lawson's lavish Star Island mansion, Zach was more than ready to throw a coat over Ana and usher her back to his car.

Every eye was on them—and he knew they weren't looking at him. The men were blatantly staring and the women were shooting invisible daggers. They had every reason to be jealous.

"Ah, two of my favorite people." Victor crossed the black marble floor from the back of the house to greet them. "I'm so glad you made it. We have drinks, food, people. All the makings of a fantastic evening."

Zach eased a hand to the small of Ana's back. A petty claim he was staking, but he wanted the oglers to take note. Why he was so damned determined to show others how much he wanted her was beyond him. Hadn't he told his brother he was only interested in Ana in an intimate setting? He simply didn't share, that's all. No reason for him to analyze this situation into anything more than what it was. Ana was the perfect woman to occupy his nights.

"We were afraid we were going to be late," Zach stated, earning him a death glare from Ana. "I told her you'd understand."

Victor chuckled. "Absolutely."

"Your house is absolutely breathtaking, Victor." Ana offered the billionaire her sweetest, most sincere smile. "Thank you for the invitation."

Victor reached for her hand, brought it to his lips. "No thanks necessary, Anastasia. You are aiding in making my next hotel the most glamorous of all. It is I who should be thanking you."

Okay, that hand-holding had been going on a bit too long. Zach was ready to go Neanderthal until Victor glanced his way. An unspoken male conversation passed between them and then Victor nodded, grinned and released Ana's hand.

"I must go see to my other guests," Victor said. "If there's something you want and don't see it, ask one of the waitstaff to get it for you."

The second Victor walked away, Ana turned to Zach. "Don't you *ever* do that again."

"I didn't want him getting any ideas," he defended. "He's a single man who's more than popular with the ladies. I just wanted him to know you were off-limits."

"I'm off-limits to you as well," she whispered between gritted teeth before she turned and headed toward the back of the house where all the French doors lining the rear wall were open to the magnificent backyard.

Zach allowed her a few feet head start then casually followed. No way was he going to make a scene, especially at the home of the man who held a multimillion-dollar deal with his family's architectural firm.

Before Zach could step outside with Ana, Victor approached him once again.

"Is Kayla still out of the country?" he asked.

"Yes. I believe she's due back within the week. Did you need to talk to her about the hotel?"

Victor shook his head. "No, nothing associated with business."

Zach didn't get a chance to reply. Victor had walked away and was already mingling with other guests.

Interesting. Victor wanted something personal with Kayla? An uneasy feeling formed low in his gut. He didn't like the thoughts of that billionaire bachelor with Ana and he sure as hell didn't like the idea of him pawing at his sister.

But that was something he'd have to get Cole in on. There was no way his sweet, soft-spoken sister was going to have any dealings with Victor other than business.

Zach walked through the open French doors and out into the garden…if such an extravagant floral garden with waterfalls trickling into small ponds could be called a garden. The simple word seemed much too tame for the amazing scenery.

Rich, throaty laughter floated through the air, sucker punching him deep in the gut. Ana. He'd know that laugh anywhere, but just how he would know was a mystery. She'd certainly never laughed that sexily around him.

He spotted her a few feet away standing beside his twin brother, Cole, and Cole's fiancée, Tamera. The women were smiling and chatting while Cole nursed a longneck. No doubt the women were discussing the upcoming wedding.

Zach didn't know if he should stand back and take in the beauty of the smile Ana offered or if he should go save his brother.

But like the magnetic force that seemed to draw him lately toward the stubborn, sexy woman, Zach found himself closing the gap and standing so close to Ana, his arm brushed hers. Even though she continued smiling, her body tensed, shivered.

"Glad you could make it," Cole stated, slapping him on the arm.

"Me, too," Zach replied, taking a bottle of imported beer from a passing waiter. "Tamera, you're looking beautiful as always. You're almost glowing you look so happy."

His soon-to-be sister-in-law beamed, slipping an arm around Cole's waist and leaning into him. "I have many reasons to be happy and they all revolve around this guy right here."

"I was just asking where they're getting married," Ana chimed in. "I'm surprised they're getting married at Cole's house."

"We didn't want anything unfamiliar or too out of the way for our closest family and friends." Tamera looked up at Cole, love radiating around them. "We plan on having a long reception and leaving for our honeymoon right after and we wanted a place for our family to stay overnight. Our house seemed perfect."

Ana smiled. "That sounds wonderful. Very intimate and personal."

Zach was certain if all this love, wedding and happily-ever-after talk proceeded much longer, he'd break out in head-to-toe hives. This was definitely not a topic he was comfortable with, nor did he want to hang around long enough to get comfortable with it. The moment would never come.

"Been by the site in the last couple days?" he asked Cole.

His twin nodded. "Matter of fact I ran by earlier today."

"The preparations are coming along ahead of schedule and the rest of Ana's crew arrived two days ago, so that will speed things along even more."

Tamera rolled her eyes. "Do we have to discuss work? We're all off, so let's just enjoy the party. I'm hungry, Cole. Let's go get a plate."

Cole eyed his brother, giving him the "we'll talk later"

look. Zach chuckled as he took a long pull of his beer. Never, ever would a woman get that deep into his life that she called the shots on his next move. Just another reason love wasn't for him.

It was something he wished he would've known before his wife ran off with another man and then continued to haunt him because her affair didn't last.

But Zach was happy his brother and Tamera had found their way back to each other and were now planning the wedding of the year.

"Don't look so sour," Ana said, snapping him from his thoughts. "If you want to talk shop, I'm all ears."

"A woman after my own heart," he joked.

A lopsided grin spread across her face. "I'm hardly after your heart, Zach."

"That's good, considering I won't give it away again."

"Again?"

Dammit. Of all the times to bring up his most vulnerable moment.

"I was married before," he said casually. "Didn't last. She wants back together, I don't. End of story."

Ana rubbed a delicate hand up her arm and shook her head. "Just another reason we're so different. Marriage is a huge deal. That's one of the reasons I never want to do it. There's no way a man would be what I need in a husband."

Interesting. "What do you want?"

She shrugged, clutching her tiny purse with both hands. "It's not so much what I want as what I need. Faithfulness, loyalty, stability, honesty. He'd have to put me first. I'm not saying spoil me and pamper me, I'm saying be attentive to my needs and know my desires."

If only she'd let him know her desires, he'd meet every single one of them. But he certainly wasn't vying for a slot in the husband category.

"Don't get me wrong," she went on, staring at all the

couples mingling hand in hand around the lavish grounds. "I'm so happy when two people who are meant to be together find that happiness. It's just not something I'll ever have. But, believe me, I'm not complaining."

The longer she talked and watched other people, the clearer it became she was lying. Oh, she may not know she was lying to herself, but she was. The longing in her eyes, the softness in her voice as she spoke of her requirements… Yes, Anastasia Clark wanted that fairy tale and one day she'd probably find it. The right man would come along and give her all of that and more.

Zach didn't want to think about Ana with another man. Not when he hadn't even had a chance to explore that passion that lurked inside of her.

"Oh, and a dog," she added.

"Excuse me?"

She turned her pale green eyes back to him. "I'd have to have a dog. If he loves animals, then that's a good sign he's caring and nurturing. Of course, in my work a dog isn't very practical, not with me traveling all over the country."

"Maybe when you meet your prince charming, you'll settle into his castle and not travel anymore." Zach couldn't help but grin as her eyes narrowed. "Then you can have all the dogs you want."

"I told you, I'm not settling down. I'm certainly not slowing down anytime soon on my work, either. I love what I do, love my independence."

Even better. She wasn't looking for a commitment. Perfect.

"I see a client of mine," Zach told her. "I need to go say hi. You're welcome to come with me."

She waved a hand through the air. "You don't need to babysit me. Go, mingle. I'll come find you when I'm ready."

Zach left Ana as she made her way toward one of the numerous tiered food tables. He chatted with one client, and then with many more previous clients his family's firm had worked with.

After about an hour, Zach scanned the area for Ana but had no luck in spotting her. Surely she wouldn't have left with someone and not told him. He wandered back in through one of the seven French doors that led into the house. This set led into the formal sitting room where more partygoers chatted. No Ana.

Then he heard that sexy laugh.

His head darted around and he spotted that red hair, that emerald dress, and his ever-present arousal smacked him in the face. Jealousy soon followed as he watched her chat with a man that Zach knew was married to a very sweet, unknowing woman. The rich, middle-aged man smiled as he pushed a stray strand of Ana's hair that had slipped from her bun.

Zach had never considered himself territorial before, but there was no way in hell he could let this go on. He had no doubt Ana didn't have a clue the man she was talking to had a mischievous gleam in his eye and had set his sights on her.

"Gabriel Stanley, nice to see you again," Zach said as he approached, not affected one bit by the glare he'd just received from the other man. "I saw your wife outside. She looks wonderful. You two having another boy?"

Gabriel shoved his hands in his dress-pants pockets. "Yes. We're having our third boy."

"How wonderful," Ana beamed, oblivious to the tension. "Congratulations. You didn't tell me that."

Zach nearly laughed. No, old Gabriel probably didn't tell his prey he had a wife and family…. That would certainly put a damper on any affair he hoped to have with her.

"She looked a bit tired," Zach added. "You may want to check on her."

The muscle in Gabriel's jaw ticked. "Ana, it was a pleasure to meet you. Zach, see you around."

"Well, that was incredibly rude," Ana said once they were alone. "Why didn't you pee on me to mark your territory?"

Zach stood directly in front of her, staring into those eyes that were as mesmerizing as any emerald. "He's married."

"And?"

"He was flirting with you."

Ana grinned and patted him on the cheek. "You're cute when you're jealous. Almost makes me want to pursue that to see if those feelings are sincere."

"I'm not jealous," he insisted, though if that got another foot inside her stone wall, he'd own up to it. "Let's go."

She opened her mouth as if she wanted to argue, but closed it and nodded. "We should tell Victor goodbye."

"He's busy talking with guests. He won't mind if we slip out."

Giving her no other option, Zach took her hand and led her through the mansion and out onto the stone driveway where they waited for the valet to bring the car up.

Strained silence accompanied them back to her South Beach condo. He didn't want her to think of him as a jerk. After all, wasn't he supposed to be showing her a different side of men?

Wait a minute. Since when had his conquest gone from getting into her bed to showing her that he was genuinely interested in getting to know her? He didn't want a relationship by any means. Then again, if they were going to be together so much, he might as well work every angle to his advantage.

"Look, I'm sorry if you think I was rude to you back there." He cleared his throat. "But I won't apologize for being rude to Gabriel."

"Yeah, that sounded sincere."

Zach shot her a quick sideways glance. "I am sincere. And I'm not afraid to apologize when I know I'm wrong or I've hurt someone's feelings that I care about."

Her sharp intake of breath shocked him. He'd better clarify his statement.

"I know how you view men," he went on. "But we're not all bad and we're not all like Gabriel. Just because some men choose to enjoy women doesn't mean they are playing them. They may just be dating around, one at a time and having fun."

"Like you," she said.

Sitting this close, with her wearing so little, Zach had to reach out to touch her. He slid his hand across the console and rested it on her thigh. "Like me. I don't lie to women, ever. If I'm with someone, she knows where I stand on relationships and she also knows that she can trust me not to be with someone else while I'm with her."

"For some reason, I believe you."

And for some reason, he exhaled a breath he hadn't known he was holding. He wanted Ana to think of him as one of the good guys. He wanted to set the bar for her so when she did go out and realize she wanted that fairy tale, she wouldn't fall for any frogs.

Dammit. He was now thinking like a five-year-old little girl. He was a man, for crying out loud. He wasn't supposed to think of fairy tales and frogs.

Bottom line, he'd show her how a real man was supposed to treat a woman. And he could certainly do that without getting wrapped up in a relationship.

Seven

When Zach pulled up to her condo, she started to get out. "Thanks for the ride."

"I'll see you up."

She began to protest as he exited the car, but he quickly opened her door and extended his hand, leaving her no choice but to accept his gesture and follow. She wanted to get away from him, away from his overbearing antics. She was a grown woman, for heaven's sake and she could handle herself. Maybe she had liked being hit on at Victor's party—though the fact that Gabriel Stanley was married with a child on the way was a bit creepy and extremely wrong.

Zach told the valet that he'd be right back, then he slid an arm around her waist and escorted her inside to the elevator.

The he-man routine wasn't quite her style, but she couldn't help but feel humbled and a bit special because he'd come up to her when he thought she may be getting in over her head with a married man.

Either Zach had really high morals about fidelity or he wanted her all to himself.

Or, the most likely scenario, both. A part of her worried she was taking this flirting too far.

Ana flicked open her clutch as the elevator dinged on her floor. Zach's hand hadn't moved from her back and the heat radiating from him had probably put a hole right through her dress.

The simple affection made her heart flip, but she knew it was only because she wasn't used to seeing that side of a man. She was used to sweaty, grimy men working all day on sites. She hadn't been on a date in months and even then, it hadn't been anything special.

Zach took the key card from her and slid it into her door. She couldn't let him in. Not only did she fear her willpower would fizzle the second he stepped over that threshold and the door slammed behind him, but she couldn't let him see all of her personal things. No one ever saw all the items she carried with her from site to site. They were her sanctuary. When he'd questioned her earlier about her pictures, she'd panicked.

Zach opened the door, gesturing for Ana to step in ahead of him.

"Thanks again." She turned, holding her hand out for the key. "I'm sure I'll see you Monday."

Zach didn't turn the key over to her like she'd expected. He kept hold of it while his eyes roamed over her face, focusing on her lips.

"I've watched you all night," he told her in a softer, huskier voice. "Watched that creamy skin slide against your dress. Pieces of your hair dance around in the breeze. I've never practiced more restraint than I did tonight."

Control had to remain with her, she knew, or they would both make a decision they weren't ready for. "Don't, Zach. Just give me the key."

He laid the key in her upturned palm, only to cup the side of her face and stroke her bottom lip with his thumb. "You don't want me to go. If you're honest with yourself, you want to know what it would be like."

The "it" wasn't in question. And, yes, she had wondered, dreamed. But that didn't mean anything could or would happen. Though she knew exactly what he was talking about when he'd said he'd practiced self-restraint. God knew she was having to hold herself back right now.

She never thought she'd be at the point of restraint. She'd always assumed when she chose to take a lover, she would be so certain, all of her doubts would vanish. Yeah, so not the case. Not that she'd decided one hundred percent to take Zach as her lover, but she was inching closer and closer.

"We're so different, Zach."

He stepped closer. "Then why aren't you pushing me away?"

Because she couldn't form a coherent thought. Between his sultry words, that crisp scent of his cologne and his potent touch, Ana only knew her body was approaching flashpoint and was racked by an ache she hadn't felt before now.

"I'll go if you tell me to," he murmured a second before his lips came down onto hers.

Both arms came around her waist as he softly coaxed her lips open with his tongue. With her dress low-cut in the back, Zach's rough palms slid over her smooth skin, proving once again how opposite they were…yet how amazing he felt.

He pressed her against his body as one hand snaked up beneath her hair and massaged her neck.

With all the assaults on her body at once, Ana hadn't even noticed Zach had backed her farther into the foyer until the door clicked shut, closing out the light from the hallway.

Ana pulled back, her hands clutching his hard biceps. A soft glow from the living room filtered around them, but the half-wall kept most of the light out.

"Zach," she said breathlessly, "I can't. We can't."

Zach's eyelids were heavy, his lips moist and swollen, his breathing erratic. "Don't be scared," he whispered as he eased her back against the wall and covered her mouth once again.

Scared happened long ago. Now she was downright terrified. Certainly not of him, but of herself for wanting something, craving something she had no control over.

Ana wrapped her arms around his neck and pressed her aching body to his. The tie behind her neck came free with ease as Zach gave the knot a gentle tug. The soft material slid down, stopping where their bodies were joined.

Zach eased back, breaking their kiss for a moment. They both looked down as the top of her halter dress slid away from her breasts.

"Breathtaking," he whispered.

Ana didn't know what to say, what to do. "Zach…"

"Shh." He laid a finger to her lips. "I won't hurt you."

She pushed just a bit more against his chest before he could claim her tingling lips again. "I've never done this before. And as much as I'd like to give in, I just can't."

Zach stared at her, as if only just registering her words. Then slowly he pulled her straps back up, tied them around her neck with shaky hands.

Ana didn't take her eyes off him as he straightened her dress. Embarrassment and shame filled her. "I didn't mean to tease you or to let this get out of hand."

He stepped back, shoved his hands into the pockets of his dress pants. "I don't know what to say."

Feeling the need for security, Ana wrapped her arms around her waist and glanced down to the floor. "It's okay. You can just go and we'll pretend this night never happened. This was my fault for letting you in."

"Nobody lets me do anything." His husky voice enveloped

her. "I wanted to come in with you, Anastasia. Nothing could've kept me out."

She couldn't look at him, didn't want to see the disappointment in his eyes. Since when had his feelings and what he thought of her really mattered? This was precisely why she didn't get involved, on any level, with men. Her emotions weren't too far below her steel surface and it never took much for them to slip out.

Zach's fingertip slid beneath her chin and tipped her face up. "Look at me."

As much as she wanted to avoid him, she knew the sooner she cooperated, the sooner he would leave and she could get past this awkward moment.

Ana lifted her gaze, but instead of finding anger or disappointment, she discovered a passionate, caring look she'd never expected in Zach's eyes.

"Why are you ashamed?" he asked. "I'm surprised, yes, but I'm even more impressed. I knew you were strong, independent, but I had no idea just how vulnerable you were."

She straightened her shoulders. "I'm not vulnerable or ashamed."

He stroked the pad of his thumb over her lips. "Don't lie to me or yourself. You think I'm disappointed, so you're ashamed you lost control. You're also vulnerable or you would've let go long ago. You're afraid of getting hurt. Who hurt you in your past, Ana? Who put this worry, this doubt in you?"

The burn began in her eyes, her nose, then her throat. When tears threatened to spill down her cheeks, she closed her eyes and turned away to break free of his mesmerizing touch.

"Leave," she whispered. "Just…leave."

"I would never force you, would never make you feel pressured. But I won't let go of this attraction between us and neither will you." Zach reached for the door, pulled on the knob. "I'm a patient man when I see something I want.

I'll wait for you, Anastasia. Because I want you more than anything I've wanted in a long time. That's new for both of us and something we'll have to get used to."

Before she could say anything else, he opened the door and left.

Ana stood bone weary against the wall opposite the large entryway mirror. She nearly didn't recognize herself. Dress sagging from the loose knot Zach tied, mouth swollen, flushed cheeks, mass of curls falling loose from her clip to hang around her face and shoulders.

She looked like a woman who'd been through a battle. Had she ever. And all this time she'd not wanted him to come in to her condo for personal reasons.

A giggle escaped her. Well, at least he didn't see her family pictures she kept on her nightstand. Though him seeing all her family she'd once had and now longed for would've been a whole lot easier to deal with than letting him in on her intimate, private secret that she'd never been with a man.

Now he was more determined than ever to get close to her. What had she done? She had to tell him she was a virgin to make him understand why she couldn't go on, but had she not let him in to begin with, none of this would've happened.

Ana readied herself for bed and for the first time in her life, she dreaded the following day on the job site.

Eight

Ana was surprised at the end of the next day when Zach hadn't stopped by. She never took him for a coward. Then again, she was relieved she didn't have to face the man who'd turned her world completely inside out with arousing caresses and captivating kisses.

She left the site later than expected because she'd lost track of time as she'd completed the payroll. She refused to admit she didn't want to go back to her condo where memories would smack her in the face as soon as she walked through the door.

But, as she slid the key card into the slot, she braced herself. It was just a room, just an incident. Zach had probably already wiped those moments from his mind.

Her cell vibrated and chirped against her hip as she entered the room. How ironic, she thought, looking at the caller ID, that Zach would call at the precise time she stood in the place where he'd broken through her line of defense.

"Hello."

"Sorry I didn't make it by the site today."

Ana leaned back against the closed door and tried to stop the chills from racing all over her body at the sound of Zach's low, sexy tone.

"That's okay," she said honestly. "What's up?"

"I've got this seating chart and it's driving me nuts. I know you've worked all day, but I need you."

He needed her. No matter what way he meant those words, she couldn't deny she loved hearing them.

"I'm fine." She walked farther into the room and began undressing. "Want me to meet you somewhere?"

"I'll pick you up. Can you be ready in thirty minutes?"

Considering she'd spent most of the day in her office with the cool air-conditioning, she didn't need a shower to rid herself of the grime and sweat she usually brought home at the end of her day.

Yeah, she just exuded sex appeal.

"Sure. See you in a bit."

She hung up before she could change her mind. Being close to Zach again was inevitable so she may as well get the first meeting after their make-out session over with.

After freshening up just a bit, she put on some mascara and lip gloss, and pulled her hair back in a loose knot at her nape. She hoped they weren't going anywhere fancy because she grabbed a pair of denim shorts and a pale blue tank, then slid her feet into white sparkly flip-flops. When she turned to look in the full-length mirror, she frowned. She looked like a teenager.

Zach knocked on her door before she could contemplate changing. That was fast.

When she opened the door, she forced a smile. She knew he'd act like last night hadn't been a life-altering moment, and it probably hadn't been for him, unlike for her. Even so, she had to put up a good front so he didn't know just how affected she was by what had happened.

"I'm ready," she told him, grabbing her purse from the small stand near the door. "I hope we're eating. I'm starving."

He smiled. "You like to eat, don't you?" he asked in a playful manner.

"What's not to like?" She closed the door and pocketed her key card. "I'd love a big steak or pizza."

Zach laughed, reaching to push the button on the elevator directly across from her door. "I've never dated a woman who didn't order a salad and then pick at it."

Her heart fluttered. She jerked to see him staring intently down at her. "Are we dating?"

"What do you say?"

Ana smiled, stepped into the elevator. "I say you're dating the wrong women if they're worried about keeping their figures the same as when they were teenagers."

Zach laughed, followed her in and punched the lobby button. "You're dodging me, Anastasia."

"You're the one who didn't show up today at the site."

Oops. She hadn't meant to sound like she'd been keeping time and waiting for him to show.

In a second, without warning, Zach turned, backed her against the back of the elevator and caged her in between his thick, muscular arms.

"You missed me."

It wasn't a question, but Ana shook her head anyway. "No, I just got used to you dropping by at least once a day."

His dark, seducing eyes sparkled. "Would you feel better if I told you I'd rather have been with you than in my office?"

"I'd feel better if you gave me some breathing room."

Zach placed a kiss on her lips and eased back just as the doors opened to the lobby. "For now."

Ana let out a pent-up breath as she followed Zach out the doors. She squinted against the sun, not seeing his Bugatti or Camaro.

"Over here," he motioned and walked toward his Harley.

She stood rooted in place. Of course he'd have a big, Alpha-style Harley with a matte black finish and just enough chrome to be flashy. "You're kidding," she said, glaring.

He pulled his sunglasses from his T-shirt pocket and slid them on. "What?"

"I'm not getting on that."

He swung his long leg over the seat, grabbed the spare helmet and held it out to her. Before she could tell him he was out of his mind, his cell phone rang. He grabbed it from his pocket.

"Hello."

She moved closer as he listened, grew concerned when he snapped toward her and asked the caller what happened.

"She's with me," he said into the phone. "We'll be right there."

"What's wrong?" she asked as he slid the phone back into his pocket.

He grabbed her hand and gave her the helmet, then tried to get her to get on the bike behind him. "Someone broke into your office at the site."

"I'll take my car," she demanded. "Stop tugging me."

"We'll go together."

She gave up arguing as fear and confusion took over. "Who called? Was there much damage?" She plopped the helmet over her head.

"That was Victor," Zach said. "He's getting ready to leave town for a few weeks and wanted to see how everything was going before he left. He swung by the property and noticed all the busted glass around your office. The windows are all shattered. He called the cops."

Zach reached around, adjusted the strap on her helmet. "Here."

Ana took a step back, holding up her hands. "You're

kidding me with this motorcycle, right? Why don't you drive a truck or something?"

"Because I live where the sun shines year-round and I like the freedom. Are we going to stand here and discuss my means of transportation or are you going to get on?"

She got on behind him and Zach started the bike.

He glanced over his shoulder and grinned. "You've never done this before, have you?"

Ana shook her head and put her arms around his waist. Thank God she'd chosen to wear shorts.

"You'll have to hold on tighter than that, Anastasia."

"Don't you wish," she yelled over the noise, but then he took off and she had no choice.

Ana didn't squeal like she wanted to, but she did shut her eyes as Zach flew through downtown Miami. The warm evening wind whipped the hair that stuck out from beneath the helmet. Slowly, lifting one lid at a time, she checked out the surroundings as they flew by.

If she weren't so worried about falling onto the pavement or the fact that some vandal had trashed her office, Ana would relish having her arms wrapped around one extremely muscular man. Beneath her palms and linked fingers lay his hard, chiseled abs under a thin black T-shirt. Wrapped by her legs, his lean thighs felt strong and sinewy. Ana couldn't help but lean forward, just a bit, and breathe in Zach's spicy, masculine scent. Between the vibration beneath her and the strong man against her, Ana was having some serious thoughts about taking Zach up on his offer and just giving in to the inevitable.

In no time they were pulling onto the site. A squad car was parked next to a sleek, black sports car. Ana's instincts went on alert as she took in the equipment, the area partitioned off for the resort. From an initial glance, everything seemed in order, except of course for the glass around her office trailer.

Zach pulled to a stop and killed the engine. "You can let go."

"Oh."

Ana jerked her hands away from his warm body, almost sorry the ride had come to an end. Even though she was a little shaky about the new, exhilarating experience, she could totally understand why Zach loved the bike so much. And the freedom he talked about, well, that just went hand in hand with Zach's lifestyle.

She climbed off the bike, waited for Zach to get off then handed him the helmet. "Let's go see what the damage is."

He walked beside her step for step. His silence spoke volumes. Zach, Mr. Always a Good Time, was quiet because he was just as scared and nervous as she—at least she assumed so. They couldn't afford disasters or setbacks on this job or any other. Earlier in the week she'd been worried about the potential threat of a tropical storm, one that had thankfully turned out to sea. But vandalism was something else again. True, it occurred occasionally on a job site, but with the rains and the firing of an employee, she hadn't had time to think about the off-hours when the site was left unattended. Besides, she'd only been gone about an hour tonight.

The epiphany hit her hard.

Ana stopped, grabbed Zach's arm to stop him as well. "What if this was revenge?"

Zach looked into her eyes. "We're thinking on the same page. You need to tell the officer exactly what Nate said about my sister, what you said when you fired him and an address where he can be found."

Ana nodded, glancing up as the officer and Victor Lawson came from inside the trailer. The grim look on Victor's face didn't help diminish her nerves.

"Much damage inside?" Zach asked.

"It's been trashed," the officer explained. "I assume you're the foreman?"

"No," Ana corrected, drawing the officer's attention to her. "I am. I'm Ana Clark and this is Zach Marcum, the architect."

The officer jotted down some notes on his pad. "You'll have to go in and see if anything was taken."

Ana turned toward Victor. "I can't tell you how sorry I am. I will hire a security guard to watch over the site in the off-hours."

Victor's generous smile eased her concern somewhat. "I assure you, this is not the first time a project of mine has been tampered with and I've already called a security team. They will be here tomorrow."

"I'll stay here tonight," Zach offered.

Ana jerked her head around. "I will. This is my site."

"Great, I'd love the company," he said with a wink.

Ana narrowed her eyes at him. If he was purposely trying to annoy her, well, mission accomplished. She wasn't going to get into an argument here and now with an audience.

She turned to her shattered office. "I'm going to check the trailer."

"Don't touch too much," the officer said. "It's still a crime scene and the crime scene unit should be here anytime to check for fingerprints."

She moved around the three men and climbed the rickety steps. They'd left the door open and Ana scanned the wreckage from the doorway. Files were flung everywhere, desk drawers had been dumped all over the floor. Luckily there wasn't too much paperwork and she knew Zach had all the duplicates in his office, but the fact that some jerk had torn apart her space made her furious.

"Could've been worse."

Zach's warm breath and voice were right behind her. She glanced over her shoulder, thankful he stood so close. His sunglasses were perched on top of his windblown hair, his dark eyes taking in the mess.

Why was her body reacting to this man? Why couldn't she have a barrier around her hormones that prevented the penetration of sex appeal brought on by cocky, overbearing men?

She'd always heard that women were attracted to men with qualities like their fathers'…. Obviously the case with Zach.

He flaunted himself, his money, his relationships, and all for the sake of a good time. He didn't care what people thought of him but, ironically, people still flocked to him.

The man thought he could have everything and no matter how attracted she was on a physical level, her emotions wouldn't go any deeper.

Still, she had to admit he was continually surprising her. He stepped closer and placed a comforting hand on her shoulder. His gentleness shocked her. She remembered last night when they were on the verge of intimacy in her condo. He couldn't have been any gentler with her. Not even as she'd dropped her bombshell when it was almost too late.

Nine

"I'll bring a couple of air mattresses." Zach urged her forward and stepped into the cluttered space. "You can bring the coffee."

Ana rolled her eyes. "We're not having a slumber party, Zach, and you're not staying."

The CSU had left powdery residue all over and she wanted to clean up and have a moment to herself without his sexy gaze on her. She was beyond pissed that someone had messed with her site.

Zach propped his hands on his narrow hips. "Oh, I'm staying. You're more than welcome to join me, but you won't be here alone."

Mimicking his stance, she rested her hands on her hips as well, more than eager to go toe-to-toe with him. "Look, this won't be the first, or the last, time I sleep in my on-site office. I don't need a babysitter. I'm sure whoever did this was just pulling a prank. We can't be sure it was Nate and even if it was, he probably feels better about getting out his frustrations. I'll bet this is the last we'll see of him."

A muscle in Zach's jaw clenched as he stepped closer. "I'm not chancing your safety. Besides, this will give us time to go over my sister's to-do list."

Ana wanted to argue, but Zach was genuinely concerned; she could tell by the low, slow voice. He wasn't joking anymore which meant he was still worried. Maybe she shouldn't be so quick to brush off the incident.

"If you stay—"

"I'm staying," he interrupted.

"Fine. You will keep your hands and all other body parts to yourself. Are we clear, Don Juan?"

The corner of Zach's mouth kicked up. "Yes, ma'am."

She found herself biting the inside of her cheek to keep from smiling back at him. Damn, the man had a contagious smile.

Her cell rang, pulling her from the moment. She pulled the phone from her bag.

"Hello."

"Oh, thank God. I've called twice this evening, Anastasia." Her mother's worried, frantic tone had Ana's back stiffening, her heart speeding up. "I'm sorry to bother you, honey. Are you terribly busy?"

"Not too busy for you. What's wrong?" She turned so she wouldn't have to look at Zach's questioning gaze.

"I don't know how to say this." Her mother's voice cracked. "Your father and I are filing for divorce."

Heart in her throat, Ana eased back against her desk, saw Zach step beside her out of her peripheral vision. "What?"

"I'm so sorry to have to tell you over the phone," her mother cried. "I just wanted to tell you before you heard it anywhere else. I finally left him."

Ana didn't know whether to congratulate her or offer her sympathies. "Mom, where are you now?"

"I'm at the last property your father hasn't gambled away... the beach house in Georgia."

"Do you need me to come to you?" Ana asked, her heart breaking for her mother.

"Oh, no, dear. I know how important this job is for you. I'll be just fine."

Would she? After thirty years of marriage, her husband's numerous affairs and being all alone in the end, how could anyone sound so positive? Pride for her mother overtook Ana. The amount of strength this woman exuded was remarkable. And the fact that Lorraine Clark hadn't committed an unspeakable, illegal action against the man Ana loosely termed "father" was a feat in itself.

"Call me anytime, Mom. I mean it. As soon as I'm done with this project, I'll take some time off and we'll go somewhere to relax."

Her mother let loose a watery laugh. "I'd really like that, Ana. I love you."

"Love you," Ana said, trying to choke back tears. "I'll call you tomorrow."

Ana disconnected the call, straightened and turned her back once again to Zach.

"I'll just go outside and speak with Victor and the officer," he told her, obviously taking the hint she needed some alone time. "They should be about finished here."

Well, that was one good thing that came from him knowing women so well. He was in tune with their feelings.

Ana swiped at a tear that had escaped. She didn't want to cry about this. Hadn't her father caused enough anguish over the years? He never seemed to care whom he hurt, so long as he got what he wanted. Women, money, the thrill of the next bet. He always took from everyone, never giving even a piece of himself in return.

And her mother had finally had enough. After thirty years.

Did happily-ever-after even exist anymore? She wished she could be there for her mother right now, but their reunion would have to wait.

"They're gone."

Ana jerked around to see Zach closing the office door. "Oh, um, didn't they need to talk to me some more?"

"I told them you had an emergency call and you'd come down to the station in the morning to let them know if anything was taken and to file an official report."

Ana tugged her rubber band from her hair, smoothed the tangled curls back as best she could and looped it back into a low bun. "Thanks. Guess I'd better start cleaning up."

Zach crossed the tiny space, stepping over files and papers, and came to stand within inches of her. "Care to tell me what put that tear track on your cheek?"

"Not right now."

He studied her face. "We're going to be bunk mates all night. I'm here when you're ready to talk."

Torn, Ana stood still as Zach began to pick up the papers and put them in stacks on her desk. Not only had he dropped the subject, he'd genuinely been concerned and offered her a listening ear later. Just like last night when her emotions and feelings were all over the place, he'd known when to give her space and say just the right words.

Okay, so maybe some good qualities did come from him being a playboy. Ana wasn't sure. But she did know one thing. She had to be on her guard where this man was concerned because if she wasn't careful, he'd cause more damage to her life than any vandalism or divorce ever could.

She was on a slippery slope and losing her grip fast falling for Zach Marcum. Each day she slid just a bit more. Unfortunately he wasn't on the slope following her down.

Cole and Tamera had brought fast food, an air mattress, pillows and a couple of lightweight blankets. After Zach assured his twin and Tam that he and Ana would be fine sleeping in the on-site office, they finally walked out.

But not before Cole motioned for Zach to join him outside.

"Could I have a word with you?" Cole asked.

"Be right back," Zach told Ana.

Cole sent Tamera on to the car and stood at the bottom of the wrought-iron steps waiting for his fiancée to be out of earshot.

"Don't screw this up."

Zach rested one black boot on the top step, the other on the bottom step. "I'm not screwing anything up."

"I know you," Cole stated. "I also know Ana isn't your type, but the two of you are shooting off some pretty strong sparks. I was serious when I told you you couldn't get her because she wasn't your type and she wouldn't be interested."

Zach shrugged. "I never take you seriously. Was there anything else?"

"She's not here for your enjoyment, Zach," Cole warned, lowering his tone. "I haven't spent much time around her, but there's a sense of innocence about her. She's a professional. Make sure you stay that way as well."

Anger bubbled to the surface. Between the break-in, Ana's upsetting phone call that he still ached to know about and Cole's fatherly warning, Zach was ready to explode.

"If you're finished letting me know how to live the next year of my personal and professional life, your fiancée is waiting."

Without another word, he turned and went back into the cool office where Ana was setting up the air mattress in the middle of the floor. Every window, save for the one with the small air-conditioning unit, had been busted. They'd boarded them up in order to keep in the cool air.

On her knees, pulling the air pump from the suction of the

mattress, Ana glanced up as he came back through. "Home sweet home." She smiled.

Even though she tried to keep her tone light, Zach caught the question underlying her statement. When her eyes darted to the bare bed, the stack of pillows and sheets on the desktop and back to him, he knew she was worried. Cole had only brought one mattress.

"Ana, you don't have to stay here." He closed the door behind him, not moving much farther into the tiny office. There was no reason to make her any more jittery. "I'll be just fine. In all honesty, I'm sure whoever did this won't be back tonight, if ever. I can call Cole back and have him give you a lift home."

Shaking her head, Ana came to her feet. "Don't be absurd. I'm not going anywhere. I meant that the first and second time I said it."

"You're nervous."

"Yes."

He smiled at her quick, honest answer. "Don't be. I also didn't lie when I said nothing would happen until you're ready. I would never push you, Ana."

"I'm not concerned about you, Zach." She crossed her arms over her abdomen. "I'm scared of myself."

"Excuse me?"

She sighed, moving around the mattress to lean against the small desk that had been shoved into the corner. Her long, lean legs extended out in front of her. Zach held his place, waiting for her to continue.

"I don't recognize myself lately," she said, staring down at her jeweled flip-flops. "You make me want things I've never wanted before. Make me have thoughts about something other than work and my family. I've never thought about…"

"Yourself?" he asked, earning him a slight nod. "You're too busy working or taking calls from your parents or helping people who need you. You can't say no to anyone, so therefore your own needs are put on hold."

Ana brought her gaze back up to his. "You're not telling me anything I don't know, but I just don't know how to let go."

Easing closer, Zach shrugged. "I can't believe this is coming from my mouth, but take it slow. I don't want you to regret being with me. And since we're here all night, and my first choice of activities isn't an option, we'll work on the seating chart for the shower."

Ana's eyes studied him for a moment. And now that he'd moved closer, he could see just how hard her pulse was pounding. Out of nerves? Or arousal?

"I never know what you'll do or say next," she murmured. "You're not who I thought you were."

That made two of them. He had no idea he'd ever want to put his social life on hold to wait for a woman who may or may not ever be ready to sleep with him. And if/when she did decide, what the hell then? He had nice words to give her about waiting and being patient, but when the time came, could he really give her everything she needed? Would he be attentive enough, gentle enough?

"Let me go get the list of names," he told her, once again heading back outside, needing some distance. "I'm going to move my bike closer to the office, too."

He walked out into the sun setting over the ocean to retrieve the list from the saddlebags on his Screamin' Eagle and couldn't help but think of how far they still had to go on this property.

Normally when a project started, Zach was in a hurry to see it completed. Not this time, though. Because when this resort was done, Ana would move on to another town, another site. Another man?

Zach kick-started his Harley to life and gritted his teeth.

No, he was in no hurry to see this project come to a close, but he wouldn't dwell on the inevitable. Right now, he was working on his master plan of seduction.

Ten

Nerves slammed around in Ana's body as she waited for Zach to come back. Was this fate's way of smacking her in the face by giving her the opportunity with a man she knew could show her everything she needed to know and more about intimacy?

Yes, Zach's willingness to be her teacher wasn't her concern. The fact that she knew without a doubt that her heart would get battered in the process was more bothersome.

Ana slipped out of her flip-flops and took the pile of sheets to make up their bed.

Their bed.

There was no way that she could sleep with Zach on this mattress. No. Way. She'd never shared a bed with anyone, much less a man.

This was a bad, bad idea. So what if Cole only had one mattress in his attic? Why didn't he just go buy another one? Probably because Zach told him not to.

Ana snapped the fitted sheet from the folded pile and

wrestled the elastic corners over the air mattress, all the while cursing the blasted person or persons who were responsible for the break-in. Not only did they make a total mess of her meager work space, but so did the cops, and now she was forced to be with Zach and his sexy smile, powerful words and arousing touches.

Just as she sent the top sheet sailing into the air to let it fall carelessly over the bed, Zach stepped back in with folded papers in hand and an expression she couldn't quite read.

"What's wrong?" she asked.

He shook his head, laid the papers on her desk. "Nothing— other than the fact that your office got trashed, I'm stuck with this guest list while my sister is out of town and this is not how I wanted to spend an evening alone with you."

Ana couldn't help but laugh. "Careful. Your bottom lip is starting to pucker. Pouting won't change a thing."

"You're right, but you asked." He glanced down to the bed in the middle of the floor, then back up to her. "You know there's no way we can sleep on that."

Yeah, she knew. She was just surprised he thought so.

"I'll take this blanket and sleep on the floor by the door," he told her, grabbing the thin cotton blanket from her desk chair.

"I'm not tired." Ana didn't want to get into sleeping arrangements right now. Her nerves were already a jumbled mess. "Let's look at the guest list and see how many people you all should expect so we can get some numbers to your caterer."

Zach spread the blanket out on the hard floor and came back over to where Ana had the papers spread across her desk. His cologne wasn't overpowering, but it was strong and dominating, just the same. Much like the man.

She knew her office was small, even more so every time he'd been in here, but now that she knew they were going to be here for hours, through the hot, hopefully silent night, the space really seemed to close in around her.

Ana stared down at the papers, resting her hands on the edge of her desk, right alongside of Zach's. Yeah, there wasn't a word on there that she could focus on. How could she when all she could think about was whether she should take this opportunity and run with it?

But at the same time, just because the opportunity was there, did that mean she had to act on it?

"…and since we're going with the ice cream social and mingling motif, seating won't be an issue so we won't have to worry about dealing with exes and people who would rather not be seated next to their in-laws."

Ana dragged her mutinous mind back to the issue at hand. Forcing herself to listen to Zach, she nodded. Zach seemed to have it all sorted out. Obviously he wasn't having an issue at all.

"The names printed in red are the ones who are coming." He pointed to another set of names. "These in green haven't sent their RSVP back in yet."

Ana cleared her throat. If he could manage this crackling tension, then so could she. "How many of these are children?"

Zach ran a long, tanned finger down the last page. "She has here approximately seventeen."

"Okay, so we'll need two dozen cupcakes at least," Ana told him, grabbing a pen from her desktop and jotting down notes on the list. "I'd say more like three dozen, though. I assume Kayla will take care of calling the caterer?"

Zach nodded. "She should be back tomorrow, so yes, she'll do that."

Ana picked up a small notepad from her desk and moved to the mattress. She sank down, crossing her legs and began to jot more notes down, trying desperately to get into the role of wedding shower coordinator and keep her distance from Mr. Tall, Dark and Yummy.

No such luck. He followed her, removed his black boots and sat next to her on the bed. Because he outweighed her by a good fifty pounds, she had to catch herself from tumbling against him.

"What are you writing now?" he asked, leaning closer to get a look.

"Just some of my thoughts for Kayla. I—"

Zach placed a hand over her hand on the pen. "You're shaking."

Ana kept her eyes diverted to the paper and forbid herself from looking up into a set of chocolate eyes she just knew were watching her every move.

But she wasn't about to act like the unknowing, naive woman who didn't know what he was referring to. "I tend to shake when I'm nervous."

"Do I make you nervous, Anastasia?"

She risked a glance over at him—so much for her forbidding herself. "Only when you're with me," she said with a slight smile.

His warm fingers stayed wrapped around her hand, but his other hand came up to the base of her throat. "Your pulse is always going so fast. Are you scared?"

"I'd be a fool not to be scared." She closed her eyes, allowing his sensual touch to take over. "You promised not to push me."

"You don't look like you're being pushed into anything." She heard the smile in his voice. "You appear to be enjoying my persuasion."

Those wandering fingers came up around her jawline, slid over her slightly parted lips and stroked them. "You like my touch, don't you?"

"Yes," she whispered.

The pen slid from her hand, rolled off her lap. The notebook slid onto the sheet as well.

"Why don't you just let your body take over?" he whispered, moving in closer. "I know you have so much passion."

Oh, how she wanted to let him take complete control over this situation. But she couldn't. If she let him in, even the slightest bit, she feared he'd leave her wanting more of something he couldn't give.

She came to her feet, nearly tripping backward as she stumbled off the mattress. "This isn't happening. It can't."

Zach's gaze started at her bare feet, traveled up her legs and body before locking onto her eyes. "It will happen, Ana. You want this just as much as I do and you won't deprive yourself for long. One of these times when we're alone, you'll lose control. And I'll be there ready and willing."

Shivers slid up Ana's spine at the matter-of-fact tone. "Are you always this sure of yourself?"

His grin was menacing, threatening. Arousing. "Always."

She stepped back once again when he came to his feet and held out his hand. "Come on," he told her. "I have an idea."

Keeping her hands to herself, she eyed him. "What?"

"Just come on." He pulled his boots back on, tossed her flip-flips her way and grabbed his keys. "I'm going to be your first one way or another."

"You can't be serious," Ana exclaimed once they stepped outside her office into the stifling Miami heat. Even though it was nearly midnight, the air was thick and Zach's idea was preposterous.

He smiled, crossed his arms over his wide chest and shook his head. "This is the perfect spot for you to learn how to ride."

Ana stared at the big, black motorcycle like it would bite her. "There's no way I'm getting on that and driving it."

"Why not? I had a first time, too."

She laughed. "I don't want to hear about your firsts and I don't want to learn."

He leaned down next to her ear and whispered, "We can always go back inside."

Ana swallowed. "Give me a helmet."

"No need." He eased back and handed the key to her. "We're just going to be around here and you won't be going fast. Besides, there are no rules on private property."

Still, fear of the unknown territory speared through her. "Zach, this is silly. What if I tear up your bike?"

He shrugged, took her hand and placed it on the handlebar. "You won't tear it up and if you do, it's a piece of metal. It can be fixed and I have others."

The warm metal beneath her palm did nothing to soothe her nerves. "Is there anything I should know before I mount up?"

Zach let out a deep-from-the-belly laugh, smacking a kiss right on her cheek before he came around the other side of the bike. "Mount up? No, there's not much you need to know. I can stand here and tell you that this is a Harley-Davidson Screamin' Eagle specially made when I ordered it. I could go through the impressive engine I had put into it, along with all the accessories, but I won't bore you.

"Right now all you need to know is how to sit on it before you start it. Get used to holding all that power between your legs."

She quirked a brow. "You're seriously not going to start with those double entendres, are you?"

Zach shrugged. "If that's the only way to ease you into everything. Now sit."

"Don't I need pants and boots or something?"

He glanced to her bare legs and flip-flops. "Nah. The engine won't get hot in the little bit of time you'll be riding. That is if you can get it started and can steady it."

Ana rolled her eyes. "Like I said. How hard is it to sit with this thing between your legs?"

When Zach merely smiled, those stark white teeth shining bright compared to his tanned skin and dark rugged stubble on his jaw, Ana knew she was in over her head.

And not just with the Harley.

Keeping her hand firm on the handle, she tossed her leg over the seat and grabbed hold of the other handle. "Okay, now what?"

He stood in front of the bike, arms crossed over his impressive chest, the hint of a tattoo on his bicep peeking from beneath his black T-shirt. Well, that answered one question. One down, how many hidden tattoos to go?

With the moon behind the clouds, this sexy, irresistible man before her looked like the polar opposite of a millionaire CEO type…. He looked like the devil wrapped in a nice, enticing package.

"Try to balance the bike between your legs. Put your weight on your feet and ease the bike so it's up and not leaning on the stand."

Her hands gripped the bars as she shifted her weight, and the bike. "Oh, no…"

He was right beside her, curling his big, strong hands around hers, shoving his rock-solid body against her side to prevent her from tilting.

"Good grief." Ana's breath came in fast pants, not just because of the near fall on this huge bike. "I had no idea it would feel that heavy. It didn't seem like that when I sat behind you."

She glanced up to see him mere inches from her face, his heavy-lidded eyes aimed right on her parted lips. "That's because I do all the work," he told her in a raspy tone.

"We're not talking motorcycles anymore, are we?"

He smiled, leaned in even closer, his lips barely a whisper

away from hers. "I was referring to everything in my life. But I like where your mind keeps wandering."

And then he didn't let her mind wander anymore. His smooth, soft lips covered hers in the kiss she'd been dreaming about for hours, for days. And Ana didn't even have the briefest of moments where she wanted to fight him or pull back. She wanted his mouth on hers.

Their hands still remained on the handles, but his fingers had slid between hers, stroking. Her shoulder still rested against the hard wall of his chest.

With a gentle sweep of his tongue, he eased her lips apart, taking the kiss to an even deeper level of intimacy.

How could he be so controlling, so demanding, yet so gentle and passionate?

Just when she thought for sure he'd put his hands someplace else on her body, he tugged slightly on her bottom lip, drawing out the kiss even more before easing back.

Her eyes fluttered open as she ran her tongue across her lips, trying to hold on to his taste.

"What about the police cruiser that's been driving by?" she whispered. "We can't—"

"He already drove by and they're only coming by every hour." Zach's bright smile cut through the darkness, and her resolve. "Plenty of time."

Nerves now settled in good and deep in her stomach. "Zach, I—"

Now his hands did come up to frame her face as he crushed her mouth under his. All words, and thoughts, were completely lost. She had no idea what she'd been about to say. Maybe she was going to tell him she couldn't go any further than heated kisses, but more than likely she was going to beg him not to stop. At least he'd saved her from begging.

Her body ached for him. Her hands fell off the handlebars as she turned to the left and reached around with her right hand to grab fistfuls of his shirt.

Zach's talented lips trailed heated kisses from her lips down her jaw and neck to the scoop of her tank top. Something in Ana took over—instincts, hormones, pure lust—did it matter? She arched into him, silently begging him to keep doing everything he was doing that made her feel so amazing.

"I can't stop, Ana. I can't stop touching you." He kissed her harder, then pulled back. "I won't push you, but I have to at least touch you anywhere you're comfortable with."

He pushed one hand up her tank and she could only groan out a "yes" when that warm palm slid up her abdomen and over her lacy bra.

Chills raced, one after the other, all over her body.

"This is for you," he murmured against her skin as he traveled back up to her mouth.

"What?"

She had no idea what he meant, but he didn't stop assaulting her shoulders, neck and lips long enough to answer.

Taking both hands to the waistband of her shorts, he made quick work of the button and zipper.

Was this really happening? Was she ready? If not, she feared in about one more second it would be too late to say so.

"Zach…"

He eased on the bike behind her. "Shh. Lean against me, Ana."

Falling back against that hard-planed chest she'd give anything to see bare, Ana tried to relax. But Zach's hands opened her shorts and one of his hands slid in.

Her body stiffened, but Zach murmured soothing words into her ear as his other hand eased back up her shirt. Ana didn't know where to put her own hands, so she rested them on Zach's thighs and squeezed when his fingertips caressed her between her legs.

"Relax, Ana. This is all for you."

Her hips jerked as she tightened her hold on his thick,

muscular legs. Easing her legs open wider, Ana did as he told and let herself go.

Zach used both of his hands in ways she'd never dreamed possible. She didn't know if he was torturing her or pleasuring her. A fine line separated the two emotions.

Just when she thought she couldn't take another second of agony, her body tightened, convulsed. Pleasure like she'd never known shot through every corner of her body.

Whatever Zach whispered in her ear was lost in the hot Miami night. His stubbled jaw rasped against her cheek as her tremors slowly died down.

Embarrassment threatened to take over, but Zach, as usual, knew where her thoughts were headed.

"So responsive." He eased his hand from her shorts, placing it on the inner part of her thigh. "That was the sexiest moment of my life."

Ana closed her eyes, wishing she could believe his words, but knowing he probably did this all the time with women. Perhaps he'd even said those exact words.

Hey, get on my bike and I'll show you how to ride.

And she'd fallen for his line. But with the way her body tingled, she'd worry about her foolishness tomorrow. Right now she was too busy relishing the way her body still hummed.

Oh, she'd made out with men, but never had she even come close to climaxing. Nothing about Zach resembled any relationship she'd had in the past. And that was the scariest part of it all. She wasn't even in a relationship with him; he was her boss.

"I think I've had enough lessons." She tried to ease away, but his arms tightened around her.

"Don't be upset."

"With whom?" she asked. "You or me?"

"Me for showing you a new side to your own body and you for thinking you lost control." He straightened her clothes, even refastened her pants, and wrapped his arms around her waist. "Sometimes loss of control is a good thing, Ana. I will apologize if you think I lured you out here for that. I really had every intention of you learning to ride."

She pried his arms from her and not so gracefully removed herself from between his legs and off the bike. "Yes, well, neither type of riding will happen again. It can't. Yes, I'm attracted to you. Obviously. But we can't have a fling while we're working and then afterward just go our separate ways. I don't do flings, Zach. And that's all you do. Surely I'm not the only one who sees the problem."

She didn't wait to hear his reaction. With jittery legs and a rapid heart, Ana climbed the rickety stairs to her office. After kicking her flip-flops into the corner, she flopped down on the air mattress and jerked the sheet up over her heated body.

He was right. She didn't know if she was upset with herself for playing right into his hand or him for making her see just what she was missing.

Ana had a feeling she still didn't know what she was missing because for some reason, even though Zach had pleasured her, she still felt cheated by not seeing him or touching him in return.

Damn that man. He'd gotten around her wall of defense, but he wouldn't get around the one to her heart.

That wall was made of steel.

Eleven

When the sun rose, Zach was still fully awake. And aroused. He'd spent the last six hours cursing himself for pushing Ana into something she mentally wasn't prepared for and pushing himself to the brink of insanity.

He'd never, ever been so adamant, so demanding about pleasuring a woman and receiving nothing in return.

But the intensity with which he'd wanted to pleasure her overrode any physical ache he'd had. He'd wanted her to see just a glimpse of the passion they could share, the desires that were swirling around them. Dancing around the sexual attraction for weeks was damn near killing him.

Knowing he'd maybe ruined any chances of getting her into his bed hurt much more than his stiff back from leaning against the wall at the foot of her mattress all night. Yes, he'd watched her sleep, trying to figure out how the hell he could get her to understand there was nothing to be ashamed of, nothing to regret. And so much more to explore.

But he knew the moment those mesmerizing green eyes

opened, he'd see regret filling them and there wasn't a damn thing he could do about it.

Zach came to his feet, picked up his boots and stepped outside, careful not to wake Ana. He sat on the top step and shoved his feet into his shoes.

Workers would be arriving in an hour or so. Some construction companies didn't start so early, but Ana didn't cut her employees slack where hours were concerned. She wanted them early, prompt and ready to get to it. Which was a smart move considering the hellish Miami heat.

Another thing he admired about her.

Dammit, he was treading on shaky ground here. He didn't want to admire her. He wanted to get her into his bed and get her out of his system. Then once the project was completed and Victor Lawson was thrilled about his first U.S. resort, then Zach could walk away feeling satisfied and one more giant leap past Melanie.

A small four-door car pulled into the dusty lot, gravel crunching beneath the tires. Zach turned to the vehicle, wondering who on earth could be here this early.

A tall, slender man with dark hair stepped from the car. The sun glinted off his hair, making the red more prominent. There was something about him that seemed familiar, but Zach knew he'd never met the man before.

"Morning," the man said as he closed the car door and approached Zach. "Didn't expect anyone to be here this early, except my girl. She's always prompt."

His girl. This was Ana's father. Zach loathed him on the spot and wondered what the hell the man could want.

"You work for Anastasia?"

Zach crossed his arms over his chest, wishing he'd woken Ana so she could be prepared for this surprise guest. "Technically she works for me. I'm the architect, Zach Marcum."

He didn't extend his hand by way of most initial meetings.

Zach had no desire to shake hands with a man who'd obviously hurt Ana on a level he couldn't possibly understand.

The man placed his hands on his hips, eyes narrowed. "Where's Ana?"

Before Zach could respond, the office door opened. Ana stood on the top step, wiping her eyes. All that auburn hair draped her shoulders in curls, and her tank and shorts were wrinkled from an uncomfortable night's sleep.

She hadn't spotted her father yet and Zach figured her eyes were still adjusting to the bright morning light. She stretched her arms above her head, baring a pale shimmer of midriff between her tank and shorts. What he wouldn't give to scoop her into his arms and take her away where they could be alone.

But he knew the second she spotted them. Her eyes, which had been scanning the horizon, now froze. She shoved her hair from her face, swept it over her shoulders and tilted her chin.

"What are you doing here?" she asked, without moving from the top step.

Zach turned so he was in between the two. He took a step back, though, to let them talk, but he wasn't going far.

"Just wanted to stop by to see my girl."

Ana rolled her eyes, rested her hands on her hips, mimicking her father's motion. "You've seen me, but I'm sure you're not here to make sure I'm okay or that I'm happy. So, let's cut to the chase, how much this time? And what are you doing in Miami?"

Zach saw the man's eyes turn to slits. "Can we talk in private?"

Looking to Zach, Ana shook her head. "Zach's not leaving unless he wants to. If you want something just come out and say it? How much are you in debt for this time?"

"Don't talk to me that way, young lady." Her father took

a step forward, putting Zach on full alert. "I'm still your father."

"You've never been a father to me," Ana said in a tone Zach had never heard from her. Pure venom dripped from her voice. "I'm just glad Mom finally came to her senses and left you, though you left her little choice when you squandered away everything she's ever owned."

"Why am I not surprised she called you crying? Look, Anastasia—"

"No." Ana held up a hand and came down the steps and closed the gap between her and her father. "You're just upset she called and told me because you know that now you have no leverage for me to fund your habit."

Zach moved toward his motorcycle, which was only a couple feet from this family feud. From the debt Ana referred to, Zach assumed her father had a gambling issue. Something he'd have to investigate on his own time.

"I just need ten thousand and I'll leave you alone," her father pleaded in a softer tone. "That's a small amount for someone like you. You've always hoarded every single dime you made and you've been at this business for a long time. I know how much you work yourself, too, so don't act like you don't have any money. Besides, I've been in Miami for a few weeks. I figured this is where all the high rollers come to play. Might as well see what I can get."

"You're pathetic to think you rank with people who actually worked for their money and were responsible enough to invest or pay off debts. I won't give you ten cents." Ana pointed a finger at her father, her tone growing louder and stronger. "If you want to play with the big boys, then step up and be one. Now get out of here before I call the police and have you arrested for trespassing."

A moment of silence stretched, but the tension still crackled. Finally her father spoke. "I can't believe you'd do this to me."

"Had you, even once, pretended you gave a damn about me and Mom, I would give you anything you wanted." Ana's voice hitched, the commanding voice she'd had seconds ago vanished as her vulnerability crept to the surface. "Had you ever told me you loved me, shown me that I mattered to you, I'd never question you and hand over everything I have without question. You didn't only gamble our money and assets, you gambled with lives. Mom and I will never get over how you destroyed our family."

Ana cleared her throat and Zach knew she was on the verge of tears. He wanted to go to her, wrap his arms around her and comfort her. But he wasn't sure how, not sure what to say. This was brand-new territory for him.

He did know one thing, though. He wanted Ana's father gone five minutes ago. But Ana had to deal with this herself. He wasn't her boyfriend. Hell, he wasn't even technically her lover, so this family reunion was none of his business.

"But you've never given me even one second of your life," Ana continued, her voice now stronger than ever, but Zach saw her eyes shimmering in the sunlight. "So I won't give you anything of mine."

Her father stood still for a moment, the muscle ticking in his jaw. "Fine. I hope you can live with yourself knowing you turned me away. I'll be in Miami for another week or so to see what turns up if you change your mind. I didn't raise you to be selfish, Anastasia."

"No, you didn't raise me at all."

He stalked away, got into his rental car and drove off the site, leaving Ana and Zach staring after the dusty trail.

"I didn't mean to oversleep." Ana turned toward Zach, pulled a rubber band from her pocket and twisted her hair back and looped it through. "I need to get to my condo and change so I can be back here before my crew shows up. Can you give me a lift?"

He lifted a brow. "Are you really going to pretend you're fine when I know you're not?"

"You know nothing about me, Zach."

Treading on shaky ground, he pushed his limit with her even further. It wasn't the brightest move to make, but he'd always gone against the odds and taken risks. No way was he going to let her brush this off when she was so upset.

"That's not true." He stepped around his bike, shoving his hands in his pockets to show her he wasn't threatening or confrontational. "I know you're hurting, I know you're vulnerable and I know you're regretting last night and the last thing you needed to wake up to was your father making demands."

His eyes held hers, saw the tears gathered there. She shut her eyes and one lone teardrop trickled down her creamy skin. The silent emotional plea took hold of his heart and squeezed. Hard.

"My personal business isn't your concern," she told him, eyes still closed as if trying to gather her courage to open them. "Can you just give me a ride back to my condo?"

Because he'd been dying to touch her the whole time her father had been here, Zach stepped forward and with the pad of his thumb wiped the moisture from her cheek. Her eyes popped open, and she bit her bottom lip and stared into his eyes.

"There's no need to hide your emotions." Zach left his hand on her cheek, cupping her soft skin in his palm. "I know you don't want to lean on anyone, but I'm here if you want to talk."

Her eyes searched his face. Surely she'd open up, let out what she'd kept bottled inside her. But she stepped back, making his hand fall to his side.

"All I need from you is a ride."

She walked around him and mounted the bike like a pro. Damn, she had a spine of steel. How could he not find that attractive? And how could he possibly stop himself from wanting her on more than a physical level?

Ana changed and was back at the site before the first member of her crew showed. As long as she kept going, didn't take time to think about her father's visit, she'd get through the day.

Oh, who was she kidding? She was used to her father always dropping in unannounced, begging for money. She needed to concentrate on work and stay busy so she didn't think about the one and only sexual experience she'd ever had, thanks to Zach and his talented hands.

Even inexperienced as she was, she had a gut feeling that he'd set the bar so high no other man could reach it.

Great. Exactly what she did *not* need.

This was just one more reason she'd never gotten involved with a man, never let him touch her body in such an intimate way. How could she work when her mind was replaying over and over the events of last night? How could she ever be alone with him again and not immediately desire to see what else he could teach her?

Zach had been so giving, so…perfect. Yes, much as she hated to admit it, he'd done every single thing right.

So why was she so ticked?

She slammed the door to her office, stared at the mess of sheets on the mattress where she'd slept. Alone. She'd rolled over last night and peeked from beneath her lids to see where Zach had gone. She was surprised to see him propped against the wall watching her.

A ripple of nerves speared through her as she recalled how he'd looked with the sliver of light filtering through the cracks in the boards over the windows.

He cared for her. Whether he wanted to admit it or not, he cared. He couldn't have been so giving, so gentle with her last night and expect nothing in return if he didn't. He wouldn't have stood by her side when her father showed up, then offered a shoulder to lean on if he was only out to take her virginity.

And the mind-blowing thought that big, bad playboy Zach Marcum was growing feelings for her scared her to death. He wouldn't like it when he realized the path his emotions had taken him down.

Of course, she could be wrong and he treated all of his women this wonderfully. That would explain why she always had so many.

But she didn't think she was wrong and now she'd just have to wait and see how the rest of their time together played out.

God help her heart when he walked away.

Twelve

Ana was back in her condo, freshly showered and in her cami/boyshort pajama set getting ready to comb out her hair when a knock sounded on her door.

She laid the wide-toothed comb on the vanity in the bathroom and walked through her master bedroom and the living area to the door and peeked through the hole.

Zach. Of course.

Being around him all day had been fine, seeing as how her entire crew was milling about. But now he chose to come to her alone, a one-on-one meeting, when he knew she'd be more vulnerable. Fantastic.

She opened the door, just enough for him to see her, but blocked his entry.

"Can I come in?" he asked.

In the span of a second, all the reasons flashed through her mind as to why he shouldn't come in. Her state of dress, or lack thereof, the pictures she never wanted to share that she had sitting around in her bedroom. Which wouldn't be an issue if he stayed out.

Oh, yeah, and another reason he shouldn't come in was the fact that she knew he'd want to discuss what had transpired between them last night and the confrontation this morning with her father. She needed armor to deal with Zach and not just in the form of more clothing.

"Now's not a good time." Wasn't that the truth?

A corner of his sexy mouth tipped up in a grin. "If I waited for a good time, you'd never let me in."

Why lie? "Probably not."

"Please," he said, all signs of joking aside.

"I'm not really dressed for company," she explained.

"If I promise to control myself, will you let me in?"

She wondered if he was capable of controlling himself, at the same time that she felt a bit disappointed that he wasn't here to finish what they'd begun last night.

What a mix of chaos her emotions were. One minute she wanted him to take her to places she'd never been and the next she wanted him to stay away.

"Ana…"

She bit her lip and eased the door open to allow him to pass through.

When she turned to face him, his gaze raked over her bare legs, her bra-free chest and her wet hair. And she just knew her nipples were now puckered. Why did her body have to betray her when she was trying to stand her ground?

Because she wanted this man. After the performance last night, she honestly wanted to see what else he would do.

"Let me get a T-shirt," she said, bypassing him and walking into her bedroom.

Thankfully all of her personal pictures were kept beside her bed and on the dresser. She would just have to keep Zach in the living room.

She grabbed an oversize T-shirt from the top dresser drawer

and was just pulling it over her head when he stepped into her bedroom.

"I didn't mean to intrude." He took a seat in the wing chair next to the window. "But at the site today, we didn't have any privacy and if we had managed to steal a moment, it wouldn't have been without interruptions."

Ana crossed over to him, leaned a hip against the window-sill. "I'm sorry you had to witness that not-so-pleasant family reunion this morning. I'd appreciate it if you didn't tell anyone what you overheard. My father... He has a gambling problem."

"I assumed as much."

Zach eased back in the chair, watching her. With very few words and an intense stare she knew he was listening as if he wanted to know what was going through her mind.

No man had ever given her the kind of personal attention Zach did. God, she didn't want to be one of those clichés. The woman who never had affection from her father fell for the first guy who showed her attention.

But in Ana's heart she knew, even if she'd had a father of the year as a kid, she'd still be tangled up with Zach emotionally.

"I'm not proud of the fact I've always paid off his debts," she continued, turning her gaze out the window to the bright pink sky meeting the clear blue ocean. "I only did because I love my mother and she's been through a hellish marriage. But now that she's left, I don't care what happens to him."

Saying those words aloud was so much different than thinking them. Ana ran her hands through her tangled hair as all of her twenty-eight years of emotions bubbled to the surface. "That sounds so cruel," she whispered, looking down to Zach. "I can't help that I don't love him. He never gave me a chance to. He's my father, but he never loved me. The first time in my life he ever paid attention to me was when I started making money. He became interested in my business...or so I thought.

"I was foolish enough to believe he saw me as an adult and we could start having a good relationship. I should've known better."

Zach reached out, took her hands in his and squeezed. "There's nothing wrong with wanting to be loved by your parent, Ana. That's something that you shouldn't have to beg for or pay for. Ever."

Tears clogged her throat as her eyes began to burn. "You're right, but that didn't stop me from paying every time he came to me. In the back of my mind I always thought maybe this time he's proud of me. He knows how hard I've worked for the money and he's going to recognize my accomplishments."

Ana didn't know why she was telling him all of this, but once she started, she couldn't seem to stop herself.

"You know, when I was a kid, I always wanted a dog." She pulled her hands free from Zach's and paced the room. "I overheard my mother begging for him to let me get one, but he told her the last thing they needed was something else depending on him."

Ana took a seat on the bed, crossed her legs beneath her as memories flowed out into the open. "I didn't ask for one again because I heard my mother crying in the bathroom right after that. Even as young as I was, I knew she was the only parent who loved me, who actually cared."

"Why didn't she leave him a long time ago?" Zach asked.

Ana lifted a shoulder. "At first I think it was because she got pregnant right after they got married and she quit working for my grandfather to stay home. My grandfather, the one I would tag along with on his construction sites, was old-school. Once you're married, you stay married, no matter what. Then as I got older, I think Mom was afraid to start a life being single, jobless and trying to take care of me. Dad still worked for Grandpa, so maybe she was just scared what that relationship would do. I honestly don't know."

"What about when you moved out?"

A question she'd asked herself many times. "I still think she was scared. She knew about his numerous affairs, his overexcessive spending habits, but she'd been living that nightmare for so long, I don't think she thought she could do better."

Zach came to his feet and Ana was sure he was coming to comfort her. Instead he moved to the nightstand and picked up a small frame.

She'd been so wrapped up in spilling her family secrets, she'd completely forgotten about the photos. But now Zach was holding one and no matter how much she wished she'd never let him step foot in her bedroom, she knew he'd taken an even bigger step into her heart.

Zach studied the picture of a young, even-more-innocent Ana and a lady who undoubtedly had to be her mother. Both were smiling for the camera, but their eyes were empty.

"You certainly take your beauty from your mother," he told her, trying to get her to think of something more positive. "How old are you here?"

Ana barely shot a glance at the picture he held. "Seven."

Gently he sat the picture back down as his eyes traveled over the others. There was another one of Ana and her mother. This time Ana was grown and the two were smiling, arm in arm sitting on the beach.

But it was the picture of Ana as a young child that captured his attention.

"This your grandfather?" he asked, pointing to the aged photo.

Ana turned and smiled at the picture as if she were looking at the actual man in the photo. "Yeah. He was the best."

Zach smiled at the toddler sitting on a bulldozer, with

red ringlets poking beneath a scratched-up hard hat. Her grandfather stood beside the machine, securing little Ana with one large tanned hand on her dimpled knees.

"He taught me everything I know," she told him. "I've never felt more alone than when he passed. It was hard for me to keep working, knowing I couldn't run to him for advice. My mother took his death the hardest, though. She truly was alone because my father was never around and I was off hopping from site to site."

Ready to make the next paycheck to send to her father to keep his habit going and keep a roof over her mother's head. Zach knew what she was thinking, but he wasn't going to intervene on this shaky ground.

"Nothing you can do about it now," he told her, trying to get that sad look from her eyes even if he had to make her angry at him. Anger he could deal with. Remorse and sadness, not so much. "Don't beat yourself up on someone else's mistakes."

She jerked her chin up, her eyes to him. "I'm not beating myself up. But I do get upset when I think of all my mother has gone through because my father couldn't control himself… in any way."

"She's a grown woman, responsible for her own actions, Ana." Zach eased down onto the bed beside her. "You're not helping anyone, especially yourself, by being depressed about this. You held your ground with your father today and he'll either straighten up or he'll pay the consequences. Either way, it's out of your hands."

She stared at him for a moment before coming to her feet and crossing to the window. With her back turned Zach couldn't help but allow his gaze to rake over all that delicate skin and the skimpy shorts that fit perfectly over her bottom.

Ironic that he'd never wanted anyone more than Anastasia. Yet here they were in her bedroom with the orange glow from the setting sun creating the perfect ambiance, and her wearing next to nothing, and they were only talking.

Yeah, this had never happened to him before. He'd come here to have another intimate encounter to get her to trust him a bit more. He had no idea he'd get in on an emotional battle she was waging with herself.

Personal issues were not things he ever allowed himself to get involved in with a woman. Families were messy, complicated—two things he didn't need when seducing a woman. He liked simple and straightforward.

"I'm sorry," she said in a soft voice, still keeping her back to him. "I didn't mean to just have an emotional dump. But with Dad's visit today, I'm just not the best company."

"Then let's talk about last night."

Zach watched her back stiffen, her body freeze as if she was holding her breath.

"What's to discuss?" she asked. "It happened, it won't again, so let's move on."

He came to his feet, slowly closing the distance between them. "When you talk fast like that, I know you're nervous which makes me believe you don't really mean what you just said."

She glanced over her shoulder, her eyes finding his. "You don't have to remind me again about this attraction, and yes, last night proves it. But we're different, Zach. I do require some commitment and even if I didn't, I can't split my time between the largest project I've ever taken on and something so personal and intimate all at once."

"That's why I'm perfect for you." He placed his hands on her slender shoulders and turned her to face him. "I'm here for you on both fronts. Ana, I'm persistent, you know that. Why fight what we both want? We'll sleep together by the end of the project anyway. Prolonging the inevitable won't change the outcome."

Her creamy cheeks reddened. "I don't know why I find

myself wanting you. You're sexy, and you've always been right by me when I've needed you, but then you pull out this arrogance that I can't stand and remind me of all the reasons I don't want to like you."

Tugging on her gently until she fell against his chest, Zach looked down into her eyes. "I don't care if you like me, Anastasia. I care if you want me."

He crushed his lips to hers, not taking the time to be gentle, just demanding. He knew no other way.

She'd driven him crazy for weeks. He was hanging on by the proverbial thread.

Ana ran her hands through his hair, holding him in place, as if he were going to go anywhere. She groaned when he nipped at her lips and then dove back in for more.

Yeah, there was no way this urge to have her would just disappear if they ignored it. His desire for her grew each time he saw her, touched her.

Zach's hands roamed down her back to cup her backside through the long T-shirt and boyshorts. What he wouldn't give to rip off all their clothes and show her just how arrogant he was. He wasn't laid-back, certainly never had been in an intimate setting, but Ana needed someone in her life to be. And, dammit if he wouldn't be that man.

Much as it pained him, literally, Zach eased back, moving his hands back to her shoulders to steady her.

"You don't need this now," he told her, never hating himself more for having morals.

She blinked in confusion. "Yes, I think I do."

As if she'd taken her small hand and clutched his heart, Zach felt the pressure deep in his chest. "You *think*. That's not enough. When you know for certain, come find me."

Zach turned, walked out of the condo and to the elevator before the ramifications of what he'd just turned down hit him.

Ana offering herself with no promises of commitment or questions about tomorrow.

He'd never turned down a woman he was interested in. Ever.

Obviously in his attempt to sneak past her line of defense, she'd gotten by his without so much as a warning.

He'd wanted to get past the complications of Melanie trying to wedge her way back into his life. Well, his wish came true. Now he just had an even bigger complication in the form of a fiery redhead with a tool belt.

Thirteen

After four infuriating weeks, Ana was ready to choke
Zach Marcum. It was either that or drag him into her office
and make him finish what he'd started on his motorcycle
a month ago. What had he called it? A Screamin' Eagle?
What an appropriate place to have such a memorable sexual
experience.

How dare he assume that just because she wanted him that
she'd act on her feelings? Granted, had he not pulled back in
her condo, she would've consented to anything and everything
he wanted. She'd been a vulnerable, emotional basket case.

But he'd gone and shocked her by leaving. Ana had no
doubt he'd shocked himself as well. The evil part of her hoped
he'd suffered because of his gallant effort to make sure she
was certain about taking the next step.

As she thought about him, Ana fingered the invitation for
the wedding shower today. For some insane reason, Kayla had
invited Ana to Tamera's bridal shower.

Silly, really. She barely knew Tamera, since she'd dealt with mostly Zach. But Kayla had been so thrilled with the whole ice cream social idea, she'd insisted on inviting Ana. How out of place would *that* feel? What on earth did she have in common with any of these socialites? She was a forewoman. She didn't get weekly manis and pedis, she didn't visit a salon on a regular basis to tame her curls and she certainly didn't have the pedigree she was sure the women at the party had.

She was just a simple girl from the Midwest who just so happened to catch the eyes of several architectural firms and built her career one beam at a time. There was nothing fancy, nothing special, and certainly nothing glamorous about her.

So why was she standing in front of the floor-length mirror in her bedroom running a hand down one of the last dresses in her closet? The knee-length purple strapless would be okay for a wedding shower. Wouldn't it?

Rolling her eyes at her preposterous way of thinking and for always second-guessing herself, Ana grabbed her gift and purse and set out for what was sure to be an interesting day.

When Ana stepped from the building, ready to ask the valet to fetch her a cab, a driver stepped from a sleek, black Jag and rounded the hood with a smile.

"Miss Clark?"

Smiling in return, Ana nodded. "Yes."

"Mr. Marcum sent me." He opened the rear door and gestured her in. "He told me you were attending a party and wanted to make sure you got there and back with no problem."

Stunned, Ana stood rooted in place for a moment, then stepped toward the car. "Zach sent you to take me?"

"Yes, ma'am."

Just another check on Zach's gentleman list. Seriously, if the man didn't want women falling head over heels, why on earth did he insist on doing such romantic gestures? She needed to put a stop to this and soon. But that was certainly not an issue she'd take up with the friendly driver.

"Thank you."

Refreshing air-conditioning welcomed her as she slid onto the cool leather seat. Zach was not making her life easy and she had a good feeling he knew it. He wanted her to come to him. Begging.

But she was already halfway in love with the frustrating man and if she gave him the last piece of her vulnerability, there would be no turning back. Which meant that when Zach moved on, and his type always moved on, she would have no one to blame for her broken heart but herself.

Today, however, would not be about her or her insecurities. Today she would make the most of being introduced to new people and celebrating the love two people found a second time around.

Ana admitted, only to herself of course, that she was excited to attend the shower. It wasn't that often she was able to mingle with women and dress like a lady all in one day. She would certainly take this moment and relish it.

Yes, she positively loved her job and all the amazing structures she'd been trusted with, but she was still a woman. And going out in public where she could show that side was always a plus and not something she often turned down.

Actually she needed this break. A break from the site, a break from the pressure, a break from her parents' impending divorce. But most of all a break from Zach.

He'd been at the site every day, but he'd never been anything but a complete professional. Some women may think he'd lost interest, but she knew better. She'd felt his stare numerous times, saw the muscle tick in his jaw as if he were grinding his teeth to keep from saying something. And he always drove the same motorcycle he'd had the night he'd given her the first "lesson."

No, he hadn't given up. If anything, he was just getting started, plotting his next course of seduction…or attack, depending on how she looked at it.

Ana nearly groaned as the car pulled onto Star Island. Because Kayla had wanted the shower to remain small, intimate, yet still extravagant, she'd chosen to have it at Cole and Tamera's house. Since the wedding was being held there, Kayla figured the shower would be perfect there as well.

The professional side of her was excited to see the home of one of the best architects in the world. Of course, she'd love to see Zach's house as well, but she figured asking him would certainly give the wrong impression.

Heaven's sake, she didn't even know what the *right* impression was anymore. She'd give anything if her emotions would settle down on this volley back and forth. But she was a realistic woman. She knew, as well as Zach did, that they would end up making love. At least, that's what it would be on her end.

Before she could process that stimulating thought any further, the Jag had come to a stop in a wide, circular driveway and the driver was opening her door.

"Ma'am," he said, extending his hand.

Ana clasped the elderly man's hand and smiled. "Thanks so much for the ride."

He tipped his head down like a true Southern gentleman. "My pleasure, miss. I'll be right here when you're ready to leave, too."

Ana shook her head. "Oh, no. That's not necessary. I can find a ride back."

"I'm just following orders, ma'am."

"But I could be here for a couple hours."

He nodded once again and headed back to the driver's door. "That will be just fine, Miss Clark."

The driver got into the car and pulled around the driveway to get out of the way of the entrance. Ana stood there for a second, amazed, humbled, confused.

Pulling her phone from her purse, she punched in Zach's cell. She waited in the shade of the oversize mansion because it felt like five hundred degrees in the sun and she wasn't ready to step inside yet. Not when she wanted privacy for her call.

"Hello."

Ana gripped the phone with one hand, settled the package under her arm with the other and turned her back on the car that had just pulled up. "Quit sending me mixed signals."

"Ana." She heard the smile in his lazy voice. "Did you make it to the shower?"

"You know I did," she snapped. "I'm sure your driver already told you that and that he's waiting for me to leave."

"Of course. He's a driver, Ana, that's what he does. What's wrong all of a sudden?"

She glanced over her shoulder as two middle-aged women stepped from the car, packages in hand. Lowering her voice, she replied, "Not all of a sudden. You haven't been anything but professional for weeks and today you send your driver to pick me up."

"Ana, I just thought you'd appreciate being able to leave when you wanted. You don't really know anyone, so if you became uncomfortable, I wanted you to have a way out."

Another piece of her heart melted at his concern for her, even though she knew in his mind it was simple, logical. Still, no one had ever taken this much care with her, this much effort to win her trust and affection.

She swallowed the lump in her throat. "You care for me."

A soft chuckle from the other end vibrated through her. "Of course I do."

"But you haven't touched me in weeks, haven't called or stopped by after hours. You've been all business." She let out a sigh, not quite comfortable with baring her heart. "I wasn't sure anymore."

She hated admitting that, but she'd always been honest in every aspect of her life and she wasn't going to stop now just because Zach had her all torn up.

"Is that what you want, Ana? For me to touch you? To stop by after hours when I know you'll be alone?"

Another car pulled up as shivers raced through Ana's body. "Yes. I do. But I think for our sanity and the sake of this project, we need to keep our personal distance."

"You're not a coward, Anastasia."

She never had been, but then, she'd never had her heart on the line, either.

"Thank you for the driver, Zach."

Snapping her phone, Ana slid it back into her purse, re-adjusted the package under her arm and stepped up the wide, travertine steps leading to the arched entryway.

Women in beautifully colored sundresses chatted, laughed and mingled. A couple of children ran through the foyer, followed quickly by a mother extending her quick apology as she chased the kids.

Ana smiled and walked toward the back of the house in the hopes of finding Kayla or Tamera and to see where to put the gift.

She didn't have to wait long. The two women, looking stunning as always, were embraced in a sisterly hug. A small tug at Ana's heart almost brought tears to her eyes. What would it be like to have a sister or a friend so close she felt like one?

Traveling down that path of thoughts would only get her into trouble. She'd come to terms years ago with being an only child, and she didn't stay in one place long enough to make any friends. And she certainly couldn't bring herself to get too attached to Zach's family. Being attached to the man was bad enough. She didn't want to have to cut any more ties than necessary when the resort was done and she moved her crew to the next location.

Shoulders back, chin high, Ana walked out onto the stone patio area like she belonged at this intimate social gathering.

"Ana," Kayla greeted with a wide grin. "I'm so glad you could make it."

Accepting the half hug from Zach's baby sister warmed her. "Thanks for inviting me. Where should I put this?" she asked, lifting the gift.

"I'll take that."

Kayla plucked the present from her and took it over to a table loaded with colorful boxes of all sizes and shapes and bags overflowing with tissue paper.

"Everything looks beautiful." Ana glanced around the lush tropical gardens that were obviously professionally maintained, then turned her attention to Tamera. "Congratulations."

The stunning blonde was literally beaming from ear to ear. "Everything is perfect. I understand I have you to thank for this creative idea. I absolutely love the relaxed atmosphere, and having desserts was brilliant. I seriously can't thank you enough for suggesting this."

Embarrassed, Ana merely shrugged. "It's really no big deal. Zach was in a bind, Kayla had business that took her away and I happened to be there. I just suggested what I would've liked."

Tamera studied her for a moment and Ana suddenly felt like she was under a microscope. She glanced around for Kayla, but saw her taking other guests' presents to the table.

"Zach's mentioned how efficient you are," Tamera said, still smiling. "I have to say, I've never seen him in such a good mood. And, come to think of it, I haven't seen him date in over two months. That's a dry spell for Zach."

Ana remained speechless. What could she say?

"Unless…" Tamera quirked a brow.

"No," Ana said, shaking her head. "No unless. We're working together, and yes, we've become friends, but that's all."

Tamera's smile dimmed down to a knowing grin. "I know how it is with the Marcum twins. Cole is just as potent as

Zach, but Cole always had that quieter, more subtle approach. Zach's is more full-force, knock-you-to-your-knees. But their effect is the same, so if you need to talk, I'm here."

Ana could only nod. Seriously, what could she say? That she'd already experienced that knock to her knees? That there was no way she could ever build up an immunity to Zach Marcum? That every time she was around him she second-guessed every personal decision she'd made about keeping her distance?

Yeah. She was much better off sticking with a simple nod and keeping her mouth shut.

"Ana." Kayla came up behind her and placed a hand on her arm. "The ice cream and toppings are through this set of double doors to the left. In the living area are all the cakes. And out here are all the finger-type desserts—cookies, cupcakes, fruit dipped in chocolate." She gestured at the tables all around her. "If you need something, don't hesitate to ask."

"I think I just gained ten pounds listening to the menu," Ana joked. "I'll walk around and see what appeals to me."

"Oh, I see one of my old clients," Tamera said. "Excuse me for just a moment."

Kayla ended up walking around with Ana, giving Ana the prime opportunity to quiz her about Zach. But Ana didn't. She was truly enjoying Kayla's company and couldn't bear to be sneaky and selfish just to gain an insight into Zach's interesting lifestyle.

But when she told Kayla about the driver Zach had sent and how the poor man was outside waiting on her, Kayla smiled and rolled her eyes and went and told the man he could leave. Since the order came from a Marcum, the driver obeyed once Kayla assured him she would take Ana home and take any of the backlash from Zach.

The shower was a huge success. Ana lost track of the time and didn't once think about Zach or how she could possibly keep her distance in a personal manner. For once, she truly felt at home, like she belonged.

She *oohed* and *ahhed* with the rest of the ladies over the gifts. Platinum candlesticks, picture frames, crystal vases, even an oil painting of the happy couple, provided by Kayla. At that gift, the entire room teared up, except for the few children who were still running their poor mothers in circles.

Ana wondered if she'd ever find that whole place in her life where she could smile every day and feel that joy of being blessed with someone who loved her unconditionally.

Before the shower, she hadn't known Tamera well, but now she got a better insight into her. The woman was obviously sentimental, very caring and extremely popular given the number of hugs from guests and lavish gifts from absentees.

One by one the guests trickled out and in the end Kayla, Tamera and Ana were left each holding a glass of champagne. Kayla sat on the floor, her petite legs stretched before her as she leaned against one of the two leather sofas. Tamera sat up on that same sofa with her legs extended across the cushions. Ana lounged across from them with her elbow propped on the arm of the couch, her legs to the side, knees bent.

"If Cole came home now, he'd have a heart attack," Tamera said, twirling her glass and taking in the wreckage of the room.

Ana eyed all the shredded paper, torn ribbons, empty boxes and laughed. "This is like Christmas morning for adults."

"I hope I get a Christmas morning like this." Kayla laughed. "I'm so happy for you two, Tam. My brother is so lucky."

"We're both lucky," Tamera corrected. "I never believed I would find love a second time, let alone with the same man."

Ana had heard bits and pieces of how the two were torn

apart and reunited, but seeing the glow on her face, the sheen in her eyes, really breathed life into the stories.

"Have you ever been in love?" Kayla asked Ana.

"I don't think so." She took a sip of her champagne, not wanting to be the focus of the conversation, especially this one. "I know I've never had feelings like that before."

Both women stared at her. Ana took the silence as her cue to keep going.

"I've had a few relationships, but with my career, it's hard to establish any type of commitment. Besides, I've never found anyone I'd want to have a deeper bond with."

"Until now," Kayla said with her sweet smile.

Ana didn't know how to respond, so Zach's sister's words hung in the air like an unanswered question. Though both women were smiling like they already knew the answer.

Finally Tamera spoke up. "If the man makes you crazy and happy at the same time, if he does unexpected things that are thoughtful and he's expecting nothing in return and he didn't do anything to have to suck up for, then I'd say it's love. Especially if he consumes your thoughts and you instantly feel that flutter of emotions kick in when you hear his voice or see him walking toward you in a crowd."

Ana eased the glass down from her lips and with a shaky hand, sat it on the glass coaster on the low coffee table.

Flutter in the belly. Check.

Thoughtfulness. Check.

Crazy and happy all at once. Check.

Oh, God.

"You don't have to say anything," Tamera said quietly. "And believe me when I tell you we certainly won't tell."

Kayla set down her glass and came to sit next to Ana on the couch. "Oh, honey, don't get upset."

Ana honestly hadn't noticed she was crying until a tear tickled her cheek. "I'm sorry. I honestly just realized it. I mean, I've been wondering if that's what I've been feeling, but hearing you talk about the emotions that come along with love…"

"Zach is a very fortunate man." Tamera smiled. "And I'm sure he feels strongly for you."

Ana shook her head. "No, no. He's made it clear he isn't a relationship kind of guy."

"Maybe not," Kayla agreed, "but I've never seen him go this long without a date or five. He's never let his driver take a woman anywhere that he wasn't there, too, and I can tell you for certain, that he's never, ever looked this happy."

Ana shoved to her feet, pushing through the pile of tissue paper and boxes. "I can't even let myself think like that for a moment. I can't get hurt."

"Love isn't easy." Tamera swung her feet to the floor and sat up. "But it's so worth it in the end. Cole and I went about it the long way. Eleven years later, we're finally getting married. So, if you feel something for Zach, tell him. Don't let time get away. This is your life and you have to take risks now and again to make the most of it."

Just the thought of opening up to Zach made Ana's stomach roll. She had no doubt numerous women had proclaimed their love to him over the years. So what made her so different?

"Don't overanalyze this." Kayla stood, grabbed Ana's hands. "My brother may be known as a ladies' man, but he's got a heart of gold and would never purposely hurt you."

Ana looked Zach's baby sister in the eyes, squeezing her hands. "I know that. It's what he could do without meaning to that scares me."

Fourteen

Zach didn't know what to do about Ana. She was nervous lately. Always talking a mile a minute about nothing in particular.

He hadn't made any more suggestive remarks, hadn't tried to touch her and certainly hadn't allowed himself the luxury of being alone with her.

And it was damn near killing him.

The shower had been a week ago and ever since then, Ana hadn't been herself. He'd asked Kayla and Tamera if something had happened, but they'd both just smiled at him without uttering a word.

Which meant something monumental had occurred and he was more than likely in the center of whatever inside joke these three women were keeping. He shuddered. Nothing was scarier than a woman keeping a secret.

Zach drove his work truck today for the special delivery he had for Miss Anastasia Clark. Sunday was normally his day to relax by his pool, enjoy a beer and think of nothing work-related.

But today he didn't want to relax. Today he wanted to see Ana and to put a genuine smile on her face. He wanted to surprise her, to earn her trust so she would give into this desire that was ready to explode between them.

Zach made a quick stop before he picked up the present for Ana. Once he had all the supplies he needed and the gift sitting next to him in the passenger seat, he headed for her condo.

He couldn't wait to see her face. A part of him was nervous she wouldn't like it or would read too much into the gesture, but he couldn't resist. Ever since she'd opened up about her childhood and her father, he wanted to do something to make her life better.

He hadn't asked, and she hadn't said, if her father had contacted her any more. Zach had already set the plan in motion to take care of Ana's father's debts, with the stipulation that he never contact her or come near her again for any reason. His attorney had drawn up all the necessary legal paperwork, so now he was just waiting until they tracked down the deadbeat to get him to sign.

But he didn't want to bother Ana with that right now. No, today was all about making her smile, seeing her laugh and maybe having her revert to being a child and letting all her worries go for a while.

Zach called Ana's cell when he pulled up to the curb outside her SoBe building.

When she answered, he simply asked, "Busy?"

"No. Why?"

He looked down to the surprise he had waiting for her. "Can you come downstairs? I'm parked right out front."

"Sure," she replied. "Is something wrong?"

"Not at all. But grab your purse or whatever you need because I'm taking you somewhere."

When she paused on the other end, Zach was worried she'd decline. "Um…okay. Give me just a minute."

He disconnected the call, cursing himself for being this anxious over a woman. Since when did he worry about rejection? He'd never been nervous before about presenting a woman with a gift.

Then again, he'd never presented something so personal or hoped to touch any woman's life in such a meaningful way.

Wow. What the hell had happened to him?

Two words. Anastasia Clark.

Within five minutes, the lobby doors whooshed open and Ana stepped through wearing a white tank and cutoff jean shorts with the frayed edges laying against her tanned legs. Her hair was pulled back in a mass of curls.

She looked positively adorable and Zach wanted to gobble her up.

Scooting the surprise over into his lap, he hit the button to unlock the doors.

"You sounded weird on the phone," she said as soon as she opened the passenger door and hopped up into the truck. "You sure nothing's wrong? There wasn't another break-in, was there?"

Without saying a word, he grinned and pulled out the surprise he had hiding between his body and his door.

"Oh, my God!"

"Do you like him?" Zach asked, handing over the furry puppy.

Her entire face softened as she cuddled the black-and-white ball of fuzz to her chest. Lucky dog, he thought.

"Oh, Zach, I love him." She continued to nuzzle her face into the dog's side. "Is he yours? I didn't know you had a puppy."

"I just got him."

Ana smiled. "When I mentioned wanting a dog, you never said you wanted one."

Much as he'd love to sit here and watch her elation, he pulled the truck back out onto the road and headed for home. A place he'd never taken a woman.

"I didn't want a dog," he corrected. "You did. You've mentioned it twice before."

She sat up straighter, turning toward him. "Zach, you can't get a dog because I want one. I can't keep him in the condo. I'm sure they have a policy and I'm not staying forever."

He didn't know why those words bothered him so much.

"He'll stay at my house, but for the duration of this project, he's yours."

Glancing from the road for just a second, he saw Ana biting her bottom lip, tears pooling in her eyes. His grip tightened on the wheel as silence settled in the cab. He didn't want to see gratitude in her eyes, didn't want her to look at him as some type of hero.

"It's no big deal," he told her. "I saw him at the shelter and knew he needed a good home."

"You went to the shelter?"

Zach shrugged. "Yeah, why?"

"I would've taken you for a purebred type."

"Just because I have money doesn't mean I don't remember where I came from." He turned off the freeway. "We were not well-off growing up, Ana. My parents died when we were all barely in high school and we had to work even harder for everything we had when we went to live with my elderly grandmother. There's no reason to give away good money when there are dogs out there who need good homes and someone to love them."

Dear Lord, he thought. All she did was ask about the dog and he turned into a Humane Society infomercial. Why he felt the need to ramble was lost on him. He needed to keep his mouth shut about his personal life and just concentrate on Ana and the fact that she had him all torn up.

While the resort was being erected and moving along swift and smooth, his progress with Ana was anything but.

"I don't know what to say," she said, her voice thick with tears. "I've never had anyone do something so... thoughtful."

Uncomfortable with her emotions, Zach grinned. "How about we give him a name?"

"What do you want to name him?" she asked.

"You tell me," he countered. "What would you call him if he was yours?"

Ana held the little bundle out from her and seemed to study him. "When I was little I always wanted a big dog and I was going to name him Jake."

Zach laughed. "Well, the man at the shelter told me this dog was some sort of a Saint Bernard mix, so he'll get plenty big. And Jake sounds like a fine name."

"What do you think?" she asked the dog, once again nuzzling her face against his. "Do you like your new name?"

Little squeaky whimpers came from the miniature puppy.

"I think that's a yes," Zach told her. "I figured we could go to my house and get him used to his new surroundings."

"What will you do with him when I leave?" Ana asked.

"Keep him, of course. But, for now, consider him yours."

Within minutes he was pulling up his long, palm-lined Coral Gables driveway. He had to admit, just to himself, that he wasn't ready to think about Ana leaving. Probably because he'd always been the one to walk away and he'd never seen the retreating back of a woman with whom he'd been intimate.

That had to be the reason a lump was forming in his throat over this woman and a puppy. Since when did he get all emotional?

"Your house is beautiful," Ana said as he pulled in front of the four-car garage.

He killed the engine and opened his door to get the bags of

supplies from behind his seat. "Thanks. I'm looking for the perfect property to build a place, but I haven't found it yet. I'd like to stay in Miami."

Ana got out with Jake in hand and let him down to sniff his new surroundings. "Why do you want to build something else? This is gorgeous."

Zach glanced at the beige stucco, three-story home with large white columns extending to the second floor where it was topped with a third-floor porch. Yeah, it was nice, but he was ready to move on. Always restless, always ready to find something better. He was done here.

"Want to buy it?" he asked, half joking.

Ana shoved her hands in the pockets of her denim shorts. "I don't need the place I have now, let alone two homes."

Curious, he studied her as she watched the dog follow his nose toward the manicured lawn. "Where do you call home?"

"Well, let's put it this way. I get my mail in a suburb of Chicago. A small cottage that my grandfather willed to me. But I'm rarely there. I use it mostly as my office. I have a secretary who comes in during the day to take calls, make appointments and such, then passes everything along to me."

They followed the dog as he moved around to the side of the house. "Your grandfather built amazing homes and businesses and he still lived in a small cottage?"

Ana smiled up at him. "He was happy and said that's where he'd fallen in love with my grandmother and they had a history there, so he never looked elsewhere. That was just home. I guess that's why I can't bear to sell it."

Zach sighed. Ana was definitely a nostalgic family girl. He certainly appreciated his brother and sister more than anything, but no material thing was that important to him that he wouldn't sell it to obtain something bigger and better.

As they walked around the house, silence settled between

them and Zach wondered what she was thinking, what she was feeling. Did she remember that he'd put the ball in her court as to whether or not they moved forward in their personal relationship? The wait was ripping him apart, but he knew Ana would be worth it. She was special and she was his. For now. And even that small epiphany scared the hell out of him. He'd never been so territorial before.

"You're going to Cole's wedding, right?" he asked.

She looked up at him and shielded her eyes from the sun. "I hadn't thought about it. Why?"

"It's next weekend." Suddenly Zach wasn't so confident. Why did this woman have that ability to sap his courage? And why was he holding his breath over his next question? "Would you like to be my date?"

Ana took a step back. "That's not a good idea."

"It's a great idea," he told her, taking a step toward her. "We're working together, spending off-hours together. You've already made a great impression on Tamera and Kayla. Why shouldn't you go?"

"The shower was one thing, but a wedding is a personal, family-or-close-friend occasion."

Before she could retreat any farther, Zach placed his hands on her shoulders to stop her. "You are a friend, Ana, and I want to get very personal with you."

Yes, he may have thrown down the gauntlet for her weeks ago, but damn if he didn't pick it back up the second his lips came down on hers.

He moved his body into hers, wrapping his arms around her waist and drawing her flush against him. She felt so perfect, so right. Her arms slid around his neck as he took advantage of her mouth by easing her lips apart.

"God, Ana, I want you," he murmured against her mouth.

She took his face in her hands and stared back at him.

"I know I'm driving you crazy. I'm doing the same thing to myself, but I have to be sure. Can you understand that?"

Having been a risk taker his entire life, no, he didn't understand, but he was willing to try. For her. He could see the desire in her eyes and knew that he could have her now if he pressed enough. But what would that get him? An evening of hot, sweaty sex? No, when he finally got Ana, he wanted more than one night to explore, to teach, to worship.

And he didn't want her to second-guess herself the entire time. He wanted her to come to him with total abandonment.

"Come to the wedding with me."

She kissed him, softly, tenderly. "Okay." Then she eased back. "Now what do you say we take Jake inside and get him fed?"

Zach smiled. He'd never had to plead for a date before, but he'd also never felt this good about one.

Ana was seriously the equivalent of every business deal he'd ever had. The ones he truly appreciated were the ones he worked hardest to get.

Cole's wedding couldn't get here soon enough. Once the wedding was over, the reception finished, Zach knew Ana wouldn't deny him. Not with an ambiance of love surrounding them and the fact that family and a select few of their friends were invited to stay at the Star Island home afterward.

Less than a week and Zach was sure Ana would take what he'd been offering.

Zach couldn't push his Harley fast enough. Finally an arrest had been made in the breaking and entering at the construction site over a month ago and seeing as how he hadn't been by yet to check on progress today, he decided to tell Ana in person.

He always got excited when he pulled onto the private property that led to the resort. The skeletal frame had been done, but in Zach's eye, he could already see the completed masterpiece.

Of course, he also got a little thrill when he pulled onto the site because of a certain sexy, albeit frustrating forewoman who always looked amazing in her little tanks and hard hat.

He was surprised to not find her out with the crew, so he made his way into her office. Empty. Zach went back out and was approached by a member of Ana's crew.

"She's not here, Mr. Marcum," the sweat-covered man said. "We had to call the ambulance—"

"Ambulance?" Panic flooded through every single part of his body. "Is she hurt? Did she fall?"

"Dehydrated," the man said. "The squad just left with her about ten minutes ago. Damn hot out here and she's always too busy making sure we all have enough water, I suppose she forgot to get some herself."

"If you need anything, call my cell," Zach said, running back to his bike. "I'm going to the E.R. now."

Not waiting around for another moment to pass him by, Zach brought the engine to life and made record time in reaching the hospital. Damn fool woman. How many times had he told her the Miami heat was nothing like what she was used to?

Anger, worry, fear, they all accompanied him to the doors of the E.R. And even though Zach knew her condition wasn't life threatening, he still couldn't get to her fast enough.

Once he told a little lie that he was family, the nurse let him into the room.

Ana, still in her white tank, cutoff denim shorts and dusty boots, was hooked up to an IV. She looked up from where a nurse drew her blood and rolled her eyes.

"Seriously? They called you to come down here?"

Zach stepped farther into the room and pulled the curtain behind him. "No, I was on my way to talk to you and one of the crew members told me what happened."

"I don't want to hear it," she told him, then hissed as the nurse pricked her delicate arm with a needle to draw blood. "I know to drink and stay hydrated, but I'm a little too tired right now to argue. Can we just say you were right and move on?"

Zach laughed and moved to the other side of her bed. "You must be tired if you can't argue with me."

"Okay, Miss Clark." The nurse tossed the trash and gathered her things. "The doctor will be in shortly."

"Wonderful." Ana sighed and settled into the bed. "What did you need to tell me?" she asked him.

"What? Oh, nothing that can't wait." He just wanted to look at her. Wanted to make sure she was really okay because when that initial shock of her being taken away by an ambulance had hit him, he'd imagined the worst.

Ana closed her eyes, clasped her hands over her flat stomach. Zach hated to see the IV sticking from her delicate wrist.

"I'm not going anywhere," she told him. "You might as well tell me what you needed to say then you can go."

He took one of her hands and nestled it between his. "I'm not going anywhere."

Opening her eyes, she turned her head and smiled. "I'm fine, Zach. I'm just going to lie here, get some more fluids and I'll be good as new in a couple of hours."

He returned her gaze, leaving no room for argument. "I'm staying."

"Then tell me what you wanted to say."

"An arrest was made in the break-in."

She sat up, her eyes wide now. "Who did they arrest?"

"Nate. Claims he was mad and wanted to teach you a lesson."

"Arrogant jerk. What took the cops so long to arrest him?"

"He'd fled the state. Victor and I had an investigator hunt him down. Nate was picked up in Michigan."

Ana gritted her teeth. "Too bad the investigator couldn't accidentally have shot him. Then we wouldn't have to worry about pressing charges."

Zach laughed, brought her tiny hand up to his lips. "Bloodthirsty, aren't you? He's going to go before a jury and pay for his crime."

"Probably with a slap on the wrist."

Feeling more confident, Zach eased down on the edge of the narrow bed. "Seriously, stop worrying about it. Don't worry about anything. Not the break-in, not your father or the divorce, and not even the resort. I can't believe I just said that."

Ana laughed. Just the response he was looking for. "Okay, Dr. Marcum. I am tired. I'm just going to close my eyes for a second. Okay?"

He nodded and continued to stare long after her breathing slowed. When the nurse came in to change the bag of fluids, Zach still remained on the edge of the bed clutching her hand. When the doctor came in to order more blood work to make sure her levels were back up, Zach thanked him.

Funny. He couldn't recall any woman in his past, other than his sister, with whom he would've sat for hours in an E.R. over something this minor.

Come to think of it, there were a lot of things he'd do for Ana that he wouldn't have done for past lovers. And that was the funniest part of all. Anastasia Clark wasn't even his lover.

Fifteen

Tonight was the night.

It was all Ana could think of as she stepped into the lobby to wait for Zach to pick her up. She took a deep, calming breath but her heart still fluttered.

She'd known from the moment she'd told him that she would be his date for his brother's wedding that she would give herself to Zach tonight. There was no denying him, or herself, anymore.

The jumble of flurries in her belly stemmed from pure excitement from the promises the evening held. She had no expectations, no thoughts as to what she wanted to get out of a night with Zach. At such a monumental moment in her life, she knew she had to take each step at a time and follow her heart.

Ana clutched her gold handbag and stared at her reflection in the lobby doors. She was so glad she'd let Kayla take her shopping for a dress to wear to the wedding. The shimmering emerald strapless matched her eyes, and Kayla had assured Ana that Zach would not be able to take his eyes off her.

Ana had even gone to great lengths to tame her mass of curls by going to the salon several hours ago. Now her hair was smoothed to a shine and tumbled down her back in soft waves. She'd never have been able to achieve this look on her own, so she'd tipped the stylist very well.

But as Ana continued to study her reflection, she wondered if maybe she should've chosen the short, gold dress with straps instead of this floor-length strapless.

A limo pulled up and Ana quit fussing with her dress and hair. Even though she was anxious, she needed to stay calm and just enjoy what life was so graciously offering.

She just hoped Zach still wanted her once he saw her. She did look different, and not just the hair. Her makeup was heavier than she normally wore, as well. Would he like the bronzed shimmer that she'd used to highlight her shoulders? Would he appreciate the brand-new lingerie she'd purchased just that morning with him in mind?

The limo driver opened the rear door and Zach emerged looking sexy, sinful and perfect in an all-black suit. The best man would look even more dashing than the groom. Of course, that was her own opinion.

She knew when he spotted her. Zach froze. With nothing between them but the glass doors, Ana could only stare in return. She didn't think having a conversation with only your eyes was possible, but she'd been wrong before.

Zach's traveling gaze over her body may as well have been his big, strong hands. Ana tilted her head, smiled and spun in a slow circle with her arms out, sending him a subtle signal that this was all his for the taking. Later. Another shiver of delight speared through her. She only hoped her newfound bravery held up through the night.

Ana walked through the sliding doors. "I'm glad you didn't bring one of the bikes."

"I'm glad you decided to go with me." He ran a fingertip across her bare collarbone. "Damn, you're sexy. Every man there will want you."

"But I'm yours."

His hand froze on her heated skin. "Ana..."

She stepped closer, leaning in to his ear so the driver and valets couldn't hear. "For tonight, I'm yours. I don't want to think about how different we are, or that in a few months we'll part ways. Tonight, Zach, take what you want."

As she eased back, she saw Zach swallow. And for once, since she'd known him, he was speechless.

Zach turned toward the open door to the car and assisted her, following her in before the driver closed the door.

"I always thought you were beautiful," he whispered, taking her hand in his. "But I had no idea you could be so stunning that my mind could actually go blank."

"Kayla helped me," Ana confessed. "She took me shopping for the dress and I went to the salon for my hair."

His eyes settled on her shadowed cleavage. "Remind me to get Kayla a very nice birthday present next month."

Ana laughed. "If you don't stop, we won't be able to get out of the car at the wedding."

He lifted a brow. "Is that a bad thing?"

"It wouldn't look good if the best man didn't show." She laughed. "Try to control yourself."

"You're kidding, right?"

Ana shrugged. "Just think about what good behavior will get you. Oh, and try to picture what I'm wearing under this."

Zach groaned and squeezed her hand. "You sure you've never done this before? You're too good at torture."

Nerves swirled around Ana's belly. "I promise. I've been waiting on the right person. Are you sure you want to be with someone who may do everything wrong?"

Zach shifted in the seat, took her other hand in his as

well. "You will do nothing wrong. We'll do this together and nothing could be more perfect. Relax."

Relax? Sure. No problem. She only had several hours to go knowing that this man was going to bring out a new side of herself tonight and they would explore that side together.

Relaxing should be no problem. Right?

Standing up as best man was pure agony seeing as how he kept looking into the crowd to make eye contact with Ana.

He wanted to be alone. With her. Now.

But as his twin and Tamera said their vows, he had to look away from Ana. She was tearing up and smiling like women do at weddings. She was no doubt wondering what her own wedding would be like someday.

And Zach instantly loathed the faceless man who would take Ana and make her his for life.

If Zach were looking to settle down—the thought was laughable—he would certainly explore where this desire with Ana would go. But he wasn't, so he would take what she offered tonight and not worry about anything else.

"You may kiss the bride," the minister said.

Finally. Zach clapped along with the other one hundred fifty guests as Cole and Tamera kissed and turned to be introduced as Mr. and Mrs. Cole Marcum.

As the sun set in the background and flocks of doves were released to fly overhead, Zach smiled. This sort of fanfare wasn't for him. But he was so happy for his brother and new sister-in-law. Happy they'd found each other and wanted to share their love with so many people.

After the receiving line was finished, Zach went in search of Ana to make sure she was okay and not feeling lonely since he had duties to see to as the best man. But once that toast was over, he was skipping out of this shindig early and taking Ana upstairs to one of the numerous guest rooms to make love to her all night.

Make love? Whoa. Where the hell did that come from? He'd never thought of sex as making love.

Must be all the holy matrimony getting to his head.

"You next?"

Zach spun around to see Victor Lawson smiling, a glass of champagne in hand.

"Hardly," Zach replied. "What about you?"

"Married? No, thanks. Too busy enjoying life." He motioned with his drink toward Tamera and Cole. "But love looks good on them."

"Yes, it does."

Zach glanced at the happy couple, then allowed his eyes to wander until he spotted Ana. All the breath left his lungs. Those mesmerizing deep green eyes were on him, half shielded by heavy lids.

And she had the same look in her eye as she looked at him that Tamera had when Cole had said his vows.

No, no, no. She couldn't be in love. Could she?

And why, when Victor mentioned love and marriage, did he automatically seek Ana?

All this wedded bliss was wreaking havoc on his mind, making him weak and vulnerable. Time to make a quick exit.

"If you'll excuse me," Zach said, nodding to Victor.

A wide grin spread across the billionaire's face. "I don't blame you for the interest in Miss Clark. She's got that quiet, reserved beauty, but knows how to make a statement when it counts. Makes a man want to take notice."

Zach didn't return the smile. "So long as *you* don't take notice, we'll get along just fine."

Victor's chuckle followed and mocked Zach across the courtyard. He didn't care. All that concerned him was Ana and the fact that she was ready to give him the greatest gift he'd ever received.

Cole may be the one to have gotten married, but Zach considered himself the luckiest man here tonight.

When he reached her side, she was chatting with some guests. He softly took her elbow and whispered in her ear, "Let's go."

The tremor that shook her also vibrated through him. Ana graciously said her farewells and allowed him to lead her back into the house.

"Did you at least tell Cole and Tamera goodbye?" she asked as they passed the marble entryway and headed toward the wide, curved staircase.

"They left an hour ago," he told her. "They were eager to be alone, too."

Instead of going up the stairs as he'd originally planned, Zach led her out the front door.

"Where are we going?" she asked. "I thought we were staying here tonight. Isn't that what Cole had planned for the family and close friends?"

He led her to his Camaro, which he'd had Cole's driver bring over, and opened the passenger door, but before she could settle into the seat, he turned her around, pinned her against the car and kissed her. Gentleness had no place here, not right now when he was ready to explode. He would be gentle later when she needed it most.

Before he could get carried away right here in the driveway, Zach eased back, but kept his body flush with hers so she would know how affected he was.

"This matters to me," he murmured against her moist lips. "I want you in my bed and I want privacy."

When he stepped back to let her have room to get in the car, she continued to stare. "Are you always this passionate?"

Her honest, whispered question took him by surprise, but he didn't even have to think. "I can honestly say I've never felt this way before."

Ana closed her eyes, sighed. "Don't say things like that to me."

He didn't know what she meant by that or why she looked so torn, so he just gestured for her to get into the car.

Months ago he was so confident, so sure he would have her in his bed. Of course at that time he didn't literally intend to have her at his home, his sanctuary. He'd planned on seducing her aboard his yacht, maybe whisking her off to his cabin in the hills of Tennessee for extra seclusion. Or maybe just a quick evening romp in her on-site office after hours.

Yeah, he'd been cocky and sure of himself. But as he settled in behind the driver's seat, Zach was hit by an attack of nerves like he'd never experienced before.

Ana was innocent and that meant this evening would be a first for him as well.

Surprisingly Ana didn't feel as nervous as she thought she'd be at this moment she'd dreamed of. If anything, she felt a sense of peace, like she was doing something right. As Zach pulled into his four-car garage and killed the engine, silence enveloped them.

Yes, she'd waited a long time to give herself to a man, but she wasn't sorry she was going to give herself to Zach. She loved him, and he cared for her as much as he could. Once upon a time, Ana wouldn't have accepted that. Not that she was settling now, not by any means. She'd never been in love before, but she was now. Was it her fault her heart chose someone who was skittish of love? He had every reason to be considering his ex had skipped out on him in such a swift, coldhearted way.

Ana opened her car door before Zach could. They walked by two of his motorcycles and the Jag and the Bugatti and finally stepped into the house, where he promptly turned off the alarm.

"Where's Jake?" she asked, setting her purse on the island in the kitchen.

"He's in the crate. I'd better let him out to do his business before…"

Ana smiled as Zach trailed off and went into the utility room to let out their dog.

Their dog. No way could Zach deny that he loved her. Oh, he may not be ready to admit it, but deep down he did. Otherwise he never would've gotten her a gift so meaningful. He wouldn't have remembered her even mentioning that in her rambling comments about her family.

Yes, Zach Marcum may be resistant when it came to commitments and relationships, but they hadn't even made love and he hadn't seen another woman in months.

That spoke volumes in ways his words couldn't. And solidified the fact that giving herself to him was not a mistake or something she would regret later. Even if they went their separate ways after the project was finished, Zach would always have a piece of her heart.

"Would you like a drink?"

Ana spun around as Zach reentered the room. "No, thanks. Did you already let Jake out?"

He nodded. "I put him on the enclosed patio. There are puppy pads for him and not much those little sharp teeth can tear up out there. Plus it gives him some room to walk around after being cooped up for several hours."

Ana walked through the kitchen and into the living area where a large flat screen TV was framed to look like a picture between floor-to-ceiling bookshelves.

The stark white walls were tastefully adorned with pictures of various sailboats out on the ocean. He also had a pencil sketch of a sailboat on an easel in the corner. The lone drawing drew her interest.

"You like sailboats?" She glanced over her shoulder to where he remained at the entryway just watching her. "I didn't pay attention to all these the other day when we brought Jake here. Guess I was too busy playing with him."

"Well, that just boosts my ego. You notice them now when I'm dying to strip you out of that dress?"

She turned fully now, more than aware of her heart beating, her palms sweating. Okay, maybe she was more nervous than she thought. "I actually have never been on the water. Too busy working, I guess."

He moved toward her, one slow step at a time, and her heart picked up its pace. Game on. Let the predator come to his prey.

"You sketched this?" she asked, turning back to the drawing before he reached her. "Your talents are endless with design."

His warm breath hit her bare shoulder as his words caressed her skin mere inches from her ear. "Are we really standing here discussing how well I draw? I have many, many more talents, Anastasia, and I want to show them all to you."

She turned, her breasts brushing against his crisp dress shirt. Yes, she wanted this man and it thrilled her beyond description that he wanted her, but she'd be a fool not to go into this with a bit of fear.

"Relax, Zach." She smiled, laying a hand on his chest. "I'm not going anywhere. Even though I'm nervous and scared, I need this to go slow. Can you handle that?"

He rested his hands on her bare shoulders, extending his thumbs down to brush against the tops of her breasts spilling from the dress. "I've watched you move all night in that dress. I've watched other men look at you and each minute that passed was too long for me not to touch you. But I don't want to scare you. I want to show you how perfect this will be. Let me show you, Ana."

Ana didn't protest when his hands slid around to her back and eased the zipper down. Emerald silk swished to the floor in utter silence.

And the look in Zach's eyes was so worth the extra money she'd put toward her new lingerie. How could she make this as good and perfect for Zach as he'd promised it would be for her? She knew nothing about pleasuring a man. But the look in his eyes told her she was about to learn very soon.

Shivers of anticipation swept through her and in their path excitement and love now replaced fear.

Sixteen

More than anything Zach wanted to run his hands all over Ana's slender body, but he knew the moment he touched her smooth skin, this night would progress at a much faster pace than he wanted. And right now, he wanted to savor this moment with his eyes and capture a mental picture of every dip, every curve of her body.

"The dress was stunning," he said, almost not recognizing his own husky voice. "But this is positively breathtaking."

A wide grin spread across her face. "I was hoping you'd like what I chose."

Wrapping a body like Ana's in clothes should be a sin. But wrapping it in a sheer gold thong and bustier was pure heaven.

"I'm glad you like it, Zach, but could you touch me or start taking off some clothes? I feel a little silly being on display."

He jerked his shirt from his pants and unbuttoned it, tossing it over his shoulder, not caring one bit where it landed.

Zach wrapped his arms around her waist, pulling her against his chest. They matched perfectly. Chest to chest, stomach to stomach, thighs to thighs.

"I don't get to give you the microscopic overview?" she asked, teasing.

"Later."

He bent down, scooped her up and made his way out of the living room, through the wide, long hallway and toward the front of the house where his master suite was located. The whole east side of his home was his bedroom, his domain, and he wanted to spend the next two days closed in with nothing and no one but Ana and her innocence.

He eased her down to her stiletto-covered feet. "Be sure, Anastasia."

She ran the palm of her hands over his bare chest, never taking her eyes off his. Slowly she eased her body closer, until her lips were a breath from his, and smiled. When her arms looped around his neck, she gave him a gentle tug until he was walking her backward toward the high four-poster bed dominating the center of the massive room.

She sank down on the edge as he towered over her. Pure, raw heat shimmered in her green eyes. The mass of red hair, usually curly and wild, was now tamed and tumbling down her back. He couldn't wait to see it spread across his sheets.

Ana licked her lips, but not in the suggestive way most women did. Her eyes darted to the ground, then back up.

That she was getting nervous humbled him. A surreal feeling, but one he was learning to live with considering Ana had become a part of his life he hadn't expected.

More than anything, he wanted to make this night, this moment perfect for her. He wanted to ruin her for any other man.

No. Those thoughts had to leave. There was only room in this bed for two. And he refused to already give her up to someone else, even if only in his mind.

Zach placed a hand on either side of her hips on the bed and leaned down to capture her mouth. Tipping her face up, she rose to meet him. She sighed deeply as she opened her mouth, giving him access. Her back arched, the satiny material over her breasts brushing against his bare chest.

Taking her shoulders, he eased her down and placed a knee on the bed. As much as he wanted to continue kissing her, he wanted to see her completely free of all clothing first. He knew he needed to take his time, something he'd never had to consider before, but he didn't know how agonizing it would be. He wanted to draw this moment out for both of them.

With one knee on the bed, one foot on the floor, Zach eased back and began unfastening the little hook and eye closures on her bustier. One by one they popped open, exposing creamy, pale skin beneath.

"You make me feel beautiful," she whispered.

Zach's eyes roamed up to Ana's. "You should never feel any other way."

He parted the shiny material, laying it open on either side of her torso. Then he hooked his thumbs in the side strings of her panties and slid them down her slender legs, over the heels and flung them off.

Laid bare before him, in his own bed, Ana looked like sin personified. Those mesmerizing eyes sparkled, her chest heaved with every breath she took. Her moist lips were parted, begging him to take more.

To know he was looking at a body that had never been touched, never been admired nearly brought him to his knees.

"I've always taken this for granted," he told her as he ran his hands up her legs, over her pelvic bone and up to her breasts. "You have no idea what you do to me, Ana."

She sat up, reached for his belt and unfastened it along with the button and zipper of his pants. "I know, Zach. I know because you do the same to me."

Once his pants were off, along with his socks and shoes, he bent to take off her killer heels. Now that she was fully naked, he kissed his way from her feet to her breasts, bypassing her most sacred part.

She wiggled and moaned beneath his touch. Zach wanted nothing more than to bury himself in her and assuage this ache he had, but he was realistic. He knew that with Ana once would never be enough. No, once she got into his system, he had a feeling it would be hard to ever get over her.

Concentrating on the here and now, he took one nipple into his mouth. When her back arched off the bed, he wrapped both arms around her waist to hold her closer. And that was another first for him. He couldn't get close enough or touch her enough. He literally couldn't wait to become one with her.

Zach turned his attention to the other nipple, then traveled up her neck and finally reclaimed her mouth. Ana grabbed his shoulders, her short nails biting into his skin as she lifted her knees around him.

He trailed one hand down her body, found the spot between her legs and stroked. He needed to make sure she was ready, and not just emotionally.

Ana's mouth tore from his as she cried out at his touch. He couldn't wait another minute. He grabbed his pants off the floor and pulled a condom from his wallet.

"Look at me," he told her as he positioned himself between her legs. "Don't ever forget this moment."

Don't forget me, he silently added.

Inch by agonizing inch, he entered her. Their eyes stayed locked as Zach allowed her body to adjust.

Ana brought her hands up to his cheeks, framing his face in between her fingers. "Please, Zach. Don't hold back."

He didn't. "Wrap your legs around my waist."

When she did, he sheathed himself in her even deeper. Her

hips tilted with each thrust and Zach had to grit his teeth to remain in control.

"I'm so glad it's you," she murmured right before she gripped the duvet in each of her fists, threw her head back and came beneath him. That's all it took for Zach to let go.

And as much as he wanted her to remember this moment, he wanted to keep it embedded in his own head forever, so he leaned down and kissed her as his body trembled and even when the tremors ceased.

Sated, Ana kept her eyes closed. She was afraid if she opened them she'd see this was a dream. Or worse, Zach was disappointed.

He shifted his body over and she instantly felt the loss of his presence, but in an instant he was lying at her side again, trailing his fingertips over her heated body.

"Are you okay?" he asked.

Ana smiled, opened her eyes and turned her head toward him. "I can't believe I'm in your bed. I never thought this would make me feel so...alive."

The look on his face was sexy, yet at the same time vulnerable. The words I love you settled on the tip of her tongue. She wanted to tell him how she felt, but she didn't want this moment to turn into guilt on his part. He wouldn't be able to say the words in return and he would probably think she was just saying it because of what had just happened.

So she kept the secret for another time. But she would tell him. Soon. He deserved to know how he'd touched her life, how he would always be a part of her even if they weren't together.

He broke the silence. "I have to say, these last few hours of you in that dress really tested a man's willpower."

She laughed, rolling to her side and mimicking his pose. With her elbow bent and her head resting in her hand, she looked at him. "It was just a dress, Zach. I'm the same person in my dusty boots and holey jeans as I was in that dress."

His brows drew together. "That's what I'm trying to figure out. How can someone look so totally different, yet amazingly sexy both ways?"

"I don't know. Why don't you tell me? You go from a CEO to a construction worker to a motorcycle rider in a flash."

His wide grin split across his face, making that stubbled jawline all the more appealing. "Are you saying we're not that different? I'm positive I wouldn't have looked that good in the dress."

Ana laughed and shoved him in his chest until he fell to his back. She came up on her knees, still laughing, took a pillow and smacked him. "Now you're making fun."

"Maybe just a little."

Zach clasped his hands behind his head, instinctively flexing those hard muscles in his arms, accentuating his tribal-looking tattoo that wrapped around one hefty bicep.

How could she not have fallen hard for this man? All that sex appeal wrapped around the heart of a true gentleman. He could have anyone, yet he'd taken time to earn her trust, show her what passion and, yes, love was. All the afterglow, all the tingling feelings swirling around inside her, and all of the confidence she had in herself were all due to Zach.

How in the world had she ever thought this caring, giving man was anything like her selfish, womanizing father?

"What are you thinking?" he asked, gazing up at her.

She shrugged, came to sit on her knees, surprising herself at just how comfortable she was naked in his bed. "Everything. Nothing."

"You were smiling, but you had a different look in your eye for a second." He rested a big, tanned hand against her pale thigh. "What was it?"

"I love you."

Silence settled so deep into the room, Ana wanted to be buried in it. "Oh, God. I told myself I wouldn't tell you."

She covered her face with her hands, praying the last ten seconds of her life would be erased from Zach's memory.

"Ana." The bed shifted as Zach sat up and took her hands in his. "Look at me."

Slowly moving her hands, she looked him in the eye. But he wasn't horrified. At least he didn't appear to be.

"I'm sure you hear that all the time," she began, suddenly trying to backpedal in a current too forceful for her to fight. "And I'm not just saying it because we made love. I told myself not to say anything, to just let this moment be and not bring my personal emotions into it. But, much as I want to, I can't take the words back. I know you don't feel the same, and I'm fine with that. I knew going in that you wouldn't love me."

He remained motionless as she rambled, except for the one corner of his sexy mouth that turned up into a smile. "Are you finished?"

Ana shook her head. "I tried not to fall for you. I really did, Zach. But do you know how much you've done for me?"

"Excuse me?" His brows drew together. "I didn't do anything."

"You gave my company this amazing job." She began ticking the list off on her fingers. "You were there for me when my office was broken into. When my father showed up, you stood by my side. You've been so patient with me even though I know that goes against everything you've probably ever done where a woman was concerned. And Jake. You gave me a dog, Zach. Something I wanted when I was a little girl and you just delivered it to me."

"Let me get this straight," he said, still holding on to her hands. "You love me because I was in the right place for the break-in and your father's visit and because I got a dog?"

Ana closed her eyes. "That is all on the surface," she whispered, knowing tears weren't far. She opened her eyes anyway, not caring she was baring all the emotion there. "You gave me a sense of hope that not all men are jerks. That not all men who can literally have it all are uncaring and selfish. You put me first, in everything. I don't think you know what that means to me."

"Ana." Zach sighed. "I don't know what to say. I do care about you. I can't even try to deny that. But…"

She'd be lying if she said a piece of her heart hadn't just chipped away. There was never any question that he wouldn't fall in love with her, but she was hoping for just a sliver of his love.

"I don't expect you to say anything," she told him. "But I can't lie to you, Zach. I'm not sorry you know how I feel. So, now that I've embarrassed myself, can we enjoy the rest of the evening or did I ruin it?"

He leaned in, touched his lips lightly to hers. "Never."

Thankful he wasn't terrified of her now, Ana smiled. "I bet you'll never ask me again what I'm thinking."

Zach slid off the bed and scooped her up into a fireman's carry. "Not for a while, I won't."

As he carried her into the glass-tiled bathroom, Ana couldn't help but smile. The words of affection were out now and she felt relieved. Scared, but relieved.

And now that the truth was out in the open, would he, could he consider something more with Ana than a fling? God, how she hoped so. She wanted desperately to see where this love could go. If only Zach would open his eyes, and his heart.

Seventeen

Zach had just finished sliding the pancakes onto a large platter when his cell rang. He grabbed it from the kitchen island praying it wasn't Melanie again. She'd left him three texts during the night, all of which he'd ignored and deleted.

Thankfully it wasn't her. It was his attorney.

"Zach, we've found Miss Clark's father."

He glanced toward the arched doorway to make sure Ana hadn't wandered in from the bedroom. He'd left her sleeping and decided to make her a surprise breakfast in bed.

"He agreed to sign the contract?" Zach asked. "That was too easy."

"Well, an IRS threat really scares people into doing what you'd like," his lawyer agreed. "All debts, legal and otherwise, are clear. Everything is taken care of."

Zach could feel the relief lifting off his shoulders. Now when he and Ana parted, he would know she could move on without that extra baggage and could live without fear. But he would have to keep his investigator on this for a while, just to make sure Ana's father held up his end of the bargain. Zach had a feeling the man would, simply because people like that were too afraid of people with power. He would slink into someone else's life and start anew with some other innocent.

"Thanks," Zach said. "Make sure you let the P.I. know how much he is appreciated and that a hefty bonus will be added to his fees for his swift, efficient work. And make sure he knows to keep an eye on Miss Clark once this project is complete. I don't want her or her mother bothered with this bastard anymore."

He disconnected the call and pulled the syrup from the cabinet. Now he could greet Ana with a simple breakfast of pancakes and juice, a morning-after kiss and the good news about her father who would no longer be a problem in her life.

Zach loaded up the tray and headed back to the bedroom. Ana was just rustling beneath the covers.

"Morning." He smiled and moved toward her with the tray. "I hope you like pancakes."

She stretched, arms high above her head, and pulled the covers back up and tucked them beneath her arms. "You know I love food, so anything is fine."

He settled the tray over her lap and leaned down to kiss her. "I like to see a woman who's not afraid to eat."

Ana's wide grin spread across her face. "I've told you, you date the wrong women."

Something settled deep in Zach's chest at her subtle joke. "I'm beginning to see that," he mumbled against her mouth before capturing it again.

He couldn't explore his emotions, not now. Maybe never. This uncomfortable state that had been plaguing him for days, weeks, was confusing him, making him lose track of what was right before him.

Zach took the kiss deeper, and Ana cupped his face and parted her lips. How could he ever let this woman out of his bed? Out of his life? Was he seriously contemplating something long-term?

Zach pulled back, more than a little shaken at the smack to the heart from the sudden epiphany. "Eat before they get cold," he told her.

"Aren't you eating?"

He shook his head. "I had some juice and fruit while your pancakes were cooking."

Placing the napkin in her lap, Ana picked up the syrup and drizzled it over her plate. "You seem off. Is everything okay?"

"Fine." Zach eased down on the edge of the bed. "Just conducted some business this morning. I wasn't expecting to wrap it up this fast."

"You're all work, Zach." She cut into the pancake and lifted a forkful to her mouth. "I thought you were only working on the Lawson project right now."

"This was something that couldn't wait." Zach scooted farther back on the bed and turned to face her more. "I'm glad it's done and came through quicker than I'd expected."

"So you can spend more time on...more important things."

Zach smiled and leaned closer. "Absolutely," he said, moving over the tray to capture her mouth.

He wanted her to know how much she meant to him, but at the same time he couldn't tell her because she would read too much into it.

Zach eased back. "Finish eating. We can take Jake out to play later and let him run some energy off."

"Can I grab a quick shower first?"

"Absolutely. You don't have to ask to use anything here."

Zach left Ana to go into his office on the other side of the house. He wanted to read the contract that his attorney had faxed to make sure there were no loopholes Ana's father could jump through in the future.

Everything had to be in order down to the final period if he expected to move on. And he would move on. He had to. As soon as Ana was one-hundred-percent safe.

By the time he read over the document, he was more than satisfied that his lawyer hadn't missed a thing. Of course, he had expected no less, but he wasn't going to take even the slightest chance when it came to Ana's future.

Zach filed the contract in his cabinet and strode back to his bedroom. He heard the shower shut off just as he grabbed the tray. He took the empty dishes back to the kitchen and left them on the counter. His housekeeper would be in later.

When he went back to his bedroom, Ana still hadn't emerged from the bathroom. He'd just raised a hand to knock when the door whipped open.

Ana's face was tear streaked and she'd donned his black silk robe that hung on the back of the door. Instincts took control as he stepped forward and grasped her shoulders.

"What's wrong?"

She shook her head and brushed by him. "Absolutely nothing. Everything is perfect. That's the problem."

Zach turned, watching Ana pace back and forth across his white carpet. "You've lost me. You found a problem in my bathroom?"

She stopped, hands on her hips, a mass of wet, red hair settling around her shoulders. "No. I'm just so happy and I started feeling guilty while I was enjoying your party-size shower. I don't think my mother experienced an ounce of the happiness I've had in the past few weeks. And that makes me sad."

Treading into unfamiliar territory, Zach took a hesitant step forward. This was a shaky part where every word he said could give her false hope for a future. "Ana, don't feel guilty. I can't imagine your mother would want you to. I'm sure she'd want you to be happy."

Ana's shoulders relaxed, her hands fell to her sides and her head drooped. "I know she would. Which is what makes her so great. She always puts others first. I wish my father would've appreciated what he had and what he's thrown away. He used his power to get anything and everything and where's it gotten him?"

"I won't lie and say money doesn't talk, but people with power can't let the power overtake their lives." Feeling a bit more in control of this shaky situation, Zach closed the gap between them and placed his hands on her silk-covered shoulders. "Money and power have ruined many lives. You have to think more of yourself and be stronger than the power…if that makes sense."

Ana looked at him as one tear trickled down each cheek. "If I didn't love you before, I love you now."

"Ana, I can't…"

Her smile broke his heart. "I know," she whispered, slipping her thumbs inside his boxers and sliding them down his legs. "Let me show you."

The loose knot she'd tied at her waist came free with just one slight tug. She dropped her arms to her sides as he brushed the robe from her shoulders.

She moved into him, wrapping her arms around his neck and kissing his stubbled jawline. He circled his hands around her waist and groaned at the slow pace she was dead set on keeping.

"Don't ever doubt my feelings for you," she whispered in his ear. "And don't lie to yourself."

The little minx knew exactly what she was doing because just as he was about to ask what she was talking about, she covered his mouth with hers and ran her hands down his sides and around to his back where she massaged him from bottom to top.

"Enough," he rasped.

Zach wrapped his arms around her waist, picked her up and walked over to the chaise in front of his French doors which he'd opened at sunrise. The ocean breeze slipped through, kissing their bare bodies.

Once he had Ana laid out, ready for him, Zach made quick work of protection and came back to stand between her legs. With no words, no kissing, he entered her. A moment later he stopped.

"Don't stop," she told him. "Don't doubt."

He clenched his teeth. "I can't control myself around you, Anastasia. I can't give you slow."

"Then don't."

When she smiled, looking up at him with desire in her heavy-lidded eyes, he was a goner. He leaned over, bracing himself with one hand on the arm of the chaise, one hand at Ana's side, and moved with her.

Desire overtook him and just as he was about to close his eyes, he saw hers. Nothing but love looked up at him and Zach knew if he could love anyone, it would be Ana. He wanted nothing more than to make her happy but he was broken and not willing to take the risk again.

So he closed his eyes and took them both over the edge.

When Ana came back to reality and Zach dropped her off at her condo, she discovered four messages on her cell from her mother.

She'd been so busy enjoying herself between the amazing wedding, the reception, but mostly the hours after. Had she really only spent less than twenty-four hours with Zach? So much had happened since she'd last been in her bedroom.

Her whole life had changed—not to mention her outlook on life.

She'd told herself, once she decided to sleep with Zach, that she wouldn't expect anything in return…. And she wouldn't have if he hadn't looked at her the same way she'd seen Cole look at Tamera.

A burst of giddiness swept through her at the fact that Zach may actually love her. She'd wondered before, but now she had a bit more hope. When they'd been one and he'd looked into her eyes, she'd seen the emotion as clearly as if he'd said the words. She seriously didn't think she was imagining things just because her own feelings were out there.

As Ana listened to her mother's messages, her excitement increased. Her mother wanted to come for a visit and to see how the new project was coming along.

Nearly six months had passed since Ana had seen her mother. She couldn't wait to show her how the site was progressing. Maybe she could stay until the end of the project since she was technically single and had no job to be home for.

Oh, who was Ana kidding? She was more excited about Zach and her mother meeting. Of course, that was a giant step into relationship territory and she didn't want to stress Zach or make him feel trapped, but she did want him to see another side of her. And she wanted her mother to meet the one man who'd touched Ana so deeply, he'd be embedded into her heart forever.

Ana called her mother and made arrangements for her to fly in on Friday. That would give her time to get Zach used to the idea of her mother's arrival.

And even though the proverbial "meeting of the parents" was a giant step in a relationship, Ana couldn't let this opportunity pass her by.

She sank down on her bed and stared out the wide window toward the harbor. Taking on this project had changed her life in so many unpredictable ways. How would she cope with leaving Miami? Would Zach want her to stay? They still had many months to go before she could pack up and go. Surely in that time he would be honest with himself.

Ana knew, at this point, the best thing she could do was just be herself. After all, she hadn't done anything to get Zach to have feelings for her, so she certainly wasn't pressing her luck by making him open up about something he feared.

No, this was a monumental decision and one Zach needed to come to on his own. And if he didn't, well, when she left and said goodbye for the final time, she'd leave a piece of her heart with him.

Eighteen

Ana called Zach's house, hoping to catch the housekeeper. Thankfully the Latina woman remembered her.

"I never see one of Mr. Marcum's ladies. I hear about them, but never see," she repeated with a heavy accent.

Okay, that was a plus in her favor, though Ana didn't really want to hear about all of Mr. Marcum's ladies. She asked the woman if she could stop by and pick up Jake for the day.

Now Ana was in a rental car, with towels placed all over the front seat and floor to help defer the mess of any accidental doggie business and she was heading to Zach's office for a surprise. Since he was always doing things for her, she decided to take half the day away from the site and spend it with him. After all, her mother would be in town tomorrow and Ana had barely mentioned the fact. What would he think of meeting her mother? Surely he knew, because she'd given her body so freely and confessed her feelings, that she wanted more from this relationship than just an occasional romp.

Ana found a parking spot directly in front of his office.

As she exited the car, she squinted against the harsh gleam of sunshine reflecting off the six-story glass office building.

A bubble of excitement popped up when she glanced in the backseat at the large picnic basket and white blanket she'd brought. She reached across the console and scooped up Jake, tucking him under her arm.

When she stepped through the double doors, the receptionist greeted her. "Good afternoon, Miss Clark. Are you here to see Mr. Marcum?"

Ana nodded. "But don't tell him I'm here. I want to surprise him."

The young woman's eyes darted down the hall toward the elevator and back as she bit her lip. "Um…okay."

That was weird, Ana thought as she headed for the elevator. Another woman, a very tall, stunning blonde, stood waiting as well.

The doors slid open just as Ana got there.

"What a cute dog," the other woman said as they entered the car together. "What's its name?"

Ana pushed the number four and said, "Jake. My boyfriend just bought him for me and I'm here to surprise him and take him to lunch."

The elevator lifted and seconds later the doors opened on the fourth floor.

"But I thought Cole just got married," the blonde said, her brows drawn together.

Ana stepped off the elevator with the woman. "Oh, he did last Saturday. I'm dating his brother."

The woman's eyes widened, her mouth dropped open. "Really? Well, I'm his wife."

Ana's hold on the dog tightened, but she was careful not to squeeze too tight. No need in causing harm to the wrong being. Surely she heard wrong or this positively breathtaking woman was delusional.

"You say Zach bought you the dog?" the beauty asked.

"Funny, he always told me he never wanted pets messing up our tidy house. But whatever. I didn't catch your name."

Ana refused to show any emotion and let this woman have the upper hand, no matter that her heart had just taken a punch. "If you'll excuse me," she muttered, purposely ignoring the request.

Just as she turned to go, the woman touched her arm. "I need to see him before you and Toto here go in."

From the corner of her eye Ana spotted Zach striding down the hallway. And, oh, joy, the ex noticed at the same time, too. They both watched an unknowing Zach as he came toward them with his head down, reading a document.

Ana ate up his looks from his shiny black shoes to his faded designer jeans and long-sleeve black dress shirt rolled up onto his tanned forearms. Even his messy, spiky hair and stubble along the jawline didn't diminish the fact that this man was sexy. Sexy and very much in trouble.

"Zach."

Ana stood back, holding Jake to her chest as the ex crossed to him.

"Melanie." He jerked to a stop, then darted his eyes over her shoulder to look straight at Ana. "Ana? What's going on?"

Ana shrugged, letting Melanie have her say. No way was she going to interrupt this. Seeing Zach's reaction to his ex would give her an insight into his true feelings—something she never doubted until now.

"I need to talk to you," Melanie said, throwing a glance over her shoulder. "Alone."

Suddenly Ana wished she'd thrown on a cute sundress instead of her white shorts and blue tank. But she figured they'd be at the beach for the picnic and she wanted to be comfortable. Melanie, however, seemed to be comfortable in her skinny mini strapless dress and stilettos.

Yeah, Ana could so see Zach wanting to spend the rest of

his life with an hourglass instead of a stick figure with a B cup…and that was on her "puffy" days.

Jake whimpered and Ana kissed his fur. "You're okay," she whispered in his little ear.

"After we talked the other day, I didn't hear from you so I thought I'd stop by and talk in person," Melanie said. "You didn't answer the texts I sent on Saturday night."

Saturday night. The night Ana had given herself to a man who was still in a relationship with his ex-wife. A viselike grip tightened around her heart and Ana couldn't hold back the gasp as air whooshed from her lungs.

Zach's eyes darted back to Ana, as if he knew where her thoughts had wandered. And if Melanie's revelation hadn't just ripped out her heart, the look in his dark eyes did.

Sorrow, shame, guilt, they all stared back at her. How long had they been talking? Is that why he'd been so patient with her? He was already getting some from his ex?

God, what a loser and gullible mess she was. But Ana refused to be the "other" woman as her mother had for years.

"If you'd just told me that you were in a serious relationship, I wouldn't be here," Melanie went on to say.

Zach looked back to Melanie and ran a hand through his hair. The other hand holding the document fell lazily to his side. "I didn't say anything because I'm not in a serious relationship."

"Really?" Melanie laughed. "Because this sure looks serious. A dog, Zach?"

If the fist around her heart hadn't been squeezing hard enough before, it sure was now. Ana refused to be the third party in whatever twisted relationship Zach and his ex obviously still had. She wanted out of here now, but she didn't want to look like she was jealous or hurt. No, she didn't want to give either of them the satisfaction of knowing how naive she'd been to believe a playboy like Zach Marcum could change.

"Go ahead and talk privately," Ana told them with a smile she knew looked just as fake as it felt. "I need to take Jake outside anyway."

She turned to go and Zach called out her name. Ignoring him, she punched the elevator button.

"Ana." He grabbed her arm. "I'm sorry."

"What? Sorry you lied or sorry that you got caught?" Venom all but dripped from each word. "Don't apologize when you don't mean it."

"I do. Don't leave like this. Let me explain."

Glaring over her shoulder at him, she jerked her arm free and brought both hands up to Jake who was now trying to get to Zach. "Don't worry. You told me when you told your *wife* exactly what we have. We're not serious, so go talk with Melanie and any other woman you desire. Just make sure it's not me."

The doors slid open and Ana stepped onto the elevator. As she turned, the doors closed, shutting her off from Zach's angry face and Melanie's triumphant glare.

Ana couldn't get to her car fast enough. She ran by the receptionist who Ana noticed gave her a quick, apologetic smile.

Finally alone, Ana sat Jake in the passenger seat and squealed the tires as she pulled away from the curb. She didn't want to be in the vicinity of Zach Marcum for a long time. She actually never wanted to see him again, but since they weren't done with the resort yet, that would be impossible.

Wonderful. Just wonderful. She would have to see him every day for the next several months. Thankfully the exterior was near completion and her men would be mostly working inside now. There would be plenty of room for her to hide in the monstrous resort when Zach came to check on things. She'd just have her second-in-command fill Mr. Marcum in on the progress.

Ana turned down another palm-lined road. She really had no clue where she was going; she just needed to drive.

All of this was her own fault. Every bit of it. So why was she mad at Zach? He'd told her up front that he didn't do relationships. Hadn't he said marriage had sucked the love right out of him? He hadn't lied to her about that. But he had lied, at least by omission.

That was the part that hurt the most. He had been talking with his ex the whole time he'd been trying to get her into bed. He'd been so convincing that he cared about her feelings, so gentle when they'd finally made love.

Made love. Yeah. That was totally one-sided. No wonder he panicked when she professed her love to him. What a total idiot, she thought, hating herself more and more with each passing moment.

Ana pulled her car off the road and parked facing the beach. With her head in her hands, she let the tears fall, one right after the other, angry at herself for letting anyone in that could cause this much damage to her heart again.

Why hadn't she seen the signs? Why? Even after she'd opened up and told him how she felt about him, that she loved him, he still hadn't confessed. His silence spoke volumes; too bad she was just now hearing it.

Jake crossed the console and slid his sandpaper-like puppy tongue along the tears that seeped through her fingers.

Yes, all of this mess was her fault and that made her a complete idiot. But the fact that she still loved him made her a damn fool.

"Oh, honey. Now don't do this to yourself."

Ana sat on her bed, sobbing into her mother's loving arms. "I can't help it. I've tried to hate him. I've even tried to push his betrayal out of my mind, but that's all I can think of."

Lorraine Clark stroked her daughter's hair and leaned back against the satin-covered headboard. "Has he tried to call?"

Ana slid her head down into her mother's lap and let the gentle stroking of her long hair relax her as much as it could. "He's tried. I won't answer. I'm such a coward. I even called out of work today. But since it's Friday, that wasn't a big deal. My crew can handle one day. Besides, I'm hoping by Monday I'll be better."

"Why can't you go to the site?" her mother asked.

Ana closed her eyes and wiped her damp cheeks. "Because he's the architect for the project. He's at the site at least once a day."

"Oh, Anastasia."

Her mother's soft tone and simple words only made Ana ache more. Even her mother noticed the severity of the situation. Of course her mother would notice. Her mother had lived through a lifetime of pure hell.

But now she was free. They both were—thanks to Zach.

Another heart-wrenching sob tore through her. Not even her mother's soothing words and comforting presence could help repair her shattered world.

She had to get this out now. No way would she show even an inkling of sadness on the site.

"I hate being weak," she murmured into her mother's long crinkle skirt. "I hate knowing that I let someone get that close to me when I knew the outcome. I knew this would happen, but I didn't care. Deep down I thought I would be the one. Foolish, really, to think the one time I find myself attracted enough for a relationship, it's with someone like him."

Her mother's hands stilled in her hair. "You love him."

"I don't want to."

Lorraine let out a soft sigh. "Unfortunately we don't choose whom we love. Right or wrong, sometimes our hearts and our heads don't communicate well."

Ana sat up, wiped her eyes again and sniffed. "I'm sorry

to have a meltdown the second you get here. You're dealing with your own problems."

Her mother smiled and reached for Ana's hands. "No matter what's going on in my life, I'm never too busy for you."

Ana studied her mother's creamy skin, the slight wrinkles around her eyes and mouth. With blond, shoulder-length hair and bright green eyes, Lorraine Clark was a beauty even at the age of sixty. The woman didn't look much over forty and Ana knew how lucky she was to have at least one parent who would drop anything to be with the ones she loved.

"What is wrong with Dad?" Ana asked before she could stop herself. "I'm sorry. That was rude."

"That's okay. I've often wondered what I could have done differently." A sad smile formed as Lorraine looked across the room out the window toward the bay. "It took me a long time to realize it wasn't me at all. He wasn't the man I wanted him to be. We didn't have the relationship I conjured up in my head."

"Why did you stay?"

Her mother's gaze came back to Ana. "Fear of being alone. I'd been with him so long that I didn't know if I could make it on my own. Plus when you were younger, I was so worried I wouldn't be able to take care of you financially. Of course, I had no idea he'd started gambling away everything we had."

Ana embraced her mother. "Let's do something for ourselves today. What do you say we take advantage of the spa in this hotel? We need to be pampered."

Lorraine eased back and smiled. "I couldn't agree more. And no more talk about love and foolishness. This is girls' day."

Ana could go the rest of the day and not discuss Zach, but that didn't mean he wouldn't always be in the forefront of her mind. The only way she could get over him was to move on.

From here on out all she would concentrate on would be work and her mother.

What else did she need?

Nineteen

Zach pulled his Screamin' Eagle onto the site.

Two weeks had passed since he'd talked, alone, to Ana. Every time he came to the site, she was inside the resort and her assistant foreman had filled him in on where the project stood. One time she wasn't around because she'd gone to run an errand—one that he could've done had she called him and admitted she needed help.

She refused to return his calls, ignored his texts. God, she was acting like…him. Zach killed the roaring engine and stared at the beautiful gigantic resort. Ana was brushing him off like he'd done to women when they got too close. Only when Ana had gotten close, he wasn't nearly as ready to get rid of her as he had been every woman in the past.

But now she acted as if nothing had happened between them, as if they hadn't changed each other's lives. And, yes, she had changed his life. He couldn't pinpoint when, but she had.

Anger flooded through him. Hadn't she told him she loved

him? That was something she couldn't just turn off. Unless she hadn't meant it to begin with. But Zach knew Ana never said anything if she didn't mean it. Could he have killed that love so quickly? He didn't want to even consider the notion.

Zach wanted to make Ana listen. Make her understand that Melanie wasn't part of his life anymore. He was over her.

Had been over her.

It just took seeing the two women side by side to come to grips with what he already knew.

Ana had been standing there in her little shorts and tank with her wild red curls, holding their dog, and Melanie had looked like the knockout she was with every hair in place, every nail professionally polished to a shine. But it had been Ana to whom his body had responded.

Zach stopped dead in his tracks on the dusty path to Ana's office. He'd called Jake "their" dog. Since when was Jake "their" dog?

Making his feet move again, Zach realized that the dog had been theirs from the get-go. Obviously even then he knew he cared for her more than he wanted, more than he thought possible.

Behind his dark shades, he scanned the area. Ana wasn't in sight, so he made his way toward her office. He tapped lightly on the door, but didn't wait for her to respond or answer. He walked right in—and froze.

Ana sat at her desk, and a woman probably around forty or so sat opposite her. The two were sharing lunch and laughing, but their faces froze and all chatter ceased when he entered.

"I didn't mean to interrupt," he said, closing the door behind him. "Ana, I need to speak with you."

Ana set down her fork in her salad and came to her feet. "I'm having lunch with my mother, Zach. Is this about business?"

Zach's eyes darted back to the other woman. Good Lord,

that woman was Ana's *mother?* She was stunning, poised; obviously she'd aged very well.

"I'm Zach Marcum." He extended his hand. "I see where Ana gets her beauty from."

The woman came to her feet, smiled and shook his hand. "She said you were charming. I'm Lorraine Clark."

Zach held on to her hand, quirked a brow over at Ana. "She's mentioned me, huh?"

"Only as a warning," Ana said, unsmiling. "What do you need?"

He dropped Lorraine's hand and shoved his hands in his denim pockets. "The same thing I've needed for weeks. To talk to you alone."

Ana mimicked his stance by placing her hands on her hips. "Surely you of all people recognize a brush-off, Zach. Isn't that how you work? Go back to Melanie or whoever else you want this week. I'm not interested."

If she didn't care that her mother overheard their conversation, then neither did he. "I'm not interested in Melanie. I want you."

Ana stared, then looked down at her desk, but he didn't miss the moisture that gathered in her eyes or the way she blinked rapidly trying to keep her emotions hidden.

"Well, we can't always have what we want." Ana's tone softened, and her throat sounded full of tears and emotions. She picked up her salad and tossed it into the garbage. "Now, if that's all, I'd like to finish talking with my mother."

Zach nodded, refusing to grovel for anything. He'd caused this damage and now he had to live with it.

"It was a pleasure to meet you." He offered Lorraine a smile even though he wanted to yell or throw something, anything to make Ana listen. "I need to speak to the assistant foreman before I leave. If you'll excuse me."

He left the office without looking back. If she was truly

done, then he would walk away and leave her be. But he didn't believe she was because she couldn't look him in the eye.

Zach did a one-eighty and got back on his bike. He didn't need to speak to the foreman that badly. There was something much more important he had to do. A plan formed in his mind and he knew this could seriously make or break his future.

For once in his life, he was putting business on the back burner, putting himself second and putting a woman first.

He didn't know another term for this insane way of thinking. It must be love.

Ana was so looking forward to a weekend with no contact with Zach. She and her mother had planned a glorious day at the beach doing nothing but soaking up the sun and catching up on some reading…something Ana hadn't done in, well, she couldn't remember how long.

While her mother changed in the bedroom of the suite, Ana threw some bottles of water, a book and a towel into her yellow mesh bag. The day at the spa they'd had together last weekend was great, but Ana needed another day of relaxation. Especially after Zach had confronted her in front of her mother.

God, she wished he'd just see what she was offering. Why couldn't he see how fake Melanie was? Ana had been in the other woman's presence for all of five minutes and was less than impressed.

If that's what Zach found attractive, then obviously she was the wrong woman for him. But oh, how she wished he weren't that shallow. She truly believed he wasn't, but he was rich and perhaps he'd gotten swept into that lifestyle. Ana had been in Miami long enough to realize that image was everything.

The ache that had taken up permanent residence in her heart grew deeper roots each day. The way Zach had listened to her, had offered advice when it came to her father and her childhood, the way he knew what would make her smile and laugh all were indications he cared for, if not loved, her.

He'd bought her a dog, for crying out loud. Hadn't his ex even said he'd forbidden a dog in their house?

She replayed every moment they'd spent together, over and over, and she never saw a spot where he acted like he didn't want to be with her.

Each flash of memory was filled with laughter and unspoken promises.

Maybe she'd just gotten wrapped up in Zach because she'd given herself to him, but Ana highly doubted it.

Dammit, she just wanted to find a reason or a person to place blame on. But she knew blame could only lie with herself. She knew going in what kind of man Zach was.

"All ready."

Her mother's cheery tone snapped Ana out of her stroll down agony lane.

Lorraine stepped from the bedroom wearing her one-piece red bathing suit with a black wrap around her hips. "Let me just grab my bag."

A heavy knock sounded on the door. "Okay, I'll get the door," Ana called over her shoulder.

Ana moved through the living area and opened the door. To Zach. Holding Jake.

"He missed you," Zach said, holding the dog out.

Taking Jake, Ana held him against her chest and swallowed that lump of emotion that came along with seeing Zach. "Thanks. Mom and I are going out. I'll take him with us."

Zach shoved his hands in his pockets and leaned against the doorjamb. "I was hoping you'd come with me. I have something to show you."

Ana didn't want to be standing this close to him, let alone go anywhere with him. The spicy, clean aroma she'd grown accustomed to from Zach wafted around her. The sexy stubble he always seemed to have was just a tad longer than usual.

His eyes were puffy as if he hadn't slept and his hair was downright unkempt. Ana knew those long, tanned fingers had run through that thick hair over and over.

As much as she enjoyed that he was looking as miserable as she felt, she still loved the man, even though she wanted to throttle him for taking her heart and crushing it with both hands.

"That's not a good idea, Zach."

"I think it's a great idea," her mother said, stepping up behind her. "Go on, Ana. We can go to the beach next weekend when you're off."

Ana turned to her mother. "What will you do?"

Lorraine smiled. "Don't worry about me. I'll just take a book and pick out a nice lounge chair with an umbrella and relax. Now go on."

Even though Ana hated to admit it, she was curious as to what he wanted to show her. And to be honest, she knew they needed to talk. They couldn't leave things up in the air even though Ana knew the outcome. Stepping out that door with Zach would just bring on more heartache, but after all she'd given him she deserved the chance to speak and let him know where she stood.

"All right." Ana turned back to Zach. "Let me grab my bag."

"You won't need anything," he told her. "Just Jake."

Hesitant, Ana decided to leave her belongings, except her key, which she slid into her shorts pocket. She kissed her mother goodbye, made sure she had the spare key and followed Zach out the door.

Silence surrounded them in the hallway, accompanied them into the elevator and settled between them once they were in his truck.

Okay, so obviously he wasn't in a talkative mood. She

could deal with that…for now. Eventually they would have to talk, but she would go with his flow until they got to the surprise destination.

When they pulled into his driveway, he hopped out and came around to help her down from the truck. She kept hold of Jake as she followed him into his house.

"Come into my office."

Ana set Jake down and went with Zach. The little puppy's paws clicked on the marble floor behind her as she entered Zach's spacious office. Ana couldn't help but admire the beauty of the floor-to-ceiling windows on the two exterior walls. His lavish, well-manicured gardens were quite the view and definitely could inspire anyone working at the oversize mahogany desk.

And it was the desk that drew her attention now. Sprawled across it were blueprints.

"Before you look at this, I need you to know something."

Ana risked taking her gaze from the harmless paper up to Zach's dark eyes. "What?"

"Your father won't be a problem for you anymore. I paid off all his debts and he signed a legal, binding document not to come in contact with you or your mother ever again. Not in person, not via the internet or phone or any other form of communication."

Ana sucked in a breath. "Why did you do that?"

The muscle in Zach's jaw ticked as he glanced down to the desk. "I want no secrets between us."

With a mock laugh, Ana crossed her arms. "Too late for that, isn't it?"

"Look over these," he told her with a roughness to his tone as he pointed down to the drawings. "I'm looking for a company to build this."

Ana swallowed hard. "Zach, after this resort is done, my company is moving on. We have a six-story office building to construct in Dallas. Besides, I don't think it's a good idea for us to work together anymore. Let's just finish these last two months and put this behind us."

"Can you just look at the plans?" he pleaded.

Stepping up to the desk, Ana looked down, but it didn't take her long to see this wasn't any commercial project. "This is a house. I don't generally contract homes." She studied the amazing plans, though, nearly salivating at the lucky would-be owner. "Who wants this done? Victor?"

"Me."

Ana looked up. "You?"

Oh, God. Just drive the knife in and give it a swift turn, why don't ya? Now he expected her to build a home where he could resume residence with his ex-wife. Yeah, she should've listened to her first instincts and not gone with him today. She should be sitting on the beach with a fruity little drink, reading the latest gossip magazines with her mother.

Instead she and her heart were here, taking another beating. Was Melanie somewhere in the house? Did she still have that smirk Ana so wanted to smack off?

Ana glanced to the door, half expecting the ex to be keeping watch over Zach. "Does Melanie know you're asking me to build her house?"

Zach came around his desk and stood within inches of her. Ana tipped her head back to look into his heavy-lidded dark eyes.

"You're not building a house for Melanie. You'd be building a house for me…and you."

Hope, hurt, stress in general all plagued her at once and Ana couldn't look him in the eyes another second. She turned, crossed the room to sit on the bulky leather couch. As much as she wanted to believe, she couldn't look at him, couldn't let herself get drawn back into the dark depth of his eyes, his world.

She curled her feet beneath her, rubbed her damp palms down the cover-up she'd thrown over her swimsuit. "Don't. Just don't. This can't happen, Zach."

"What can't happen?"

Ana shoved her stray curls from her face and lifted her gaze to his. "Whatever you have planned. You aren't over your ex, that's obvious. And that's okay. I knew you weren't long-term when I got involved with you. Part of this mess is my fault, but please don't make me believe in something you can't give."

Zach closed the gap between them, crouched down to take her hands in his. "You're right. When we first met I wasn't in a place where I could, or even wanted to, get involved with someone. I was hung up on Melanie even if I didn't admit it to myself."

Hearing those words, knowing he meant them didn't help the tight band around her chest. If anything, he'd just pulled it tighter.

"But you changed everything," he admitted. "I never wanted another relationship, but I can't deny myself. I can't walk away from you."

Ana stared into his eyes, saw the shimmer of his own unshed tears. "How can I believe you? How do I know you don't just want me because you lost me? What if you decided next month you're ready to move on? You've even admitted yourself that you're always looking for something better."

He nodded and tucked a curl behind her ear before squeezing her hands. "I was, but I found something better. You. You're the something I'd always been looking for."

That hope that had started forming in her heart when she'd seen the house plans grew just a bit more. "What about Melanie? You love her."

"No, I don't." He eased up next to her on the couch and

faced her fully. "I thought I loved her, and maybe I did on some level, but whatever I felt for her is absolutely nothing compared to the feelings I have for you."

Ana leaned in closer to Zach. She wanted to look in his eyes when she asked the next question. Wanted to look for any doubt, and lie.

"What do you feel for me?"

"Love." A wide smile lit his face. "I admit, when I first realized I loved you, I denied it to myself. I didn't want to get hurt again."

Ana didn't even try to stop the tears from falling now. "Hurt? You destroyed me when I found out you'd been talking with Melanie. To know that you love me… God, Zach, that's more than I ever thought you'd feel for me. I want to believe…"

Zach cupped her damp cheeks in his palms, pulled her against him for a hard, loving kiss. Yes, loving. She felt it in every part of her. He did love her.

Ana wrapped her arms around his neck, unable to control her emotions a moment longer.

"Believe," he murmured against her lips. His forehead rested against hers. "Ana, believe in everything I'm telling you. Don't doubt my love for you. Ever."

Ana couldn't speak for the tears, so she nodded.

"Is that a yes that you'll build our house?" he asked.

"Y-yes." She sniffled. "I knew you loved me, Zach. I just never knew if you'd see it yourself. Months ago when I poured my heart out to you about my childhood you listened. You've been so patient, so understanding. I know what I've found in you will make me happier than I deserve to be for the rest of my life."

He eased back, wiping her tears with the pads of his thumbs. "I have another condition."

"What?"

"We only have a couple months left on Victor's resort, then you can send your crew on to Dallas, but I want you here for a while."

Ana drew her brows together. "I'll have to go get things started, Zach. I can't just forget this project because you asked me to. What is so important?"

"Marry me," he said with a smile. "Tell me you'll stay in my life forever."

Stunned, elated, nervous. Ana didn't know what label to place on all the feelings whirling around in her mind, her heart.

"Are you sure?" she asked, praying to God he was. "You married before and swore you'd never marry again."

"That's because I married the wrong woman. Everything about you, about us, is right."

Ana grabbed hold of Zach's strong hands as he continued to hold her face. "I want babies and more dogs."

Zach kissed her again, his mouth hard, possessive. He wrapped his arms around her waist, pulled her tight against him.

"More of anything with you is fine with me," he told her as he eased her back against the couch, already working her sheer cover-up off. "I have another surprise for you."

"I've seen it." She laughed.

"Oh, well, I do have that," he joked. "But I bought you your own bike. It's in my garage."

She held a hand to his chest to stop him. "My own motor-cycle?"

"Well, yeah. I want you riding with me."

Ana ran the possibility through her mind and nodded. "I suppose since you were my first with everything, you may as well teach me to ride. Provided we can get to actually start the engine this time."

Zach's smile remained in place, but his eyes grew serious as he explored her face. "You were my first, too. Love never meant anything to me until you, Anastasia Clark."

Ana knew this journey she was about to embark on with Zach was just the start of many firsts to come.

* * * * *

THE
MILLION-DOLLAR
QUESTION

KIMBERLY LANG

To Marilynn, Terri, Sunny, Angela, Stacey, Marbury, both Melissas, Anna, Andrea, India, Kelly, Buddy, Chris, Susan, Nelson and the whole ASFA dance department for all the stories that start with, "There was this one time, during *Nutcracker* . . ."

CHAPTER ONE

"SOMEBODY'S GOT A hot date."

It was hard for Olivia Madison to both roll her eyes and apply mascara at the same time, but she managed it—just barely. Rehearsals had run long today and she was now running late. She didn't have time for this. "It's not a date."

Her roommate, Annie, flopped across the bed and examined the outfit Olivia had laid out for tonight. "Hmm…Silky top, the 'good butt' jeans and 'take me' boots. You curled your hair, you're wearing makeup, and…" She stopped to sniff the air delicately. "I smell perfume. All signs point to a hot date. And it's about time. I was getting afraid we'd have to get a couple of cats soon and the lease doesn't allow pets."

"First of all, neither of us is in Cat Lady territory just yet. Getting married and having babies is what your thirties are for. Second, it's just dinner. Pretty much a business dinner, at that."

Annie still wasn't convinced. "In that outfit? Please. Did you shave your legs?"

Olivia had, but that was neither here nor there and had nothing to do with the person she was meeting for dinner. "It's with my brother's college roommate, for goodness sake."

"Is he cute?"

Olivia had to admit he was. She'd looked him up online to see if he'd changed much in the past nine years, rather hoping to find that he'd developed a paunch or lost a lot of hair, only to be disappointed in that hope. If anything, the past decade had been quite good to Evan Lawford, maturing his features—and even the attitude he projected in the photos—light-years past the frat rat she remembered. The sun-bleached hair had turned darker, probably meaning he didn't spend as much time on the beach as he used to, but the color offset his blue eyes nicely. The cheekbones and the jawline she remembered quite well, only the two-day stubble look was also gone. The difference between boy and man was stark and startling at first.

Objectively speaking, Evan Lawford was *hot*. Male-model-broodingly-advertising-expensive-suits-in-a-glossy-magazine hot. "It doesn't really matter. He's a jerk."

"Which means he *is* a hottie, and that's just wrong." Annie sighed and rolled to her back. "Why can't the really nice guys be drop-dead gorgeous, too? Is that really too much to ask?" she pleaded to the universe.

"All signs point to *yes*." Olivia tossed the mascara tube back into her makeup bag. *Jerk* was a nice word for Evan. He was a cocky, arrogant, ego-ridden player.

But he was a *successful* cocky, arrogant, ego-ridden player, and that was what was important at the moment. She'd have to suck it up and deal with the rest.

"So why are you having dinner with him then?"

Because I'm forced to sell myself out in order to further my career. That wasn't entirely exactly true: no one at the Miami Modern Ballet Company expected her to actually sleep with someone for their money, but the trade-off still gave her icky vibes. "I need him to sponsor me."

Annie's forehead wrinkled in concern. "Like a twelve-step kind of sponsor? Are you okay?"

Olivia kept the sigh—and the smart-ass comeback—behind her teeth. It wasn't all that unexpected of a speculation, and at least Annie was asking it from a place of concern. Olivia had left home at fifteen to spend the next decade in studios and on stages, driving herself to reach this point: a contracted principal in an established, prestigious ballet company. Therefore, everyone assumed that she had to have something wrong with her—drug habit, an eating disorder, or even just a flat-out psychotic break à la *Black Swan* picked up along the way. She nearly snorted. There probably *was* something wrong with her, only they didn't have an official diagnosis for it yet.

And while she'd known Annie for only a few months—trading the privacy of having her own place for the opportunity to live near the beaches and nightlife of Miami, even with an unknown roommate—they were getting along very well. "Not that kind of sponsor. An actual please-donate-your-money kind of sponsor."

Annie looked confused. "You're fundraising?"

"In a way. Money is tight all over, and the arts are really feeling the pinch," she explained, slipping into her jeans. Annie averted her eyes as Olivia dressed, but Olivia had lost any kind of modesty years ago through one too many quick changes backstage in view of the entire corps and stagehands. "Our state funding has been slashed, ticket sales are down and corporate sponsorship in general is not as strong as it used to be. So nowadays, rich people can adopt a dancer of their very own. In return, they get all kinds of perks—tickets, backstage passes, first dibs on tables at the En Pointe Ball and for the big spenders," Olivia continued, as she pasted a smile on her face and added a chipper tone, "the chance to have their dancer appear at their corporate—or sometimes private—events."

"That sounds cool." Her forehead wrinkled. "But kinda creepy, too."

"Tell me about it."

"And you need one of these sponsors? I thought you had a contract."

Annie, who worked as a Spanish-language interpreter for the city, was getting a crash course in the state of the arts in America these days. "I do, but my contract isn't cheap. And while MMBC has the option to pick up my contract for next season, there's no guarantee that they will—especially if I'm the only one without sponsorship to offset my cost. Sponsorship doesn't guarantee anything either way, but it won't hurt."

"I see. So you're hoping your brother's college room-mate has that kind of money?"

"I know he does. I haven't seen Evan in years, but he and Jory are still real tight." Why that was, she didn't quite know. Evan had nearly succeeded in turn-ing Jory into a carbon copy of himself in college, and while Jory had turned out okay anyway, she didn't re-ally understand what the two men could possibly have in common. "He's got the money." She frowned at the mirror as she finger-combed out the curls and sprayed her hair into place. "I just need to figure out how to ask him for it."

"Why can't you just ask him outright? It seems pretty straightforward, and it's a tax deduction to boot."

"Yeah, but it's…" She wasn't sure how to explain it, even if she wanted to. Which she really didn't. "It's complicated."

"Complicated?" Annie's forehead wrinkled again, then smoothed out as understanding dawned. "*Oh. That* kind of complicated."

"Let's just say that it's not complicated enough to keep me from asking, but complicated enough to make me want to handle the situation delicately."

"If it's going to be awkward, why not just call your brother instead? Get him to play middleman."

"No." *No way.* That was a can of worms she defi-nitely wasn't going to open.

"Then maybe your brother or your parents could sponsor you, instead?"

She knew Jory. Telling him she needed sponsorship—or any money, really—would lead him to opening his checkbook. He'd tell Mom and Daddy, and they'd want to do the same. And that was *not* going to happen. Jory needed to be investing his money into his own business, and Mom and Daddy needed to be saving for retirement.

Mom and Daddy were comfortable enough, but they'd sacrificed greatly over the years to support her dream. So had Jory, in fact. She wasn't going to take another blessed dime from them. Any of them.

She shook her head. "They're in Tampa, and the sponsors need to be local." Even as she said it, she had no idea if it was true. The company probably assumed sponsors would be local—and that was how the donor rewards were structured—but she couldn't imagine any company turning down money, regardless of the source. Still, it was a clean and quick explanation, and Annie accepted it at face value.

"That's a problem, then."

"And I've been in Miami for only three months. I don't really know anyone else." She paused in zipping up her boots to look hopefully at Annie. "Unless you happen to have thousands of dollars tucked away and a hidden, burning desire to support the arts in your community?"

Annie shook her head. "Uh, no."

"Then I'm off to dinner with Evan." She took one

last critical look in the mirror, then turned to Annie. "How do I look?"

"Amazing, as always. And, as always, I kinda hate you for it. If you can't win Evan over with logic or reason, you should be able to flirt his checkbook right open." Annie rolled off the bed and got to her feet. With a cheeky grin, she added, "I won't wait up for you."

Olivia had no intention of flirting with Evan at all. She could be polite and friendly, but this was merely business. She'd flirted with him that one time, and the lessons learned stuck with her to this day. But she was older now, wiser, and she could look back on it for the educational experience it was, without feeling the pain or shame.

Much.

The restaurant Evan chose to meet her at was only about six blocks from the condo she shared with Annie, and Olivia elected to walk it. Eventually, she'd have to buy a car—an expense she'd managed to avoid for at least the past five years—but for now, Miami's public transport could get her pretty much anywhere her feet couldn't.

It might be November, but she didn't need a sweater. However, she grabbed a pashmina in case the air conditioning in the restaurant was set on "Arctic." After spending so many winters in more northern climes, it was so *so* nice to be back in Florida, with her winter gear shipped home to Tampa to the storage unit she kept there. The sun had been down for an hour, but the temperatures were still in the high seventies, perfect for a walk, but it was a little jarring for it to be that warm as businesses took down their Halloween decorations and replaced them with a mix of turkeys and Santa Claus.

She could come to really love Miami. MMBC was a highly respected company with a great mix of classical and contemporary in their repertoire. It may be not as prestigious as some in New York, but the trade-off was a lower cost of living and fewer up-and-comers nipping at her heels all the time. She could still do the occasional guest artist thing when the traveling bug bit her or things started to feel stale, but Miami was a great base.

And she needed to start thinking about the future, anyway. If all went well, she could get another six, maybe seven, years in before retiring, but she was feeling the effects of the past two decades already and her chances of injury increased each year. She needed to be building some kind of foundation, and Miami was ideal for that.

Plus, it was only four hours from home.

All this was great. Provided she could keep the job she'd worked so hard to get. The fact she was willing to turn to Evan Lawford proved how much she wanted her contract picked up for next season. That would give her time to build a reputation and network here in Miami and increase her chances of further seasons exponentially.

She just had to get through dinner with Evan and get his agreement first.

Easy-peasy, right?

Oddly, Evan hadn't asked many questions when she'd emailed him, saying hello and asking if he'd like to get together. She'd provided her phone number, but he'd stuck to email, setting up the place and time with the minimum amount of communication necessary. She wasn't sure if that was a good thing or a not.

It had taken courage—more than she thought she'd need for something so simple—to email him in the first place, but he'd accepted so quickly that she'd only had forty-eight hours to figure out how to actually pull this off.

Evan and Jory were friends, practically brothers. Although she'd not been there to see it, she knew Evan loved her parents and had spent a lot of weekends and holidays at their house instead of his own. Her parents loved him. But that had nothing to do with her, and she couldn't cash in on her parents' kindness or Jory's friendship like some kind of promissory note owed to her.

But *they* weren't friends. They were just two people in Jory's orbit, basically little more than strangers.

Okay, they were *more* than strangers. She just wasn't sure where on the hierarchy of relationships to place her brother's roommate when he was also the guy you lost your virginity to in what turned out to be only slightly more than a one-night stand.

Ugh.

While she'd felt hurt and used at the time, perspective could offer the balm that it probably hadn't been personal. And realistically, he'd most likely saved her from making a similar mistake later on—when she would have been alone, surrounded by strangers, and even more vulnerable. Naïveté was a dangerous thing.

The truly embarrassing part was that she'd known exactly what he was going in to it. Hell, he'd taken Jory into his decadent world of wine, women and song, debauching him quite thoroughly. But with the arrogance only a teenager could have, she'd believed she was different. *Special.*

Combined with Evan's combo of charm, good looks and raw sensuality, that arrogance had easily overwhelmed and shouted down anything she'd known merely intellectually.

That was the rational, reasonable part of her brain. The same part of her brain that turned that burn into something useful, allowing her to focus on her training instead of getting wrapped up in messy entanglements that could have complicated her life unnecessarily. So that was good.

Parties, boyfriends…all those things she'd been told she'd have to sacrifice for her career didn't seem like so much of a sacrifice after that. Or at least not an overly painful one.

Her inner eighteen-year-old still held a grudge about it, but she'd need to keep *that* safely hidden away.

Even if *Evan* felt remorse over the whole sorry incident, she wasn't sure that was something she could—or wanted to—play on, either. She'd look foolish and

ridiculous and hopelessly naive—and petty and ma-
nipulative to boot.

Nope. That little lost weekend needed to stay lost.

She was an adult; he was an adult. This was a purely
business transaction, albeit with a personal glaze. But
there was no crime in networking the contacts you had,
personal or not.

Be friendly. Be businesslike. Evan was a successful
businessman. According to Jory, Evan's advertising
agency was growing in phenomenal leaps and bounds,
and he should appreciate a professional approach. There
was no need to jump right in with the request—a little
pleasant small talk always greased the wheels nicely.
She would put the sponsorship out on the table early,
giving him plenty of time for questions and plenty of
time for her to convince him. If all went well, she could
walk out of here tonight with his commitment and the
ballet's business manager could get the good news by
class tomorrow.

If all went well.

And there was no reason why it shouldn't.

"Good evening, Mr. Lawford."

The valet at Tourmaine opened Evan's door and
greeted him with a smile. Tourmaine was his go-to
place for entertaining clients—modern enough to feel
on trend without being trendy, music loud enough to
hear and enjoy without hindering conversations, and,
most importantly, good food and a staff that knew

him—and his tipping habits—well. "Good evening, Brian."

"Enjoy your meal."

"Thank you." A banal, basic exchange of pleasantries, but one that he needed to remind him that the world hadn't, in fact, gone insane.

Because barring that, he had no idea why Olivia Madison wanted to have dinner with him.

He knew, of course, that she'd moved to Miami. Jory had been ridiculously proud of his sister's accomplishment, and they'd had dinner back in the fall when Jory came to see Olivia's first performance with her new company. But Olivia hadn't joined them, and Jory didn't bring up his sister unnecessarily.

Evan hadn't seen Olivia since she was eighteen, and that was definitely intentional. The only thing that had ever come between him and Jory was Olivia, and they'd nearly come to blows over her, doing damage to their friendship that had taken time to repair. He didn't know how twitchy Jory might be about it these days, but it wasn't something he wanted to stir up—not until he at least knew why Olivia had contacted him in the first place.

Miami was plenty big enough for them to never come in contact with each other at all, and he assumed that was exactly how Olivia—and Jory, as well—wanted it.

So an email out of the blue from her with a dinner invitation had to be viewed with some level of suspicion, yet there was no way he could not have come. If only to find out why.

Yep, that was his story and he was sticking to it.

He was a few minutes early, but Olivia was already there, the unusual coppery-blond hair both Madison siblings inherited from their mother easy to spot in the small crowd of people around the bar. She was in profile to him, reading something on her phone, giving him the chance to examine her at leisure.

She'd been baby-faced at eighteen, but far more mature in some ways than others her age—by then, she'd already traveled and lived abroad, a professional in her career when most others were still figuring out their future. She'd said she'd wanted a taste of real college life, the same as anyone else, and there hadn't been a good reason not to indulge her—and himself at the same time.

The baby face was now gone, replaced by chiseled cheekbones and winged eyebrows that gave her a classical, elegant look, emphasized by the impossibly good posture and movements that were effortlessly graceful—even those as simple as ordering a drink or walking toward him…which she was now doing, a hesitant smile on her face.

"Evan. It's good to see you."

While her tone sounded sincere, he doubted it was completely true. There was a moment of hesitation, then she leaned in for one of those air-kiss things. Her cheek touched his accidentally and she jumped back as if she'd been scalded. He wouldn't deny it: it sent a bit of a jolt through him, as well. He cleared his throat. "And you."

The initial pleasantries finished, they stood there in an awkward silence, and he wasn't used to awkward silences. "You look good," he managed.

There was a small tug of her lips that stopped short of a smile. "So do you."

More silence.

Thankfully, the hostess arrived to save them. "Mr. Lawford, we have your table ready."

Following Olivia to the table gave him another chance to study her, and goodness, she was thin. She'd always been on the slight side, a necessity of dancing, but *wraithlike* was the word that came to mind. It was a good thing they were in a restaurant, because the need to feed her something was nearly overwhelming. She was also taller than he remembered, just a couple of inches shorter than his six-two, and only part of that height came from the boots she was wearing.

Long soft curls hung to the middle of her back, and a gold chain belt hung loosely around her tiny waist. Mile-long legs ended at slightly turned-out feet, giving her walk an unusual cadence that was still somehow graceful and smooth. Chin up and shoulders back, Olivia had presence.

He couldn't take his eyes off her. And that had gotten him in trouble before.

He shook his head to clear it. *Of course* the woman was thin and graceful. She *had* to be. That was a job requirement, and from what little he did know, Olivia Madison was good at her job.

Safely seated in the high-walled booth he favored

for its privacy, the awkward silence that had started in the bar was easy to fill with menu discussions and ordering. He couldn't stop his eyes from widening as she ordered a meal almost as big as his, and as the server walked away, she noticed. "What?"

"That's a lot of food."

She shot him a look. "If it's a problem, I'm perfectly happy to pay for my own dinner."

"That's not what I meant."

An eyebrow arched up. "Really? What did you mean then?"

Her tone could be called innocent and inquiring, but he realized the danger underneath just a second too late to pull the words back. "It's…well, you…" He usually wasn't foolish enough to bring up weight and diet with any woman, but he'd already stepped into it. "I guess I expected you to order a small salad with dressing on the side."

She snorted. "Maybe for the *first* course. But I spent six hours in rehearsals today. I'm hungry."

"Okay, a *large* salad, then," he teased.

Olivia folded her hands primly on the table, and as she spoke, her tone clearly said this was a speech she'd given many times before. "I eat. I have to. I work my body hard, and my body needs fuel to do that work. I stay aware of my weight, but not in an unhealthy manner. Since I'm not obsessing over it, I'd appreciate it if you didn't either. Okay?"

Duly chastised, he nodded. "Okay."

Then she leaned forward. "And seriously, they put

blue cheese *cream* sauce on a *steak* here. How am I *not* going to order that?"

"Fair enough." She talked a good game, but he'd withhold judgment until he actually saw her eat something. He worked in advertising, for goodness sake. He knew about models and the things they did to lose weight, but he had to admit that Olivia wasn't skeletal or starving—she was very slim, yes, but she didn't have the hollowed-out sickly look. "It's just surprising."

She inclined her head, and reached for her water.

"But not as surprising as hearing from you."

Olivia's hand froze, making him suspicious all over again. She recovered quickly, though. "I'm just full of surprises then. Honestly, I feel I've been rather rude not getting in touch before now. My only excuse is that I've been unbelievably busy the last few weeks—getting settled, with rehearsals for the fall performance, and then straight into *The Nutcracker* and the winter special that's coming up in January…I haven't had time to even think."

He'd known Jory for over twelve years, and his sister shared many of his mannerisms, making her somewhat easier to read than the average person. Olivia wasn't fully at ease in this conversation, which wasn't surprising. There were many reasons—beyond the busyness of her life—not to have been in touch before now, but there was no sense bringing those up just yet. That piqued his curiosity further, but he found that he wanted to make her comfortable, nonetheless. The past was bound to come up eventually, and it would be better to have a friendly footing before that happened. "But you're feeling more settled in now?"

"Yeah. I'm not getting hopelessly lost every time I leave the house these days, which is good. And it's nice to be home in Florida, where I can go to the beach anytime I want. Even in November."

Via Jory, he knew Olivia had done recent stays in Chicago and Boston, where the snow would be enough to drive any Florida native to the brink of insanity. "Which beach is your favorite?"

Her mouth twisted. "I haven't actually gone, yet. Like I said, I've been busy."

"Are you some kind of workaholic?"

"I believe that when you love your job, it's not exactly drudgery to put the time in."

"That's not an answer."

"I work a lot, and I like it. How's that?"

"That's a good answer. I might have to use that myself in the future." He paused as the server brought their drinks. Then he lifted his glass to her. "And congratulations on landing the new job."

She accepted his toast, a real smile replacing the hesitant one. "Thanks. It's exciting. MMBC—the company—normally chooses its principals from inside, but they decided to open the search this time. I knew one of the company members from years ago when I first went to New York, and he brought my name up to the artistic director. All the stars just aligned perfectly to get me here." She seemed as if she was just winding up, but caught herself instead, reaching for her wineglass and sitting back against the leather seat. "But what about you? Jory says your agency's doing really well."

"I can't complain. We're only three years old, and we still have some growing to do, but we're good."

"That's great to hear. I'm happy for you." Olivia stared at her glass, pondering the depths of pinot gris, and silence settled again. Then she looked up at him again with that smile he was beginning to think was definitely fake. "Jory's coming down with my parents in a couple of weeks to see the performance."

"I know. We're planning to get together while he's here."

"Oh, good."

"He says your parents are very excited."

"They don't get to see me in action very often because I'm usually so far away. I send videos and stuff, but it's not the same for them. And honestly, I'm excited they're getting to come, too. You know," she added casually, "if you'd like to come with them to the show, I can get you a ticket."

"Oh, hell, no." The words slipped out before he could check them. *Damn it. Insult the woman's career. That's always a great dinner conversation topic.* "I mean, no thank you. I'm not really a fan."

"Of *The Nutcracker* or ballet in general?"

"Both. No offense," he added. "It's just not my thing."

"None taken. We like what we like." She was being gracious, but he still felt as though he'd offended her. "Are you into the arts at all?"

He shrugged. "I used to have a membership to the art museum. I like the Egyptian stuff. There are a few local bands I keep up with." Lord, he sounded like a cultural wasteland. He justified it by saying, "Getting the agency off the ground has kept me pretty busy."

"I'm not judging."

Her smirk implied otherwise. "Yes, you are."

She shrugged a shoulder. "Okay, maybe a little. The arts celebrate what makes us human. They are the cornerstone of civilization and the heart of a community."

He nearly laughed, but swallowed it at the last second. Olivia obviously believed what she was saying. "You should work in advertising. That sounds like copy straight from a fundraising brochure."

She inclined her head. "That doesn't make it less true."

"That doesn't make them less boring, either."

Her eyes widened. "No offense intended again?" she asked.

"Of course."

"You could still support them financially, you know."

He shook his head. "Don't look at me like that."

"Like what?" she asked innocently.

"Like I'm some kind of miser. I give to charity. I just lean toward the more practical. You know, like food, housing, medical care…"

"Those are all very worthy causes."

"Is that sarcasm?"

"No. It's hard to enrich the mind and soul when the

body is hungry. I'm sure your philanthropy is much appreciated."

Evan felt as if there was something else that needed to be addressed. An undercurrent he was missing. But they were interrupted by the arrival of their meals.

Olivia greeted the food with a genuine, "That looks amazing." She inhaled the aroma with a blissful look on her face before taking a bite.

The steak with cream sauce was one of Tourmaine's signature dishes, and rightly so. Olivia obviously agreed; chewing her first bite with her eyes closed while making little happy noises. "Oh, man. That's *so* good."

He swallowed hard. He knew that look. Remembered it as if he'd seen it yesterday. But Olivia hadn't been eating steak with cream sauce the last time he'd seen it. *He'd* put that look on her face.

His blood rushed to his lap with a speed that left him feeling slightly light-headed. That one look had opened a floodgate of memories—memories he'd safely locked in a box to forget until just now. But that look…

He could practically feel those long, strong legs wrapped around him.

When she opened her eyes and saw him staring, she looked a little abashed. "I said I eat. I can't eat like this *all* the time, though, so I enjoy it very much when I do."

If she was going to enjoy her entire dinner like that, he'd be dead by dessert.

Thank goodness Olivia couldn't read his mind.

CHAPTER TWO

EVAN FOUND THAT concentrating on his food helped. Some. Tourmaine's owner, Harry, came by, nicely distracting his attention as he introduced Olivia and she complimented everything from the steak to the music. Harry was duly flattered and invited her back to try everything on the menu.

By the time it was just the two of them again, Evan had himself basically back under control, thankfully.

They ate for a little while, the conversation carefully kept to the simple topics of the excellent food, Jory's successes, her parents and the weather. It was oddly easy. Even fun, at times. There was the occasional overlong pause, but they didn't last. He'd nearly forgotten how smart and funny Olivia could be, and that had only improved in the intervening years. They had very little in common—no overlapping tastes in music, TV or movies, and some widely differing stances on politics and social issues—but that worked in their favor, keeping the conversation moving and interesting. And while he might be shallow, *this* was what had actually tipped the attraction all those years ago and made him risk Jory's wrath.

And it was almost enough to let him ignore that little voice nagging him now.

Almost.

When he decided they'd had enough of the small talk, he charged ahead. "Well, you seem to be settling in fine, so you don't need anything from me in that area, everything is okay with the people we have in common, and," he couldn't help but say through a chuckle, "I don't want to buy season tickets to the ballet. Care to tell me why we're actually here?"

She chewed, but he figured that was more of a stalling tactic than anything else. Finally she swallowed. "To eat dinner?"

"Come on, Liv, you've been in town since when? August? If you'd wanted my company for dinner, you'd have called long before now."

"Therefore, I must have nefarious reasons to do so now?"

"I wouldn't necessarily assume your reasons are nefarious, but you must have at least *one* above and beyond a free meal."

She shrugged a shoulder again.

Fine. There'd been two elephants in the room and Olivia had been talking around them both for over an hour now. If she wouldn't address the specific *why* of this dinner, he'd simply address the problem he did know. He leveled a look at her across the table. "After all, the last time we spoke, you called me a cold, heartless bastard."

She blinked, somehow caught off guard by the blunt statement. "True. I was mad and my feelings were hurt."

At least she was honest about that much. "So why would you want to have dinner with a 'heartless bastard'?"

"I'm trying to make my home here. I thought it'd be nice to expand my network of people outside just the dance world, and you are the only person in Miami—outside my roommate and the company members—that I know. Since I'm not the same person I was nine years ago, I'm assuming you aren't either." The corner of her mouth twitched. "I guess I'm hoping you outgrew that."

"Not really," he said, causing her to choke slightly on her wine.

"Wow." She cleared her throat and thought for a minute. "Well, at least you're honest about it."

"Those aren't exactly bad qualities to have in my line of work."

She thought for a moment, and then nodded. "If that's the case, then we just won't do this again. It's okay. You're friends with Jory and that doesn't automatically include me simply by extension. You have a life, and I can't just intrude upon that."

Well, now he felt like a heel. And the one possibility he'd been steadfastly ignoring as implausible was beginning to win out: Olivia had *wanted* to see him. He'd hurt her and yet she'd still gotten in touch after all this time. It was equal parts flattering and mystifying.

It was also extremely complicated. Jory had put his sister firmly off-limits nine years ago. Not that Evan blamed him. He'd been seriously messed up back then, not nearly good enough for Olivia. Hell, he probably still wasn't what someone like Liv needed, and he had to assume that prohibition was still in place. Of course, Olivia didn't know about any of that. It put him in a very awkward situation. There was a huge difference between an eighteen-year-old and a twenty-seven-year-old, but she was still Jory's sister.

Maybe she was just lonely and in need of a friend. Just because *he* was having flashbacks to happier, more naked times, there was no reason to assume she was, as well. And while he'd broken a major tenet of the Guy Code by sleeping with her before, there was an equally important tenet of the Code that required him to look after a friend's sister when she was new and alone in a big city. There were as many possibilities as pitfalls here. "Well, I guess if you're fully aware I'm *still* a heartless bastard and are willing to accept that, then there's no reason we can't be friends anyway."

Olivia's eyes widened at the baldness of his words, but he could rest easy either way knowing she was coming in with her eyes wide open. The ball was in her court, and he was frankly very curious to find out how she'd play.

Because she couldn't say he hadn't warned her.

You're a coward. A fool. A screaming idiot who should be kept on a leash for her own safety.

Olivia stared at herself in the mirror of the ladies' room and frowned. She'd had such clear, simple goals for this dinner, and she'd failed to accomplish even one.

Instead, she couldn't have made a bigger mess if she'd tried.

In a just and fair world, anger and hurt feelings would not fade enough over time to allow the person who caused those feelings to have the same effect on her that had gotten her into the situation in the first place. Instead of being hit with all the things about Evan she'd hated him for, she'd been overwhelmed with all the things that had sucked her into Evan's bed in the first place.

It was easy enough to say he was charming and good-looking, but it was another to face that head-on. The way that baritone slithered through her insides, turning them to jelly; the way those blue, blue eyes could make the most casual glance feel like a caress. It was even more devastating because he wasn't *trying* to seduce her. That was just his default setting, a natural part of his personality that made him catnip to women.

It was humiliating. She might not have Evan's legions of former lovers, but she wasn't an innocent anymore either. She'd taken lovers, had flings and summer romances, so why was Evan able to reduce her to a simpering virgin again?

Mercy.

She'd been rattled and ready to run for the door the minute she'd laid eyes on him. She should have known then that the whole idea was insane, made her excuses and left instead. But *no*, she just had to try.

Wandering up to a random stranger on the street and asking if they wanted to support the MMBC and adopt a dancer might have been less nerve-racking and equally as successful. And she'd probably like herself a bit more afterward than she did right now.

It hadn't been a completely crazy idea, just one that worked much better in theory than in practice. Regardless of how sensible it sounded on the surface, she hadn't been able to shake that uneasy feeling that swirled underneath, and she was now very glad she hadn't followed, though.

Maybe I'm not a coward. She was a decent human being who'd got carried away for a minute, but pulled back in time. Points for that. And she'd made it through dinner without making a complete fool of herself, so bonus points could be awarded, as well.

Thank goodness Evan could be so blunt, or else she might have tried to pull off this stunt—which she was now viewing as pretty gauche and tacky. She was now going to say good-night and go home, thanking her lucky stars she wasn't leaving in shame.

She'd sort out the other confusing stuff later. Much later, and when she was alone. She took a deep breath and squared her shoulders. *Time for a dignified end to this farce of an evening.*

Evan was waiting for her out front. "Thank you for dinner," she said. "It was good to see you." *Handshake? Air kiss?*

"And you. Do you have your valet ticket?"

"I walked."

"I'll drive you home, then."

"It's only six blocks," she protested, but it sounded weak even to her own ears.

"It's about to rain." As if to punctuate his words, a raindrop landed on her shoulder. *So much for dry Miami Novembers.* It felt like revenge for her tackiness.

Was it worth a standoff? Probably not, and she'd look foolish wanting to walk home in the rain. She was just feeling ashamed of herself in general and didn't want to drag this out any further. Of course, they *could* stand here and continue to argue, but the ridiculousness of that would only exacerbate her foolishness. "Okay. Thanks."

The timing bordered on eerie, as the moment the words left her lips, a car coasted to a stop at the curb and Evan was reaching for the door. The man had to be half genie.

This car was a far cry from the beat-up, perfect-for-trips-to-the-beach Jeep he'd driven in college. Black, low-slung and convertible, it looked expensive and classy, and it suited this adult Evan perfectly.

She wasn't surprised that the valet knew Evan's name—she'd gotten the feeling at dinner that he was a regular here—but the fact Evan knew the valet's name did surprise her. Her experience with rich donors had proved that most of them couldn't be bothered with the little people. He couldn't be *entirely* selfish if he remembered the names of valets and servers.

His car proved that Evan *definitely* had money—regardless of his modest "we're still growing" comments and it was almost enough to make her rethink her original, now aborted, plan.

No. Now she had her mother's voice in her head, reminding her that anything she thought might be a tacky or bad idea probably *was*, and she bit her tongue as Evan put the car in gear.

"Which way?"

"Left at the light," she answered absently. The traffic was bad and the streets were crowded, slowing their progress to a crawl. She definitely could have walked home faster than this. Her original refusal seemed less foolish now, as she was trapped in a small, enclosed space with Evan, his hand only inches from her thigh as he shifted gears.

It created an intimacy she wasn't quite prepared to face at the moment, and in the small space, the silence rapidly gained weight.

When Evan sighed, she knew he felt it, too. "Liv..."

No one but Evan had ever called her Liv. Jory called her Livvy sometimes, but Liv sounded more grown-up and more intimate, somehow. And all things considered, "Liv" carried a lot of baggage straight into the conversation.

She tried to keep it light, nonetheless. "Yes?"

Evan turned his head toward her, but his face was unreadable. "Just so you know, I'm sorry for what happened. Particularly the way I treated you."

She had to swallow her shock. *That* certainly was the last thing she'd ever thought she'd hear. She'd given up hope of an explanation or apology years ago. "Thank you," she managed after a long pause.

He seemed genuinely surprised at her response. "For what?"

"For saying that. It means a lot."

He shrugged a shoulder as he changed lanes. "I know it doesn't change anything, but I can still regret my behavior. The apology may be years too late, but it is sincere."

It was oddly much easier to have this conversation side-on, instead of having to look directly at him. She kept her eyes front and said, "For an admitted bastard, that was a nice apology."

She cut her eyes toward him just in time to see the corner of his mouth twitch as if he found that funny. "Thank you."

I won't ask for details. Asking would sound pathetic and whiny. And there was a very good chance she wouldn't like what she would hear. "Can I ask why things ended the way they did between us?" she said, wincing even as she did.

"Beyond the fact I'm cold and selfish?"

This time, she did turn to face him. "You're saying there's *not* one?"

He looked at her as though he was sizing her up and coming to a decision. Then his eyes went back to the road as traffic began to move again. "Not that I'm willing to share."

"Like that's not going to drive me crazy now," she

muttered, really not caring what it might sound like to him.

"If I tell you it was genuinely me and not at all you, would that help?"

He sounded sincere, and something panged inside her, reminding her of the sweet side of him she'd seen and gone cow-eyed over in the past. Jory had been uncharacteristically closed-mouthed about Evan's background, but she'd known his childhood had been difficult and that he spent time at her parents' house because he was estranged from his own family. She easily painted him as wounded, and being naive and smug and influenced by too many romantic movies, she'd cast herself as the woman who'd heal the misunderstood bad boy's heart. "Maybe. But—"

A skater shot out in front of them, nearly invisible in the mist and dark, and Evan jammed on the brakes, throwing her against her seat belt. His hand flew out at the same time, landing painfully on her chest, and the effect of both managed to knock the breath out of her. The skater didn't even look back as he sped away.

Evan cursed, then asked, "You okay?"

"Yeah." She purposely looked down to where Evan's hand was still pressed against her chest, pretty much copping a feel. Evan moved his hand quickly, without comment *and* without the decency to look even a little abashed or surprised at where it ended up. She, however, felt branded, the imprint of his hand seeming to linger. In hindsight, she should have worn a bra tonight whether she needed it or not. "Dude has a death wish," she said to break the tension she felt even if he didn't.

"You were smart to walk. Traffic down here is abysmal."

"It'll clear some once you turn." The sudden stop had sent her purse into the floorboard, and she leaned over to gather the contents back up. Her lipstick, though, had rolled under the seat and she had to contort herself to get to it. Realizing the solution to both her physical and emotional situation, she gave one last stretch and got it, then sat up and said briskly, "I can walk from here, save you some time."

"Don't be ridiculous."

So much for that idea.

As she promised, the traffic was thinner on her street, and Evan pulled up in front of her building a minute later. "These are nice condos. I'm glad you're not doing the starving artist thing."

"I ate half a cow covered in cream sauce for dinner, so I think we've already covered the 'not starving' part," she said with a laugh. "And I have a roommate to help cover the rent. It's a great location for me. It's fifteen minutes on the bus to the studio, and I can walk pretty much everywhere else."

She had her purse over her shoulder and a hand on the door, and that horrible how-to-end-the-evening tension returned. Evan's face was partly shadowed and unreadable, giving her no help there. Not a date, not friends, not business associates.... She didn't know the protocol.

To her ever-loving surprise, Evan got out of the car and walked around to open her door. Her jaw was still hanging open as he extended a hand to help her out.

For someone who purported to be selfish, he'd been raised right when it came to good manners.

That shock, though, caused her to stumble as she climbed out, pitching herself straight into Evan's arms. He caught her easily, his arms strong and solid around her. He was warm, and damn it, he smelled good. Her heart jumped into her throat.

Over her head, she heard Evan chuckle. "That was graceful."

Kill me now.

He set her back on her feet. "You okay?" Evan asked.

"I'm fine. Just clumsy."

His eyebrow went up. "Maybe it was the wine."

"Yeah, maybe." Shaking it off, she rushed ahead with forced cheer and casualness. "Well, thanks again for dinner. And for the ride home."

His lips twitched. "Take care, Liv. And if you ever need anything, give me a call."

Oh, the irony. "Good night."

Evan waited until the security door closed behind her before driving away. It had been a really, really strange evening, where nothing had gone as planned, but it hadn't been bad either. The beginning and end hadn't been fantastic, but the middle part, like the over-dinner chitchat, had gone pretty well, all things considered. Had she not gone into it with a specific agenda, she'd have called the evening a success.

But even with that failure, the evening still wasn't a total disaster. She *did* live in the same city with Evan, and they might run into each other on occasion; having a truce in place made good sense. And when Jory came to town, he wouldn't feel as if he had to divide his time so precisely. *All good things*, she thought, as she climbed the last few stairs to her floor.

Everything else could just be ignored.

Annie was sprawled on the couch, flipping through TV channels, but she sat up when she heard her come in. "How'd it go?"

"Not bad."

"So he's going to sponsor you?"

"No."

"He turned you *down*? Jeez." Annie went to the counter and got a wineglass, filling it and handing it to her. "That sucks."

Olivia accepted the glass gratefully and sank into the cushions on the opposite end of the couch. "He didn't have to turn me down. I didn't ask."

"What? Why not?"

With a sigh, Olivia ran through the evening, all the small things that added up to tip the scales in the direction of keeping her mouth shut. She glossed over her rather disturbing reactions to him, because, for her own sanity, that was best left unexamined.

"I can't say I blame you. I see where you're coming from, and I'd probably feel the same way. But," Annie continued, as she cocked her head, "what, then, did you say to explain why you suddenly wanted to have dinner after all these years?"

"New in town, don't really know anyone..."

"Olivia, really?" Annie sighed. "He's going to think you still have the hots for him."

"What? No. Not likely."

"You said he has an ego."

"He does."

"Then he *will*. It's actually the only logical conclusion he could come to, to explain it."

"He might think I'm insane now, but that's about all." *And he might not be wrong.* She stood and handed her glass to Annie to finish. "I'm going to bed. I've got Pilates at eight tomorrow."

"I'm sorry it didn't work out."

"Me, too."

It was a shame, but there was always plan B. Plan B involved making sure that everyone from the chairman of the ballet board all the way down to the stagehands loved her *and* working her butt off to prove her value to the company. She'd also talk to the business office to see if they had any ideas of how she could land sponsorship—and to suss out how important that sponsorship really was.

That's what I should have done in the first place, she told herself as she got ready for bed. That was a far more sensible idea than a half-baked plan to talk Evan into it. Hell, plan B should have been plan A. Too bad she didn't think of it first.

At the same time, she didn't regret their meeting.

It would make things easier for Jory when he came to town. She didn't know exactly how much Jory knew about her and Evan, but her brother had made it very clear he considered his roommate off-limits to his little sister. He'd been unhappy and grumpy about it. She hadn't asked him to take sides, but he always seemed uncomfortable bringing up Evan around her after that, giving the whole thing a patina of awkward wrongness—at least to her mind. That, as much as anything else, had led to making it a *thing*—which, now at least, she realized it really didn't need to be.

So, in that sense, dinner wasn't such a bad idea, after all.

The wine, the food and a long day—both physically and mentally—were catching up with her, and the bed beckoned.

As she climbed in and pulled the covers up, she realized she'd gotten distracted by the near miss with that skater and hadn't followed up on his mysterious "genuinely me, not you" statement.

What could he have possibly meant?

The next morning, just outside Boca Raton, the sudden blaring of "Born This Way" caused Evan to swerve dangerously in his lane.

What the sweet hell? The news program chattered on from his car speakers, but that was undeniably Lady Gaga coming from…under the passenger seat?

Pulling off onto the shoulder, he searched under the seat until he found the source: a phone that went silent about the time he got hold of it. It had an overly sparkly rhinestone case, and when he pressed the home button to wake it up, Olivia and Jory smiled back at him.

He couldn't figure out how Olivia had managed to leave her phone in his car, but now the question was what to do with it. The screen had a long list of missed calls from "Annie" and "Theo." Presumably those calls were Olivia using her friends' phones to locate her own. But the phone was locked, so he had no way of calling back.

Based on the sheer volume of calls, though, if he waited another thirty minutes or so, Olivia would be calling again. Sliding the phone into his shirt pocket, he pulled back out onto the interstate.

Last night had certainly been odd. And while he still didn't have a good explanation for why Olivia had contacted him, he didn't regret it. He just wasn't sure what, if anything, it meant, and what, if anything, he should do about it.

It wasn't a feeling he liked. In fact, he intentionally avoided these kinds of situations. Everything needed to be up front and clear, without mystery or games or prevarications. Jory was a straight-up, no games, kind of guy, so he'd assumed Olivia would be the same. Why then did he feel so bothered at the idea she might not be?

He snorted. Maybe because he wasn't sexually attracted to Jory.

Of course, the next question was if Olivia was still attracted to him? He'd like to say yes, and there had been moments, but that could be wishful thinking on his part. But she had left her phone in his car...accidentally or intentionally?

He was pulling into the parking lot of Riley Construction when Olivia's phone rang again. "Hello?"

"Hi." There was great relief in her voice that didn't sound fake. "My name's Olivia, and you seem to have my phone."

Accidentally. That knowledge came with unexpected disappointment and made his words sharper than intended. "Because you left it in my car last night."

There was a pause, then a confused, "Evan?"

"Who else?"

"I thought I'd left it at the restaurant or something. I didn't even think to call you." He heard her sigh. "I'm *so* glad you have it, though. My life is in that phone."

"I know how you feel."

"We should be breaking for lunch soon. Can I meet you somewhere and get it?"

"I'm in West Palm Beach for a meeting and won't be back until later this afternoon."

"Oh." She sounded disappointed. "Well, let me know when and where would be good for you."

"I can drop it by the studio later, though, on my way home," he offered for some reason.

"That would be awesome. I'll be here until around five-thirty or so. The studio is in Wynwood."

"Then I can find it."

"Thanks, Evan. I really appreciate it."

He silenced the phone's ringer before putting it in

his briefcase. Although Olivia would quit calling her phone now, other people might, and he really didn't want that annoying song blaring out during the meeting. If he was remembering correctly, the MMBC studio wasn't too far out of his way home, and he could swing by easily.

But, jeez. She was at the studio already and would be there until five-thirty? When Olivia said she worked her body hard, she hadn't been kidding. Granted, he knew next to nothing about the subject, but he would have guessed the job would be part-time at best. How long could it take, really? He had to assume she knew all the moves; putting them in a specific order for a performance shouldn't take all *that* long.

She'd said yesterday that she'd been in rehearsals for six hours. He'd assumed that was either an exaggeration or at least unusual. Six or seven hours in a dance studio couldn't be easy, much less doing that every day. Or maybe she didn't dance the whole time? He had no idea. A six or seven hour workday didn't seem like much, but then Olivia wasn't exactly sitting at a desk.

Regardless of what his father might say, he wasn't averse to hard work. He'd nearly killed himself to get through school and graduated with enough debt to buy a decent-sized house. Honestly, it was one of the things he and Jory had first bonded over—although for different reasons. The Madisons weren't rich—their family restaurant in Tampa was popular, but hardly a gold mine—and Jory's work ethic was rooted in the love and support of a family that wanted him to succeed.

Neither Jory nor Olivia knew what it was like to drive themselves out of spite and desperation, but they drove themselves nonetheless.

He had to respect it.

Jory, though, had needed to learn to let go, to come out of his shell and trust his instincts. Evan liked to think he played a big part in that, even if it had been mostly through bad influence and serving as a cautionary tale from time to time. But being too serious, too focused and too sure had a downside—and all Evan had to do was point in the direction of his own family for an example.

On paper, his family sounded great; in practice, they were insufferable. He far preferred the Madisons; Jory had brought him home like a stray, and Gary and Dee showed him what real families could be—fun, accepting and loving without reservations or conditions. There was very little he wouldn't do for the Madisons. They'd probably saved him from himself.

Which was why he'd walked away when Jory asked him to—and why he'd done it the way he had. He didn't want to cause tension between Jory and Olivia. If Olivia had ever told her parents about it, Jory must've said something to keep him okay in their eyes. He'd taken the blame, been the jerk, hurt Olivia for her own good. But it had all seemed to work out.

But with Olivia back in his orbit, however tangentially at the moment, it made things a little complicated. Again.

He had a meeting in less than ten minutes and he

needed to focus. There was a lot of money riding on this pitch, and he couldn't risk blowing it because his brain was elsewhere. He wanted Riley Construction in his stable.

Three hours later, he had them. He emailed his assistant and his office manager the good news, then stripped off his tie, tossed it into the backseat, unbuttoned his collar and his cuffs, and put the top down for the ride home.

His brain was buzzing, high on the adrenaline rush of success and future plans, and he forgot he still needed to drop off Olivia's phone until he was almost past the exit.

The parking lot was much busier than he expected, packed with cars. He followed a very tall, very slender teenager and her mother to a set of glass doors and inside into an alternate dimension.

Dozens of young girls—from early tweens to just-licensed-to-drive—packed the hallway. All were tall and slim with their hair pulled severely back. They all wore black bodysuits and pink tights as they contorted themselves into various stretches. They looked like a small bun-headed robot army, ready to invade.

The noise was at a level painful to adult ears, with an occasional squeal rising above the din to make him wince.

He waded through the chest-high crowd, dodging swinging arms and flying feet, to a door marked Office. A middle-aged woman sat behind a desk, seemingly unconcerned with the melee right outside her door. "Can I help you?"

"I'm looking for Olivia Madison."

The woman was professionally distant. "She's in rehearsals. Can I help instead?"

"I'm Evan Lawford. I have her phone."

Her voice warmed immediately. "Oh, good. She mentioned you would be coming by. You're welcome to leave it here with me, and I'll see that she gets it. Or you can wait. They should be done in another fifteen minutes or so."

Wait? In that hallway of overly excited children?

The horror must have shown on his face, because the woman laughed. "*The Nutcracker* gives young dancers from the community the opportunity to perform with a professional company. It's a tradition, albeit a sometimes noisy one."

He reached in his pocket and handed over the phone. "I think I'll just leave the phone with you."

She winked at him. "Smart move. I can't say I blame you."

Back out in the hallway, he tried to move toward the door, but was blocked by adolescent Bun-Bots huddled in a pack near a large window he hadn't noticed on his way in.

None of them were taller than his shoulders, so he could easily see over their heads, and he wondered what was so attention-grabbing that it deserved their awe.

The window offered a side view into a studio with painted cinder block walls and a gray floor. Mirrors lined the front wall and metal bars were bolted to the other three. It was frankly depressing. A dark-haired man in street clothes gesticulated wildly with his hands, obviously trying to make a point to the two dancers standing in the middle of the room. The walls absorbed most of the sound, muffling the words but not the volume or the emotion behind them.

It took him a second to realize that the woman dancer was Olivia. Her hair was scraped back from her face, but small tendrils had worked themselves loose and clung to her face and neck—which were flushed pink from exertion.

She was wearing a one-piece black thing that clung to her like a second skin, emphasizing the long, clean lines of her torso and the length of her legs. Yes, she was thin, but street clothes had hid the truth of her body from him last night. At eighteen, she'd still been growing into herself, but now, Olivia was solid, sculpted muscle, more like an athlete than his mental picture of a dainty, fragile ballerina.

Both she and her partner—who had all of *his* attributes on display as well in just tights and a tank top—were dripping sweat. Yet neither of them seemed phased by the other man's enthusiastic diatribe; they both just nodded as he went over to a stereo and started the music.

Olivia took a breath and started to dance.

Seriously, the studio doors *had* to have been a portal to another dimension, as Olivia seemed able to defy the laws of gravity, physics *and* biomechanics.

She could spin like a dreidel on her toes, then melt into the arms of her partner, her back bent over his arm like her spine was made of rubber. Those long legs extended to impossible heights, her foot easily higher than her head, and her jumps would be the envy of NBA players and world-class hurdlers.

He found himself holding his breath as Olivia's partner lifted her high over his head, supporting her with only one hand in the small of her back. An impressed gasp rose from the crowd in front of him. He didn't blame them one bit.

It was truly the most amazing thing he'd ever seen the human body do, and Olivia did it all with a serene smile on her face, making it look easy and effortless.

Something heavy and hot landed in his stomach. He couldn't quite define it, but it was powerful and impossible to ignore. It was different than just desire: he'd wanted her nine years ago, and that want had nudged at him all last night, but this ran deeper, somehow.

He felt himself starting to sweat, and he left quickly, ending up in the front seat of his car. Seeing Olivia in action, even just for those few minutes, shifted his entire perspective about her.

Jory had said she was good, and he'd had no reason to doubt that, but this showed a side of Olivia he never really knew about. No one got that good at anything without hard work—*really* hard work, the kind few people, including himself, would ever experience or understand. He had to respect that level of determination and discipline. It made his own drive seem pale in comparison.

And Jory had been right to expect Evan to leave her alone. Their affair would have ended—and probably badly, too—in quick enough time, only Olivia would have ended up hurt worse. He knew himself too well, both then and now, to think he'd have been a positive influence in her life at that point.

He still wasn't much of a prize. All anyone had to do was ask any of the past ten women he'd dated, and they'd provide a long list of his flaws. Which, again, he was well aware of—and even if he hadn't been, those flaws had been listed for him repeatedly, usually at top volume mere moments before the woman stormed out.

He should walk away. Quickly and to a great distance.

But he wasn't sure if he wanted to. And he was not one to always do the right thing when the wrong thing held much more appeal.

And Olivia was definitely appealing.

CHAPTER THREE

BEING SEPARATED FROM her phone all day had Olivia feeling twitchy and disconnected. Getting it back made her feel like a junkie who'd finally found a fix. Not that she'd really missed all that much, but it was the feeling she *could* have that caused detox jitters.

She wished she'd been able to tell Evan thanks in person; after all, he had gone out of his way to return it to her when she'd been silly enough to leave it in his car in the first place. That would just be good manners.

At the same time, it was probably easier this way. All things considered, she'd had a good time at dinner last night. Evan could be funny and quite charming when he wanted to; even with his assurances he was cold at heart. And she had to question her sanity at her willingness to appreciate that charm when he'd treated her so badly. It made her feel shallow, as if she was desperate and able to fall for good looks and flattery over substance.

It had always seemed strange to her that Jory could be so close to someone like Evan, and she'd been horrified to see Jory adopt some of Evan's partying and hell-raising ways, but Jory was a good man, and he wouldn't be friends with someone completely irredeemable.

And it *had* been a long time. She wasn't the same person she'd been nine years ago, so even with his denials to the contrary, Evan probably wasn't either.

Good grief, she was being ridiculous. She was either lonely or insane or sex-starved—or possibly a combination of the three. Why else would she be having this argument with herself?

Evan had dropped her off last night with "Call me if you need anything," which could be loosely translated as "Have a nice life," so it wasn't even an issue worth stressing over. To assuage her inner Miss Manners, though, she emailed him a quick, simple, "Thank you," and then pushed the whole thing out of her mind to protect her sanity.

She wasn't in a hurry, and there was no good reason to fight the masses on the bus during rush hour. So she showered, picked up her shoe allotment, checked the board for photo calls and rehearsal changes, and spoke to a few of the young girls waiting for their turn to rehearse—general dithering.

She'd make a quick trip to the grocery store for dinner supplies, then head home to an evening of TV and sewing.

It wasn't the most exciting of evenings, but her life didn't exactly suck, either. She'd signed on for this life, so she couldn't complain.

Outside the studio, she stopped to get a barrette

to pull her hair back. When she heard her name, she looked up.

Evan was leaned up against his car, arms crossed over his chest. It was so unexpected, she had to do a double take to make sure it was him, and even then she couldn't be sure he'd actually been the one to call her name. But there was no one else in the parking lot, and the chances of him waiting for someone else had to be pretty slim. She changed course and headed toward him.

Evan looked like an advertisement in a magazine. His collar was loose and his sleeves were rolled up, but it was very much the "businessman after hours" look. Expensive clothes, expensive sunglasses perched on his head, expensive car.

His hair was messy, as though he'd been driving with the top down, and just a hint of five o'clock shadow traced his jaw. *Hummina.* He was picture-perfect, and she wouldn't lie to herself by denying it wasn't working on her. A little shiver slid through her insides. Whatever he was selling, she might be convinced to buy.

Down, girl. She wasn't a naive eighteen-year-old anymore; she knew better. And she knew exactly *what* he was, too, but sadly, that wasn't the bucket of cold water her good sense might hope for. In fact, knowing made it *worse.* If she wanted to, she could walk, eyes wide open, right into that place where what he was willing to give met up with what she wanted to take—with no misunderstandings or heartaches this time.

That was a big *if,* though.

Frankly, her brain was twisted to even go there. Hadn't she *just* gotten all this sorted out in her head?

Guess not. Or at least not entirely.

He looked so good that her vanity kicked in. She was quite glad she'd showered, but she wished she'd known he was here so she could have spent a little more time on herself. Maybe at least dry her hair so it wasn't hanging damp and limp down her back.

She'd gotten her phone from the office *before* her shower. *Before* she'd dithered around in the studio. Which meant Evan had been waiting out here for a good half hour or more, at least.

She felt a little bad about that, but also a little flattered, too, and she smiled as she got closer. "Hey. Thanks for bringing me my phone."

"You're welcome. It must have fallen out when I had to dodge that skater last night."

"Yeah, probably. I didn't expect to see you to thank you in person, so I sent you an email."

"I saw it."

This was weird. Evan looked completely comfortable, at ease even, but the conversation felt awkward. Forced. Since he was standing here, though, she had to assume he had *some*thing to say to her, but there was no nice way to ask "What do you want?". Grasping for conversational straws, she said, "And thanks again for dinner. I had a nice time."

"I did, too. We should do it again."

Well, that was an improvement from the "have a nice life" feeling of last night. The wisdom of another dinner could be examined another time; right now, she'd take it as a compliment. "Sure."

"Are you hungry?"

Whoa. Okay. That was fast. "Now?"

"I watched rehearsals for a little bit. It looks like a good way to work up an appetite."

"Well, um…" She paused as the full statement registered. "You watched rehearsals?"

"Just for a few minutes. You're really good."

She examined his tone for flippancy and didn't find any. If anything, he seemed genuinely impressed. "Thanks."

"I don't know much—anything, actually—about it, but it was still pretty impressive."

She wasn't going to play with false modesty—she'd worked too hard for that—so there wasn't really much to say to that other than "Thank you" even if she'd already said it once.

"So *are* you hungry?"

She was, but…she gestured to her outfit. "I'm not really dressed to go anywhere."

He held up his phone. "According to Siri, there's a great deli-bistro-type place just a couple of blocks from here. I assume it's casual."

"Huey's? Yeah, it's a great place."

"Okay, then. Can we leave the car here?" She nodded, and he opened the trunk. "Then drop your stuff."

Flattery had given way to confusion and uncertainty. They had a past, but it was past. Was he just being friendly or was he hoping he might get lucky tonight?

Was it a little of both? Or neither? Or something else entirely? And why couldn't she decide where her feelings on those possibilities fell on the spectrum?

Oh, jeez. How could Evan mess with her head so easily? And what kind of fool was she to let him?

"Liv? Are you okay?"

She snapped her head up to see Evan standing next to his open trunk, his hand out waiting for her to hand him her stuff and a confused look on his face. "Yeah." She handed over her bags, and he locked them inside. "Thanks."

She took two steps, then stopped. This wasn't an ideal time or place, but it would have to do. "What are we doing?"

Evan looked at her as if she'd lost her mind. "Going to dinner? At least, that's what I thought we were doing."

"No. I mean, why? Why *now*? Considering…"

The confusion cleared and he nodded. "I could ask you the same thing. You're the one who made first contact."

He had her there. And she still didn't have a plausible alternative reason for why she did. "Maybe I didn't realize there'd be a second time."

"There doesn't have to be. I'm not going to drag you to the restaurant and force-feed you—even if you do look like you really need a sandwich."

"Evan, be serious."

"I am."

"Do you honestly believe there's nothing we need to discuss? No air to clear?"

Evan sighed, his face the perfect picture of resigned exasperation. "I feel I'm safe assuming the answer you're looking for is not 'yes.'" He shook his head. "I apologized. What more can I do?"

That was a good question, and one she should have answered for herself *before* asking him. She'd beat herself up over it, except Evan was far too good at scrambling her higher brain functions, turning her into a babbling idiot. "So we're going to be friends now?"

"I kind of thought that was the point of dinner last night."

Nothing ventured, nothing gained. "*Just* friends?"

"You're a beautiful woman, Olivia. Talented, smart, charming." He looked her up and down. "I'm not going to deny there's still an attraction."

"So not just friends, then?" Why did that possibility send a little thrill through her?

"That would be entirely up to you." The wicked little half smile held a challenge and that didn't help.

"And if I did want to be just friends?"

"I'd respect that." He thought about it for a second. "It'd be a novel experience for me."

"You're saying you don't have any platonic female friends?"

"I don't have many friends period."

She could relate to that, but still... "So you're telling me you've slept with every woman you know."

He grinned. "Not *all* of them. Some of them are married."

"You are insufferable."

He grinned. "So I've been told."

She felt off balance. "And this is supposed to encourage me?"

"Nope. I'm just being honest."

How could she be annoyed and intrigued at the same time? In fact, it was almost a challenge. But Evan *was* charming, and hadn't she decided that a peaceful coexistence with him would be a benefit all around?

"So are we going to dinner or not?" he asked.

She had to think about it for a minute. She needed to give herself the chance to weigh the pros and cons and decide if she wanted to shake things up a little bit. Because she had a suspicion that being in Evan's orbit—in whatever way—would not be boring. And now she understood what had drawn her bookish brother into his orbit, as well. The man was just irresistible—and not just in a sexual way. His attitude could be grating, but it was refreshing. And his ego, while quite large, made him fun to spar with. And while *she'd* had a problem with Evan and Jory's friendship, Jory never had, which said a lot about Evan as a person, giving clues to facets of his personality she wasn't aware of.

Oh, she might regret this later, but she might not, either. She might decide that they, too, could be friends, and it would be nice to have another friend. If she wanted to cross that line later? Well, she'd know what she was doing. And if, in the process of this new friendship, she decided that Evan was still a jerk, she could get out easily enough.

She nodded, trying to look regal and haughty—which was a little difficult when wearing yoga pants and a T-shirt with wet, wild hair. "We are."

"Then let's go."

Had he really just agreed to be just friends with Olivia? Considering the rather adult nature of his thoughts recently, that bordered on insane. But that seemed to be Olivia's choice. Could he keep her at arm's length? Maybe being friends would make the attraction wane.

Or not, he thought as he watched the sway of her hips as she walked. While Olivia was elegant, she also had a girl-next-door wholesomeness about her—especially right now, barefaced, uncoiffed and yet comfortable in her skin. Normally, that wasn't an attraction for him, but on Olivia it worked. A little *too* well. Oh, he'd created a challenge for himself. He'd have to play this carefully by ear with the full knowledge he might regret it later.

The MMBC studios occupied a converted warehouse on the fringe of the Wynwood Arts District. Wynwood was still primarily a mecca for the visual arts, but the performing arts were getting a toehold in the area, too. He wasn't overly familiar with the district, but Olivia seemed to be, and she pointed out items of interest as they walked. She was passionate about the arts in general, not just dance it seemed, as well as very knowledgeable, and she told him about shows and upcoming artists and the growth of the area.

"That looks like graffiti, not art," he said as she showed him a mural she claimed was a favorite.

"It can't be both?"

"I want to say no, but I'm starting to think that's not the correct answer."

She laughed.

"You must think I'm an uncultured troglodyte."

After a long pause that bordered on offensive, she finally answered. "Troglodyte? No. Uncultured? Maybe." The mock-haughty tone and twitching lips took the sting out of her words.

"You'll have to pardon me then, and blame it on my childhood. There wasn't much in the way of what you'd consider culture of any kind in Arrowwood, Florida."

"What does that have to do with anything? Beyond being an argument for improved arts education in Florida public schools, that is."

Looking pointedly at a sculpture that looked like salvaged bedsprings from a fairy's junkyard, he said, "I'm thinking art may be something that you have to grow up with to truly appreciate."

She shook her head. "No, it's not. It's for everyone. You just have to expose yourself to it. You don't always have to understand it to appreciate it for what it is. As you learn more about it, the more esoteric stuff will start to make sense. But something is bound to speak to you, if you give it time and the chance to."

"Since I'm reevaluating my mind-set about ballet, I just might believe you."

"That's very flattering." She grinned and it lit up her entire face. "I'd be happy to help you in your quest to expose yourself to what's out there. What do you think of this?"

The bedsprings? "It's um…interesting?"

"See, you're becoming more cultured even as we stand here."

"You know, I feel it." He put a hand to his chest dramatically. "It's like a flower blossoming in my heart, filling me with color and joy and wisdom all at the same time. This piece…it shows the waste and futility of society while celebrating the, the *resilience* of um, *springiness*. And purple."

"Smart ass." She shook her head as she led him away from the sculpture. "So where is Arrowwood, anyway?"

"North of Ocala, south of Gainesville, middle of nowhere."

"And your family is still there?"

"Yep." He didn't elaborate, hoping she wouldn't ask.

"Do you get to go home often?"

"No." It came out sharper than he intended. He could tell by the look in her eyes that Olivia caught the hint that time, and while she gave him an odd look, she didn't press further. The ensuing silence was a bit awkward and noticeable after the easiness of the conversation before, and he needed to find another topic before it either got worse or Olivia decided to ask more questions. Thankfully, he found it quickly. "Hey, look at that."

That was a poster-sized advertisement for *The Nutcracker*, featuring a full-color picture of Olivia in a white-and-silver tutu and tiara. The man holding her up looked vaguely as if he might have been the same man she had been dancing with earlier. "Good picture. Cool pose."

Olivia looked a little embarrassed. "Thanks. That's a fish."

"You're a fish? I thought it was a Christmas-type story."

"It is." She laughed. "That *move* is called a fish, but I'm the Snow Queen—in that picture, at least."

He was getting more confused, not less. "So you're *not* the Snow Queen?"

"Oh, I'm the Snow Queen, but I'm also a mother in the party scene and I alternate Sugar Plum Fairy and Arabian in the second act."

"Is that all?"

He meant that as snark, but it seemed it wasn't. "I also had to learn Dew Drop, just in case, but I wouldn't do them all in the same show." Olivia also must have misunderstood the look in his face, too, as she quickly added, "*Nutcracker* is a big show and we're not that big of a company. I'm just lucky we have a large enough corps to cover Waltz and Snow."

Very few of her words made sense, but her tone was easy enough to understand. "You don't sound very excited about the show."

She shrugged. "It's *Nutcracker*. There's no escaping it."

"Escaping?"

"Almost every ballet company does *Nutcracker* at Christmas. It's a tradition, and because so many people consider it part of their Christmas tradition, it makes a lot of money in ticket sales. So that's great and all, and I'm so glad people love it so much, but you have to understand—this is my twentieth year doing this ballet."

Twentieth? His jaw fell open a little bit, causing her to grin.

"When I was eight, I went with a friend to *Nutcracker* auditions in Tampa, even though I'd never set foot in a studio before at that point. I was cast as a Bon Bon in act 2, and all I really had to do was skip around the stage and look cute. I was hooked, though, from that moment on, and my folks enrolled me in ballet classes in the January. I have danced *Nutcracker* someplace on this planet every single year since then."

"Wow."

"Exactly. I did the math once, and when you consider that rehearsals for a December show start in late September or early October, I've spent nearly five *years* of my life preparing for and dancing in that one show." She leaned in and whispered, "Don't spread this far and wide, but I'm kinda over it."

"But…"

She raised an eyebrow at him. "Are you going to tell me that there's *no* part of your job that you don't find boring or monotonous or frustrating? Or wouldn't be after you'd done that one thing for five solid years?"

There were plenty, but he didn't call himself an *artist*, dedicated to his craft. "No, but—"

She lifted her hands as if to say *there you go* and opened the door to the restaurant.

"Wait a second." He motioned her back from the door. "You're telling me you don't enjoy it?"

"Dancing? Yes. Performing? Yes. *Nutcracker?* That gives me hives. Just hearing the music is enough to make me start to twitch, and it's *everywhere* this time of year."

"If your marketing and PR people knew how you felt, they'd put a gag order on you before they let you out in public."

"Hey, now, I can behave in public." As if to prove that, Olivia lifted her head and in an interview-perfect tone said, "I'm so thrilled to be making my first appearance in MMBC's production of this classic and timeless ballet. It's truly a Christmas tradition, enjoyable for people of *all* ages, and I encourage *every*one in town to come see the show."

"That's better," he admitted as Olivia grinned at him again. No one would be able to tell she hadn't been grumbling about it five seconds before. "You're a good liar."

"I'm not lying," she protested. "Every word of that was true."

"You're good at lies of omission, then." A strange look crossed Olivia's face, and he wondered if he'd insulted her somehow. "But I respect that. I'm in advertising, remember? It's all about the image." He opened the door to the restaurant and motioned for her to go in. "Now let's eat."

Olivia's order tonight was far more in line with what he'd expect—a hummus and veggie pita with a side of fruit and iced tea. "I can't eat like I did last night *all* the time," she explained with a shrug. Then, over his protests, she insisted on buying both their dinners. "If we're going to be friends, you can't buy all the time either."

Evan couldn't quite find his balance in all of this. Olivia's grudge had somehow been appeased, but he still felt as if he was on probation with her—regardless of her easy, friendly attitude. It was the quick switch that bothered him. People didn't just adapt like that.

But he saw no danger in enjoying it, as long as he didn't forget who she was.

And there was no danger of *that*.

CHAPTER FOUR

TONIGHT WAS EASIER by far than last night, Olivia thought. Having an understanding—even if she didn't fully understand it—with Evan helped, and she was actually able to relax. His very bald "it's up to you" kept a flirty undercurrent running under the dinner conversation that was actually kind of fun.

Plus, after watching that little bit of rehearsals, Evan suddenly had an interest in ballet and peppered her with questions.

"Have you ever been dropped?" Evan had a keen interest in the lift he'd seen.

"Yes. But not ever from that particular lift and never by Theo."

"So you trust him."

"With my life." She laughed. "I've known Theo since we were really young. He was my partner when we took silver at Nationals. We've done thousands of lifts together."

"But you *have* been dropped before."

"Of course. It's not fun, but it does happen. I even

ended up with a mild concussion once." She took one last sip of her drink and started cleaning up the debris of their meal.

Evan wasn't quite letting it go, though. "You say that like it's nothing."

"It was an accident. Like I said, it happens. Sometimes it's something I did, sometimes it's something he did, but there's no sense assigning blame. You learn from it and go on."

"And if you get hurt?"

"You're much less likely to make that mistake again, that's for sure. But it's his job to do his best to catch me before I hit the floor. Partners who goof around and make it more likely someone's going to fall will soon find themselves without partners at all."

"Are there men you won't dance with?"

She nodded. "But most of the time, I just do what I'm supposed to do and trust my partner to do his part." She stood. "You ready?"

Evan stood, too, and led her toward the door. "But to let some guy hold you upside down with one hand? That's a lot of trust."

"It goes both ways, you know. If I mess up, he could get hurt. I could injure his back or his shoulders or kick him in the head. Or he could get hurt trying to keep *me* from getting hurt from something that was my own fault." It was fully dark outside now, cool, but not cold, and the neighborhood's nightlife was warming up. "We have to trust each *other*, or else we'll both end up hurt."

"How very Zen of you," Evan scoffed, as he fell into step beside her, adjusting his pace to hers.

"I know it sounds cheesy, but it's the truth."

"Trust has to be earned," he said seriously, causing her to do a double take at the emotion in his voice. Before she could answer though, he continued. "It takes time. You just show up and trust that this guy is not going to drop you on your head."

"That's not how it works."

"No?"

"Of course not. It's like sex."

It was a common joke in the studio, and she said it without really thinking how Evan might interpret it. When he stumbled, then looked at her with wide eyes, she regretted saying it. But when he reached for her elbow and pulled her out of the flow of foot traffic next to a Picasso-inspired mural to ask, "*Sex?*" she lost the regret. *This might be fun.*

She couldn't quite name the look on his face—horrified interest? shocked interest?—but it was enough to spur her on. "Just like you shouldn't jump into bed with someone you just met, you don't introduce yourself to a new partner and then do the most complicated lift in the program." She tried to put the right amount of earnestness into her words. "It would be all awkward, you know, feet and hands in all the wrong places, and getting frustrated because it's not feeling right and it's not any good for either one of you. And what's the point of having sex if you're not going to enjoy it? Sex is great, but good sex is *better*, and *great* sex takes an investment. *That* kind of great sex requires a little trust in your partner."

Evan cleared his throat and Olivia felt wicked.

"So you start slow and simple, feeling each other out." She ran a hand lightly over his chest. "You look for quirks that you'll need to adapt to and learn how his body moves." She ran her hands up his arms and squeezed his biceps gently. *Wow.* "You have to find your partner's strengths, learn how his hands feel, and how you'll fit together…that's the foreplay. And you can't rush that, can you?" Evan shifted uncomfortably as she moved her hands up and over his shoulders, but he shook his head. She leaned in, lowering her voice, moving slowly around his body, trailing her fingers. "You've got to get in sync with your partner first, and then…*then* you can trust him to do what needs to be done. *Then* you're free to go at it hard, full-out, over and over, until you're sweaty and exhausted, but satisfied with what you accomplished. And that feels *amazing.*"

Evan's breath had gotten shallow as she spoke. More surprisingly, so had hers. She dropped her hand as Evan swallowed hard and gave himself a small shake. "You are evil, Olivia Madison."

"Whatever do you mean?" she protested with as much eyelash-fluttering innocence as she could muster.

When Evan lifted his eyes to hers, she saw heat there. It fanned embers she'd been trying to smother, and they flared with an intensity that rocked her back on her heels. Regretting she'd let bravado lead her into the deep end, she stepped back to let some air between them. The option may have been put out there, but she wasn't ready to decide whether to exercise that option or not.

But Evan certainly looked ready. And, *damn*, that was tempting. "So, anything else you want to know about ballet?" She tried for a light and airy tone and started walking again. "Pointe shoes? Tutus? Turns?" she tossed over her shoulder as Evan caught up.

"As a matter of fact, I do have more questions."

"Ask away."

"I'm curious about positions. Beyond the basics, of course." An eyebrow went up in challenge. "And what about your flexibility? Stamina?"

Jeez, she really was in over her head. She should know better than to play games with a master. "What about them?"

They were back at Evan's car, where her stuff was in his trunk. Figuring he'd have one of those fancy keyless entry things, she reached for the trunk latch and was rewarded when it popped open. Grabbing her bag, she tossed it over her shoulder and turned to face him. *Big mistake.* Evan was close. *Very* close. She could smell him, feel the heat of his body. And she was trapped between him and his stupid fancy car.

His smile was wicked. "Or you could just tell me more about that foreplay."

Over his shoulder, she could see her bus arriving like a gift from God to get her out of this. She focused on the relief of that and tried to ignore the little shiver that went through her. "Another time, maybe." She shim-

mied out and ran toward the bus stop, hand up to signal the driver to save her simply by stopping. "Bye!"

She looked back over her shoulder as she climbed
aboard, only to see Evan leaned against the trunk of
his car, grinning at her. When he saw her looking, he
shouted, "Coward!"

Maybe so, but I'm not stupid, too.

Surprisingly enough, Olivia got in touch a few days
later with an invite to something called "Margaritas
and Melodies," which turned out to be a fundraiser for
the symphony. She was taking his arts education seriously, it seemed.

He'd been torn, unable to decide, when her invite
first landed in his in-box. He recognized danger when
he saw it.

He might have agreed to just being friends, and she
might be on board for that, but it was going to be very
hard. He wanted her; he wouldn't lie to himself about
that, but *three* outings? He either needed to nip this in
the bud, or accept the direction this was heading and
the possible consequences of that.

He wanted to be a better person and a good friend
to Jory, but his big head wasn't exactly in total control.
He'd accepted the invite before he'd really thought it all
the way through and now, here he was—consequences
or no consequences.

It was a casual affair, held in one of the larger gal-
leries in the art district. They had a good-sized crowd
packed in there, and the conversations nearly drowned

out the background music of the symphony playing pop tunes given a classical twist. There were the usual fundraiser things—silent auctions, raffles, light refreshments and an overpriced cash bar.

He knew a lot of the people in attendance, though, and all of them seemed surprised to see him there. It was a good place to make new business contacts. He should have gotten more involved in the arts sooner.

He mentioned that to Olivia, and she gave him a pitying look. "I can't believe you're just now figuring that out. But," she corrected sternly, "you're not here to do business. You're supposed to be absorbing the atmosphere and appreciating the culture."

"The music is nice."

"It is. Our symphony is great and we're lucky to have that talent here. What do you think of the art?"

Frankly, he found it garish and ugly, as if the artist had randomly stuck household trash to a canvas and flung paint at it. "It's…unusual."

"I think it's hideous," she whispered.

"Wait, what? It's art."

"Yes, it's art, but that doesn't make it *good* art. The value in the piece often lies in the eye of the beholder, but I think it's derivative, amateurish and ugly." She leaned in to read the artist's name. "And this Jackson Pollack wannabe is…Damien Hoffman. Ever heard of him?"

"No."

"Looking at this stuff, I'm surprised anyone has."

"I thought you artsy types stuck together. Feeling the muse and all that jazz."

"I work really hard to perfect what I do. This guy rolled out of bed, stuck rubber bands to a canvas, called it art and had the nerve to slap a two-thousand-dollar price tag on it." Olivia sounded personally insulted.

"Ooh, do I hear some interdisciplinary infighting? Paintbrushes versus pointe shoes at dawn," he teased.

She cleared her throat. "The music is nice, though."

"So we said. Here, have a snack. You're getting grumpy." He offered her his plate, piled high with bite-size hors d'oeuvres.

"No, thank you."

"It's not bad stuff."

She wrinkled her nose. "That's okay."

"First you insult the art and now the food? *Tsk, tsk.*"

"If I'm going to load up on carbs and fat and calories, I'm going to go get a piece of cheesecake from the bakery and really make it worth my while. Not all junk food is created equal, and I'm picky about my splurges." She smiled. "But I will take another margarita."

"That, I can handle." He tossed the plate and offered her his arm. They headed toward the bar, only to be waylaid by a couple of his clients.

When they finally got past, she said, "You seem to know a lot of people here."

"I've lived in Miami for six, nearly seven years now. It happens."

"Since so many of them seem to be plugged-in to

the arts community, I'm surprised your friends haven't dragged you to these kinds of things long before now."

"Oh, man, I'm going to be on every mailing list in the city now, aren't I?"

She nodded without sympathy. "Yep. That's what friends are for."

"I know them," he explained, "but I wouldn't say we're friends."

She nodded. "That I understand."

"Really?" Olivia seemed friendly and outgoing. She shouldn't have a hard time making friends. Jory certainly didn't, so he assumed it was just part of the Madison DNA. "I don't like a lot of people. What's your excuse?"

"I just don't normally stay in one place long enough to make a lot of friends."

"You sound like you're on the run from the law or something."

"I have commitment issues," she confessed matter-of-factly. "I've never been able to agree to anything that locks me in longer than a season. And even then, I have small panic attacks before I sign the contract."

"I'm not sure that's healthy. Have you talked to a psychiatrist?"

"I'm not crazy." He looked unconvinced, so she added, "At least not in any clinical sense, thank you very much. But see, when I was accepted into the National Ballet Academy, I realized dance was what I really wanted to do with my life, and I began to believe I could actually make it my career. So, I made a list of all the places in the world I wanted to dance and all the things I wanted to achieve. I've been checking that list off ever since."

"Like where?"

"New York, Boston, San Francisco, London, Paris, Rome, Prague—"

"Prague?"

She nodded. "Great city. They have wonderful support for their ballet companies."

And he'd lived in Florida his entire life. "You're quite the traveler."

"Jory says I have itchy feet, and it's true. I do."

"That's got to be tough, though."

"It can be. It's got its problems, but it makes up for it in other ways. This is the life I chose, and I don't regret it. I've gotten to see and do a lot."

But there was a cost to everything, he knew. "What's your record?"

"My second time in New York. I stayed eleven months, but only because I stayed on to do summer stock."

"And the shortest?"

"Honolulu, six years ago," she answered immediately. "I signed a six-month contract, but broke my foot three weeks after I got there, and they released me from it. I knew some folks in Dallas, so I went there to recuperate and finished out the season with their company as a guest artist once I was well."

He ordered their drinks. "I didn't hear Miami on that list."

"It wasn't, but priorities shift as you get older. I'm ready to slow down a little, start looking ahead to retirement and what happens after that."

The absurdity of that made him laugh. "You're talking about retirement while everyone else your age is just starting their careers."

"Yes, but that gives me the chance to do something completely different if I want—I don't even have to stay in the arts. I could go school and learn about..." she said with a grin, "advertising, maybe."

"I don't recommend it."

"You seem to be doing pretty well."

"Exactly. The Lawford Agency would crush your little upstart biz like a bug." He handed her the drink and lifted his in a mock toast.

"How very pleasant of you."

"Hey, you're not the only one who made a list of things they wanted to accomplish."

"Really? What's on yours?"

"The only one you need to worry about is number two—making my agency the biggest and best in Miami."

"What's number one?"

"Making it the biggest in the world."

"Oooh, I like a man with big plans. Why don't—"

He didn't hear the rest of that statement because he caught sight of Elaine headed toward him like a missile. *Hell.* He hauled Olivia up against his side, ignoring her shocked "What on earth...?" as he anchored an arm around her waist.

"Evan." Although Elaine was pretending to be friendly, she lacked control over her tone of voice.

"Elaine."

"You're the last person I expected to see here."

"Well, I'm full of surprises."

Elaine looked at Olivia expectantly, and Olivia seemed to finally understand the situation, relaxing into him and smiling at Elaine.

"I don't believe I know your friend."

"This is Olivia Madison. She dances with the Miami Modern Ballet Company. Liv, this is Elaine MacDonald. Elaine's a software designer."

Olivia extended her hand. "Lovely to meet you."

"I'm afraid I don't follow the ballet. It's so old-fashioned at times, and I prefer my arts more modern and cutting-edge." Elaine was taking out her jealousy and hostility toward him by insulting Olivia, who didn't deserve it. He bristled.

"Well, ballet's not for everyone," Olivia answered quickly. Although she'd said almost exactly the same thing to him, her tone was different, landing the insult easily, yet without sounding like it. He was impressed, and waited to see where Olivia would go next.

"I prefer the visual arts," Elaine explained condescendingly. "For instance, I've been following Damien's career since the beginning. The energy and innovation in his work is so exciting," she gushed in the direction of the paintings. "It's very avant-garde, and not for everyone."

Olivia nodded in agreement. "I agree it's not for

everyone, because its over-derivative nature shows an immaturity in the artist that concerns me—or maybe it's just a lack of knowledge." She turned to Evan and smiled sweetly again. "What's coming out of New York right now in this medium is incredible. I guess it just hasn't made it to Miami yet."

Boom. That was a direct hit and Elaine's face reddened. Maybe she would think twice next time before picking a fight with someone who didn't deserve it.

Or maybe not. Elaine was taking a deep breath. And he stepped in before things got really ugly. "Good to see you, Elaine, but we must be off. Take care." He steered Olivia to the other side of the room. "I'm liking this friend thing," he whispered in her ear.

"Do you want to tell me why I just got in an Art 101 competition with that woman?"

"Because you are amazing and delightful and I could kiss you right now. That was brilliant and Elaine totally deserved it."

"But I didn't," she reminded him.

"I know, and I'm sorry. That was her way of trying to needle me."

"What did you do to her?"

He hesitated.

"*Oh*," Olivia said, nodding as understanding dawned. "If I'd known *that*, I might not have taken her down like that. After all, I understand where she's coming from."

"It's not the same thing at all. I mean, you just met her. She's not a nice person."

"But you slept with her anyway?"

He could see her estimation of him sliding south even as she spoke. "I didn't know she wasn't a nice person when I did," he said in his own defense.

"I see. But still…"

"It would be one thing for her to take it out on me because I can handle it and I possibly even deserve it."

"*Possibly?*" Olivia snorted and rolled her eyes.

He cleared his throat. "But attacking another woman just because I might be sleeping with her now? That's bad form."

"You should be more careful about the women you get involved with, then."

"We weren't 'involved,'" he corrected. "We went out a few times."

"And you slept together."

"Well, yes. She's beautiful, and I promise I didn't know she was crazy at the time."

"So you were keeping everything casual."

"Yep. Always do."

"And she didn't know that?"

"Guess not."

Olivia cocked her head. "Why?"

"Why didn't she know? Beats me."

"No," she corrected gently, "why do you keep everything casual?"

"So many questions. What difference does it make?" Olivia just stared at him. Finally, when he couldn't stand the silence another second, he said, "Because I make a terrible boyfriend. Ask any of my exes."

"At least you admit it. That's the first step, you know, admitting you have a problem."

"Oh, I'm selfish, unable to commit…"

"Egotistical, a womanizer, smug…" she supplied.

"Gee, thanks."

"If we're going to be friends, I have to be able to be honest with you," she said primly.

"Maybe I should rethink this friend thing," he muttered.

"The truth hurts." She patted his arm. "But think of all the opportunity you have for personal growth. Then you can have a real relationship one day."

"Oh, you're one to talk."

Olivia's mouth fell open. "I beg your pardon?"

"I don't see you in a relationship."

"I told you. I move around a lot. That, in and of itself, is an issue," she explained, "but I'm also very committed to what I do. I love my job and it comes first. A lot of guys can't handle that."

"We're both just doomed to be forever alone, then, huh?"

"Yeah." She sighed. "It's a good thing we're pretty."

He looked at her and they both burst out laughing.

"Come on," he said, "Let's get out of here. I've had enough culture for one evening."

"And I'm hungry," she added.

"Why am I not surprised?" At least he could let go of any worries he might have about her eating habits. "The pigs in a blanket would have at least filled you up, you know."

"Yuck. There's another place I like about three blocks from here. Will you eat falafels?"

Ugh. "Art *and* falafels in one night?"

"Yes. Good brain food and good body food."

He sighed. "Fine. If I must."

She sighed and took pity on him. "There's a pizza truck just down from the falafel place."

"Then lead on."

About a block later, he remembered what else he wanted to ask. "By the way, what *is* going on in the New York art scene right now?

She shot him a look that questioned his sanity. "How the hell would I know? I'm a ballet dancer."

He burst out laughing. This friend thing…it wasn't always easy to remember just to be friends, but it wasn't as bad as he thought it would be, either.

But then, Olivia had never been what he expected anyway.

And he liked that.

A couple of days went by and Olivia didn't hear from Evan at all. She couldn't decide if that was a good thing or not. It was probably the *wise* thing, but still….

They were friends, and those weren't dates, so it wasn't like he owed her a follow-up call. At the same time, there'd been those *moments* which made the lack of contact now seem like a rejection. So while lack of contact seemed the wiser option, it didn't feel like the better option and bordered on slightly insulting.

Evan—or actually his agency's page, but still—had

liked her Facebook page, and she'd returned the "like," but that meant less than nothing.

It was all too weird. Annoying. Of course, then she got annoyed at herself for being annoyed in the first place. So juvenile.

This was definitely a sign that she needed a group, a posse, something. The lack of a large social circle wasn't new for her—because she moved around a lot, she tended to have more acquaintances than actual friends—but the disappointment over it *was* new. Maybe it was because she really did want to put down roots here, and knowing *that* made her more aware of the sparseness of her life in general.

She owned no furniture—another reason why she'd chosen to live with a roommate in a furnished apartment—and very little "stuff." She'd moved her entire life to Miami from Chicago in a rented Subaru Forester with room to spare. Memorabilia and keepsakes and that kind of stuff had always lived in a rental shed in Tampa, waiting for the day she'd settle down or retire.

If Miami was going to be that place, then she needed to start building a life here—one beyond the studio. It was a little scary to contemplate, and the fact she was annoyed at Evan of all people drove home how much she needed to just commit and get started on that. She'd been here three months already; what was her excuse? *Beyond* the niggling worry that her contract wouldn't be renewed next season. She'd never been without a job or an offer before; she wasn't going to be unemployed.

Maybe the fact she wanted this so much was driving the fear she wouldn't get it.

But she also knew that worry was just asking for failure. *If you worry you will fall, you will fall.* It was advice she'd passed on to hundreds of young dancers—and it was *good* advice. She needed to listen to her own platitudes.

She'd just have to work under the assumption that everything would work out the way she wanted and that Miami would become home. The worst-case scenario? She'd have to rent a bigger truck when she moved.

So by Friday, she'd made her first major purchase, and she luxuriated with her laptop on the wonder that was a new mattress and bedding and surfed the internet in well-supported, high-thread-count comfort. She felt oddly grown up.

She'd given up on wondering what kind of friends she and Evan were supposed to be, so she was quite surprised when her phone rang and Evan's name popped up on the screen. "Hey."

"How've you been, Liv?"

"Good. Busy as always. You?"

"The same."

They were the masters of inanity. And she was getting the feeling that Evan did it on purpose, just to throw her off balance. But for someone who'd been wondering if or when Evan was going to call, she was remarkably without a topic of conversation. "So what's up?"

"Do you work tomorrow?"

"I've got rehearsals until three, why?"

"Would you like to go to a party tomorrow night?"

She needed a minute to process that question. Dinner was different than a party. Dinner was simply food, and people had to eat. She was helping Evan expand his arts education. They could make as much or as little out of those as they needed. A party with his friends was a whole other animal. That might be an actual "date" and did she want to go there?

Evan had to be a mind reader because he seemed to pick up on the thoughts whirling through her mind. "It's a business thing. One of my clients is having their holiday party early to beat the after-Thanksgiving rush, and it's so much easier if I bring a date."

So it was a date, but not a "date." She wasn't sure how she felt about that.

She started to ask how a date would make it easier for him, but stopped herself before she asked the single most ignorant question ever. Evan was young, good-looking, successful and single. "So, in reality, you need a beard."

He laughed. "More like a shield."

"Do I get combat pay?" she teased.

"Free food and booze—and this client goes all out, so it should be quality food and booze. Well worth the splurge."

"While I do the arm-candy-small-talk-thing? Um…I don't know."

"One, while I'm sure you'll make great arm candy,

don't feel you need to hang on mine every second of the evening. Two, Matt Abrams is a big supporter of the arts scene, so between him and his family, friends and clients, there's a good chance you'll find some arty and cultured people there to talk to."

That got her attention. "Matt Abrams as in the Abrams Corporation?"

"Yes. Why? Is that a problem?"

The Abrams family were like gods in the Miami arts and humanities scene. A concert series, a lecture series and an entire *wing* of the art museum carried their name. The MMBC ballet board genuflected at the mere mention of the family. They were already donors, of course, but meeting and mingling in a social situation—well, it wouldn't hurt her to be personally known by any of them.

And, a little voice reminded her, she was still in need of a sponsor. An Abrams corporate event *had* to be a good place to find one.

"Olivia?"

She'd been spinning too long again. Evan was going to think she was mentally deficient in some way. "Formal or semiformal?"

"Cocktail is fine. Do you have a dress?"

"Of course."

"Then I'll pick you up around seven-thirty."

"I'll be ready."

Hanging up, she gave herself a congratulatory mental pat on the back. Seems she hadn't been making such bad choices, after all. Her reward for not being tacky and asking Evan for the sponsorship was entry into the very social circle that could provide exactly that.

Being Evan's friend definitely had benefits.

CHAPTER FIVE

OLIVIA WAS A HIT at the Abrams's party, and Evan congratulated himself on his excellent idea. She was elegant and charming, mingling easily with the other guests and a whiz at party small talk. She'd confessed in the car on the way over that meet and greets were as much a part of her repertoire as *Swan Lake*, as they were essential for...*something*. He hadn't been paying as much attention as he should have because Olivia in a little black sparkly number had fried much of his brain. A simple back sheath that looked demure from the front dipped low in the back to show the sculpted muscles of her shoulders and the long line of her spine from her upswept hair to the small of her back. The hem stopped high enough on her thigh to showcase those amazing legs without looking trashy. Although he'd managed to get his tongue off his toes—eventually—every now and then he'd catch sight of her unexpectedly and all his blood would rush south again.

He wasn't sure he'd be able to hold up his end of this "friends" deal—simply because he couldn't guarantee he'd be able to keep his hands off her for much longer. Not and keep his sanity intact, too. He had to be a masochist to even consider it. Olivia's uneven, hot-and-cold flirting was an added stumbling block, as he couldn't quite tell where her thoughts were heading.

But tonight, they were here as "friends," and repeatedly introducing her and explaining their relationship—"my best friend's sister"—*should* be enough of a reminder to keep his hands in his pockets. But since he rarely brought women to business events, questions about the true nature of their relationship were clear in everyone's eyes.

It was probably in his, too.

Olivia didn't require constant attention, which was nice, allowing him to socialize and mix business in as needed. These people were potential new clients for his agency, and he needed to work the room. But she was also usually near enough to function as that all-important shield, keeping enough speculation alive to prevent any other women from making their move.

A couple of hours into the evening, Matt Abrams made his speech, thanking everyone for another great year. Then the band started playing and people headed for the dance floor.

Olivia was chatting with a woman he vaguely recognized as the wife of one of the city managers as he sidled up beside her. They exchanged pleasantries for a few minutes, then the woman made her excuses with a smile and left them alone.

"Having a good time?"

"I am. Thanks for bringing me. And you were right—the food is great."

He hadn't seen her go near the buffet, but that was neither here nor there. Olivia was also going easy on the booze, nursing a glass of champagne while others were starting to feel their buzzes. When he offered to get her another, she shook her head. "I'd rather stay sober. I don't want to make a fool of myself in front of all these people."

He inclined his head toward the dance floor. "Then why don't we go dance?"

Olivia shook her head. "I said I *didn't* want to make a fool of myself."

"No one's expecting any fancy moves out of you, Twinkletoes."

"Well, that's good."

He reached for her hand, but she shook her head. "I don't really dance."

"You don't *dance*?" He was waiting for the punch line.

"Not like that, I don't."

"Wait…you're actually serious, aren't you?" When she nodded, he couldn't stop himself from laughing, which earned him a withering look from Olivia.

"If I go onto the dance floor, people expect a lot out of me," she explained. "Like I'm supposed to be Ginger Rogers or something, even though my idea of a waltz is a lot different than theirs. It's embarrassing when I can't deliver what they expect. All dance training is *not* equal."

"I'll lead then."

Her eyebrows went up. Slightly suspicious and disbelieving, she asked, "*You* can dance?"

"Well enough not to step on your feet." He held out his hand again. She still looked suspicious. "Come on. What happened to trusting your partner?"

She cut her eyes at him, but didn't acknowledge that conversation otherwise. "You'd better not make me look bad," she warned, but she put her hand in his and let him lead her to the dance floor. Once there, he was able to pull her decently close to him in a special sort of torture. She smelled amazing and his hand found warm bare skin above the deep drape of her dress.

At first, Olivia was stiff in his arms, but after a few minutes, she relaxed a bit and followed his lead. It was nothing fancy—he stuck to the basic steps and she picked them up quickly—but Olivia was obviously impressed when she smiled at him. "You're good."

"You sound surprised."

"Because I am. I didn't peg you as the dancing type." The teasing smile took a little of the sting out of her words.

"Ah, well, I like women, and women *love* a man who'll take them dancing."

Olivia laughed. "That explains it, then. I knew there would be a good reason. So where'd you learn to dance like this?"

He led her through an easy turn and into a shallow dip. "The Recreational Dance Society of Jacksonville. Beginners always welcome."

"*Really?* In college?"

"Yes, really. Why the disbelief?"

She shook her head. "I just can't picture eighteen-year-old Evan Lawford taking time out of his partying to take dance lessons."

"Like I said, the ladies like it."

"I believe it, but you need a better story."

"Why?"

In all seriousness, she said, "Because the lady might not like to hear that you only dance in the ongoing quest to get into her panties."

He had to respect her blunt honesty. "Then what story should I tell?"

She really seemed to be thinking about it. "Um… Like your mom teaching you when you were little. Maybe dancing around the kitchen with your feet on hers. It's a sweet image and would work nicely."

He snorted at the idea and Olivia gave him an odd look. "There's no way I could say that with a straight face," he explained. "I come from a very conservative religious household. No dancing allowed."

"None?"

"No. Dancing inspires lust." He said it with snark, but his father *was* being proven partly right even as he spoke. Evan was certainly lusting after Olivia right now. Much more of this and he was going to have to loosen his hold to put more space between them before Olivia felt that lust.

To his surprise, she collapsed into giggles. "What's so funny?"

"You. Taking dance classes to rebel against your parents. That's got to be the strangest, yet most civilized form of rebellion I've ever heard of."

"Hey, there was plenty of other rebellion," he said in his own defense. "And long before college, thank you very much. There was just no place I could learn to dance in Arrowwood."

Her eyes narrowed suspiciously. "A whole *town* of people who don't dance? Did you grow up in that town in *Footloose* or something?"

"Yes, as a matter of fact, I did. Call me Kevin Bacon." When she continued to stare at him, waiting for his response, he finally shrugged and offered, "When your father is a hellfire preacher in the town's biggest church, no one is going to teach you to dance, even if you ask nicely."

Olivia was incredulous. "*You're* a *preacher's* kid? Oh. My. *God.*" She started to laugh, but pressed her lips closed instead, making the sound come out as an unladylike snort. "That explains oh-so-much about you."

Damn it. He'd assumed she knew, but this proved that Jory had kept his promise and that information to himself. But the last thing he wanted was amateur psychology from Olivia. "Actually, that explains nothing about me."

"I beg to differ."

"Well, you'd be wrong." To throw her off-topic and off balance, he led her into a more complicated pattern that had her nearly tripping over her feet to catch up.

She shot him a dirty look, clearly aware of why he'd

done it. But "I thought you said no fancy moves," was all she said about it.

"Sorry. I thought you could handle it."

"You thought wrong. I still don't know what I'm doing."

There was a sigh in her voice that changed the subject nicely, even if she didn't mean for it to. But they'd been dancing—literally and figuratively—long enough.

He leaned close enough to drop his voice but still see her face. "Do you need a bit longer to feel me out, learn how my body moves and how we fit together?"

He felt her stiffen at the reminder of the words that had been haunting him, and she stumbled slightly again. She'd put the idea out there, though, so she had to have been expecting it to come back on her. A pink flush, evident even in the low light of the room, crawled up her chest to her neck. "I'm not sure we're quite in sync yet."

His thumb stroked the soft skin of her back, and he felt the muscle beneath jump in response. "I think we're getting there. You just need to let go and trust me to do my part."

That flush had made it to her cheeks, and he could see her pulse fluttering in the base of her throat. But when she lifted her eyes, they met his evenly. "That's the thing, Evan. I'm not sure I can."

And, that, sadly, was the truth. Even if Evan looked shocked to hear it.

She knew perfectly well what Evan was capable of—

and honestly, it only made it more difficult to make decisions. She had plenty of memories of exactly how they fit together, what his hands felt like and how he moved. And since he'd had nine years to improve on his technique, the possibilities made her knees a bit wobbly.

But knowing what he was capable of cut both ways, because she knew what he *wasn't* capable of, either. *That's* where she'd gotten burned before. And while she could talk a good game this time, she had to be honest with herself, too, and she wasn't completely sure she trusted herself to be okay with where that limit of capability was.

Evan was the scariest kind of womanizer: he genuinely liked women, and he could be caring and sweet—up to an extent. She didn't think it was an act he pulled just to lure women into his bed, because he didn't need to pretend anything to get women to accept a no-strings fling. The fact that easy, sexy charm probably *wasn't* an act was what made him so dangerous. Even knowing what she knew, even after he'd hurt her before, even telling herself exactly where the line would be going in…it still didn't bode well for her in the end.

And she'd be a fool to set herself up for the hurt—however unintentional—this could cause.

"You can't what? Let go? Or trust me?" Evan asked. There was tight humor in his voice—he didn't seem angry or hurt, just curious, surprised and maybe, just *maybe*, a touch offended.

The song changed, and Evan altered his pace, but not the steps—which they'd now repeated enough that she didn't have to think too much about her feet. But it did remind her that they were not alone: a couple hundred of Miami's wealthy and elite surrounded them. "This isn't an appropriate place for this conversation, Evan."

It was a viable, reasonable excuse—and she'd jumped on it for exactly that reason.

"There's loud music and lots of booze. No one's paying any attention to us, sweetheart."

Okay, different tack. She might as well be up-front and honest. "I thought we were going to be friends."

"We are. Look at us. Perfectly friendly."

"Then why are you making a pass at me? I thought you said you'd respect my wishes."

"I said I'd respect it if you said 'no.' I didn't say I wouldn't ask." He pulled her a little closer and the effect was devastating. "And you haven't said 'no,' yet."

And that was a glaring and very telling lack of action on her part. While Evan might be lots of less-than-gentlemanly-things, she didn't doubt he would back down as soon as she said it. Yet somehow the magic word wouldn't make it past her lips. She was a fool, but she'd put herself in this position willingly, knowing she'd have to make the choice sooner or later.

She had weaknesses—plenty of them—and she always had to balance the want against the price she might later pay for the indulgence. Everything was a trade-off: she might have a slice of chocolate cake, but skip the bread, or she'd do extra sit-ups the next day to work off some of the extra calories. As long as she didn't eat cake every night, it wasn't a problem.

Everything in moderation. Splurge occasionally because life was short. You only live once.

Evan was a splurge. And far more tempting than any chocolate cake. The big question, though, was could she enjoy Evan in moderation this time?

Evan hadn't said a word the whole time she went over things in her mind. He'd just kept dancing, kept stroking his thumb over her back and raising goose bumps on her skin, waiting for her to answer.

She took a deep breath and met his eyes. The heat there should have scorched her. "I haven't said no, but then, you haven't actually asked me a question, either."

Evan finally stopped moving. The hand he was still holding shifted slightly, keeping them palm to palm but allowing his fingers to thread through hers and squeeze gently. "Do you want to get out of here?"

Moment of truth time.

She only hesitated for a second.

"Yes."

Evan seemed genuinely surprised at her answer, and for a split second, Olivia wondered if he'd just been messing with her, teasing her and flirting without expectation.

Because if so...well, she'd have to kill him.

But then she noticed the way his fingers continued to tighten around hers and the slow, sexy smile. "Good."

Their exit was hurried and as sly as possible. Evan mumbled something about not wanting to make the entire rounds and Olivia agreed. She grabbed her wrap and purse and tried to look dignified—just in case—as they slipped out the door and into the stairwell headed to the parking deck.

Her heels clacked on the metal stairs and it echoed in the emptiness. Evan kept a hand on her elbow to steady her down the first two flights, but on the next landing, he stopped, trapping her between his body and the wall and causing her heartbeat to kick into double time.

Then his hand was cupping her cheek and tilting her head to his and…

Sweet mercy. This was probably a big mistake. A decision she was going to regret.

But the regret would come later, and right now, she had this. Her purse dropped to the floor, forgotten, as she gripped the lapels of his jacket.

Evan's kiss was everything she remembered and more. Unhurried but hungry, it promised all kinds of pleasures to come, and pure *want* drowned out any cautions from her higher brain functions.

He tasted like the whiskey on the rocks he'd been drinking earlier, only hot and far more potent. Then he leaned into her, pressing her back against the cool cinder block wall, deepening the kiss and blocking out everything that wasn't him.

And his hands…one was gentle against her cheek, but the other was strong against her hip—both of them caressing and stoking the fire kindled by his tongue.

She slid her hands under his jacket to feel the hard muscles of his stomach hidden under fine cotton, then wrapped her arms around his waist to pull him against her.

A groan echoed off the walls, and she wasn't sure

if it was hers or his. Evan's lips were hot against her neck, sending shivers over her skin. Hooking a foot around his calf, she pulled his thigh between hers and squeezed, trying to release some of the tension building inside her.

"Liv." Evan mumbled against her neck as a tremor rocked his body against hers. The hand that had been kneading her hip reached for hers as he pressed another hard kiss against her lips, then he bent down to get her purse and pushed through the door into the parking deck.

Olivia followed on shaky legs. At the car, Evan stopped to kiss her again, and she nearly climbed him like a tree, wanting more. Whispering a promise that made her blush, Evan opened her door. She scrambled inside as Evan went to the driver's side.

Some of her hair had come down—or been pulled down by Evan's hands—and she could feel the French twist now wobbling drunkenly on her head. Not caring or bothering with a mirror, she searched for the other pins and let it all fall loose around her shoulders with a big shake. Evan paused as he put the car in gear to run his hands through the messy curls, then used it to tug her over to his side for another kiss. "I don't know how I'm going to get us home."

"Drive fast."

Evan grinned at the command, and tires squealed as he accelerated. They were both quiet, and Olivia wondered if the pounding of her heart was audible to Evan as his hand landed on her knee and moved up to gently stroke the sensitive skin of her inner thigh. Her nails dug into the leather seat as the muscles began to quiver. She let her head fall back against the headrest and closed her eyes as his fingers moved slowly, maddeningly, *dangerously* higher.

But was it actually dangerous? A little voice inside her was shouting a warning, but it was easy enough to ignore. Dumping old emotions on top of this would be a mistake. She was an adult, not some starry-eyed kid, and *this* was not the same as last time at all.

Evan was hot and sexy and occasionally sweet, and there were far worse reasons to have sex. There was no reason to overthink this. Evan's fingers moved another crucial inch. Hell, why was she even thinking at all when she could just *feel*?

Mercy.

All that attention to *feeling* meant Olivia had no idea how long she'd been in the car or even where they were, but Evan was killing the engine and coming around to open her door. The breeze and the play of the lights told her they were near water, but she had no idea *which* water and she lacked enough knowledge of Miami as a whole to even hazard a guess.

Wherever they were, it was gorgeously landscaped and lush—the building not brand-new, but not shabby either, and the fact it wasn't a high-rise meant they might be off one of the canals, but not right off the bay. She had no idea. But, really, it didn't matter. Evan paused long enough to give her another kiss before leading her up the path to his door.

She half expected Evan to grab her, sweep her off her feet and carry her to the bedroom the second the door closed behind them, but instead, she found herself pulled gently into a long, unhurried kiss. He took her purse and wrap and laid them on a table before tossing his keys on top and shrugging out of his suit coat. She took a deep breath as an anticipatory shiver ran over her.

"Can I get you a drink or something?" he asked as he loosened his tie.

The air rushed out of her lungs. *Was he kidding?* She was so primed that one more touch might do the trick and Evan was playing Gracious Host? Hell, the only thing keeping her from dragging *him* to the bedroom was the fact she didn't know where the bedroom *was*.

"I'm good, thanks," she lied. More accurately, she felt like an idiot, standing in his foyer like an unsuspecting prom date who'd just been friendzoned.

"You sure? Wine? Water?"

"I'm *sure*." She didn't like the tone of her voice, but it couldn't be helped.

In a snap, the Gracious Host was gone, replaced by an almost predatory look that weakened her knees. "Good. That way," he pointed.

"Finally," she said honestly, slipping out of her shoes and following him. "I thought we were about to have a tea party."

"Hey, I was just trying to be nice."

"Noted. Appreciated."

Evan backed into a room, pulling her with him, and she could see the bed just over his shoulder.

"But I didn't come here for nice," she added.

A split second later, she was flat on her back on that bed with Evan looming over her. "Since you put it that way…"

She wasn't sure if that was a warning or a promise, but she was okay either way. Evan straddled her hips, his eyes watching hers as he unbuttoned his shirt and tossed it aside.

Oh yes. Very nice. It might be shallow, but Olivia spent every day in the company of men who, by the nature of their careers, had excellent bodies. *That* set a standard difficult for an average guy to meet. But Evan…oh, he'd do *nicely*. Plenty of definition and strength on display without being overly brawny or muscle-bound. A light sprinkling of hair accented his pecs before narrowing to a trail that bisected a nice set of abs and disappeared into the waistband of his pants. Her fingers itched to trace that line, and she did, following it from his belt buckle to his sternum, loving the way the muscles contracted under her touch.

Evan tugged her dress up over her hips, nearly to her ribs, before pulling her up to slide it up and off. Olivia had that one moment of self-consciousness but tried to push it aside. Evan had seen her naked before; he knew what he was getting. She had no breasts to speak of, no "womanly" curves. She was just as far from the lingerie model ideal figure as any other woman. It was a double standard, she knew, to expect a certain physique from a man while she offered a bony, boobless body in return, but Evan didn't seem to mind any more now than he had then.

If anything, Evan seemed to like it, his eyes hooded and dark as his hands mapped a path for his lips to follow. Her breasts might be small, but they were very sensitive, and the rasp of his tongue over her nipple had her arching off the bed, begging for more.

She'd been a virgin the first time with Evan, too naive to not confuse love and sex, and too nervous to fully appreciate the experience. But tonight...*mercy.*

Her hands were shaking with need, making her attempts at his belt and zipper clumsy. Evan finally took over, shucking his clothes and giving her the skin to skin contact she craved. His skin was hot, his body heavy on hers, his fingers and tongue working black magic on her until she wanted to scream.

So she did.

Olivia's thighs squeezed him like a vise, threatening to crack a rib as she came against his mouth. Evan felt the shock wave roll through her body and redoubled his efforts, working his tongue until she was tugging at his hair, pulling him up and over her and wrapping those long powerful legs around his hips.

The sight of Olivia nearly stopped his heart. That golden-red hair was wild and tangled, and her skin was flushed pink and glistened under a sheen of sweat. She opened her eyes, dark with desire but focused directly on his, and used those legs to leverage him closer.

He knelt between her thighs, indulging his need to

touch her. Her skin was so soft, but it draped over steel-hard muscle that fluttered as his fingers touched it. He'd seen her in action; he knew she was strong and had seen what she could do with her body, and it gave him a primal level of satisfaction to see her body react so strongly because of him.

But that strength put him in a tug-of-war—her pulling him closer, him holding back, wanting to touch and explore with leisure—that he wasn't entirely sure he'd be able to win, even if he really wanted to.

He anchored himself and slid his hands over her ribs to her breasts, tracing light circles around her nipples. Olivia's eyes rolled back in her head and teeth caught her bottom lip.

"Ev-*an*..."

The breathy, exasperated plea made him smile. He squeezed a nipple gently, causing her to groan. "Yes, Liv?"

Her hand grabbed his wrist. "Don't tease."

"But you said not to rush the foreplay, remember?"

"You're evil." A tiny tremor shook her body and she released his wrist. "And you're killing me."

He wanted to feel smug, but Liv's hand had slithered down between them, palming him and working him with gentle, insistent pressure that threatened to snap his control. His hands were shaking as he reached for the nightstand drawer and grabbed a condom. "I know the feeling."

That earned him a smile that turned wicked as she took the condom from him, turning a simple, usually perfunctory action into an erotic one that left him groaning and wheezing for air.

"Now who's teas—?" The question was cut short as Olivia lifted her hips and guided him in.

He lost the ability to speak—the ability to even *think*—as all his higher brain functions shut down, narrowing his focus to one thing, and Olivia's deeply satisfied sigh echoed his own.

He moved slowly at first, taking his time, loving the way Olivia responded—earnestly, wholeheartedly and enthusiastically—the little moans spurring him on. He wanted to savor, prolong it, but he'd been waiting for nine years to have Olivia in his bed again, and that resolve was weakening under the need to lose himself in her completely.

She was thrashing, fisting the sheets and moving her hips frantically, trying to increase the pace. Rolling to his back, he pulled Olivia atop him to let her take the lead.

Her hair fell like a curtain around them, blocking out everything else as she rocked against him, finding her groove and driving him insane. When her eyes glazed over and her rhythm faltered, he grabbed her hips and took over, slamming into her again and again until she arched nearly in half, her whole body shuddering and shivering as her orgasm moved through her.

It was beautiful to watch, but her climax pushed him over the edge, causing him to explode with enough force to make his vision go fuzzy at the edges.

When he was finally able to think again, Olivia was

draped over his chest, her breath still heaving. Care-fully, he pushed her hair out of his face and hers, gath-ering it into a loose ponytail and wrapping it around his fist.

Olivia smiled, but her eyes stayed closed. "Thanks. It was bothering me but I couldn't be bothered to find the energy to move it."

"Well, that was about all the energy I had left. I may be dead now."

Her fingers stroked slowly over his chest, then she opened her eyes. "Pity."

Amazingly, that was enough to stir his blood, if no other part of his body. "Just give me a minute or two."

"Yay." After a heavy sigh, she asked, "Am I too heavy? Do I need to move?"

The woman weighed nothing, and she felt amazing anyway. "No."

"Good." After another sigh, she seemed to doze off.

Since the only remaining option was for him to lie here and think—which he really didn't want to do—he did the same.

CHAPTER SIX

OLIVIA EASING OUT of bed woke him up. Sunshine streamed in through curtains he'd forgotten to close, telling him they'd slept pretty late.

But then they hadn't gotten much sleep before the sun came up, either. He felt wrung-out and sore in muscles he didn't know he had, but the deep, sated satisfaction well made up for that.

Olivia stretched, bending herself into another of those impossible positions. It was kind of sexy, until he heard a sharp crack.

"Ouch."

She started, then looked over her shoulder. "Just wait," she said with a weak smile and proceeded to crack seemingly each and every joint in her body—including some he didn't know *could* crack. "Ah, that's better."

"Good lord, Olivia. It sounds like you're falling apart."

She shrugged. "I'm in pretty good shape for my age, so I'm lucky."

She was in excellent—amazing—shape. "For your *age*?"

"Sadly, I can't be twenty-one forever. A couple of my friends have already retired, but they had injuries that tipped the scale a little early. If I make it to thirty-five, I'll be happy." She reached for the shirt he'd thrown on the floor last night and slipped into it. "I need water. I'm as dry as the Sahara this morning. Do you want anything?" she called as she disappeared down the hallway.

He grabbed a pair of boxers and followed her. "I'll make coffee."

"Oh, that will be excellent. But water first." She poured a full glass and drank deeply as he filled the pot and measured coffee. The initial morning-after awkwardness that they avoided by Olivia's snap-crackle-pop routine settled in belatedly and they stood there silently as the coffee brewed.

Finally, he asked, "Do you need to be home at a specific time today?"

"Not really. I've got some sewing and laundry to do, but I have Sundays off unless we're performing or something. But," she quickly added, setting down her glass, "I don't want to keep you from whatever you need to do today. I can call a cab or..."

"I've got no plans." He paused and reached for the hem of the shirt she wore, tugging her a few inches closer. "Yet."

"Well, all I have is the dress I wore last night. It rather limits my options."

"You don't need clothes for what I'm planning."

"I'm intrigued."

"Good."

Olivia was angling in for a kiss when a loud, fast guitar riff played and her purse began vibrating against the table. She pulled back as if she'd been burned.

"It's okay," he said, "You can answer it."

"I'd really rather not."

In that second he recognized the tune and realized why it was familiar. At that point, he wanted to put even more space between them. There was really only one person Olivia would assign that particular song to on her phone because it was one of his favorite songs: Jory.

He didn't know why she might not feel like talking to her brother at the moment, but it served him up a heaping load of guilt for his behavior. Not for sleeping with Olivia—he had no regrets—but because he knew he *should* feel bad for not staying away from Jory's sister. It was a fine hair to split—but one he'd been splitting all his life. He might be sorry what he did was a sin, but only *because* it was a sin. But he wouldn't be sorry he did it because he'd enjoyed it and would do it again if the opportunity presented itself. His father, needless to say, hadn't been pleased with that bit of amateur theology runaround. Where he and Olivia were concerned, he doubted Jory would be impressed with that logic either, and forgiveness wouldn't be easily given.

"That's Jory's ringtone," Olivia explained unnecessarily, then she shook her head. "Maybe I shouldn't have brought him up right now. You know, all things considered."

"Well, one of us had to."

"But my brother and my sex life aren't really something I like to discuss in the same conversation."

"I'm sure Jory feels the same way. But," he added, "You and me? It's kind of hard *not* to bring him in."

"Ew. Gross."

"Liv," he chided, "You know what I mean."

"I do. I also know that I'm an adult and it's none of my brother's business who I sleep with."

"True."

Olivia looked uncomfortable. "How much does Jory know? About before, I mean."

"You don't know?"

"I know he knows something, but he certainly doesn't talk about it, and he wasn't keen on even the *idea* of us hooking up." She shrugged. "But you two are friends."

Evan had no idea where to go from there. "Does it matter? That's ancient history."

"Except that it's news now, isn't it?"

"Is it?"

Olivia sighed. "Look, I'll be honest with you if you'll be honest with me."

That was almost ominous. "Seems fair," he said carefully.

"Honestly, the less Jory knows about my sex life the better. And as I said, it's none of his business who I sleep with."

"I happen to agree with you on that."

"So, I don't see the need to tell Jory about this. Do you?"

"I can assure you that your brother does not want me anywhere near you, so no, I don't see the need to tell him anything either."

Instead of agreement, he got a surprised look from her. "Why is that?"

"Because as you said, it's none of Jory's business."

"No. Why do you say Jory doesn't want you near me?"

"Because you're his sister." Surely she understood that.

"But you're his friend. If you're good enough for him to hang out with, why aren't you good enough for me?"

Oh, where to begin. "Because."

"Because?"

He poured coffee, stalling, and when that didn't work, he tried to shrug it off. "Yeah, because."

"Is this some kind of weird guy thing?"

"Yes," he said, hoping she'd leave it at that. "It's a guy thing."

"How juvenile. It's like you're still teenagers."

He was beginning to agree. Hell, hadn't he already convinced himself there was a big difference between an eighteen-year-old sister and a twenty-seven-year-old sister? But that might just be wishful thinking on his part.

"So sisters are completely off-limits?" she asked

and waited until he nodded. "That's insane. What if we were to fall in love?"

Evan spit his coffee across the counter, burning his lip in the process. "Whoa, there. Liv, I—um…"

She waved a hand and passed him a towel. "Oh, calm down. It's purely a rhetorical question. It just seems unfair. Does he get to put other, nonrelated women off-limits?"

"No."

"Then that's just ridiculous. Either it's his business who you sleep with or it isn't."

"It's more complicated than that."

"Only because boys are weird."

"Oh, and girls aren't? One of your girlfriends would be okay if you slept with her brother?"

That gave her a second's pause. "I wouldn't know. Unless that girl's brother was also dancing in the same company, the chances of me meeting him are slim. Anyway, dancers are a small community. Chances are whoever you're sleeping with has slept with someone else you know anyway. The grown-up thing to do is to butt the hell out of any sex that doesn't currently involve you."

She had a refreshing, mature approach that didn't help at all in this instance. "I'd agree, but the last time I slept with you, Jory practically broke my nose. Right, wrong or indifferent, Jory *does* have strong opinions when it comes to me and you."

Olivia blinked. "He did *what*?"

He cursed. "Nothing. You want some breakfast?"

"Oh, no, you can't drop something like that and just move on. So Jory does know we hooked up?"

He could lie. It only depended on which Madison sibling he wanted to anger today. From the look on Olivia's face, it was probably safer for him to tell the truth to her. "Yes."

"And he was mad about it."

"Yes."

"Why? And don't give me any 'because of a Guy Thing' crap."

"Aside from the 'Guy Thing crap'—which is not crap, by the way—you don't screw around—literally or not—with someone's sister when you have nothing to offer."

"Every woman is someone's sister."

"Then let me rephrase—"

"No need," she interrupted. "It'll never make sense. But if Jory was so mad about this, how come he never said anything to me about it?"

"Because once it was over and done with, there was no need." He could hope she'd accept that at face value.

"That little..." She shook her head slowly. "I'm going to kill him."

"Olivia..."

"Don't," she warned. "Jory told you to back off, didn't he?" She didn't wait for his answer. "*That's* why you dumped me like that."

"In all fairness, you were leaving for London—"

"New York," she corrected.

"—or wherever in another couple of weeks or so. What difference did it make?"

"It made a hell of a difference to me. *Jory* makes a decision, *I* get dumped and *you* get to be the bad guy. He comes out smelling like a rose. I'm going to *kill* him."

"Liv, be serious. You're getting all worked up over something that happened years ago. And Jory really did mean well."

"Oh, as long as he *meant* well, that changes everything," she snarked. "I'll just forget all the hurt and shame and stuff since he 'meant well'."

Somehow he was the rational person in the conversation. Jory owed him big-time. "How would you going off to New York feeling like you had some kind of attachment to me have been at all good for your career?"

"I wasn't 'attached' to you," she mumbled.

"Really? Then why did it hurt?" Her lips flattened and she looked deep into her coffee cup. His point made, he continued. "But that way, you went off, with nothing holding you back. And being mad at me was far preferable to you being mad at Jory, right?"

"Why are you being so damn reasonable about this?"

"Because I happen to think Jory was right." It had been the right thing—for everyone.

That took some of the wind out of her sails. "Wow. You really are a cold, heartless bastard."

"So you've said."

She lifted her chin. "So what about last night, then?"

"There's a big difference between then and now. Not

only are you an adult, you're established in your career and your life—there's not much for me to screw up for you now. I've been very honest about what I wanted, so if you did make that choice, my conscience could be clear."

Olivia rubbed her temples. "I'm not sure how to process this."

"Then or now?"

"Either. Both. It's going to take a little time for me to make sense of it." She looked at him. "Here's the thing about now, though—*I'm* not worried about Jory or what he thinks. Are you?"

There was a clear challenge there that was impossible to fully answer. "I brought you home last night, remember? But, no, I don't see the need to rub Jory's nose in it. I may not be the best of friends, but I hope I'm better than that."

"If it makes you feel better," she said quietly, the quick change of mood surprising him, "I think you're a really good friend to Jory."

He certainly didn't feel like it. "Yes, because sleeping with his baby sister is the true sign of friendship."

"But you don't want him to be upset, so that says something. Does it make me a bad sister to sleep with my brother's best friend?"

"Well, when you put it like that..."

"The thing is, I can see where the idea of possibly being put in the middle or forced to choose sides comes into this, but that's an issue *any* time two people you know—especially if you know them independently of each other—are involved. It's selfish to demand other people adjust *their* behavior so that *you* aren't made uncomfortable at some point. And it's insane to think you *could* put those demands on people. It's like telling a married couple they can't get divorced because it will mess up the seating charts at your future dinner parties." He started to argue, but Olivia lifted a hand to stop him. "I don't like to think about my brother having sex, either, so you know what I do? *I don't think about it.*"

He couldn't help but laugh. "That's very logical, Olivia."

"Thank you."

"But people, as a whole, aren't logical. Especially about people they love. Or sex."

"Then it's your call. I'll leave now, if that's what you want."

"I didn't say that. But Jory won't forgive me if you get hurt again."

"Your ego is simply astounding." She shook her head.

"It has nothing to do with ego."

She sighed, then shrugged. "Well, if you don't think you can handle me, that's fine." She set her coffee cup on the counter. "I'll go get dressed. Call me a cab, will you?" she called over her shoulder as she headed back down the hall.

He caught her in the bedroom and tackled her to the bed. "Can I handle you? Liv, honey, I thought I proved that last night. *Repeatedly.* The real question is…can you handle me?"

"I think that was proven last night, as well."

He pretended to think as he worked the buttons of her shirt open. "Maybe we should try it one more time. Just to be sure."

"Might take more than *one* more time," she said. "You know, to be *absolutely* sure."

His conscience sent up a small protest, but Olivia was sliding out of that shirt and…

Well, at least he could say he tried.

There was nothing quite like orgasms to completely change a girl's outlook on life.

It was rather silly, actually, as nothing else in her life had changed at all, but Olivia had to admit she was in a much better mood. Like a pressure valve had been opened.

Endorphins, she thought. *Amazing things.*

There was a slight soreness to muscles that hadn't been used like that in a long while, but the little frizzle of energy remaining in her blood was well worth the trade-off. And while Evan had brought her home early last night, the sheer amount of energy expended on what would normally be her lazy day off left her feeling a little tired and hungover as she warmed up at the barre Monday morning.

But even with that, she still felt it was worth it. No regrets at all.

She wasn't sure she could say the same about Evan,

though. She had to respect the level of loyalty to Jory that would make a player like Evan think twice about sleeping with a woman, but it dinged her pride as well—as if she had to talk him into it or something. Her inner femme fatale was a little miffed.

But everyone kept asking her about the smirk on her face, so she couldn't be *too* miffed about it. Or stay that way for very long. After all, once Evan had gotten past the whole Jory's-sister thing, she could make no complaints about his performance.

She even felt a bit better about the way Evan had treated her before. It still stung, and she still needed to kill Jory, but she had to look at it in a different light now. If nothing else, it made it a little easier to reconcile her attraction to Evan *now*. At least she didn't have to feel completely shallow or masochistic about it anymore.

As for what would happen next…possibly the best part of this was that she didn't *need* to worry about "next"—no matter what it might be. There was a very nice freedom in that.

"Earth to Olivia?" Theo waved a hand in front of her face. "Can you move so we can put the barres away?"

She'd spaced out, moving through the warm-up by rote and habit, and now she was busted. "Sorry," she muttered and went to stretch, figuring she'd use the time to get her head back in the studio where it belonged before she hurt herself.

Theo followed her. "You okay?"

"Yeah." She put her foot on the barre and lay over

her leg. "Just a little out of it today," she offered as an explanation.

"Career, money or sex?"

"Excuse me?" she asked.

"It's got to be one of the three. The smirk on your face means it's probably good, so that strikes worries about family and health off the list of topics to space out over."

"I'm putting my money on sex." Tina, one of younger soloists, propped her foot up onto the barre next to them.

"Oh, really?" Theo asked eagerly, totally ignoring the shut-up-please look Olivia shot him. "And why is that?"

"Leslie, that new apprentice—"

"Which one is she?" he interrupted.

"Kinda short, dark hair. Bad feet but pretty turns?"

Nodding, he said, "Okay, go on."

"Leslie works for a catering company that did the big Abrams Corporation party Saturday night and Olivia was there. With a very good-looking guy, too."

Olivia hadn't seen anyone she knew, but then there'd been a lot of people there, and she hadn't been paying all that much attention to the staff. *Damn.*

"How interesting."

"I know. Leslie didn't recognize the guy, though. Then she got busy and forgot to ask."

Good lord. They were gossiping about her as though she wasn't even there. She stood up. "*Ahem.*"

"Shh," Theo said, pushing her back down over her leg. "You stretch." He turned back to Tina. "*And...?*"

"*And* Olivia left early with Mr. Tall, Hot and Anonymous."

"So definitely sex, then. Okay, 'fess up, Olivia," he said, tapping her on the back. "Who is he?"

She didn't even bother to lift her head. "Oh, so *now* I get to be a part of this conversation?"

"Yes, please. We want details."

"The juicy ones," Tina added.

She didn't want to be the subject of dressing room gossip, and demurring to answer all but guaranteed she would be. But that did not mean she was willing to confirm speculations about her sex life for the company to further discuss at their leisure. "He's my brother's college roommate."

"Oh." Tina looked disappointed, and Olivia bit back a smile. While the truth of that statement might be causing *her*—and Evan—problems, she had to love it a little, too. A complete, concise, easy-peasy speculation shut down without any of the "he's just a friend" vague denials that would be met with even *more* probing. "But if he's hot *and* important enough to get an invite to the Abrams's do, give him my number."

Hell, she wasn't sure she had Tina's number even if she did want to offer Evan up like that. "I'll let him know you're available."

"Please do," Tina said and went back to the other side of the room, presumably to tell the others what new info she had.

She smacked him, hard. "Gee, thanks, Theo."

"What?" he said, rubbing his arm.

"Did you really *have* to encourage her? She's still annoyed that I got 'her' contract. Way to give her more ammo against me."

"That contract was only Tina's in her dreams. She's lucky her big butt ever made it out of the corps." He waved it off. "So are you going to tell me about this guy or not?"

"I need to go change my shoes."

"Come on."

She sighed. "I already told you. He's my brother's college roommate. He needed a date for the party, and I had nothing better to do. So I went. And I met Matt Abrams, so that's not too shabby, either."

"And your smug mood today is caused by...?"

"I had a good time." She wasn't going to offer more than that, and Theo could infer anything he liked from it. She trusted Theo not to provide grist for the rumor mill. Of course, it helped that she had some dirt on him, and he knew it.

After a moment, Theo nodded. "Good for you, sweetie. Now, I'll let you go change your shoes, as I'm pretty sure Sylvie is going to want to run through the *adage* first."

Olivia took a second to check her phone while she was at it and found a text from Evan: You busy tonight?

It made her smile and put a sizzle in her blood at the same time she gave it a mental side-eye. There was a definite overtone of booty call to the message, which part of her felt she *should* be offended by. At the same time, the memories of yesterday were fresh enough to make her glad of an encore.

Theo was calling for her, forcing her to make a decision. I'll be done by 5:30, she typed quickly and dropped the phone back into her bag. There was no sense second-guessing herself, and there was no reason not to enjoy herself while she could.

With the decision made and the rationale accepted, she found her mind much clearer and her usual concentration returned. In fact, she almost forgot about Evan all together until later that afternoon when Leslie-the-apprentice mentioned seeing her at the party. That sent her back to her phone during the water break to see if he'd responded.

I'll pick you up at your place on my way home. 6:30-ish.

The rest of the afternoon dragged by.

Broiled chicken and steamed veggies. It wasn't exciting, but Olivia was forcing him to eat better these days. Well, not *forcing*—she actually hadn't said anything about his diet—but a man could only eat junk while his dinner partner ate healthy so many times before guilt set in. He'd buckled under in less than a week. Olivia still hadn't said anything, but she'd smirked when he told her tonight's menu.

"It's ready," he called, setting the plates on the coffee table. Olivia came out of the bedroom in yoga pants and a tank top, braiding her hair as she walked.

"Good, I'm starved. Thank you for cooking."

As she settled beside him, he noticed her bright pink socks. "Are you cold?"

She paused, a forkful of chicken partway to her mouth. "No. Why?" He indicated the socks and she shrugged. "Oh, that. I've just got ugly feet."

He honestly hadn't paid that much attention to her feet before—he'd been too busy focusing on other, more interesting parts of her anatomy. "They can't be that bad."

"Oh, yeah they can. This is yummy, by the way."

He'd seen pointe shoes. There was no way they didn't do bad things to her feet. "Let me see them."

She crossed her legs, tucking her feet under her thighs. "No way."

"Come on," he cajoled. She shook her head and took a bite. "I'm going to see them eventually."

"Maybe. But not now. It'll kill your appetite."

"One of my first jobs in college was at a restaurant. I cooked, washed dishes, scrubbed the grills. It tore my hands up."

"My parents own a restaurant. I'm well aware of what it does to your hands."

He put his fork down. "Well, my first college girl-friend dumped me because she said my hands were troll-like, and she didn't like them touching her."

"What a witch."

"True, but my point is, I understand."

"Look, even *I* think my feet are gross. I'm not showing them off. *No*," she added when he started to protest. "End of subject."

"It's not like I can't sneak a peek later."

"That's up to you. I can warn you, but I can't stop you." She shook her head. "You might regret it, though."

"You've got some weird hang-ups," he mumbled.

She smiled at him angelically. "Everyone's crazy in their own special way. The trick is to find the person who thinks your special brand of crazy is kinda cute."

"You've got a special brand there, that's for sure," he mumbled toward his chicken.

"Where did you work?"

He let her change the subject, since she obviously felt strongly about it. "The Carousel."

"That place on the beach where the waitresses wear bikinis?"

"That's the one. How do you know about The Carousel?"

"Who in Florida *doesn't* know about that place? It's legendary. I never got to go, of course, but I've heard stories from friends and other people who went to Jacksonville for spring break." She shook her head. "Wow. When you decided to rebel against your upbringing, you went all out, didn't you? Dancing, drinking, women, working in a place like that. Were you trying to mark off all seven deadly sins or just break half the Ten Commandments?"

"I had a punch card. Every tenth sin earned me a free ice cream cone to enjoy in my front row seat in hell."

"So much for a 'civilized' rebellion."

"It takes more than a few dance lessons to really rebel."

"What did your parents think?"

"I didn't tell them anything, but this girl from high school was also going to school in Jacksonville and come summer break, she went home and told *everyone* all my sins."

She shook her head in sympathy. "I hate people like that."

"Me, too. My father threatened to disown me, my mother cried because they were so embarrassed I'd turned my back on everything they'd tried to teach me. Big drama."

"But look at you now. You're certainly doing well for yourself. They can't be too upset with how you turned out."

He shrugged.

"They're not? Why?"

"Honestly, I have no idea if they are or not. I don't even know if they know how I turned out. I haven't been back to Arrowwood since the day I left, and I haven't spoken to my parents in ten, maybe eleven, years."

"I'm so sorry."

Of course Olivia would think that a tragedy. She had great parents. "I'm not. It's better this way. Everyone's much happier, I promise."

Carefully, she asked, "So there's no chance for reconciliation?"

He leaned back and studied her. "Show me your feet."

"What?"

"If you want to talk about my parents, you have to show me your feet. It's only fair if we *both* do something we don't want to."

She actually seemed to consider it. "Point taken. I won't pry anymore. But I *am* sorry you have unreasonable and judgmental parents."

"Thanks, Liv. Now you know why I've always preferred yours." That reminded him, especially since Olivia hadn't mentioned it yet. "Speaking of your parents, have you talked to them today?"

She shook her head. "Mom called earlier but I was in rehearsals. She left a message for me to call tomorrow. Wait—why do you ask?"

"I normally go to your parents' for Thanksgiving, you know."

Olivia looked at her plate. "I'd forgotten about that."

"Dee called today and asked me to give you a lift to Tampa."

"You're kidding."

"You don't have a car, Olivia. It makes sense."

"But I've lined up a rental. I *want* to drive."

"They're just worried about you driving Alligator Alley on your own at night."

"I'm an adult. I've been on my own for years. I've navigated foreign cities where no one speaks English. I think I can handle a four-hour drive through central Florida all by myself."

"But the cell reception sucks through there. I see their point, even if you are too skinny for the alligators to bother eating."

She shot him a sour look for that crack. "I'm going up on Wednesday, but I have to come back Friday night. I'm in the Santa parade on Saturday. You shouldn't have to cut your holiday short because of me."

"I've got plans on Saturday myself. It works out fine."

Olivia muttered under her breath.

"Give in graciously to make your parents happy, and I promise I won't look at your feet when you're naked later," he offered as a compromise.

"But I *wanted* to drive. I haven't driven since August."

"Fine. I'll let you drive part of the way. Will that make you happy?"

She grinned. "Oh, I was hoping you'd say that. Deal. I can leave anytime after four on Wednesday."

CHAPTER SEVEN

IT TOOK THEM longer than expected to get to Tampa. They blamed it on traffic, and everyone accepted that explanation without question. Thankfully, no one seemed to notice they were a bit more rumpled than they should be after the drive.

Evan, though, felt a little bad about the delay when he dropped Olivia at the Madisons' and saw the genuine excitement and misty eyes of Olivia's homecoming. They were truly an ideal family, straight out of a greeting card commercial—Dee fussing when she found out they hadn't eaten yet, and Gary offering him gas money for the trip. He declined both the money and the offer of food and left for Jory's place. Olivia thanked him for the ride politely and with the right amount of distance, but she had a small, I've-got-a-secret smile on her face as he left.

He got another helping of guilt when he got to Jory's twenty minutes later. He'd delayed seeing his best friend in order to see his best friend's sister naked—which he wasn't about to admit. He tossed his gear into Jory's "guest room"—which was more of a weight room with a twin bed from Jory's childhood bedroom tucked in the corner—while Jory got them both beers.

Like his sister, Jory chose to live downtown, doing his part to help gentrify an area trying to reinvent itself. It was a stark contrast to his parents' suburban lifestyle, but Jory had taken to it perfectly, all the way down to the local microbrewed beer he offered. A perfect example of a young, upwardly mobile lawyer with a hipster bent.

They caught up on a few things, then Jory said, "By the way, thanks for driving Livvy up."

"Not a problem."

"I told Mom not to ask you, but she still worries about Olivia."

"I was coming this way anyway, so it made sense."

"And it went all right?" Jory asked carefully.

That was probably as close as Jory was going to come to bringing up Evan's past with Olivia. He hadn't mentioned it since the day Evan had agreed to leave Liv alone. "It was fine. It's been a long time—too long for old grudges."

Jory snorted. "You obviously don't know my sister very well. She can carry a grudge with the best of them."

He'd say he was getting to know Olivia pretty well these days. And while Olivia could carry a grudge, she seemed equally capable of letting it go. But there was really no way to offer that information to Jory. "She didn't bring it up today, so I didn't either. I'm pretty sure she's over it." That wasn't a lie. They'd talked the whole way up, but not about that. "By the way, I brought wine for tomorrow," he said to change the subject. "Don't let me forget it."

Jory nodded. "Livvy didn't need that kind of baggage back then. She'd have gotten far more attached to you than you to her, and it would have ended badly. Who knows how that could have thrown her off, and she was just starting out. A clean break was the only way for her."

"In retrospect, I agree with you."

"I appreciate that. And, seriously, I wanted my sister to like you—and you her—just not like that." He laughed. Evan tried, but he was having a hard time seeing the humor. "I'm not counting on you two being friends, but it'd be nice to know you could at least stand each other. We'd all feel better knowing there's someone close by she could call if she were ever in a pinch."

So Jory's ban on Evan and Olivia contact wasn't complete. Just with the assumption they'd remain vertical and clothed. Evan bit back a smile—at least once, they had. It'd been quick, but far hotter than anticipated. "She has my contact info, and I've told her not to hesitate to call if she needs anything."

"Good. And thanks. Did she happen to mention anything about a boyfriend to you?"

Evan nearly choked on his beer. "No. Why?"

"Livvy's been hard to get in touch with lately, so I called her apartment and talked to her roommate.

Annie was a little cagey about her whereabouts, so I'm assuming she must be seeing someone."

Liv was spending a lot of time at his place these days—after all, he didn't have a roommate to make things awkward and she did. She rarely spent the night though, as he had to leave a lot earlier than she did and the bus didn't run anywhere near his place. But it wasn't *every* night. They each had lives they had to live. It *was* a lot of time, though. He'd tell her she needed to quit ignoring her brother every time he called while she was with him. "I wouldn't know."

"Well, could you somehow work it into the conversation on your way home?"

He nearly choked. "Why are you so concerned about your sister's love life? That's a little disturbing—not to mention really none of your business."

"That's what Livvy says, too." He laughed and shrugged. "I'm just curious. I want her to be happy, and I refuse to feel bad about that."

Evan liked to think that Olivia *was* happy—maybe not in the way Jory probably meant, but she certainly seemed happy enough for the time being.

And he liked to think that part of that was because of him.

It struck him that he was happy, too. More relaxed. That was definitely Olivia, he decided. It was a weird kind of thing—more than the average friends-with-benefits, but not a *relationship*—but it worked for them. And he was having a very good time. "I'm sure she's fine, Jory. Leave her alone and let her live her life. You two have always been pretty tight. She'll let you know if she needs you."

"I can hope." Jory went to get another round from the fridge, and by the time he got back he'd moved on to other topics, thank heavens. The weird uncomfortable feeling that settled on his shoulders from talking about Olivia lifted and everything felt normal again.

But when he finally stumbled into bed, bleary-eyed from drinking half the night with Jory, he realized he was missing her.

And frankly, drunk or not, that scared him a little.

Olivia was all smiles and teary hugs goodbye when he picked her up Friday afternoon, but the smiles faded as soon as they turned the corner and she collapsed back against the seat and rubbed her temples. "I love them so much and miss them tons, but *whoa*...I knew there was a reason I moved to Miami and not Tampa."

He laughed. "Beyond the fact Miami offered you a contract?"

She shot him a level look. "You're assuming Ballet Tampa never offered."

"So they did?"

"Of course they did. I just didn't want to go back to Tampa. I've had offers from lots of different companies over the years, and I've been fortunate enough to be able to be picky. I already told you I had a list of places I wanted to dance—both foreign and domestic—and as long as those offers were coming in, I wasn't about to move home." She pointed a finger at him and warned, "But don't tell my folks that or I'll have to kill you."

"I've got no room to talk, so we're good."

"I want to see them and spend time with them, but I can only handle short periods of it before I feel smothered. I know the smothering comes from me being gone, but because I've been gone so long, I'm not used to being smothered. Does that make sense?"

"Yep."

"Good, because I'm not sure I fully understand it."

"You've lived away from home for a long time and you're very independent. It doesn't mean they're not great people or that you don't love them."

"They are, and I do." She sighed. "Ugh. I'm a terrible child."

"No, you're not. You're living your life—which is exactly what you should do. *And* exactly what Dee and Gary *want* you to do. They're so unbelievably proud of you."

"Thank you for that. I feel a little better." She reached over and squeezed his hand. He returned the squeeze. Then Olivia pulled out her seemingly bottomless bag of pointe shoes and ribbons and threaded a needle.

"You just sewed a bunch of shoes the other day. How many pairs of those things do you need?"

"More than you might think." She was quick and efficient, finishing with one ribbon by biting off the thread. Then she tied a new knot and started on another ribbon. "Did you and Jory have a good time?"

"Yep. And I'm supposed to ask you if you're seeing someone."

"*Ouch.*" Olivia pulled the needle out of her thumb and sucked on the wound to soothe it. "Are you kidding me? Why would he care?"

"Hey, your mom asked me the same thing. You know, you could really save me some awkward moments by returning their calls."

"I *do*. Eventually. I've just been a bit busy recently and there are only so many hours in a day. Given the choice between being with you and calling my family…" She shot him a sly smile. "I chose you."

"I'm flattered." And he was. More than he really should be. More than he was comfortable with, actually, for a multitude of reasons.

But it was still kind of nice.

And that was also was also a little scary.

Thanksgiving pretty much marked the end of any kind of normality in Olivia's life—until at least after Christmas. She was prepared, though. She'd done her Christmas shopping in October and had had her Christmas cards addressed and ready to go since Halloween. She was used to the craziness of December—the run outs to various schools, the photo calls, music rehearsals, tech rehearsals, dress rehearsals, appearances on morning shows, the evening news and at half a dozen area events. That was on top of the usual classes, doctors' appointments and the like. Oh, and the sixteen or so actual performances they'd do over the next three weeks,

of course. It was nonstop between now and Christmas
Eve, but once the curtain closed that night, she could
retreat to her bed and not be required to surface again
until after the New Year.

It was the nature of the business—especially now
that she was a principal—and while the schedule was
grueling at times, she loved it.

But she'd never tried to do it before while she was
seeing someone—or at least someone who wasn't also
doing *The Nutcracker* and keeping a schedule equally
as insane as hers. And *that* was a problem.

Evan, bless him, said he understood, but anyone
would get frustrated when they were being shoehorned
into a schedule—meals had to be grabbed during holes
in that schedule, but they weren't exactly leisurely affairs at nice restaurants. Late nights with endless hours
of athletic, sweaty sex were out of the question, too.
She needed sleep—lots of it. She wasn't complaining—
much—as it was still *good* sex, but it was rather like
being put on a restricted diet after unlimited trips to
the dessert bar.

After a week of rushed encounters and last-minute
cancellations, Olivia was sure Evan would be over it.
Surprisingly though, he wasn't. She had to give him
credit for that.

The real problem, though, was that she was worried
about it at all. She'd had more than one guy hit the road
when faced with the truth of her priorities—and where
they ranked on that list. It hadn't bothered her before.

So while it was sweet that Evan was trying to handle it, the scary part was that she was juggling, trying to create time just for him. It created stress she didn't need, but she couldn't not see him, either.

She had most of today and all of tonight off to rest up before tomorrow's opening. She could make it up to him—at least a little.

Funny, since when did she care?

She left class, ran her errands and went home. After a fast shower, she pulled a T-shirt on and crawled under the covers for a quick nap before Evan got off work.

"Olivia. Liv. *Olivia*."

She fought her way back to consciousness. Evan sat on the edge of her bed, shaking her gently. Groggy and disoriented, she squinted at him. "What are you doing here?"

"Annie let me in. When you didn't show for dinner or answer your phone, I thought something bad had happened to you."

Details came into focus. Her room, which had been flooded with daylight when she lay down, was now dim and shadowy. A glance at the clock told her she was supposed to meet Evan over an hour ago.

"Sorry. I was up at four-thirty this morning to do *Wake Up, Miami!*. I only meant to lay down for an hour or so." She reached for the bottle of water beside her bed—gone warm a long time ago—and drank deeply to wake herself the rest of the way up. "Let me change and we'll go."

"Are you actually hungry?"

"Not really," she answered honestly. "But you probably are."

He shook his head. "Why don't you go back to sleep, then. You look tired. I'll talk to you later." There was a strange, almost annoyed, undertone to his voice.

"I said I was sorry."

"I know."

"This is a really busy time for me. I warned you," she reminded him.

"I know."

"Then why are you mad?"

"I'm not," he insisted.

"You seem like it."

"Olivia, what do you want me to say? No, I'm not loving the situation, but—"

"It's only going to get worse once we open."

"And I said I understand. I can live with it, even if neither of us likes it very much."

And this was where the problems began. She sat up and faced him. "That's the thing, Evan. I *do* like this. I *love* it. I got my dream job, and I don't regret anything I gave up to get here or begrudge anything I have to do to stay here. And I can't have a boyfriend who can't accept that this is who I am and what I do."

Evan looked shocked. "I didn't realize that's where we were."

The comment didn't make sense, and the way Evan was avoiding eye contact and looking distinctly uncomfortable had her mentally replaying what she'd said. "Sorry, I didn't mean *boyfriend* boyfriend. It's just easier and quicker to say that than 'the guy I'm sleeping with'."

"Oh. Okay then."

Was that disappointment in his voice? The moment got really heavy and awkward and tense. She swallowed, sucking up her courage to go out on that limb. "I like you, Evan. I always have—except when I didn't," she corrected. "And I like *this*. What we have and what we're doing. But I'm not in a huge rush for it to be more, and I certainly don't need it to be less."

"I like this, too." He smiled, and it was possibly the sweetest, most vulnerable smile she'd ever seen on his face. She felt her heartstrings twang. "And I like you, too."

This was now officially a *moment*—bed head and all. But should she address it? Was it something she really wanted to explore right now? She didn't even fully understand what she was doing and deep contemplation—much less talking about it—might just screw it up.

She took the easier path. "Sorry I stood you up." She ran a hand down his arm. "But I do feel much better after my nap."

"You do, hmm?" Evan crawled onto the bed on all fours. Once in front of her, he sat back on his haunches and brushed her hair off her face, tucking it behind her ears. Then, holding her chin, he leaned in for a kiss. It was sweet, gentle even, with a new wealth of meaning behind it that caused her heartstrings to twang again.

She deepened the kiss, hooking her fingers in his

belt loops to hold him in place, and Evan's hands eased gently over her shoulders and down her back to gather her shirt in his hands and pull it up and off, leaving her completely naked.

Evan, though, didn't seem to be in any rush. He laid her back, watching her with hooded eyes as his fingers tickled over her skin—cheekbone to collarbone, sternum to navel and hip to hip before reversing course and ending up at her lips. It definitely had the desired effect—revving her engines and causing her breath to shallow. But there was something else, too; something new and unusual and unexpected going on inside her. She didn't want to examine it too closely, but it gave everything an additional buzz.

With Evan taking his sweet time covering nearly every inch of her in hot kisses, that buzz amplified to all-out tremors, leaving her a quivering mess barely able to return his kiss when he finally returned to her lips. In the process, he'd shucked his clothes without her noticing, and skin slid over skin in a hot caress. She reached for him, only for him to move her hands over her head and press them into the pillow. "I got this," he whispered.

That promise was nearly enough to push her over the edge without any additional assistance, but Evan was far from done. It was slow, delicious torture that left her biting her fist and gasping for air as the shock waves rocked her.

When he finally knelt between her thighs, sliding inside her with one smooth thrust, she came hard and fast. Evan didn't let it break, pounding into her, keeping her orgasm rolling longer than she dreamed possible, the intensity nearly causing her to black out.

It took forever for her breath to slow and for her vision to clear, but the sound of Evan's heart beating nearly out of his chest told her she hadn't gone there alone.

Good.

This was new, different and kind of scary. But it wasn't *bad* either, so she wasn't sure what to do…

When Evan pulled the covers up over them both, she figured she'd rest for a little while, then they'd go down to the diner for a late—make that very late, she corrected herself after glancing at the clock—dinner.

She slept straight through 'til morning and woke up alone.

There was a note propped against the clock, though.

When you've got time, I've got time. Have a great show. *E

That afternoon when she went back to her dressing room after warm-up class, she found a huge bouquet of flowers that brightened the room and filled it with the most wonderful smell.

The card read, *And you've got this. Be amazing tonight.*

For someone who said he made a terrible boyfriend, Evan wasn't doing too badly at all.

That freaked her out a little.

The fact she was liking it, though?

That freaked her out a lot.

* * *

Evan didn't expect security to stop him at the stage door. In retrospect, it made sense, but who would have thought backstage crashers would be such a problem at the ballet? The security guard called down to Olivia's dressing room for permission, made him sign in and then *finally* gave him directions down a labyrinth of hallways to a door with Olivia's name and picture on it. She called "Come in," seconds after his knock. "That was fast."

"I brought you your lunch…" He trailed off. Olivia was in sweats, barefaced and reclining on a leather doctor's-office-style couch, one foot submerged in a bucket on the floor, steam rising off the water. "What happened?"

She shrugged. "Stupid new shoes rubbed a blister. I'll be fine by showtime. The hot salty water helps."

Hot salty water on an open wound? "You're insane."

Keeping her foot in the bucket, she sat up. "Actually, I'm *starving.*" She held out her hands for the bag he was carrying. "Please and thank you."

There was another rather ratty-looking chair, and he sat as Olivia tore into the bag. Looking around, he said, "This is not at all what I pictured your dressing room would look like." It was a small room, with the couch and chair on one side, and a table with a mirror surrounded by lights attached to the far wall. A metal bar hanging from the ceiling held an assortment of colorful costumes. The table was cluttered with makeup and the flowers he'd sent last night. But the cinder block walls and painted concrete floor were drab and gray and depressing and he told her so.

"Hey, this is like the Ritz compared to what the corps is in downstairs. At least I have some privacy. And my own bathroom."

"How was the matinee?"

"Good," she answered around a mouthful of hummus and veggies.

"Even with the blister?"

"I've had worse. So what have you been up to? You're kind of dressed up for a Saturday."

He leaned back and watched her carefully. "I went to the ballet."

Olivia paused mid-chew to look at him. When he nodded, she swallowed. "Seriously?"

"Yep."

"You were in the audience? For the matinee?"

"Yeah. You were great, by the way. I couldn't tell anything was wrong with your foot at all."

She looked pleased. "Wow. I thought you didn't like the ballet."

"I like *you*," he clarified. "The jury's still out on the whole ballet thing."

"See, it wasn't as awful and boring as you expected."

"It had a few moments there that were a little tough, but overall, no. And you're just amazing to watch."

Her cheeks turned slightly pink. "I'm impressed. And very flattered you came."

"I thought you were starving."

"That, too." She started to take another bite, but

stopped. "Is that why you were able to get here so quickly?"

"Yeah. I was going to come backstage and surprise you, but you texted me first. By the way, I had no idea the TSA guarded your doors."

"There are some people who like the ballet a little too much, but mostly security's there to keep random people from wandering in just to see what's going on."

She popped the last bite of her sandwich into her mouth and sighed contentedly. "That was perfect and much appreciated. I'll save the fruit for later. Can you hand me that towel?"

Once she'd dried her foot off, she crossed behind him to the door. The click of the lock got his attention and, a second later, Olivia was climbing into his lap, her thighs straddling his.

"Don't you need to conserve your energy for tonight's show?" He asked the question seriously, but his hands were already cupping under her butt to pull her closer. This wasn't what he'd come for, but watching Olivia dance still had a powerful effect on his libido.

"I think I've got *just* enough energy for a quickie *and* tonight's show." She started unbuttoning his shirt as she spoke.

"Good, because I expect my money's worth out of my ticket tonight. It's supposedly a very good seat."

Her fingers paused. "You're coming again tonight?"

"Yep. I wanted to see you do all your parts."

She leaned forward to kiss his neck.

"Is this because I brought you food or because I watched a ballet?"

She grinned. "Both." Her fingers quickly finished with the last few buttons. She pushed his shirt open and ran her hands over his chest. Then she caught his eye. "And, more importantly, it's *neither.*"

CHAPTER EIGHT

OLIVIA HAD CHANGED out of her tutu into a robe and was removing her makeup when the security guard at the stage door called down to get approval for her parents to come backstage. A few minutes later, there was a knock at her door.

Mom was misty-eyed as she wrapped her in a big hug. "You were wonderful, baby."

"Thanks, Mom."

Daddy handed her a bouquet of roses, his big smile saying all that and more as he hugged her. Jory hugged her, too, then made a crack about how sweaty she was. "But you just get better each time I see you. Great show."

"I'm so glad y'all could come." That was true. Knowing that family or friends were in the audience gave her a little extra boost and a real reason to smile.

"They told everyone in the surrounding two rows how talented and amazing you are and how very proud they are of you," Jory said. "It was all I could do to hush them when the Overture started."

"Because it's true," Mom insisted, completely un-ashamed of her behavior.

"Yes," Jory agreed, "but if you keep annoying peo-ple around us, they're going to make us start sitting in the top of the balcony."

"Why don't you go change?" Daddy said. "I'm sure you're hungry." Ever since her very first show, her par-ents always took her out afterward for pancakes. She was too far away for many years for it to happen as often as she liked, but it was something she was defi-nitely looking forward to doing more often now. The family made themselves comfortable as she grabbed her clothes and took them to the bathroom to get dressed.

When she came out a few minutes later, her mom was hanging up her costumes neatly and tidying her makeup table. "You don't have to do that, Mom."

"Old stage mom habits die hard. But now that you're out, I'll get some water for the flowers."

The theater provided a couple of vases just for this reason, and Mom arranged the roses they'd brought as Olivia took her hair down and brushed it out the best she could. Jory and Daddy were flipping through their programs.

"So many pretty flowers," Mom said.

The bouquet she'd received onstage tonight sat in water on the small table in front of Daddy and Jory, ready to be reused tomorrow. A smaller bouquet of violets and daisies from Theo sat on the shelf above her mirror next to the bouquet Evan sent on opening night—which was now looking a little worse for wear, but still pretty. The flowers Evan sent last night were on her makeup table, taking up too much room, but she liked them there.

Mom set the new flowers next to Theo's bouquet. "So who's this 'E' that's sending you flowers?" she asked.

Olivia sent up a silent thanks that Evan signed the cards in the flowers with just the one initial. And while the handwriting was masculine, she assumed Mom wouldn't recognize Evan's handwriting... *Crap, but Jory would easily.* She should have pulled the cards out and hid them away.

She kicked her "getting ready" mode into high gear before Daddy or Jory decided to join this conversation. "Just a friend."

"A *special* friend from the looks of those flowers." Mom smiled as she said it.

"A supportive friend," she corrected. She tied her shoes and stood. "I'm starved. Who's ready for IHOP?"

"Are you sure you wouldn't rather go someplace nicer?" Mom asked. "Evan sent us a list of restaurants that were open late."

Daddy shook his head. "We can't break tradition. Dancers are a superstitious lot."

"Exactly, Daddy. Dinner anywhere else could jinx the whole run of shows."

"Well, I guess we can't have that."

Most of the conversation in the car and after they arrived at the restaurant revolved around the show—the differences between this choreography and the choreography in other productions she'd danced. Her family weren't necessarily experts, but they certainly had a higher than average knowledge of repertoire, thanks to her.

Over pancakes, Jory changed the subject. "We were looking through the program during intermission and some of the dancers have a 'Sponsored by Such-and-Such Company' under their bios. What's that about?"

Just a reminder that she still didn't have one. "It's just another way for the company to raise money." She explained the program briefly, while downplaying its importance and her own need.

"Well, if you need a sponsor, honey," her dad said, "The Bay Café would be proud to. No one needs to know it's your family."

Since that was exactly what she *didn't* want, she was glad that lie she'd told Annie was easily available and believable. "Thanks, Daddy, but the sponsors need to be local. I'm still new in town and people don't know me yet. But after *Nutcracker* is over, folks will know who I am. I'm sure I'll get one in the New Year." *Fingers crossed.*

"So are you thinking you'll stay here for a while then?" he asked.

"That's my plan. I love Miami, it's close to y'all, and MMBC is great. I've decided if they offer me a multiyear contract, I'll take it."

Jory laughed. "*You?* Commit to a multiyear contract? My world is askew at the thought."

She punched him in the arm. "I've even been looking at getting my own place—an actual home where I can have my stuff and grow flowers and things. And when I retire, Miami will be a good place to launch my next career."

"We really didn't realize that when we sent you off at fifteen that it would take you twelve years to find your way back. Not that we're not proud of everything you've accomplished," Mom added quickly, "but it's nice to hear you're wanting to settle down close to home."

"What about your itchy feet?" Jory asked.

She shrugged. "There will always be guest artist appearances or touring troupes, so if my feet get *too* itchy, I can do that. If not, I'm still good. I've checked off most of the dream cities on my list, and that's more than most people can say."

"Most people aren't as good as you."

"Thanks, Daddy. But this decision means that maybe next year when you come and see me dance you won't have to stay in a hotel."

"But it's a tradition," Mom protested, "and you don't need company in your house when you need your rest more. And," she said, looking at her watch, "that's probably our cue to take you home so you can get a good night's sleep. Is it just a matinee or do you have an evening show too, tomorrow?"

"Just the matinee."

"We'd love to see it, sweetheart, but we've got a big party to cater tomorrow evening and need to get on the road early."

"It's that time of year. Busy for everyone. I'm just glad you could come." She meant that.

"I'm staying at Evan's tonight and heading for a meeting in Key West tomorrow," Jory said. "Can I grab you for brunch or a cup of coffee?"

"Maybe. I've got an eleven-thirty call time, so it really depends on how early you get up."

Jory dropped their parents back at their hotel, then took Olivia home on his way to Evan's—which she'd carefully purged yesterday of any of her personal items left there. She didn't like the stealth and deception, but Evan was adamant about it.

It felt juvenile and it annoyed her, but right now was not the time to make that stand. She had enough on her plate at the moment, and there wasn't a rush. She was having a good time with Evan, but for how long? Why stir up a mess if this was just going to spin itself out? If it turned into something else, something stronger, then they'd *have* to address it, and she'd deal with that when the time came.

She waved Jory off, not expecting to see him in the morning. Knowing him and Evan both, there'd be much drinking tonight and hellacious hangovers in the morning—at least for Jory.

Sure enough, a text pinged into her phone as she was getting up the next morning. The lack of capitalization, punctuation and basic grammar skills spoke clearly to the pain of Jory's hangover and his need for more sleep. She laughed, then texted him three more times, twenty minutes apart, just to bug him.

That's what siblings were for, after all.

Evan texted her a couple of hours later, offering to pick her up after the show, which told her Jory had finally gotten up and on the road. It was a nice, bright, sunshiny day, so Jory had to be hurting for his drive down to the Keys. Evan, though, claimed to be fine.

It still sat wrong on her—basically *your brother's gone now, so we can have sex again.* But she told herself there'd be plenty of time to dive into that later on.

After all, this was the biggest, most exciting time of the year for her, job-wise, *and* she had a pseudoboyfriend on the side. Her life didn't suck, that was for sure.

So she should just enjoy it.

Evan left work early on Monday, eager to get home. He'd left Olivia asleep in his bed when he left this morning—which was a new and unusual experience for him—and, according to her, she was going to be lazy all day and he just might still find her there when he got home.

He wouldn't mind that at all, he thought with a grin.

But he had no such luck. Instead, Olivia was on his living room floor, one leg pulled up over her head in a stretch that made his hamstring hurt just looking at it. But, *damn*, she was flexible, and that, as always, stirred up his blood.

She didn't acknowledge his arrival, but then he saw the wires running from the iPod strapped to her arm to her ears. She had a light sheen of sweat on her forehead and chest, and her cheeks were flushed. When he squatted down next to her and nudged her, Olivia jumped—nearly kicking him in the face as she did.

"Sorry," she said, pulling the buds out of her ears. "Didn't hear you."

"I thought you were just going to have an easy day and relax."

"I am." She lay back down and pulled her other knee to her chest, unfolding her leg until her toes touched the ground behind her shoulder.

"And you consider this relaxing?"

"Just some Pilates and stretches so I don't get all stiff. Plus, I can only nap and read for so long before I get bored." She peeked at him around her ankle. "I was planning to shower and get dressed before you got home, but you're earlier than I thought you'd be."

He couldn't help himself. He ran a hand over the thigh displayed so beautifully in front of him. "I gotta say, this is a nice view to come home to, though."

She grinned, releasing her leg and hooking it around his shoulder to pull him closer for a kiss. "You're so easy to please."

He kissed her long and slow, loving the way she wrapped herself around him like a vine. It was a nice thing to come home to. Actually, *she* was nice to come home to. Nice and not at all as awful as he'd always thought it would be. It was something he could get used to. The realization pulled him up short.

Olivia untangled herself with a sigh and a moan. "I'm going to go get cleaned up and changed. I'm hungry."

"For someone so skinny, you eat a lot."

"That's because you keep helping me burn off all the calories. It's excellent cardio." With a wink and a sexy smile, she disappeared into his room. He heard the water running a second later.

There were various bits and pieces of exercise equipment and dance gear lying around, his fridge was full of healthy snacks and the whole place smelled vaguely of Olivia. He liked that, too. Especially how that scent clung to his sheets—and sometimes his clothes—giving him a whiff of her even when she wasn't around.

And he wanted her around more often.

He was man enough and honest enough to admit he was in strange, uncharted waters, but he had no regrets. Things had moved quickly—almost disturbingly so—but it wasn't as if they'd started off five weeks ago as strangers.

Ending things with Olivia nine years ago had been the right thing—he still stood by the intention if not the execution—but neither of them had been in the right place anyway. Now maybe they were. It was worth a shot, right?

As if he'd just tempted the Fates, his phone rang— Jory's ringtone, reminding him of a possible problem ahead, but one he was willing to tackle this time.

Just not at this moment. Not yet.

He took the phone to the patio to answer.

"Hey. How's the head?"

"I don't know what the hell you put in my drink, but

I'm just now feeling human again. I had to go to dinner last night feeling like death warmed over."

"The tequila was your idea."

"Sometimes when I'm around you I seem to forget we're nearly thirty, and I can't drink like that anymore."

"Just keeping you young at heart, my friend."

Jory made a sound suspiciously like a snort. "Anyway…I've got a big favor to ask."

"What kind of favor?"

"It's about Olivia."

Carefully, as if Jory would somehow be able to tell that Liv was currently in his shower simply by the tone of his voice, he said, "Okay."

"She was telling us the other night about some kind of sponsorship thing the company does. Businesses or individuals give money to sponsor a particular dancer and in return, get all kinds of perks the regular donors don't get. Looking at the program I got the other night, Olivia's the only dancer—outside the corps—who doesn't have one of those sponsors. She tried to downplay it, but I think it's something she needs—especially if she's going to get to stay in Miami."

Something crawled over his skin and warning bells went off in his head.

"Dad offered, of course," Jory continued, "but Livvy said it needed to be local businesses."

"How much?"

"I'm not sure exactly and the website doesn't say, but based on what I've been able to research online, several thousand dollars, at least."

"I see. And you're asking me to sponsor her."

"If not you, maybe you know someone who could? She's still new in Miami and doesn't know a lot of people with that kind of money."

But she knew me. "I'll see what I can do." It was all he could manage to say right now.

"I know it's awkward, but…"

"Not at all," he lied.

"Thanks. I'll see you next week when I'm headed back through."

"Yep. Have fun down there."

This was what it felt like to have a bubble burst. He didn't want to believe the dark thoughts creeping in, but they had merit and couldn't be dismissed out of hand. If Olivia needed this sponsorship, why hadn't she mentioned it? The fact she hadn't mentioned it at all—directly or indirectly—seemed glaringly, suspiciously *off.*

All those happy thoughts from earlier slammed into this new information, making him wonder if he'd been a fool.

A few minutes later, Olivia joined him on the patio. She was casually dressed, hair braided back off her face, minimal makeup. She took the other chair and propped her feet—in socks of course—up on a planter. "It's nice out here."

"Yeah."

She looked at him funny, but kept her voice light as she tried again. "We should eat outside tonight. Maybe grill something."

"If you want."

"You could even have a nice steak. Give the chicken a break for the evening." She laughed, then got quiet when he didn't join her. "What's wrong?"

He had neighbors, so he wasn't going to have this conversation outside. "You want a beer?"

"Sure." She followed him inside, leaning against the counter as he opened the beers and handed her one.

"I was just thinking," he started in a conversational tone, "You never did tell me why you got in touch after all these years."

For a brief second—literally a flash he would have missed if he hadn't been watching her so closely—Olivia looked uncomfortable. *Yeah, there was something she was hiding.*

Just as quickly, she was shrugging as if it was nothing. "It seemed weird to be in the same town and not get in touch. And I thought it might make things easier for Jory in the long run if we had a truce in place. And I'm glad I did. Think how awkward Thanksgiving *could* have been otherwise."

"For Jory. Who we're not telling about us."

An eyebrow went up. "That was more your idea, not mine."

But she hadn't fought too hard about it either. He let that pass for the time being, wanting to get his biggest suspicions confirmed or denied. "But why? It's not like we parted on good terms."

"I guess I decided to get over it and let go of a ridiculous grudge."

"Jory says you never let go of a grudge."

"Jory's not the expert on me he seems to think he is." She placed her beer carefully on the counter and met his eyes. "What is this all *really* about?"

Well, he wasn't getting anywhere the indirect way. "I understand you need some kind of sponsorship."

She blinked in surprise. "How do you know about that?"

"Because Jory just called me and asked if I'd do it."

"Darn. I'm sorry. He shouldn't have done that." She shook her head and reached over to touch his hand. "I told him not to worry about it, but I should have known he'd call you."

"Of course he did. He says you need a local sponsor and hey, I'm local."

"I only said that so that my folks—and Jory for that matter—wouldn't try to do it."

"But you do need the sponsorship."

"I don't *need* it," she corrected, withdrawing her hand. "It would be nice to have it, but—"

"And just like Jory, I was the one person in Miami who you knew would have the money. Was that why you contacted me wanting to get together?"

He could almost see the wheels turning in her head as she decided how to answer. Finally, she took a deep breath and exhaled slowly. "Yes, but—"

That hurt worse than expected. "I'd have given it to you, Olivia. All you had to do was ask. You didn't have to sleep with me first."

"*Whoa.* Don't even go there. One has nothing to do with the other." He could tell he'd offended her, but that didn't give him any truths. "I'd gotten myself into a panic thinking I *had* to get that sponsorship if I wanted a contract for next season, and yes, I figured you would be the obvious choice."

"Because of my friendship with Jory? Or because you felt I owed you after what happened with us?"

She didn't address that statement, making him assume he'd scored there, too. "It was a bad plan. I admit that now. I decided—at dinner, after I actually saw you again and talked to you—that it would be tacky to even ask because there was too much other stuff between us. And you made it very clear you had no interest in donating. I let it go and I was okay with that."

"So leaving your phone in my car was just a happy accident?"

"Of course it was." Her eyebrows pulled together. "How conniving do you think I am?"

"Honestly, Olivia, I don't know anymore. I was led blindly into this."

"Oh, *please*. You all but made a pass at me at Tourmaine's. You flat-out propositioned me the very next night. It was clear what you wanted."

"What was I supposed to think? You called me out of the blue. I thought that was what *you* wanted."

"So your feelings are hurt because you feel misled? Or is it because I hadn't been pining over you all these years?" She turned to look at him evenly, and some of the snark and the heat left her voice. "What difference does it make why I called you *then?* It has nothing to do with where we are now."

"It doesn't?"

She pulled back as though he'd slapped her. "Excuse me?"

"Surely you were planning to ask me for it eventually."

Olivia's jaw tightened. "If you don't quit implying that I'm some kind of prostitute, I'm going to kick your butt so hard you'll be coughing up ribbons from my pointe shoes tomorrow."

He'd definitely hit a nerve. "I don't know why you're so surprised I'd think that."

"Maybe because we've spent a lot of time together and you should know me better than that. Or at least be willing to give me the benefit of the doubt."

"My apologies. I'm a little thrown by this. I mean, at least I came into this honestly, with the mistaken assumption you were, too. You know, like mature adults."

Her jaw dropped. "Oh no, don't you dare start tossing out words like 'honesty' and 'maturity' like you have a clue what either one of them means. *I'm* not the one who's lying to my supposed best friend because I don't want anyone to know that we're sleeping together."

"That's different."

"How?" she snapped. "Either you're an adult or you're not."

"You're changing the subject."

"Not really. I may have come into this a little dishonestly, but you're still wallowing in the lies. And you're making me your accomplice when I have nothing to hide." Her eyes narrowed as she crossed her arms over her chest. "Or am I just a convenient bed buddy with an expiration date looming, and *that's* why you don't want to tell Jory?"

"You're not exactly pushing hard to tell him either. I could assume you don't want him to know his sweet baby sister is sleeping with his best friend again when it'll all be over once you get your money."

She slapped him. Hard. The crack echoed in the room. "I'm *not* sleeping with you for money. Right now, I'm not sure why I'm seeing you at all." She stormed out of the room.

There'd been a delay between the sound of the slap and the sensation, but as blood rushed to his cheek, it began to sting. He rubbed it gently. He couldn't get too angry about it, though; she *had* warned him.

He wasn't sure who was in the right and who was in the wrong, but it wasn't pretty either way.

He could hear Olivia talking, but to whom was the question. As he came out of the kitchen, Olivia nearly ran him down in the hallway. She had her phone to her ear and her bags draped over her shoulder. "Thank you," she said and hung up, shoving the phone into her pocket.

Dodging around him without a word, she gathered up her stuff out of the living room.

"You're leaving?"

"Yep," she snapped.

"How? You don't have a car."

"I've got a cab on the way." She didn't have that much stuff, and it didn't take her long to load it up.

"Olivia…"

She spun on him, her eyes hot with anger. "I'm not going to stay here and let you continue to cast aspersions on my character just for the opportunity to be another notch in your bedpost. Not again. It's not worth it." She paused at the door. "And just to be clear… I don't need your money. I'm very good at what I do and *that's* what matters most. But even if I had to choose, I'd rather go home and teach preschoolers at the local Toe, Tap and Twirl than take a dime of sponsorship money from you. Goodbye, Evan." She slammed the door hard enough to shake the frame.

Well, that wasn't what he'd planned for this evening, and it was a big turn from where he'd started just an hour ago.

But what else could he have expected?

CHAPTER NINE

RAGE AND INSULT propelled Olivia into the parking lot of Evan's condo, where she paced while waiting for her taxi to arrive. Her eyes burned, but the anger was too strong to let the tears fall.

The fact there were tears at all shocked her. There was so much to be angry about, but tears meant something else. Tears meant she was hurt, and she didn't want to be hurt. She shouldn't even be in a place where Evan *could* hurt her. But those tears threatening to fall meant she was in that place—even if this was the first time she'd realized it—and that knowledge only made everything worse.

But maybe it was better to know now, before she got in any deeper. Evan hadn't changed all that much after all—*the selfish, egotistical jerk*. She'd at least admitted where she was wrong; Evan couldn't even see that he might be, much less admit it.

Maybe Jory had been right all along, trying to keep her and Evan apart. She'd been too caught up in her own infatuation and hormones to realize that Jory might have sound reasons. Maybe Evan knew those reasons were sound as well and *that's* why he'd been so adamant about keeping Jory in the dark. Jory might have told her more than Evan wanted her to know.

Not everything you wanted could be good for you, and sometimes you needed someone else to smack your hand away from the cookie jar.

In a fair and just world, men like Evan would come with warning labels tattooed on their washboard abs. She sighed. There was no reason to think she'd have paid any attention to a written warning when she'd done such a good job ignoring the real-life examples and lessons she had. Man, she was stupid.

She'd walked right into this, honestly believing it would somehow be different just because she wanted it to be. She could pass some of the blame to Evan, but she was equally as responsible for her own hurt.

Maybe a little more so, since he'd even tried to warn her.

The cabbie asked if she was okay, and after a couple of assurances on her part, he finally seemed to accept it and remained silent as he took her home. She tipped him extra, though, for his concern.

It wasn't that late, but the living room was dark and quiet as Olivia locked the door behind her. *Good.* She sighed in relief and went to the fridge for something to drink. She really tried to limit her alcohol during performance weeks, but the wine beckoned and she gave in. Taking a big swallow, she headed down the hall toward her room.

"Olivia?"

She jumped at the voice, nearly dropping her glass. "Annie! I didn't know you were here. Did I wake you?"

"No, I was just…" She changed tacks abruptly. "I thought you were staying at Evan's tonight."

"Not anymore."

Surprised turned instantly to concern. "Is everything okay?"

"Between me and Evan? No. That's pretty much over."

"Oh, Olivia, I'm sorry."

"Thanks, but I'm okay."

Annie put a hand on her arm. "Do you want to talk about it?"

Did she? Just for the sympathy even though justice was out of the question? "Thanks, I—"

"Annie?" That was a male voice. Olivia looked at Annie, who gave her a slightly embarrassed smile and shrugged. The man the voice belonged to stepped into the hallway a second later. He was shirtless and barefoot and oh-*my*-pretty to boot. Belatedly, Olivia noticed that Annie was slightly disheveled herself. "Is everything okay?" he asked.

"Stephen, this is my roommate, Olivia. Olivia, this is Stephen. We met through work."

"It's nice to meet you," she said lamely.

"And you," Stephen said. "I took my mother to see *The Nutcracker* last week. You were very good."

"Thank you." She wasn't as completely stupid as she thought, because she could still tell when she was a fifth wheel. "Please don't think I'm rude not to hang out and chat, but I'm going to go to my room now and listen to some music. Very loud music. I'll use headphones so it won't bother you."

"Good night, then," Stephen said, reaching for Annie's hand.

"Are you sure?" Annie asked. "If you need to talk, I can…"

"No," she insisted. "I'm thinking a long hot bath and an early bedtime is the probably the best thing for me right now. Good night."

Headphones on and music cranked up, Olivia turned the water on and left the tub to fill. In a way, it was good that she and Annie not talk it to death and obsess over Evan or what he did or did not do. It was what it was. Wallowing wasn't good for anyone, now was as good a time as any to let it go. It had been only a little more than a month, so it wasn't as if she was deeply invested or anything.

So why the hell was she crying?

Although Evan didn't like himself much for thinking it, Jory was really the last person he wanted to see at the moment. He already felt bad enough for sleeping with Olivia and lying to Jory about it—which made it a little hard to face him—but now he had the added guilt of wanting to avoid his best friend. It was a big spiral of guilt, and he didn't like feeling guilty about anything.

And Jory made him think about Olivia—they had the same hair color, same features, same mannerisms—

when he was quite determined *not* to think about her. He felt foolish for not realizing her ulterior motives—regardless of when she abandoned those motives, and more than a little annoyed that she'd think his motives were anything more than protection for all of them.

He might be selfish occasionally, but he usually had a good reason why.

If not for Olivia, he'd be happy to have Jory here. It was just difficult to act as if everything was perfectly normal, the same as it was before Olivia decided to walk back into his life.

And while Jory had spent the week on a half business, half scuba diving trip in Key West, *he'd* spent the week working on *not* thinking about Olivia and trying to forget the past month or so. They were in vastly different moods because of this.

They'd gone easy on the booze last night as Jory was still cussing him for the hangover last Sunday, and he'd stated early on in the evening that he would *not* be doing the four-hour drive home today hungover, too.

Evan was drinking coffee and half watching the news when Jory, freshly showered, shaved and not hungover, came in carrying a cup and staring at his phone.

"Mom says to tell you she's moving Christmas dinner to the twenty-sixth this year," Jory said, reading off his phone. "Olivia has a Christmas Eve performance, and Mom doesn't want her to have to rush home on the twenty-fifth. So everything is shifting a day later."

"Actually, I don't think I'll be able to come this year."

"Why not?"

The surprise tinged with disappointment made him feel a little better. "I've had another invitation."

"From who?"

"I do have other friends, you know."

Jory sat. "You've had Christmas dinner at our house for nearly ten years. If you have other friends, they've been stingy with the invites up to now."

Olivia had always been in another city, usually unable to make it to her parents' until after he left. It had worked fine in the past, but this year...definitely not. "Maybe it's a new friend."

Jory snorted. "Because you make *those* so easily and often."

"Hmm, I'm beginning to think I might have one friend too many right now."

"Mom will be disappointed."

He'd rather have Dee disappointed than horrified. Olivia obviously hadn't said anything to her family about what happened—and he was grateful for that—but that might change if she were forced to share her holiday with him now. If he wanted to salvage what he had with the Madison family, he needed to stay away. He should have stayed away from Olivia altogether if for no other reason than respect for Jory and Gary and Dee.

But he was selfish, as usual, and arrogant, as well, thinking he could have his cake and eat it, too.

"Is it Olivia?"

Was Jory a mind reader now? "What?"

"Y'all seemed okay at Thanksgiving, but I realize now that may have been just for Mom and Dad's benefit. If that was all an act, I can understand why you wouldn't be up for another round."

"Look, I had to tell Olivia the truth about what happened. She deserved to know that it wasn't about her." He couldn't tell Jory the full truth, but he should—and could—tell him that much. There were enough secrets in this freaky triangle, and *that* one needed to be put to bed for good.

Jory coughed. "I'm surprised she didn't come after me with the carving knife."

"She wasn't happy about it, but I think I got her to see your point. You weren't wrong, and you did mean well."

"I'm sure the fact I 'meant well' went over splendidly." He rolled his eyes.

"Oh, yes, of *course* that made all the difference to her."

Jory picked up on his sarcasm. "Maybe I'll apologize then. I never really brought it up before, simply because it was easier not to."

Damn it, that wasn't what he wanted. "She's let it go. I've let it go. Why bring it up at all?"

Jory leaned back and rubbed his eyes. "You know, if you'd been *this* guy nine years ago, maybe I wouldn't have minded it so much. You and Olivia, I mean."

Evan nearly fell out of his chair, but recovered quickly. "I am the same guy."

"Nah. You're not as angry or as hell-bent on breaking every one of your parents' rules. Raising hell is fine and good—and something you needed to do for your own sake—but you were taking it to extremes. And seducing every girl that got within twenty feet of you like it was your mission in life…"

"No one wants their sister mixed up with a guy like that. I get it, Jory. No need to beat that dead horse."

"Want to hear something funny?"

"Yes, please." *Anything to change the subject.*

"About five years ago, Mom got this idea that you and Olivia would be a good match if she could ever get you two in the same room."

Evan choked.

"I know, it's crazy, huh?" Jory laughed at the thought. "She just wants you in the family, and since you're too old to formally adopt, that was her next idea. But now that Livvy is finally contemplating settling down in one place…" He let the implication hang.

Evan, though, was still sputtering and couldn't talk, which Jory seemed to read a completely different way. "Don't worry. I don't think Mom will actually push that idea, so it's safe if you change your mind and decide to come for Christmas, after all."

He coughed and cleared his throat. It was all just too much to even process.

Jory, thankfully, didn't seem to need a response. "And unless you need the Heimlich maneuver, I should probably be hitting the road."

Evan walked Jory out.

Jory tossed his overnight bag in the backseat. "Oh, by the way," he said. "I owe you an apology."

"For?"

"Dropping that sponsorship thing on you. When Olivia mentioned it, you were the first person to come to mind, and I called without thinking it through all the way."

Liv and Jory were definitely two peas in a pod. According to her, she'd done the same thing but backed out before actually making the request. "Don't worry about it."

With a nod, Jory got in his car. "And if you change your mind about Christmas, just give Mom a call and let her know. She'll make you the cookies you like."

It was barely noon and he already needed a drink. The entire Madison family seemed determined to drive him insane—but for different reasons in completely different ways.

It was insult to injury. Had he wanted Olivia partly because she was forbidden fruit? Maybe, but now that she might not be so forbidden after all, he wanted her still.

But he still couldn't have her. What had she said about men she wouldn't dance with again because they'd dropped her? Well, he'd dropped her twice. She wouldn't trust him again.

This sucked.

It also hurt more than he liked to admit, but considering the amount of hurt he'd thrown on people in the past... Well, his dear old dad would love to know Evan was reaping exactly what he'd sown, just as warned.

Call it payback, karma or divine justice—it sucked no matter what he named it.

But he'd earned it. Fairly. Olivia had every right to walk, and he couldn't fault her for doing it.

And it was probably better for her that she had.

The real question was whether he could just let her go.

Wednesday afternoon, Olivia was in the studio working on her variations for the winter special. She didn't have to be there—the rehearsal schedule was cut way back during performance weeks—but it was pretty much the only thing she knew to do with herself.

She hadn't heard from Evan in over a week. She'd rather expected—maybe *hoped* was a better word—to hear *something*, but there'd been nothing but silence. It was both good and bad.

If this really had run its course, a clean break was better in the long run—no need to draw it out. Because the past week had proven one thing to her quite clearly: although she'd let her hormones lead the way, sticking around for good sex and good times, she'd gotten in deeper than expected. Deeper than was wise.

She'd obviously learned nothing in the past nine years because she was pretty much right back where she'd been before with Evan: hurt.

Screw it. And screw him.

She'd gotten all attached to the idea of settling down

in Miami and taken it too far, insanely believing that Evan could be a part of that.

Maybe she'd been dropped on her head too many times.

It was horrifying enough to have her trolling websites from other companies, thinking a change of city might be nice.

No. She wasn't leaving Miami. Not because of him. She'd never let her emotions drive her decisions about her career, and she wasn't going to start now. Not over a guy.

She'd never had to live in the same city with an ex before—at least not for very long—but people did it all the time. It had to be possible. Miami was a big place.

Hell, as long as Jory and Evan were friends she'd never be fully away from him anyway. He'd continue to be on the fringe of her life.

She'd gotten over him before, and she'd get over him again.

She stretched and shook her legs out. *This* was what she was good at. Anger and hurt feelings could be pushed down and forgotten for a while when her feet were moving too fast for her to focus on anything else and the details required her full concentration.

This was who she was. She'd made her choice years ago.

She cued up her music.

Olivia always felt a little deflated when the curtain closed on a show for the last time—even when that show was *The Nutcracker*. Months of work and prep-aration—over. The adrenaline rush of performing, the energy of the audience, the lights and costumes and music—that was her drug of choice and she was a junkie.

And like a junkie who'd been riding on a major high, the crash would come. But she had a couple of hours yet to enjoy the ride. As she left the stage, Theo ran up beside her. "We have a Christmas Eve tradition here at MMBC—a greasy, high-fat, carb-loaded feast at Lucy's Diner. Do you want to come?"

"Sure." Annie had left this morning to go to her mom's in Fort Lauderdale, so she'd be going home to an empty house anyway. "When?"

"It'll take at least thirty or forty-five minutes for ev-eryone to get packed up, but I'll come knock on your door when we're ready."

"Great." In her dressing room, she scrubbed the makeup off her face and started packing up her stuff— well, more tossing it haphazardly into a bag to be sorted later. She'd taken home all but the essentials yesterday, so there wasn't that much to pack.

Loraine, the costume mistress, came in to pick up her costumes, followed a minute later by Richard, the artistic director, who handed her a card and wished her a Merry Christmas.

"And I didn't have a chance to tell you before the show, but we got a call yesterday from a business want-ing to sponsor you. That's pretty impressive for some-one who's still relatively new in town."

She fought to keep her face still and her tone light. "That's wonderful. Can I ask which business?" *We've done sixteen performances, dozens of public appearances, and the* Times *did a big write-up last week. Any one of those things could have landed me a sponsor.* She realized she was holding her breath.

"The Lawford Agency. It's a newish advertising agency, but it's getting big. They haven't donated before, so extra congrats for landing us a new one."

Evan. As soon as Richard had told her she'd gotten sponsorship, she'd known it would be him. Somehow she managed to keep a smile on her face and make the proper responses, hiding the wave of mixed emotions inside her. Once Richard left though, she collapsed onto the couch and rubbed her temples.

She'd told him she didn't want his money. So why'd he do it? Was it a peace offering? Guilt money? Bribery? Payment for sexual services rendered? That one made her feel a little nauseous.

And while there was a definite feeling of relief that came with the knowledge he'd all but guaranteed that MMBC would offer her another contract, it was riding uneasily on top of the other clashing emotions.

She was still sitting there, trying to sort it out, when Theo stuck his head around the door. "You ready?"

"Yeah." She grabbed her bags and followed him out. A crowd of company members were gathered by the stage door. "Wait," she said, reaching for his elbow. "I'm going to have to pass. I just realized I have something I need to do."

Disbelieving, he blinked at her. "At eleven o'clock on Christmas Eve?"

"I know, but yes."

He gave her a careful look. "Is this something you need help or backup for? Maybe a driver for the get-away car?"

"No, but thanks." She rose up on her tiptoes and kissed his cheek. "Merry Christmas, Theo."

"Merry Christmas, Olivia."

She waved at everyone as she passed them and went to the parking deck where she'd left the car she'd rented for the drive home tomorrow. Halfway to Evan's house, she realized how very, very stupid she was being. Even if it weren't beyond rude to show up unannounced at someone's house after eleven o'clock—on *any* night, much less Christmas Eve—there was no guarantee that Evan would be home. He wasn't heading to Tampa to-morrow to be with her family, she knew that much, but that didn't mean he was staying in Miami over the holiday, either. He could be anywhere on the planet.

But she was already pulling into the parking lot, so she had nothing to lose at this point.

Evan's car was in its spot, so that improved the chances of him being home exponentially. But as she rang the doorbell, she realized that he might not be home *alone*.

Dear Lord, would she *ever* learn to not run off half-cocked on half-cooked plans? But unless she was going to ding-and-ditch, it was a little too late now.

Half an eternity passed before she finally heard

him unlocking the door. The irritated look on his face quickly turned to surprise, though, when he saw her. But he didn't say anything.

He was barefoot and wearing battered jeans and the T-shirt she sometimes wore when she was there because it was extra soft from years of washing. Although his hair was mussed and adorable, he didn't look like he'd been asleep.

At this point, she wasn't sure anymore whether she was angry or curious or what, and since she hadn't given a second's thought to what she actually wanted to say now that she was here, they ended up staring at each other in silence for a long moment.

"Olivia?"

"I told you I didn't want your money." The words just tumbled out, unplanned and very ungracefully.

"Well, it's a good thing I gave it to the Miami Modern Ballet Company and not you, then."

"You know what I mean. I never asked you to sponsor me."

"But Jory did. So I did it for him. And your parents. A small way to pay them back for all their kindness over the years."

"So it had nothing to do with me." He shrugged, and it grated over her last nerve. She hadn't wanted to cash in her family's relationship to Evan like some kind of IOU, yet she'd ended up exactly there. Hell, she should have just stuck with plan A—it would have been tacky and awkward as hell, but it would have been quicker and less painful than the long way around she took to get here. "Well." She cleared her throat, feeling like a complete fool. "Welcome to the MMBC family. Your generous donation is much appreciated, and we hope you enjoy the many benefits your sponsorship includes."

"Why are you here, Olivia?"

Such a loaded question. And one she wasn't sure she had the guts to answer. "I needed to know why you did it."

"It's only money, not arms and legs. And as you said, it's a tax deduction, and it's good PR for the agency."

A reasonable answer, even if she wasn't sure what it meant for her. Hell, she wasn't sure what answer she'd been hoping for, but that one left her feeling like a leaking balloon. "Okay, then. Sorry I bothered you. Good night and um…Merry Christmas."

She turned away before she made this any worse or more humiliating. She wouldn't run, but she could damn sure walk away quickly.

"Olivia, wait." Evan caught up with her and put a hand on her upper arm. When she turned around, he stepped back, hunching his shoulders and putting his hands in his pockets, but he didn't speak immediately. He leaned against his car. "Do you have any idea…" He stopped and thought for a second. "Your parents are better parents to me than my own. And Jory's like a brother to me."

"Yes, I know." She wouldn't mess that up for him or damage that relationship, no matter how angry or hurt she was. She was going to tell him that, but he spoke first.

"Then can you imagine how disloyal it feels to want you? Carnal exploration of their only daughter and sister seems a poor way to pay back that kindness. And wanting any more than that feels like taking too much. I'm a heartless bastard, but even I know that's a step over the line."

"I see."

"On top of that, I know that if screw things up with you, I risk losing it all. Of hurting everyone I care about in one fell swoop. It's a bad place to be in."

Lovely. She'd been doomed to this by her own loving, wonderful family. The same family she took for granted.

He sighed and stared up at the sky. "So, yeah, I tried to play both sides of the game and have it all." He shook his head and shrugged. "But I managed to screw it up anyway, which is pretty amazing even for me. I can't have you and I can't be around them without being reminded of that, so now I can't have them, either."

This was twisted, but she knew too much to not see Evan's logic. And it made her mad. "That's bull."

Another slap would have been far more preferable. In fact, *anything* would be preferable to this Greek tragedy. "No, that's the truth."

"If you won't give me any credit, at least give some to the family you claim to respect so much."

Why couldn't she see that he was just trying to do

the right thing for once? "I do respect them. And you, too, believe it or not."

"Then grow up," she snapped.

"Excuse me?"

"So your parents suck. I hate that for you, and I'm glad mine could be there for you instead. You should know them well enough to know that no matter what, they won't turn their backs on you. So drop the martyr act. Either you want me or you don't."

She made it seem so easy. "I already hurt you once. Wasn't that enough?"

"I like how you think this isn't hurting me now."

"See? You've just proven my point."

Olivia's lips thinned. Then she nodded. "Well, I guess got my answer." She turned her back on him and walked quickly toward a small black sedan.

And there it was. At least it was done and they could move on. It was for the best, really. But his feet were already moving in her direction, catching up with her before she could open the door.

When she turned around, he kissed her, fully expecting her to push him off and slap him again, so Olivia kissing him back felt like a Christmas miracle. It went on and on—desperate, but more sweet than carnal.

He steadied her as he set her on her feet and loosened his grip without letting her go. "No. *That's* your answer."

She smiled. "I like that one much better."

"Me, too, but—"

Olivia put a finger over his lips. "Let's just take this one step at a time."

"Figure out the basics, how we move together, before trying the harder stuff?" he teased.

"Exactly."

He grinned at her and got one in response. "Does that mean you're learning to trust me?"

"Maybe," she hedged.

"Then we'll have to keep working at it."

"Practice makes better."

"And I'm looking forward to it."

"IT'S ONLY SIX WEEKS." She stared at the contract. She hadn't gone looking for this. She was happy in Miami. The spring show was only a couple of weeks away, and then she and Evan were going on their first official vacation as a couple. These were exciting, heady times. But now that the opportunity presented itself, her feet were itching to go.

Evan barely looked up from his tablet. "I know. You should sign the contract."

"You could come to Paris and visit me, if you wanted," she offered.

He smiled at her. "Maybe I'll do that. Sign the contract."

She refilled her wineglass, stalling for time. Things had been going so well between them the past couple of months, and she didn't want to screw it up now. Hell, she'd just moved in last week—although that had been partly precipitated by Annie wanting to move Stephen into their condo. He might think she was having second thoughts. "It's just an amazing opportunity and it fell into my lap."

"Which is exactly why you should go." He seemed calm and unbothered by the idea.

"Maybe I shouldn't. I mean, I just signed my new contract with MMBC." *Argh.* The indecision was killing her. "Maybe I should stay here and do their summer stock."

That finally got his attention. "No, you shouldn't. Sign. Go. Summer in Miami versus summer in Paris? Paris wins." He held up the pen, but she didn't take it. "Sign it. You know you want to," he said, waving the pen like a hypnotist.

"Are you trying to get rid of me?"

He rolled his eyes. "If I say yes, will you sign the contract?"

She shot him a dirty look. "Six months ago I wouldn't have thought twice about this. What is wrong with me?"

He grinned at her. "Six months ago you didn't have me."

"And *there's* the ego. I should go just because you said that."

"Exactly. *Go.*" He took her hands. "Yes, I will miss you terribly, but you should still go. I'll be here when you get back. You don't have to choose between me and your career. You can have both."

Both? She hadn't thought she'd wanted both. But now she did.

"I'll probably be ten pounds heavier because I'll

be eating whatever I want for six weeks, but I'll be here."

She leaned in to give him a kiss. "I'll still love you anyway."

Evan pulled back a little in shock. "You love me?"

Ooops. She'd been thinking it, but hadn't worked up the courage to say anything, and now.... But Evan didn't seem panicked or poised for flight, just surprised—and maybe a little pleased. That gave her courage. "Yeah. I'm pretty sure I do."

"Oh. Wow."

"Just 'wow'?" That wasn't exactly a rousing endorsement. Maybe she'd gone too far, too soon.

"I didn't know that you felt that way, I mean."

"Why would I put up with you otherwise?"

"I'm good in bed?"

She pretended to think, then shrugged. "Meh."

An eyebrow went up. "Oh, really?" Evan scooped her up and over his shoulder like a sack of potatoes, carrying her down the hall to their bedroom, where he dropped her on the bed. Climbing on top of her, he said, "That sounds like a challenge."

She was trapped between Evan and the mattress, caged by his arms—not that she was really complaining. He dropped his forehead to hers. "I love you, too."

A happy bubble filled her chest. "Wow."

"So will you go to Paris?"

She felt safe saying, "Yeah. I think so. Will you come to visit me?"

He thought for a second. "I'll come at the end to see your show. And then we'll take a week or so for vacation. How's that?"

"That sounds good." She leaned up far enough to kiss him. "*Two* vacations planned, and it's barely May. What will we plan for the fall?"

This time he didn't stop to think at all. "How about a wedding?"

She couldn't have heard that correctly. But she couldn't think of anything else that sounded like that. "A wedding?"

"Yeah. I'm thinking small and tasteful. Or big and ostentatious, it's totally up to you."

"Wow."

He looked surprised. "Just wow? That's not actually an answer, Liv."

"You haven't actually asked me a question, you know."

He grinned, and it was contagious. And while she wouldn't have thought ten minutes ago she was ready for this, she was sure it was the right decision.

"Do you trust me?"

"Yes."

"Do you love me?"

"Yes."

"Olivia Madison, will you marry me?"

"Yes, Evan, I will marry you." He kissed her then and happiness made her toes tingle. She pulled her head back and made him look at her. "One thing, though."

He pulled back, worry on his face. "What's that?"

"You get to tell Jory."

* * * * *

DARE SHE KISS & TELL?

AIMEE CARSON

To my dog, Akiko, who is really just
a cat incognito.

Thanks for the entertaining attitude.

CHAPTER ONE

ARMS crossed, legs braced shoulder width apart, Hunter Philips stood in the Green Room at Miami's WTDU TV station and studied the woman on the monitor, mentally preparing for the upcoming clash. On screen Carly Wolfe smiled at the talk-show host and the audience. The little troublemaker was prettier than he'd imagined, with long, glossy brown hair pulled forward over one shoulder and elegant legs crossed. Her leopard print slip dress was flirty and seductively short, matching a pair of killer heels. An outfit perfect for the host's live midnight show, but mostly for visually seducing a guy into a stupor of compliance. Every man in the viewing area with a functioning libido was quite likely licking their TV screen about now.

Clearly smitten, the blond talk-show host leaned back in his chair, his mahogany desk catty-corner to the leather love seat where Carly Wolfe sat. "I enjoyed your daily blog accounts of your...shall we say..." Brian O'Connor's smile grew bigger "...*creative* attempts to obtain Hunter Philips's comment before running your story in the *Miami Insider*. Owning a network security consultant business must leave him little time for the press."

Her smile was warm and genuine. "I was told he's a very busy man."

"How many times did you contact him?"

"I called his secretary six times." The woman laced her fingers, hooking them at the end of her knee, and sent the host a delightfully mischievous look. "Seven if you count my attempt to hire his company to help with my social networking security settings."

The wave of laughter from the audience blended with the host's chuckle. He was clearly charmed by his guest, and Hunter's lips twisted in a humorless smile. Carly Wolfe's fun-loving nature had the audience firmly twined around her delicate pinky finger, which meant Hunter was in some serious trouble.

"I don't know for sure," Brian O'Connor said, oozing the easy sarcasm that made him so popular with the heavily sought-after twenty-to-thirty-five-year-old demographic, "but I imagine Hunter Philips's company usually deals with more complicated accounts than simple social networking settings."

A playful twinkle appeared in her gaze. "That's the impression I got from his secretary."

Hunter stared at Carly's captivating amber-colored eyes and creamy skin, his body appreciating the entire package. Physical attraction he'd learned to ignore, but these last few weeks he'd grown intrigued and amused as Carly Wolfe's attempts to get his comment had proved increasingly more ingenious. Unfortunately the sassy sex appeal and the spirited sense of fun was an irresistible combination.

No doubt she'd learned to use her charms to her advantage.

Despite the need to pace, the urge to *move*, Hunter remained still, mentally running through his options for handling the journalist as he assessed her on the monitor. Years ago he'd undergone extensive training, learning how to wait patiently and ignore the chaotic pump of adrenaline surging through his body—no matter the danger. And what did it say about the sad state of his life when danger now came in the form of a pretty reporter?

Hunter forced himself to listen as the host went on.

"Ms. Wolfe," Brian O'Connor said. "For those few Miamians who haven't read your article, tell us about the program Hunter Philips created that has you so upset with him."

"It's a break-up app called 'The Ditchinator,'" she said. There was a second ripple of laughter from the audience, and Hunter's lips twisted wryly. Leave it to Pete Booker, his partner, to choose an insulting name. "Voicemail, text messages, even email," she went on. "We've all been dumped coldheartedly before." She turned to the audience with an inviting smile that called for solidarity among the rejected. "Am I right?"

A rousing round of applause and whistles broke out from the crowd, and Hunter grimaced. His reason for designing apps on the side was to fight his growing restlessness—an uneasy edginess he couldn't explain—*not* to bring about a potential PR problem for his company. Especially with a program he'd created eight years ago during a moment of weakness. He never should have given his partner the go-ahead to rework the idea.

Forcing his attention back to the monitor, Hunter listened as the host addressed Carly. "Are you still interested in speaking with Mr. Philips?"

"I'm *more* than interested, Brian," Carly Wolfe said. "I'm dying to talk to him—if only for a minute." She turned her winning expression toward the audience, and her beguiling charm reached through the television screen and tugged hard on Hunter's libido. "What do you guys think?" she said. "Should I keep pursuing Mr. Philips to hear what he has to say for himself?"

It was clear from the whoops and cheers that the audience was ready to string Hunter up, and his muscles tightened with tension, like rubber bands stretched to the max.

Long ago he'd been secretly tried, convicted, before being

metaphorically hung for being the bad guy—all thanks to another beautiful reporter who had needed her story. This time he had every intention of fighting back...with any means necessary.

"Mr. Philips?" a crew member said as he entered the room. "You're on in one minute."

With the announcement of a commercial break, Carly relaxed in the love seat arranged diagonally to the host. She hoped Hunter Philips was watching the show and saw that the audience was as fired up about his insulting app as she was.

She was no stranger to humiliation—was becoming quite the expert, in fact. And who *hadn't* experienced an impersonal break-up these days? But the memory of Jeremy's insensitive Ditchinator message boiled Carly's blood. If he'd simply broken it off with a quick text message she would have been over him in about forty-eight hours. Okay, probably less. The way she'd learned Thomas had dumped her—via a newspaper article and, worse, to save his financial bottom line—had been a theme park ride of embarrassment, minus the thrills and fun. The Ditchinator took the experience in a different direction. It was heartless, for sure. But the worst part? It was so...so...*flippant*.

And just how horrendous would it have been if she'd actually been in *love*?

There was no way she was going to let the elusive Hunter Philips remain in the shadows, raking in money at other people's painful expense.

The commercial break over, the host said, "We were lucky to receive a surprise phone call today. Ms. Wolfe, you're about to get your wish."

Carly froze, a strong sense of foreboding and inevitability curling in her chest, and she forgot to breathe as the host went on.

"Ladies and gentlemen, please welcome to the show the creator of The Ditchinator—Mr. Hunter Philips."

An electric flash zapped Carly's every nerve, leaving her body numb. *Great*. After chasing Hunter Philips for weeks, he'd trumped her maneuvers by turning up when she was most unprepared. Crafty little devil.

Stunned, and irritatingly impressed by his move, Carly felt her heart hammer, and she forced herself to breathe as the man appeared, heading toward her amid the audience's applause. He wore dark pants and a classy black, long-sleeved knit shirt that hugged a chest too delicious to contemplate. Talk about feeling unprepared. Delectable torsos could definitely prove to be a distraction.

His dark hair was short on the sides, with just the right amount of thickness on top. His tall frame, replete with lean muscle, moved with a sinewy grace that exuded a lethal readiness—conjuring images of a night prowler poised to pounce.

Carly had the distinct impression she was the target.

Brian O'Connor stood as the man strode toward the couch and the two shook hands across the desk. The applause died down as Hunter Philips sat on the love seat beside her. The leather cushion dipped slightly...and Carly's stomach along with it.

The host said, "So, Mr. Philips—"

"Hunter."

The man's voice was smooth, yet with an underlying core of steel that triggered Carly's internal alarms, confirming that this was not a man to treat lightly. But after all the stunts she'd pulled, well...it was too late to back down now.

"Hunter," the host repeated. "Miami has been following Ms. Wolfe's blog updates as she tried several unusual techniques to get you to comment before she ran her column, and I'd like to know what you thought of her attempts."

Hunter Philips shifted in the seat to face her, his intense

iced-blue eyes landing on Carly. A static energy bristled along her nerves, paralyzing her. A classic "deer meets headlights" moment.

Hunter's smile was slight. Secretive. "I was disappointed we couldn't accept your social networking job. It sounded fascinating," he said dryly. "And sadly," he went on, "I wasn't able to use the *Star Trek* convention tickets you sent as an enticement to accept your offer."

An amused murmur moved through the audience—most likely because Hunter Philips was so far from the stereotype to attend such a function it was laughable.

Which was probably why Brian O'Connor was chuckling as well. "Thoughtful gift."

Hunter Philips studied Carly, his brow crinkling mockingly. "It would have been even better if I were a fan of the franchise," he said, his nerve-racking gaze pinning her down.

Mentally she shook herself from her stupor. *Now's your chance, Carly. Just keep it cool. Keep it easy-breezy. And for God's sake, whatever you do, don't let your emotions get the best of you again.*

She tried for her standard disarming smile, the kind that usually won people over, holding out little hope that it would sway this darkly dangerous man next to her. "Sci-fi isn't your thing?"

"I prefer mysteries and thrillers…"

"I'm sure you do." He was mysterious, all right. "I'll keep your genre preference in mind next time."

His lips curled at one corner, more in warning than humor. "There won't be a next time."

"Pity." Those watchful eyes made the hair at her neck prickle, but she refused to back down from his gaze. "Even though chasing your comment ultimately proved fruitless, it was still fun."

The host chuckled. "I liked the story of when you tried to deliver a singing candy-gram."

"That didn't even get me past Security," Carly said wryly.

Hunter lifted an eyebrow at her, even as he addressed the host. "My favorite was when she applied online for a position at my company."

Despite her nerves, and the smoldering anger she was beginning to feel building inside her, she tried injecting a little more false charm into her smile. "I'd hoped a job interview would at least get me personal contact."

"Personal contact is good," Brian O'Connor commented slyly.

Hunter's gaze grazed purposefully across her lips—setting off a firestorm of confusion in her body—before returning to her eyes. "I can see how Ms. Wolfe's charms would be more effective in person."

Carly's heart contracted, and her anger climbed higher as comprehension dawned. He wasn't simply checking her out; he was accusing her of flirting with intent. And the warning in his gaze made it clear he was less than amused. But engaging others came naturally to her. She liked people. Especially *interesting* people. And the fascinating Hunter Philips was overqualified for the title.

"Well…" She struggled to keep her irritation from showing. "While *you* specialize in avoidance, I'm much better at one-on-one."

"Yes." His tone held an intriguing combination of both accusation and sensual suggestion, setting her every cell thrumming. "I imagine you are."

Her lips flattened. If she was going to be accused of using flirting as a tool, she might as well give him her best shot. She leaned a tad closer and crossed her legs in his direction, her dress creeping higher on her thigh as planned. "And you?" she said, as innocently as she could.

His glance at her legs was quick but hair-raising, followed by a look that acknowledged both her attributes and her attempt to throw him off. In contrast to the wild knocking in her chest, he was cool and collected as he went on. "It depends on who the other 'one' is."

She wasn't sure if he was truly attracted to her or not. If he was, he clearly could control himself.

"I'm good with a face-to-face with someone I find intriguing and clever," he went on. She got the impression he was referring to her. And yet somehow…it wasn't a compliment. "The encrypted résumé you sent to my office was interesting and creative. The simple substitution cipher you used was easy to decode, but still…" a barely perceptible nod in her direction "…it was a genius touch that ensured it got passed directly to me."

"As one who seems overly keen on protecting information," she said with a pointed look, "I thought you'd appreciate the effort."

"I did." His tiny smile screamed *Caution! Trouble ahead!* and his words made it clear why. "Though my silence on the matter should have been response enough."

"A simple 'no comment' would have sufficed."

"I doubt you would have settled for that." His powerful gaze gave her the impression he knew her every thought. An impression made even more annoying by the fact that he was right—she wouldn't have been satisfied with that easy getout. "And since I declined your offer of a meeting," he went on, "I'm returning the secret decoder ring you sent as a gift."

As another twitter of amusement moved through the studio audience, Hunter reached into his pants pocket and then held out the tiny object, his gaze on hers. For a moment she detected a faint light in his eyes. Despite everything, he *had* been amused by her attempts to meet with him.

Stunned, she stared at him blankly.

Hunter patiently continued to hold out the ring and said dryly, "I half expected you to show up and request membership at the boxing gym I use."

He almost sounded disappointed she hadn't.

Feeling more confident, she smiled and held out her hand for the gag gift. "If I'd known you frequented such a facility I'd—" He placed the ring in her palm, warm fingers brushing her skin, and the electric current upped her prickly awareness of him by a billion watts. Her traitorous voice turned a tad husky. "I'd have been there."

"I suspect you would have," he murmured.

Carly had the feeling the man was noticing, cataloguing and storing away every detail about her. To what dark purpose she had no idea. The thought sent an illicit shimmer of excitement down her spine. Trapped in his gaze, Carly struggled for a response, but Brian O'Connor spared her the effort, announcing they were cutting to commercial.

During the break, Hunter leaned closer. "Why are you chasing me down, Ms. Wolfe?"

The confidential conversation emboldened her, and she lifted her chin. "To get you to publically admit your mean-spirited app sucks."

He cocked his head in caution. "You'll be waiting a long time."

She ignored his response. "Eventually—" her smile held zero warmth "—I'm going to get you to pull it off the market so no one else has to suffer."

"I'm curious..." His lethally secretive smile returned. "How much of your body will you expose for your cause?"

Clearly he was trying to get her riled. She fought to maintain her cool. "Which parts would prove most effective?"

"I'm open to suggestions."

"My middle finger, perhaps?"

"I prefer rounder..." his eyes skimmed her breasts, leaving

her sizzling "...softer parts." His gaze returned to her lips. "Though your sharp tongue holds a certain appeal."

She considered sticking her tongue out at him until his eyes returned to hers—seemingly unaffected, still unerringly focused, and full of a dangerous warning that left her breathless.

Fortunately the host announced the end of the commercial. Desperate for oxygen, and a break from Hunter's maddening effect on her body, she tore her gaze from him back to Brian O'Connor as he addressed her.

"Now that you have Hunter's attention," the host said, "what would you like to say?"

Go to hell came to mind. Unfortunately this wasn't cable—no swearing allowed.

But if she couldn't speak her mind, she could at least get him to face the music—off-key notes and all. "On behalf of all those affected, I'd like to thank you personally for the creation of The Ditchinator and the message it sends: 'It's over, babe.'" In keeping with their interaction to date, she lifted an eyebrow that was outwardly flirtatious but heavy with biting subtext. "You're quite the poet."

"You're easily impressed."

"It must have taken you hours to compose."

Hunter looked as if he wanted to smile. Whether despite her insult or because of it she wasn't sure. "Only a few seconds, actually. But at least it's short and to the point."

"Oh, it's *extremely* pointy, all right," she said. She twisted on the love seat to face her opponent more directly, refusing to let him get an outward rise out of her. "But what makes the experience *super*-fun is the bulk email the Ditchinator sends, notifying friends and social network followers that you're now single and available." Her smile turned overly sweet. "Nice feature."

"I thought so," he said, as if she was being serious. But

Hunter Philips was the sort of man who didn't miss a thing, not with that disturbingly calculated gaze that bored into hers.

"It certainly is a time-saver," the host said, clearly trying to rejoin the discussion.

Hunter's intense focus remained on Carly. "I admire efficiency."

"I'm sure you do," she said.

"It's a fast-paced world we live in," Hunter returned.

"Perhaps too fast," she said, aware they were still shutting Brian O'Connor out. Hunter wasn't playing nice with the host. She doubted he *ever* played nice. And she was too engrossed in this visual and verbal duel to care.

"Care to hear my favorite feature of your app?" She threw her arm across the back of the couch and leaned closer. His woodsy scent filled her senses. "The extensive list of songs to choose from to accompany the message."

The host chimed in. "The one I'd hate to be on the receiving end of is Tchaikovsky's *Nutcracker*," he said with an exaggerated shiver, clearly for the benefit of an amused audience.

She looked past Hunter to address Brian O'Connor, her tone laden with sarcasm. "Mr. Philips *is* very clever, isn't he?" Her eyes crash-landed back on Mr. Ditchinator.

"Hunter," the man insisted, his gaze trained on her. "And *your* ex-boyfriend's choice of songs?"

"It was an extra-special title. 'How Can I Miss You When You Won't Go Away?'"

Though the audience gasped and snickered, Hunter Philips didn't register the musical slight, and Brian O'Connor said, "Obscure. But effectively rude."

"Which leaves me curious as to why Ms. Wolfe is using her column in the *Miami Insider* to target me," Hunter said.

Hunter faced Carly again. Though braced for the impact, she felt the force of his gaze to her core.

"You don't seem particularly angry at the man who sent you the message," he said smoothly. "Your ex-boyfriend."

"We hadn't been together long," she said. "We weren't seriously involved."

His eyes held hers as he tipped his head. "I find that hard to believe."

"Why?"

"'Hell hath no fury' and all..."

Suddenly she realized he'd turned the tables and the attack was now on *her*. Subtle, so as to not raise the crowd's ire, but there nonetheless. The insinuation increased the tension in the air until it was almost palpable, and their host remained silent, no doubt enjoying the show they were providing.

But Carly let Hunter know with a small smile that she was on to his game. "This isn't a scorned woman's vendetta."

"You haven't flipped the coin from love to hate?" Hunter said.

"Love is one emotion I've yet to experience," she said. Although she'd come close once.

"I'm sorry to hear that."

"Oh?" She feigned surprise. "Does that lessen the fun of your app for you?"

He was clearly biting back a smile. "Not at all."

"Or is it entertaining simply to use your program to dump all your girlfriends?"

"I don't sleep around," he said.

Her brow bunched at his tone. Was he implying *she* did?

"I'm more..." He paused, as if searching for the right word. But she knew it was all for show. "*Prudent* in my choices."

If her lips pressed any tighter at the obvious dig they would merge into one.

The light in his eyes was maddening. "Nor am I vindictive when it ends."

She longed to knock the coolly lethal, amused look from

his face as he continued to bait her. "Trust me," she said. "*If* I'd wanted vengeance against my ex, I would have taken it out on him—not you."

"So why the need to lay your break-up at my feet?"

"It wasn't getting ditched that bothered me." Heart pounding under his scrutiny, she barely restrained the anger that begged to be unleashed. She held his gaze. "It was the method in which he chose to do it. And *you* created the app."

"Yes, I did," he said smoothly.

Her irritation rose. Damn it, his response was so deviously *agreeable*. His simple, matter-of-fact confirmation knocked her accusation to the ground, leaving it less effective. And he *knew* it. "My boyfriend was simply an insensitive coward. You, however," Carly said, her voice low, hoping for a loss of his tight control when faced with the brutal truth, "are exploiting people's callous treatment of others simply to make money."

The worst of the worst. A bottom-feeder, as far as Carly was concerned.

There was no flicker of emotion in Hunter's cool, hard gaze—just like Thomas after he'd dumped her to save himself. Hunter's I'm-in-control smile was infuriating. And right now he was the poster boy for every unpleasant break-up she'd ever experienced.

"Unfortunately," he said, "human nature is what it is." He paused before going on, a single brow arching higher. "Perhaps the problem is you're too naive."

Resentment burned her belly, because she'd heard that before—from the two men who had mattered most. Hunter Philips was a member of the same heartless club as her father and Thomas—where ruthlessness ruled, money was king and success came before all else.

Her sizzling fuse grew shorter, the spark drawing closer to her heart, and words poured out unchecked. "That's a rotten excuse for fueling man's sprint toward the death of human decency."

The words lingered in the stunned silence that followed, and Carly cringed.

Just perfect, Carly. A nice over-the-top histrionic retort, implying you're a crazy lady.

She'd let her emotions get the best of her...again. *Jeez*, hadn't she learned anything in the last three years?

Hunter's relaxed posture remained in place. His eyes were communicating one thing: her wild words were exactly what the infuriating man had planned. "Are you saying I'm responsible for the downfall of human decency?" The lines in his brow grew deeper. "Because that's a pretty heavy accusation for one frivolously insignificant app," he said, and then he turned his small smile toward the audience, drawing them in. "If I'd known how important it was when I designed it, I would have paid more attention."

A ripple of amusement moved through the crowd, and she knew her role in the show had just gone from lighthearted arts and entertainment reporter to bitter, jilted ex—with a generous dose of crazy.

Hunter returned his gaze to her, and frustration tightened its fist on her heart. There was such a feeling of...of...*incompleteness* about it. He'd swooped in, deciphered her like the easy read she was, and figured out just which buttons to push. He was more than an unusually cool, good-looking computer expert—his demeanor was a killer mix of cunning arctic fox and dangerous black panther. Obviously this was no simple network security consultant.

So why had Hunter designed such a personal app? The facts didn't square with the self-controlled man she'd just engaged in a battle of wits. Carly coming in last, of course.

"Unfortunately we're running out of time," the host said, disappointment in his voice.

Hunter's gaze remained locked with Carly's—a gut-twisting, heart-pounding moment of communication from victor…to loser.

"Too bad we can't come back again," she said provocatively, and held Hunter's gaze, hurling daggers meant to penetrate his steely armor, but sure they were being deflected with ease. "I'd love to hear what inspired the creation of The Ditchinator."

For the first time a hard glint flickered in his eyes—a look so stony she had to force herself not to flinch.

The host saved the day. "I would too." He turned to the audience. "Would you like to hear the story?" The audience went wild, and Brian O'Connor became Carly's newest BFF. "You up for it, Carly?"

"Definitely." She turned her attention back to Hunter, her tone silky, as it always was when she tried to control her anger. "But I'm sure Mr. Philips is too busy to participate." Although he hadn't moved, was as coolly collected as ever—God, she wished she had his control—he had to be mentally squirming as he searched for a way out. The thought was much more satisfying than near-miss daggers, but her fun ended when he shocked her with his answer.

"I'm game if you're game," Hunter said.

CHAPTER TWO

A SECOND show. Why had he agreed to a second show?

After a brief conversation with Brian O'Connor's producer, Hunter strode toward the TV station exit, ignoring the corridor walls filled with photos of previous guests as he homed in on the glass door at the end. He'd set himself a task, achieved his goal and won. Carly Wolfe had fought the good fight, but her anger had gotten the better of her. So Hunter should be walking away in triumph. Done. The issue behind him.

But when the talk-show host had mentioned returning, Hunter had looked at Carly's amber-colored eyes that had sparkled with challenge, the high cheekbones flushed with irritation, and he'd hesitated. Her quick-fire responses laced with biting sarcasm were entertaining. And when she'd flashed him her delightfully unique blend of charm-and-slash smile, daring him to a second go around, he'd been driven completely off course. What man wouldn't be captivated by the winningly wily Carly Wolfe—especially after her cheeky crossing-of-beautiful-bared-legs attempt to trip up his focus?

He wasn't worried he'd lose their second round of verbal tag, or that he'd succumb to her allure, because touching her was out of the question. The sexy firebrand was a problem, but one he could comfortably control—because he'd lived with a pretty reporter once, and to say it hadn't ended well was a gross understatement...

There was no better education than a negative outcome. Although with Carly around the view was admittedly five-star.

He heard Carly say his name, interrupting his thoughts, and looked to his left, appreciating her lovely face as she fell into step beside him.

Heels tapping on the wood floor, she struggled to keep up. "Interesting how you were too busy to give me five minutes of your time." The smile on her face didn't come anywhere near her eyes. For one insane moment he missed the genuine warmth she'd exuded early in the show. A warmth that had ended the moment he sat down beside her. "Yet here you are, going out of your way to come on this program, Mr. Philips."

"Hunter," he said, ignoring her enticing citrus scent.

She shot him a you-can't-be-serious look and stretched those beautiful legs, clearly determined to match his stride. "Why do you keep insisting on the use of your first name? To pretend you have a heart?"

Biting back a smile, he trained his gaze on the exit door, feeling a touch of guilt for enjoying her reaction and her struggle to keep pace with him. "You're just mad you lost."

"All I wanted from you was a few minutes of your time, but for weeks you were too busy. Yet you turn up here and then agree to a *second* show." Her tone was a mix of irritation, confusion and curiosity, as if she truly wanted an answer to the burning question. "Why?"

"Maybe you charmed me into it."

"Aphrodite herself couldn't charm *you* into going against your will," she said as she continued walking beside him. "So why *now*?

"The time suited."

She stopped in front of him, forcing him to come to a halt or plow her over. "Saturday at midnight?" Her tone radiated disbelief. "But you must be exhausted after spending the week protecting your big-name clients from sophisticated hackers and designing those heart-warming apps." Apparently she couldn't resist another dig. "I do hope you're well compensated."

Keeping a straight face was hard. "The money is excellent."

He could tell his response ticked her off even more. The slight flattening of her full lips was a dead giveaway. But eight years ago he'd painstakingly begun the process of rebuilding his life. The main benefits of the business he'd started were financial, and he wasn't about to apologize to anyone for that.

"The real question is..." She stepped closer and the crackling electricity was back, heating him up and breaking his train of thought in a disturbing way. "How much has your humiliating app made you?"

"Less than you'd think."

"I'd settle for less than I'd hoped."

He tipped his head. "And how much would that be?"

She planted a hand on a hip that displayed just the right amount of curve. "How far below zero can you count?"

This time he didn't hold back the small smile as she tried to restrain her anger. "Depends on the incentive," he said, feeling an irresistible need to bait her further. "You can try hiking your dress higher again and see how low I can go."

At the mention of her previous maneuver she didn't flinch or seem sorry—which for some reason pleased him.

"What would be the point?" she said, and her smile leaned more toward sarcasm than humor. "You aren't the type to get distracted by a little leg, are you?"

He couldn't afford to get distracted. Getting used by a woman twice in one decade would qualify him for a lifetime achievement award for stupidity. However, his body was taking notice of Carly in every way possible. Despite the years of practice, this time, with this particular woman, he struggled to seize the wayward responses and enclose them in steel even as he appreciated the sun-kissed skin, the silky brown hair and the slip-dress-covered figure built to inspire a man's imagination.

She leaned closer, as if to get his full attention. Which was ironic, seeing as how he was struggling *not* to notice everything about her. "I'm still waiting on an answer," she said.

"To which question?" he said. "If I'm susceptible to a woman openly flirting to gain an advantage or whether I have a heart?"

"I'm certain you don't have a heart," she said, and he recognized the silky tone she adopted when anger sparkled in her eyes. "But you know what else I think?"

Hunter stared at Carly. The bold challenge in her face reminded him of how far she'd gone to hunt him down. He'd pulled his punches tonight, because anything more would have agitated a crowd that was already against him. But right now they were alone, so he wrapped his tone in his usual steel. "What do you think?"

Her lids widened slightly, as if she was having second thoughts. Her words proved otherwise. "I think you're a soulless, cold-hearted bastard whose only concern is the bottom line," she said. "The very sort of man I can't stand."

He dropped his voice to dangerous levels. "In that case you shouldn't have dared me to come back."

Her chin hiked a touch higher. "It was a last-minute decision."

"Having trouble controlling your impulses?"

Her chest hitched faster, as if she were fighting to control her anger. "I have no regrets."

"Not yet, anyway."

"I suspect your reasons for appearing tonight were less

about convenience and more about the free advertising for your heartless app."

His pause was slight, but meaningful. "But I wouldn't be here if it wasn't for you."

He was certain she was smart enough to decode his message.

A message that must have infuriated her more, as her eyes narrowed. "If you benefit financially because of tonight, you should send me flowers to show your gratitude."

The thought brought his first genuine smile. "Perhaps I will."

The muscles around her beautiful mouth tensed, as if she were biting her cheek to keep from spilling a retort. "Orchids, not roses," she said. "I like a bouquet that's original."

She crossed her arms, framing her breasts and tripping up his thoughts. Hunter wasn't sure if it was intentional or not.

"I'm easily bored," she said.

As he stared at his lovely adversary, her face radiating a mix of amusing sass, honest exasperation and barely caged antagonism, he realized why he'd agreed to come back. It wasn't just his inexplicable restlessness of late. Despite the threat she posed, he was enjoying their duel. In truth, he was in danger of liking her—and, with all his money, it was one of the few things in life he couldn't afford to do.

He passed around her, heading for the exit. "I'll keep your floral preferences in mind."

Late Monday afternoon Hunter weaved his way through the crowded, opulent lobby of SunCare Bank. His cell phone rang and, recognizing the number, he answered without a hello. "I just finished delivering the SunCare proposal. I thought you were going to try and make it?"

"*You* have smooth negotiating skills," his partner said. "*I'm* lousy with clients."

"Perhaps because you expect everyone to speak fluent binary code."

"It's the language of the future, my friend," Pete Booker said. "And I might have crummy people skills, but I'm brilliant at debugging our cross-platform encryption software. Which I finished in record time, so round of applause for me."

Hunter suppressed the grin. His friend, a former whiz kid and quintessential technogeek—the stereotype Carly Wolfe had clearly been expecting—hated meetings of any kind. And while Hunter had a healthy ego, was comfortable with his skills as an expert at cyber security, "mathematical genius" didn't even touch Booker's capabilities. Unfortunately what Mother Nature had bestowed on Booker in brains she'd shortchanged him in the social graces, leaving Hunter the front man for their business. Still, theirs was a formidable team, and there was no one Hunter trusted more.

"But I didn't call for applause," Booker said. "I called to tell you we've got trouble."

Familiar with his friend's love for conspiracy plots, Hunter maintained his role as the straight man. "More trouble than those secret silent black helicopters?"

"Chuckle on, Hunt. Cuz when Big Brother comes to haul you away, you won't be."

"I promise I'll stop laughing then," Hunter said dryly.

"Do you want to hear my news or not?"

"Only if it's about another sighting of Elvis."

"Not even close," Booker said. "It's about Carly Wolfe."

At the mention of the delightfully charming menace, Hunter frowned as he pushed through the revolving bank door and was dumped out onto the bustling, skyscraper-lined sidewalk. "Go on."

"As per your suggestion I did a little research and found out her dad is William Wolfe, founder and owner of Wolfe Broadcasting. You know—the one that owns numerous media outlets throughout the country." Booker paused as if to emphasize what came next. "Including WTDU TV station."

Hunter stopped short, instantly alert, and people on the sidewalk continued to stream around him. He hadn't completely recovered from his mental tango with the lovely Carly Wolfe. But the little troublemaker suddenly had the potential of being a much *bigger* troublemaker than he'd originally thought. "The station that airs Brian O'Connor's show," he said slowly.

"One and the same," his partner said.

Hunter forced the breath from his body in a slow, smooth motion, fighting the odd feeling of disappointment. So far he'd thought Carly Wolfe had been blatantly frank about all that she'd pulled. Her moves had been amusing because she was so upfront in her attempts to get what she wanted from him. Unlike his ex, whose manipulations had all been done behind his back. And while there were clearly no rules to the game he and Carly were engaged in, there was a sort of unwritten gentleman's agreement—if she'd been a man, that was, which she most clearly wasn't.

In Hunter's mind Carly had crossed the line into unfair play. Because she *hadn't* had to charm her way onto the show—a thought Hunter had found intensely amusing. No, she'd just picked up the phone and called her father. Making her more of a user than a wily charmer. The disappointment dug deeper.

"The second show is the least of our problems," Booker said seriously. "With that kind of connection she could maintain this public fight forever. Enough to eventually hurt the business."

Hunter's cheek twitched with tension. Firewell, Inc. wasn't just about money and success. It was about redefining himself after his old life had been stolen from him. The pause was long as Hunter grappled with the news.

"I hope you have a plan," Booker went on. "Cuz I'll be damned if I know what to do next."

As usual, the weight of responsibility sat hard on Hunter's shoulders, and his fingers gripped the phone. But eight years ago Booker had stuck by Hunter when no one else had, believing in him when most had doubted his honor. On that truth alone Hunter's business, his success—even the contentment he'd eventually found in his new life—*none* of it would have been possible without the loyalty of his friend.

Hunter forced his fingers to loosen their grip on his phone. "I'll take care of it."

He didn't know how, but it was going to start with a discussion with Ms. Carly Wolfe.

After an unsuccessful attempt to find Carly Wolfe at her office—followed by a successful discussion with a Gothically dressed coworker of hers—two hours after Booker's call Hunter drove through a rundown neighborhood lined with derelict warehouses. What was Carly thinking of, doing an interview *here*? It was far from the upscale, trendy end of Miami, and the moment he'd turned into the questionable section of town his senses had gone on alert.

Hunter pulled in front of the metal building that corresponded with the address he'd been given, parking behind a blue Mini Cooper that looked pretty new, and completely out of place. He turned off his car and spied Carly coming up the alley bisecting a pair of ramshackle warehouses. Her attention was on her cell phone conversation.

His moment of triumph was replaced by an uneasy wariness as two twenty-something males exited a warehouse door behind her, following Carly. Both looked big enough to play defensive end for a professional football team. With sweatshirt hoods covering their heads, shoulders hunched, and hands shoved into their pockets, their posture was either in defense against the unusually chilly air...or because they were hiding something.

Their steps cocky and full of purpose, the menacing-looking duo called after her, their intent clearly on Carly, and Hunter's senses rocketed from his usual tensely cautious state straight to Defcon One: battle is imminent.

Sonofabitch.

Pushing all thoughts of confrontation with Carly aside, heart pumping with the old familiar adrenaline of a pending threat, Hunter reached for his glove compartment.

"Abby," Carly said into her cellular, plugging her other ear as she tried to hear over the garbled reception and the city noises echoing along the graffiti-covered alley. "Slow down. I can't understand a word you're saying."

"He came by the office, asking where you were." Abby's voice was low and ominous. "Things are about to get ugly."

Carly grinned at the doomsday prediction. Abby, Carly's beloved Gothic friend, colleague—and perpetual pessimist—never failed to disappoint. Despite Abby's predictions that it would end with Carly being bound, gagged and stuffed in the trunk of a car, the interview Carly had just finished with the two graffiti artists had gone better than expected. Outwardly they might resemble your basic gangsters, but their raw artistic talent had blown her away.

"*Who* came by?" Carly said.

"Hunter Philips."

Carly stumbled slightly, and her heart sputtered to a stop before resuming at twice its normal rate. Gripping her phone, she tried to focus beyond the noisy traffic and a distant call from someone, somewhere. "What did you say to him?"

"Sorry, Carly," Abby said with a moan. "I told him where you were. It's just, well...he caught me by surprise. And he's so...so..."

"I know," Carly said as she puffed out a breath, sparing her friend the impossible task.

"*Exactly,*" Abby said, leaving Carly relieved his beyond-description effect wasn't just on her.

He was too edgy and guarded to be a charming playboy. Too chillingly in control to play the bad boy. Beyond the iced stare he was criminally beautiful, with a dangerous appeal that was so flippin' fascinating Carly had had a hard time focusing on her morning's dull assignment about a new nightclub. Another earth-shattering story to add to a gripping portfolio filled with articles on the latest club, gallery or silliest hottest trend. But who could concentrate when there was someone like the enigmatic Hunter Philips filling her thoughts?

Tonight, hopefully she could keep her mind off Hunter by slaving away on her piece about the graffiti artists. *Another* in-depth profile article her boss probably wouldn't publish.

With a sigh, Carly said, "Thanks for the warning, Abby."

"Be careful, okay?" Abby said.

Carly reassured her she would and signed off, still so caught up in her attempt *not* to think about Hunter Philips that she didn't notice the man who stepped in front of her, failing to adjust her stride. She smacked into a solid chest, triggering an adrenaline surge that shot her nervous system straight to nuclear meltdown…until she looked up at Hunter Philips's face and the whole hot mess got a gazillion times worse.

While her heart added additional force to its already impressive velocity, Hunter put an arm about her waist, pulled her around, and plastered her to his side. Carly's senses were immediately barraged with several competing sensations at once.

Hunter's frosty slate-blue eyes were trained on the two men she'd interviewed. There was an utterly steely look in

Hunter's face. His lean, well-muscled—and protective—body was pressed against hers. And beneath his sophisticated hip-length leather jacket a hard object at his waist dug into her flank.

Alarms clanged in Carly's head. She was aware she should recognize the article biting into her, but she couldn't place it.

Hunter's words reeked with cool authority as he addressed the men. "I think you two should take off," he said, looking ready, able and more than willing to fight if need be.

Thad, one of her interviewees, took a step closer, his bad attitude reflected in his tone as he spoke to Hunter. "Who asked for your opinion?"

Wary readiness oozed from Hunter's every pore. The two beefy young men looked as if they'd been in a brawl or two, or maybe fifty, but Hunter's low voice remained smooth, without the tiniest hint of fear. In truth, Carly got the impression he was almost enjoying himself.

"No one asked," Hunter said, with an undeniably dangerous edge to his tone. "But I'm giving my opinion anyway."

Thad bristled, but Marcus, his graffiti-painting partner in crime, glanced at Hunter uneasily, as if sensing the new arrival wasn't someone to mess with.

"Ease up, man. We're good," Marcus said to Hunter as he grabbed his friend by the sweatshirt and pulled him back a step. "We just wanted to tell Carly she left her recorder."

"Yeah," the other replied with an even worse attitude. "And we ain't asking for *your* help."

Carly's stomach tipped under the tension of this testosterone-fest run amok, but the vicious surge of flight-or-fight response had finally ebbed, leaving communication possible.

"Hunter, back *off*. This is Thad and Marcus," she said, nodding at each in turn. "I just finished interviewing them."

Hunter looked down at her, his expression confirming that he thought she'd just crawled out of the deep end of crazy.

She held out her hand toward Thad, waiting for her digital recorder. Clearly she was more distracted than she'd thought.

Thad, still glaring at Hunter, began to remove his hand from his pocket, and Hunter's body instantly, *reflexively*, coiled protectively tighter. Damn, did the man *ever* ease up? The hard object at his left hip bit deeper into her flank, reminding her of its presence.

What the hell *was* that?

But focusing wasn't easy with the feel of his body pressed against her, the smell of his woodsy cologne, and his hand curved around her hip.

As Thad placed the recorder in her hand, Carly said, "I'll call next week to set up a time to finish."

After a nod at Carly, Thad tossed Hunter a venomous look, and the two friends headed back down the alley toward the side door to the warehouse.

After a few seconds of watching them go, Hunter said, "You can't be serious?"

"About what?"

"Interviewing them."

"Why not?" Carly looked up at him, not sure if she wanted to kick his butt for insulting her tetchy interviewees or kiss him for taking them on while thinking they were a threat to her. Even with the touchy situation resolved, not a single one of his tensed muscles had relaxed—as if he didn't quite trust it wouldn't turn ugly. Of course, *her* senses were still very much in tune with every inch of his body.

And there were a lot of inches. All of them hard.

Her shoulder was jammed against a solid chest. The arm wrapped around her waist held his lean hip to hers, and his long, powerfully built thigh pressed against her leg. This was no laid-back, artsy type—her usual preference. There wasn't a single soft spot on him. Every part was honed to perfection. And if his demeanor during a perceived threat was any indication, in a pinch his body could be used as a weapon..

With a clarity that smacked her system into heretofore unknown heart-rates, the identity of the object digging into her side suddenly became known. Ignoring the mutinous thrill she whispered fiercely, "Is that a *gun* at your hip?"

It was a rhetorical question, because she knew the answer. How was she supposed to stop obsessing about the man when he showed up going all action-hero on her? And just which side of the law was he on?

Without blinking, he stared at her for a long moment, as if searching for the right way to respond. And then his lips twitched. "Perhaps I'm just happy to see you."

After a split second of stunned adjustment, she rolled her eyes at the ridiculously old joke. "Only if there's something seriously wrong with your anatomy." A spark of amusement briefly lit his eyes, and she knew a comeback was forthcoming. "And forget trying to weasel your way out of my question by assuring me that there is nothing wrong with your anatomy."

His amused tone was intentionally bland. "There's nothing wrong with my anatomy."

She knew that all too well, but she was also perfectly capable of admiring masculine beauty without succumbing to the appreciation. And she hoped to heaven Hunter wouldn't wind up being the exception, because his ultra-cool aura wrapped in hard-edged alertness provided a kind of excitement no man had before. Ever.

Just remember what happened the last time you found a man intriguing and fell victim to your emotions, Carly.

She wouldn't let her fascination sway her again. She *couldn't* let her fascination sway her again. Her career was only just now recovering.

"Who *are* you?" She pulled herself from his grasp and

turned to face him, ignoring her crushing disappointment at the loss of his touch. "And don't tell me you're a simple network security consultant because by the end of that show I knew you were more. And today proves my instincts right."

He looked down at her with the intense focus that always set her on guard. "What else do your instincts tell you?" he said.

That she'd never met anyone like the enigmatic Hunter Philips. That no man had ever intrigued her so thoroughly. But mostly that he was a force to be reckoned with.

"That you could have taken those two guys down with your bare hands," she said, staring up at him, knowing in her heart it was true.

After a long pause with no response from Hunter she debated her next move. She was dying for a visual confirmation of the object that adorned his hip, and there was only one ploy she could think of to accomplish her goal. He was decidedly more dangerous than she'd originally believed, which meant she should pass on the plan. Her palms were growing damp at the thought.

Don't do it, Carly. Don't do it.

Oh...what the hell.

Tamping down her nerves, she stepped even closer, his nearness providing her with a forbidden adrenaline rush. "I think you could have taken them on bare-handed without so much as wrinkling your clothes." She began circling him slowly, not having to work hard at the sensual tone. "Not a mark on your pressed white shirt..." As she rounded his side his alert gaze followed her with a keen interest that prickled her skin. Sweat pricked between her breasts. "Not a crease in your dark pants..." She ignored his probing, assessing eyes, afraid she'd lose her nerve. "Or the classy black leather jacket..."

Heart thumping harder, she stopped in front of him and

began to run her fingers down the edge of his sleek coat, as if to feel the material. What would he do when she tried to take a look?

"Am I right?" Fingers on his lapel, she risked a glance at those oh-so observant eyes, now lit with awareness, and an exhilarating rush skittered up her spine. "Would you have delivered two right hooks and emerged victorious and wrinkle-free?" Tense with anticipation, she began to lift the edge of his coat to get a peek at his hip.

Brow creased in subdued humor, Hunter pulled his jacket back in place, blocking her view. "Maybe."

Good God, he was a tease.

She dropped her hand to her side, the disappointment intense. Damn. The more she learned, the more captivating he became—and the more she wanted to uncover.

In light of everything, an interesting possibility suddenly dawned bright. She narrowed her eyes. "Are you a former crook?" Her answer came in the form of a quizzical eyebrow. "You know…" She tipped her head curiously. "One of those high-tech, illegal hacker guys who gets caught, serves his time, and then starts a security firm helping businesses protect themselves from people like them."

Hunter leaned back against the graffiti-plastered alley wall, crossing his arms. He seemed entertained by the question. Truthfully, he seemed entertained by the entire situation. And he appeared intent on driving her crazy by not answering, along with goading her every chance he got.

"What does your gut say?" he said.

"My *gut* says there is more to you than meets the eye." Carly crossed the pavement and turned to lean a shoulder against the metal wall beside him, close enough to get his attention. Hopefully his *full* attention, without compromising her own.

She had to hike her chin to meet his gaze. Flirting with a

nan your own height was so much easier. Flirting with a guy when you weren't sure which side of the law he fell on...?

She lifted a brow. "Are you going to answer my question?" Not one of those beautifully wrought muscles moved. His ready-for-anything aura was undeniably fascinating. "For all know you're a threat I should run screaming in the other direction to avoid."

Her statement finally triggered his response. "I'm not a threat," he said.

"Then why are you packing a—?"

"I used to work for the FBI."

She bunched her brow, disturbed that her interest hadn't been quelled. And neither had his electrifying effect on her. She'd hoped that learning the truth would put the kibosh on it. Help her focus again. She should have known better.

"And why is an ex-FBI agent chasing me down?" she said.

He shifted to face her, his imposing presence no less intimidating after the truth. Just like love and hate, lawmen and criminals were just the flipside of the same dangerous coin. He said, "To ask how long you plan to use your family connections to harass me."

Stunned, she tried not to gape as a flush washed through her body. Use her family connections? Apparently he was under the mistaken impression her father was an asset to her. And any discussions regarding her dad were bound to get intensely uncomfortable.

She hiked her chin, glad her excuse was real. "Unfortunately I don't have time for a discussion. I have another interview to get to."

His previously amused expression had crossed into decidedly *un*-amused territory, making him more intimidating than before. Apparently he had no intention of letting her go so easily, and her heart sank as her attempt at escape was nixed.

"In that case," he said, "I'll tag along."

CHAPTER THREE

HUNTER sat in the back row of the old theater, empty save Carly, sitting beside him, the crew, and the three naked men on stage, dancing and singing Shakespeare to an electric guitar. *"Hamlet, The Musical!"* was unique enough, and he supposed nudity added that extra edge needed in a town as jaded as Miami. But if there was a god, and s/he was benevolent, this would end soon and he could get back to his regularly scheduled confrontation.

He shifted in his seat uncomfortably and whispered, "When are you supposed to interview Hamlet?"

Carly whispered back, "As soon as the dress rehearsal is over."

He stared at the three actors, bereft of clothing. "They still call it that?"

"They have to do a run-through in costume. Or, in this case, in the nude."

Hunter flinched as one of the male actors twirled across the stage, his male parts a victim to centrifugal forces. "This goes beyond nudity," he muttered.

Her voice held more than a hint of humor. "Wednesday I'm interviewing a participant in the Pink Flamingo's annual drag queen pageant, if you want to accompany me there as well."

He shot her a skeptical look. "What kind of reporter are you, anyway?"

"A lifestyle journalist. I do arts and entertainment pieces."

On stage, the actors formed a brief chorus line, and the image of the three naked gentlemen doing a cancan almost caused Hunter to throw in the towel and leave. "You're a little liberal with your definition of entertainment," he said dryly.

Carly leaned closer, her fresh scent teasing him, her amused voice almost...hopeful. "Are you feeling uncomfortable with the play?"

He stared down at her, not knowing which was worse: the intentionally flirty vibe emanating from her beautiful face or the monstrous scene on stage. One sight scorched his vision, and the other could leave him scarred for life.

She was a manipulator who used her charms at will, yet a part of him was impressed with her courage. A person had to be either stupid or brave to enter that alley in such a dangerous section of town. Initially he'd thought she was the first, but it was evident now that it was the second. And that hint of seduction beneath her pretense of assessing his clothes—all to get a look at his gun—had both tickled him and turned him on when it should have ticked him off. He was dismayed to realize he'd crossed the line. He *liked* her.

An unfortunate complication.

"No. I'm not uncomfortable with the play," he lied, convinced she was hoping the outlandish musical would get him to bolt. But he had no intention of leaving without finishing their discussion. Like her or not, he would protect his interests. He turned his focus to the stage, hoping he had the fortitude to stick it out. "I will, however, admit I'm more comfortable in the back alley of a crime-infested neighborhood."

"Two artistic gangsters are preferable to three actors?"

"They are when they wear clothes."

"I suppose it makes it easier to hide their weapons if they're hostile," she said, obviously amused he'd misinterpreted the men's intent.

"At least I have a concealed weapons permit. I doubt those two did. And I'm ninety-nine percent positive they were carrying," he said. Then he nodded in the direction of the stage. "That's a pretty hostile sight right there."

"Just promise me you won't shoot the actors."

"My Glock is back in the glove compartment." He risked a glance at the stage, wincing at an eyeful of a bouncing Hamlet dancing a Scottish jig. "Though I *am* tempted to retrieve it."

"I never knew network security consulting was so dangerous it required a weapon," she said.

Though her words were laced with her usual dry sarcasm, genuine curiosity radiated from her face, giving her amber eyes a warm glow, and the thrum of attraction settled deeper in his gut. Up until he'd pulled her against him in the alley she'd been just another beautiful woman he could ignore. After experiencing the dip at her waist and the soft curves firsthand, he was less confident. Since Mandy, and with the demands at Firewell, Inc., his relationships had been few and far between. Brief, superficial and uncomplicated worked best.

And it didn't get any more complicated than Carly Wolfe.

Awareness burned through him, reaffirming that his vow not to touch her again was vital.

He pushed it all aside, and said, "My day is typically weapon-free. The Glock is only in my car because I visited the firing range before work."

She shot him a look that went beyond mere curiosity. "Keeping up those skills, huh?"

Hunter's stomach lurched and he turned to stare at the stage, grateful the increase in volume of the music gave him a reprieve from responding. His weekly trips to the firing range were unnecessary, but he couldn't seem to let go of the last routine he'd maintained since he'd been forced to leave the FBI, leaving a massive hole in his life.

The sharp ache resurfaced and his jaw clenched. He enjoyed what he did now, but lately he'd been chafing at the monotony...

Carly must have decided he refused to respond to her indirect question. "Why did you leave the FBI?" she asked.

He turned to study her face. Though she was clearly digging for information, the genuine warmth he'd seen on the TV monitor that first day was back. What would she say if he told her part of the truth? There were bad parts he could share, and there were worse parts he could never divulge. In an effort to protect sensitive information the FBI had kept their investigation of him private. Outside of Mandy's newspaper article about the case he'd been working on, no other information had been made available to the public.

"Off the record?" he said.

She hesitated longer than he would have liked. "Off the record."

"I was stripped of my security clearance and put on administrative leave without pay."

A shocked silence followed, filled with awful music, until she said, "Why?"

"I was working on a case that involved a group of hackers that specialized in acquiring credit card numbers. A branch of Russian organized crime was laundering their money." He took a moment to steel himself for the words that followed. "I was accused of leaking information to the mob."

The pause was painful as she stared at him, wide-eyed. "And did you?"

The words punched hard, his stomach drawing tight with anger. He'd seen the doubt in his colleagues' expressions. The questions in their eyes. Outside of his parents and Pete Booker, no one had believed the truth—not a hundred percent, anyway. Not even after he'd been cleared. So why should *she*? But somehow her doubt took a larger chunk from his already ragged pride, and left him dangerously close to the edge. He leaned closer, and a flicker of desire swept through her eyes. For some reason the thought of a payback appealed. And there was no greater payback than refusing to answer a nosy woman's question.

"What do you think?" he said.

Carly hardly knew him, and had no reason to believe in his honor. But for one terrible moment he realized he was holding his breath, hoping she would.

"I don't know," she said softly, the tone doing little to ease the doubt in her eyes. "Why don't you tell me?"

The seconds that ticked by felt like minutes to Carly, and she held her breath as she waited for Hunter's response. The news about his past had dumped a truckload of fuel on an already burning fire of curiosity, but the impassive look on Hunter's face—so close to hers it was difficult to concentrate—revealed nothing.

And then his eyes flickered with an emotion that came and went too quickly to identify. Finally Hunter leaned back in his seat, but there was a coiled energy simmering beneath the falsely relaxed air. "I think I'll let you draw your own conclusions."

Carly stared at Hunter, quietly sucking in a breath. Damn, the man was determined to drive her down crazy lane. "What eventually happened?"

"The matter was investigated and dropped for lack of evidence," he said evenly. "After that I left the force voluntarily."

From the tone in his voice it was obvious he was done with the discussion. But his response didn't make it clear if the charges against him were accurate, but couldn't be proved, or if they were false. The truth lay buried beneath the impossible-to-ruffle gaze, and her mind kept drifting back to the hard, lethally cool look on his face in the alley.

She cleared her throat, trying to ease the tension. "Being ex-FBI must have helped your business."

He shot her a pointed look. "As much as having William Wolfe for a father has helped *your* career."

The statement was like an elbow-jab to the gut, and Carly's stomach folded protectively into a knot. Her dad was her least favorite subject, and she wished the Shakespeare-singing and dancing men in the buff *had* driven Hunter away. Clearly he didn't scare easily. The next few minutes were going to be rough.

Remember the mantra, Carly. Cool. Easy-breezy.

"It didn't help as much as you'd think," she said lightly. "My dad always insisted I make it on my own." Which she had confidently set out to do, back when she'd believed hard work alone was enough. "When I landed my first job at one of his California papers no one learned who my father was until a year later."

He studied her face, as if surprised. "That must have caused a few ripples."

"My boss was certainly nicer after he found out."

Or he *had* been nice up until she'd made an iffy decision and scandal had rocked her world—both personally and professionally. And, true to his word, her father had never intervened on her behalf...not even when she'd needed his help the most.

The pain sliced like a freshly whetted knife, and Carly clutched her armrest and stared at the stage, grateful the music was loud as Hamlet belted out his monologue, bare-assed and lifting Yorick's skull further skyward with every high note. Her father's approval had always felt unattainable. But if she earned her current boss's confidence, and a little leeway to choose her stories again, she'd regain a bit of the dignity she'd lost after her mistake.

"California is a long way away," Hunter said when the

music died down. "Your dad must have been happy you were hired on at the *Miami Insider* and moved back to town."

Carly bit back a bark of humorless laughter, staring at the stage. "You would think so," she said. "But you'd be wrong. My father thinks a weekly online paper will fail. He's convinced I made a disastrous career move."

Or, more accurately, a *second* disastrous career move. As always, his lack of confidence in her rankled. But after his prediction she wouldn't leave even if the *Miami Insider* did take a nosedive at perilous speeds. She was hell-bent on proving her dad wrong.

"As a matter of fact—" Carly sent Hunter a wry smile "—he's probably eagerly waiting for the paper to fold just so he can be proved right."

Hunter narrowed his eyes skeptically. "You're saying your father had nothing to do with you winding up on Brian O'Connor's show?"

This time there was no holding back the harsh laugh. The suggestion was so absurd it hurt. "My father would never show me that kind of favoritism."

"Seems a big coincidence we ended up at the very station your father owns."

"He had nothing to do with it. I contacted the producer of the show—"

"Who wouldn't have given you the time of day if not for the family name."

She wasn't so foolish as to deny it. "Okay, so that part is true." Having the last name Wolfe had to be good for something, because the parental aspect wasn't so hot. "But Brian O'Connor is a fan of my column and was on board with the idea from the start."

"On board for what?" he asked dryly. "Ganging up on me?"

She blew out an exasperated breath. "You handled us as

asily as you handled Thad and Marcus. And you know," he said, fed up with the entire conversation as she twisted in her seat to face him, "I asked to come on Brian's show imply to state my beef with your app. *You* weren't even sup-osed to be there."

His brow creased with suppressed amusement even as his eyes remained unyielding. "Too bad for you I showed up."

Carly's lips pressed flat as she remembered how he'd goaded her into losing her temper. Was that his intention now?

His intense gaze was relentless as he went on. "I want you to end this public dispute."

"Well, I want you to admit The Ditchinator sucks."

"Fine. I admit it."

She shook her head. "Not good enough. Which is why 'm so pleased you agreed to a second show." She sent him her best winning smile—the one that flirted at the possibil-ty for more. "You can go on air to admit it sucks *and* share he inspiration behind your app."

He leaned close again, a spark of awareness in his gaze hat sabotaged her smooth-talking abilities. "I won't do ei-her," he murmured silkily.

Desire constricted her throat, making breathing difficult. She knew he was attracted to her, and God knew he thrilled her like no one had before. She could never mix business with pleasure again, but a part of her longed to know if she could ver get him to act on his attraction. "Well, then, you'd best be on your guard, Mr. Philips."

His gaze dropped to her lips. "Hunter."

Awareness pricking her skin and scrambling her brain, he repeated obediently, "Hunter."

"With you around, I'm always on my guard." His lips urled at one end. "On guard against your sharp sarcasm. The cutting words. The arsenal of charm. And…" his gaze dropped to her legs this time, kicking up her body's response and then lifted to meet her eyes "…the intentional flash of little more thigh."

"Come this second show I'm going to pull out all the stop to use that charm and get the history behind your app."

The hard light in his gaze set her body on fire, and hi secretive smile sent a shiver up her spine as he said, "Ther isn't a dress short enough to pull that off."

She bit back the genuine smile that threatened. "Is that challenge?"

"There *is* no challenge." The light in his eyes gre brighter. "I will, however, take the opportunity to beat yo again at your own game."

Despite herself, she let out a quiet laugh. The man migh be tightly controlled, but she sensed a playful side in him One he kept carefully in check, only allowing it to surfac occasionally to tease and provoke her. "I'll accept that as th dare that it is. So how about this?" she said. "If I manage t get the answer out of you, I win. And if you can resist me… She sent him her most charming smile—the one that had al ways worked up until she'd met him. "You win."

"What's the prize?" he said softly.

Danger and desire intertwined again, leaving her bod with a now familiar unsettling attraction that was uniquel his. She was traversing a very narrow line—one so thin could double as the edge of a knife. And it was hard to focu over her heart's incessant thumping. "I haven't decided o the prize yet."

"Okay, but I expect you to keep the contest fair."

"What does that entail?"

"Leveling the playing field," he said. "No more capitaliz ing on your father's name as a resource. Which means ou side our second show any and all Wolfe Broadcasting medi outlets are off-limits in your effort to publically harass m into cooperation." The man gazed at her, his eyes no less intense in the dim light, the hint of humor dwarfed by the thread of steel in his tone. "And no more below-the-belt punches."

Intrigued, she hiked her eyebrow a little higher. "What are you going to do if I break the rules? Fit me with a pair of concrete shoes?" She leaned closer, trying to be heard over the music and desperately ignoring the sensual lips mere inches from hers. "Send me an ankle bracelet attached to an anchor and take me for a boat ride out on the Atlantic?"

His gaze was dangerously daring, lit with humor, and infused with an undeniable heat. The combination provided an edgy thrill and a sense of the unknown that shouldn't have had her so captivated.

Jeez, Carly. You really are your own worst enemy.

His smile morphed from mysterious to killer. "I'll think of something."

"Carly, you know you're heading straight for disaster, right?" Abby—doubting Thomasina friend that she was—shot Carly a worried frown as she clomped across the parking lot towards the Pink Flamingo bar. The heels of Abby's hip-length leather boots were more clunk than spike, and her black leather dress with its flipped-up collar screamed *undead.* "After your blog today, Hunter Philips is gonna be seriously annoyed."

"Why?" Irritation welled for the umpteenth time that day, and Carly frowned. "The Ditchinator just hit the top ten list for app sales."

"Yeah, and *you* just used your blog and your sarcastic wit o share your opinion about that." Abby shot her a sideways ook. "Creating quite a furor, I should add."

Carly battled the bothersome regret trying to worm its vay in. "It was a couple of rogue comments that started the rouble."

Abby let out a snort. "I've met Hunter, remember?" She began to weave through the noisy crowd toward the front door. "And I doubt he's gonna care *who* started the trouble. He's only gonna remember where it happened."

True. Because Abby's attire might conjure images of vampires, but who wound up resembling the real bloodsucker today? Carly Wolfe, daughter of the notorious William Wolfe, the ruthless man who put results before all else.

Even his own daughter.

She pushed the bitter memory aside and concentrated on the guilt that had been trying to hijack her all day. When a few of the blog commenters had taken up the virtual vitriolic pitchfork and called for Hunter's blood Carly's heart had sunk. *She* had no problem with tossing a few, or twenty, truth-filled sarcastic jabs in his direction, but the vicious turn of the comments had been awful.

But it was done. Time for the pesky little guilt gnats to swarm around someone else.

Carly followed her friend into the old bar. In anticipation of its fifth annual drag queen pageant every inch was packed, from the scuffed wooden floor to the sea of tables and the long bar lining the wall, crowded with patrons of all ages and walks of life. Instantly her tension eased. It was the perfect place to put today behind her.

But Abby clearly wasn't on board. "I'm worried about you, Carly." Hardcore and gloomy on the outside, creamy sensitive filling on the inside, Abby went on. "Hunter Philips is trouble."

Let me count the ways, Carly thought as she trailed Abby through the crowd. He was irritatingly sexy, intriguingly mysterious and possibly criminal, just for starters. "I just want to interview last year's pageant winner and forget about today, okay?"

"Good luck with that," Abby said as she came to a halt

and Carly almost plowed into her back as she continued.
"Because *he* might have something to say about your plans."

Her throat suddenly tight, Carly peeked around Abby. Her
gaze landed on Hunter, leaning against the bar. She let out
a groan.

Her day had officially gone from bad to worse.

From across the room, his frosty gaze slid to hers, landed,
and claimed her attention—something the man excelled at.
Her body vibrated and her heart thumped louder than the
subdued music pulsing through the speakers hanging from
the ceiling.

"What are you gonna do?" Abby said, staring at Hunter.

Nerves scrambling for cover beneath the force of his gaze,
Carly said, "I'm thinking."

From his position at the bar Hunter stared at Carly, disappointed in himself. Even after today's blog posts, he couldn't
help but appreciate the miniskirt hugging legs that had
taunted him during the first show. The hot pink blouse left
her shoulders bare. And her sleek brown hair was loosely
pulled back, displaying the elegant curve of her neck.

"Now that she's here," Booker said from beside him,
breaking Hunter's mental listing of her attributes, "are you
going to go over there?"

"No." Elbow on the bar counter, Hunter kept his gaze
on Carly as he answered his friend. "I'm going to make her
come to me."

"How do you know she will?"

Despite today's online disaster, despite everything this
troublemaker had put him through, Hunter's lips tipped up
at one end. "She won't be able to help herself."

"Does she have a problem with impulse control?" Booker
said dryly.

Memories of her crossing her legs on that first show and

circling him in the alley brought a faint smile to Hunter's face. "You might say that." His gaze lingered on the pretty reporter—a frustratingly fascinating mix of good humor, determination, moments of genuine warmth…and the occasional sultry come-hither vibe. "Impulse control is especially difficult when her curiosity gets the better of her or she's backed into a corner."

"Dude, she's backing *us* into a corner. After her post today, my secretary fielded no less than ten calls from clients asking about the negative publicity." Booker's eyes narrowed in suspicion. "I still say the worst of those comments came from blog trolls planted by our competition."

"I think our business competitors have better things to do with their time," Hunter said, suppressing a smile, and then he eyed the lovely Carly Wolfe again. "But it's definitely time to forgo the defensive and embrace the offensive." Something he hadn't done in a very long time.

An unexpected anticipation surged, and eagerness permeated Hunter's every cell with the old familiar thrill of the chase. He was looking forward to carrying out his plan…

CHAPTER FOUR

CAUGHT in Hunter's intense stare, Carly felt her stomach rock with nerves as she ran through all her options. Leave. Stay and ignore him. Or choose confrontation.

His leather jacket was sleekly urbane, not Harley-riding-belt-and-spike. Paired with dress pants and a tailored blue shirt left open at the throat, he looked movie star classily casual. And this time when he'd tracked her down he wasn't alone. Next to Hunter a gangly man slouched unceremoniously against the counter. Despite the crowded room, apprehension skittered up her spine at the thought of facing Hunter after today's debacle. He was clearly here to see her, and ignoring him would only prolong the agony.

Because how could she interview last year's winner and enjoy herself with him assessing her from afar, producing the goosebumpy awareness he always generated?

"Let's just get this over with," she finally said to Abby.

Carly forced her feet in his direction, her nerves stretching tighter with every step. As she drew near, she managed a bright smile.

"Mr. Philips." She stopped in front of the two men. "Amazing how I keep running into you. If I'd known you were coming I would have worn a shorter skirt."

"Pity I didn't call you ahead."

"This doesn't seem like a place you'd usually hang out," Carly said. "Are you here to compete in the pageant?"

Hunter's gaze swept across the room and landed on a contestant—a drag queen sporting a figure-hugging miniskirt and a pair of killer wedge shoes even Carly would be afraid to wear lest she break an ankle. "My collection of miniskirts isn't up to the task," he said dryly. A second participant joined the first, sporting a Marilyn Manson look made of red latex. Hunter turned his iced blue eyes back on Carly. "Interesting job you have."

"I'm trying to convince my boss to expand my column to include interesting community members." Her smile grew bigger as she stepped closer. "Today I proposed I do a story on you. She said no, but I think once she watches our second show she'll change her mind." Ignoring his disconcertingly alert eyes, she leaned close, hoping to get a rise out of him. "I don't think she'll be able to resist the fascinating Hunter Philips."

His cool demeanor didn't budge. "Unfortunately she'll have to."

Carly stared at him. Was he furiously irate, mildly fuming or calmly annoyed at her for her blog post today? Damn it, she shouldn't care. All she wanted was to interview last year's drag queen winner, move past the ridiculous remorse and get her confident mojo back.

"If you're so eager for my company you could just ask me out," she said. "Instead you keep hunting me down." She finally tore her gaze from Hunter to his scraggy brown-haired friend, eyeing him curiously. He wore a gaming T-shirt emblazoned with the words 'Carpe Noctem'—Seize the Night—well-worn jeans, and ratty athletic shoes. "And this time you brought backup too. How very FBI of you."

Hunter ignored her quip and nodded at Abby, as if he remembered her, before training his eyes on Carly. "Abby,

Carly—meet Pete Booker," he said, tipping his head in his friend's direction. "Conspiracy theorist, computer genius, and—" he held Carly's gaze as that secretive smile appeared "—my business partner."

Unwanted remorse bloomed bigger in Carly's gut as polite greetings were exchanged around her. Great, now she was looking at *two* reasons to feel guilty. Pete was cute, in a boyish kind of way that defied his description. Juxtaposed with the coiled, darker edges of his partner, he appeared downright innocent. And both men were looking at her with veiled accusation.

"I suppose your presence tonight is in response to the discussion on my blog," she said.

"Discussion? The dialogue after your post was more like a…" Hunter's voice died out, and he looked to his partner as if he needed help.

Carly knew very well he didn't.

"Firing line?" Pete suggested helpfully.

"Bloodbath," Hunter said.

"Or maybe a feeding frenzy?" his partner went on.

Hunter said, "Better still—"

"No need to go at it all night, boys," Carly said dryly. She blinked back the wave of regret that had swelled the moment they'd started their repartee, but a small resigned sigh still escaped. "That wasn't my intent."

Despite the surrounding chatter, the electrically charged atmosphere popped. Two pairs of eyes were trained on her. Carly was only concerned with one set. Hunter's.

"What *was* your intent?" Hunter's voice was deceptively soft, with the same steely tone as when he'd faced the threat in the alley. "To lose our bet?" he said.

Her smile grew tight. "I'm sure the money your app is now making will make up for today's below-the-belt punch."

"Except *now* I'm getting called by every journalist in

town," he said, and then he lifted a brow with the first hint of amusement of the evening. "And it's not my fault your efforts have shot the app sales to number ten."

"Eight," she said.

He hiked a brow. "Even better."

Oh, he knew the number. Carly's lips flattened, which made maintaining her fake smile difficult. "I should probably thank you for the flowers you sent me today, expressing your appreciation." When the delivery boy had dropped the bouquet off at work, there had been no way Carly could receive the smugly sent flowers without retaliating via her blog. "But I won't."

Hunter's eyes lit with full-on humor now. "I hope the orchid and miniature bamboo arrangement I sent was unique enough for you."

Her mouth tightened. He *would* remember her words and get it just right. Just like he'd remembered her mention of tonight's pageant. Boy, he was the first man in her life to really muck with her mojo. Carly's lips compressed further, practically blocking bloodflow now, but she managed to bite out, "They were beautiful too."

As Carly maintained Hunter's gaze the tension blanketing their small foursome reached a smothering capacity until Abby broke the spell.

"Hey," Abby said, "you two are killing my end-of-the-workday happy place." With a less than happy frown on her black-lipsticked mouth, Abby turned to Pete Booker. "I'm going to enjoy a drink at a table that just opened up. You can join me if you want. And when you say no could you at least send the message via The Ditchinator to *abby_smiles@gmail.com?*" With that, Abby headed toward the empty table.

"Uh…" An awkward expression crept up the brown-haired man's face, and his gaze shifted from the back of Carly's creature-of-the-night friend to Hunter, and then to Carly. Most likely he was trying to decide which was worse—sharing a drink with a pessimistic lady simply dressed like a vampire or the two people who were actually going for each other's throats. "Excuse me," he said, and then headed off to join Abby.

Hunter watched the two with curious interest. "She doesn't bite, does she?"

"Trust me," Carly said, maneuvering into the empty spot at the bar left by Hunter's partner. "She's all doom-and-gloom bark on the outside and no bite on the inside."

"Does she write for the lifestyle section too?"

"No. She's an investigative reporter. Me..." Carly gave a slight shrug. "I find people more interesting than facts."

"Like the renowned photojournalist turned California State Senator Thomas Weaver?"

The name cuffed her on the cheek with all the force of a full-on slap, and Carly's face burned. "You've been checking up on me again."

"You haven't left me any choice." His face had an expression she'd never seen before: curiosity. "The news media speculated you fell for the senator and gave him a free pass in your article. Is it true?"

Guilt and humiliation resurfaced, and she curled her nails against her palm. She hadn't completely fallen under Thomas Weaver's spell, as accused, but she'd cared about him. Had her actions been unethical? Technically, no. Her story had been done and published *before* they'd gotten involved. Inappropriate? Probably. Stupid? Most definitely. Because she should have avoided even the appearance of a conflict of interest. Something William Wolfe, founder and CEO of Wolfe News, Broadcasting—procreator and father of Carly Wolfe, The Disappointment—never let his daughter forget.

"I didn't fall in love." She hiked her chin. "It was closer

to a very intense like." He tipped his head in humor, and she went on. "And I didn't give him a free pass."

"I didn't think so."

She was surprised and pleased he believed her, but the feeling of validation ended when his enigmatic smile returned.

"Did you sleep with him before or after you got his story?" he said.

Her angry retort was cut off when someone squeezed into the space behind her, pressing her forward…and against Hunter's hip. A firestorm of messages bombarded her: heat, steel and a hard-edged awareness. A faint flicker of eyelids was Hunter's only reaction.

"And I wonder…" His voice was low, controlled, the scent of his woodsy cologne subtle. "If I slept with you, would you drop your little vendetta?"

Along with anger, a fierce thrill seared her veins. All from a suggestive comment meant to provoke. Despite his words, she knew he was too self-controlled to follow through on his suggestion. God help her if he ever did. She struggled to maintain a bland tone. "Depends on how good you are."

"Compared to who?"

"Everyone else."

His intense gaze held a hint of amusement. "Hopefully that's not as many as the number of stories you've written."

"Did you come tonight to insult me?"

Someone bumped Carly from behind, pushing her more firmly against Hunter, and he cupped the back of her shoulder to steady her. Every blood vessel in her body grew thick, the blood forced to pulse in jetstream fashion. His hand was warm and seductively smooth, free from calluses that would snag her skin during a caress.

"I didn't come to insult you," he said, staring down at her, his eyes lit with definite humor now. Was he amused by her attempt to continue breathing despite their contact? "That's your MO, not mine," he said.

Carly stared up at Hunter's sensual mouth, the square cut jaw, and eyes that were either icy fire or fiery ice. Carly wasn't sure which. Her voice was strained. "Then why are you here?"

"I came to give you fair warning," he said.

All sorts of warnings were ringing in her head. Professional ones. Personal ones...

She knew she should reply, but the sizzling feel of his palm cradling her from behind was fascinatingly protective and yet unyieldingly hard at the same time. She finally pushed the words past her tight throat. "Fair warning?" A repeat of his last two words was all she could manage.

Brilliant. Now you sound like a stupid, mindless parrot.

His gaze scanned her face. "Maybe putting you on notice is a better description."

Her mind spun. On notice about what? That her body was turning traitor? Trumped by her own libido. *Damn.* As if she wasn't already privy to that disturbing piece of news. She stared up at him, fascinated by the restrained, coiled stillness of the body pressed against hers. Outside an electrifying gaze alive with awareness, and a hard chest that slowly rose and fell—a marked contrast to her increasingly shorter gasps—he didn't move. No swooping in for a kiss, pushing his advantage.

And a very small part of her was...disappointed.

"Notice?" she said, dismayed she was down to single-word responses.

Hunter leaned forward to speak at her ear, his voice low, her pulse pounding.

"You started this war, Carly." The shimmer of his breath on her cheek sent a fresh wave of hot prickles down her back. "I just hope you're ready for the fight."

Without warning he turned and headed off, leaving Carly reeling in the aftermath. And with the sinking feeling he'd just become infinitely more dangerous.

Saturday night, Hunter turned into the WTDU TV station's parking garage, dark save the lights hanging from the concrete beams overhead. He pulled into a space, turned off his car, and sat back in the leather seat, settling in to wait. He'd shown up early with the plan of catching Carly before she entered the studio for the show.

The thought of seeing her again wound Hunter's insides tight. He struggled with the now familiar combination of distrust, amusement, and ever-growing attraction. In the theater, her fascination with his past had been unmistakable…even as she'd questioned his relationship with the mob.

His lips twisted wryly. Carly Wolfe was an unusual woman. With her around, boredom was certainly no longer an issue. At first it had been easy to write her off as nothing more than a vindictive, publicity-driven journalist. But he'd seen her remorse over the results of her blog. He'd thought her outraged innocence during the first show was an act, but this confident, modern woman had a kernel of naivety at her core. He was beginning to realize she truly believed in what she was doing. Worse, her zest for the unusual—and unfortunately for her *job*—made her all the more attractive. He couldn't remember the last time he'd felt so passionately about something.

Before his ex had gotten her story and left? Before he'd been forced out of the FBI? The memories still felt like a vacuum, threatening to suck him down. Unfortunately there was no telling what Carly would say on the show about his app, or in an attempt to learn the inspiration behind its creation…

His insides churned at the memory. But that had been eight years ago, and some things were best forgotten. He'd been stripped of his gullibility, so he needed to do what he did best. Focus. Concentrate. And protect what was his.

The problem he'd been mulling over the last few days was how to throw Carly Wolfe off her game. She was too quick to be bested during the most heated of banter, and she had no qualms about using every weapon at her disposal. Unfortunately she was also getting harder and harder to provoke.

Drumming his fingers on the steering wheel, he remembered the mute look on her face when they'd collided at the bar. For a moment her confidence had wavered, and the confused, dumbfounded expression that had followed had been the most telling of all. Apparently the wily Ms. Wolfe was as susceptible to their attraction as she'd hoped *he'd* be.

She might be a beautiful woman, and hot enough to melt the deepest winter chill, but he hadn't suffered at the hands of his ex without taking away a few hard-earned lessons. Attraction, the electric pull between them, was something he was certain he could control. And to date it was also the only thing that had truly shattered Carly's sassy confidence.

If he had to go toe-to-toe with her on the talk show, then he was going to utilize his every advantage. If he upped his game and started *truly* coming on to her he might throw her off kilter—at least enough to keep the loaded banter, and the *questions*, under his control.

Pleasure sluiced down his spine, heating vital parts, as he contemplated pursuing the lovely Carly Wolfe. But hot on its heels was the vague impression that what he was about to do was reminiscent of the stunt his ex had pulled.

Doubt fisted in his stomach—and then he saw Carly's Mini Cooper pull into the garage and park. She exited her car, and instead of fresh and flirty tonight she was dressed to kill—namely, to kill him. And any qualms he'd had regarding his strategy died.

Her silver-sequined halter top sparkled in the light, her

tiny skirt exposed fabulous legs, and the expanse of tan skin on display was truly impressive as she headed his way. Heart pumping appreciatively in response, now looking forward to his plan, Hunter slid out of his car, shutting the door behind him. The slam echoed in the concrete garage, capturing Carly's attention. And when she caught his gaze, she froze.

Yes, he was going to enjoy besting Carly Wolfe at her own game.

Surprise, intense caution and awareness hit Carly at the sight of Hunter leaning against his car, hands in his pockets. Given his parting words to her Wednesday night, the twirl of excitement in her belly was totally inappropriate—because she couldn't afford to be less than her best.

His tone was smooth, low. "You ready for another show?"

The comment was drenched in undertones, conjuring memories of the bar, but Carly ignored the hot curl of awareness. "Interesting choice of attire for a fight." She stepped closer, taking in his exquisitely cut black suit. The white dress shirt, minus a tie and open at the collar, gave him the perfect blend of elegant evening attire with a casual attitude. "Tonight could get messy," she said. "I hope you're wearing a bulletproof vest beneath that expensive outfit."

His mouth didn't smile, but his eyes did. "I suspect it *will* get messy."

The unknown promise in his gaze left her a little uneasy, and a whole lot disturbed. What trick did he have up his sleeve? The question had haunted her since his warning at the bar, and her heart thumped as all sorts of possibilities flitted through her head.

Just don't go getting all flustered when he flashes those cool blue eyes in your direction, Carly.

"Unfortunately I left my Kevlar-coated vest at home," he said.

She resumed her walk in his direction. "Too bad for you."

"Will you be slaying me with your words or your gaze?"

"Both." She came to a stop in front of him and leaned back against the car parked beside his. "Maybe white wasn't an appropriate choice of a shirt for you," she said with a smile she hoped looked confident. "Bloodstains being so hard to remove and all."

"I know. I had to throw away the one I wore the day of your blog."

"Are we still discussing that?"

"With one difference," he said.

"Which is?"

"At first I thought you'd enjoyed the bloodbath." His gaze held hers. "But after our discussion at the bar I realized I was wrong." He tipped his head, his eyes focused intently on her. "I think the potential for such a vindictive backlash against me never crossed your mind."

It hadn't. Then again, Thomas cutting her loose to save himself had come as a shock too. But that hadn't been nearly as devastating as her father's silence when she'd needed his support.

She stared up at Hunter as she fought the depressing memories, her heart beating a little bit harder. "You know, a part of me hates that you're right. But a part of me is proud too. Yes, I'd expected a healthy online debate, not a mean-spirited, vindictive slug-fest." She crossed her arms. "But if being naive means I reserve negative judgment until I've been proven wrong, it's a label I'm willing to live with."

"The trouble with your approach is that you experience a whole lot of bad."

"The trouble with your cynical view is you miss out on a whole lot of good."

He studied her for a moment, as if considering her words, and then his forehead crinkled in suppressed amusement.

"Maybe the answer to that particular dilemma lies in whether the water in the glass at the midway mark is worth drinking or not." He paused before going on, his voice a fraction lower, bordering on...*husky*. "And how thirsty you are."

The way he was looking at her made her sit up and take notice—even more than she had when she'd first laid eyes on his casually elegant self. He seemed different. She couldn't put her finger on how, except his demeanor was less distant than usual. More approachable. With a faint hint of sensual promise that left her on edge. And she realized since his fateful words at their last meeting she'd expected him to arrive tonight with all his metaphorical guns blazing. Instead, there was a distinct suggestion of something infinitely more subtle, almost...seductive.

Worry and desire slithered up her limbs, and she tucked her hands behind her back, hoping to quiet her damp palms and now fidgety fingers.

His secretive smile was small but instantaneous. "I'm making you nervous."

It wasn't a question, and that fact alone made the tension worse. How could she prepare for a fight when she had no idea what his plans were? But a part of her knew, and her heart tripped faster at the thought even as she grew disgusted with her inability to control the excitement. A heated flush filled her body. "Was reading body language part of your training, Mr. Agent Man?"

"*Ex*-Agent Man," he corrected.

She tipped her head, giving the words consideration as she slowly shook her head. "There's nothing ex about you. You have a very natural way with your understated powers of intimidation."

"I don't believe in bullying people. I'm just very sure of the choices I make in life. If that intimidates others..." He gave a slight shrug.

She hiked a brow meaningfully. "You're very sure of *all* your choices?"

He stared at her as if the question had hit home, his face momentarily doubtful, but then he seemed to recover. "Reading people is a skill I still use every day. Interpreting body language is useful while pitching a proposal to a potential client. It can help you tailor your presentation to make the most impact."

"That must give you an advantage over your techie competition."

"And others."

Did he mean her? He took a step forward. His eyes zeroed in on her face, and her stomach tightened into a smaller knot. Which conveniently made navigating its trip to her toes easier.

"Take you, for instance," he said.

Unfortunately right now she was wishing he would, but she pushed the mutinous thought aside as he went on.

"Placing your hands behind your back is a sign you're hiding something and on your guard," he said. "Advantage point...mine."

He leaned closer, his gaze too close for comfort as he scanned her face.

"You're breathing faster than usual, you have small beads of sweat on your upper lip, and your pupils are dilated."

She suspected he was right, because her eyes were so busy trying to take in every aspect of his handsome face that they were straining mightily—refusing to miss a thing. Every sharp plane, every angular edge was heightened in the play of shadow in the light.

He said, "Advantage to me again. Because it either denotes anxiety..." the loaded pause killed her "...or desire."

Her body sizzled with heat, yet she succeeded in sounding as cool as he did. "Mr. Philips, is this a lawman's way of coming on to a woman?"

"Ex-lawman." His lips tipped into a lopsided grin that was the most delicious Hunter smile to date. "And I'm just being observant," he went on smoothly.

A wave of heat left goosebumps on her arms. Her skin resembled a cobblestoned street.

No doubt he could see those too.

"Maybe I should remind you that women don't sweat." She cocked her head when he opened his mouth to respond. "And I don't like the term 'glow' either," she said.

"What do you prefer?"

"I prefer incandescence."

Before she could react, Hunter reached up and placed a finger at the corner of her mouth. Eyes wide, Carly stared up at him as he slowly stroked the skin above her lip...curling her toes as he went. A feat she would have sworn was a myth until this very moment, but her toenails were busy trying to dig a hole into her high heels. Hunter's finger dipped lightly into the groove bisecting the middle of her mouth, slicking away the few dots of sweat that were immediately replaced by others. Her heart pumped overly heated blood that surely had her glowing by now.

Damn him, he was right. She was drowning in both anxiety *and* desire. Her breaths came in short, tight increments that sounded embarrassingly like small gasps. As she stared up at him Carly's mind ran through every reason—and there were many—why she should step away. Despite her previous attempts at flirting Hunter had hung back, watching her with cool eyes, a hands-off attitude, and that emotional wall that was always present. Only a fool would believe he'd suddenly changed his mind. And William Wolfe hadn't raised a fool.

So why was she standing here, frozen like an idiot? She knew very well this was part of some master plan he'd cooked up. Had the partners at Firewell Inc. met, given the matter consideration and then voted unanimously to muck with her mind?

His eyes crinkled in muted humor. Clearly enjoying his effect on her, Hunter said, "You're definitely incandescent now."

Paralyzed by the sensual havoc he created, breathing was all she could manage as he cupped her jaw and finally placed his mouth on hers. Carly's heart thumped in her chest as her body concentrated on the hand on her face, and the lips that slanted softly, yet insistently, over hers. The rest of his body remained disengaged. Only his warm palm and warmer mouth were involved. With just enough restrained heat to melt her tenuous reserve. Until she was kissing him back, her mind whirling from the barrage of emotions.

Doubt. Distrust. And a whole lot of desire.

Being the dominant one of the three, desire seized her in its grasp, and Carly placed her palms on his chest, frustrated by the distance. Longing to feel the hard length of his body again. Why didn't he pull her closer? Even worse, why was she mad that he didn't?

She pulled her mouth from his, her breathing labored, and stared up at the slate-blue eyes. "You're holding back, G-Man." The need to feel more was driving her on, despite the embarrassing knowledge the whole thing was a ploy. "That's no way to seduce a woman."

"Maybe my goal was to frustrate, not seduce."

Desire still pulsed through her body, but her mouth went flat, the moisture left from his lips momentarily disrupting her thoughts. "Score one for the former FBI agent and his tactics," she said, as lightly as she could.

But now she was doubly annoyed. At him for being so damn honest it forced her to confront just how caught up in the moment she'd been, and how easy it was for him to maintain his distance. That emotional wall was just as frustrating when it was a sensual one. But mostly she was annoyed at herself, for knowing all of the above and *still* being so turned on she could barely think beyond the feel of his smooth shirt, the hard plane of muscle beneath her hand.

Gazes locked, she pressed on his chest. "Your mission was a success." If he wanted to resist her efforts he didn't let on, allowing her to push him back until she'd trapped him against his car.

"Feeling frustrated already?" he said.

In every way imaginable. "Very."

"Now you know how it feels."

Why was she so ticked about his control? She ignored the crippling doubt, beat back the voice that kept telling her to walk away...and popped open the top button of his shirt. Her beef with this closed-off, enigmatic man went beyond his heartless app, now including his ability to arouse her with so little effort. And why *him*—the man whose story she sought?

It's just lust, Carly. Show him you're not afraid. Leave him shaking.

Rationalization complete, unable to wait any longer, she lifted up on her tiptoes and took his mouth, pressing his lips open with hers. Hunter didn't resist, meeting her pursuit—at this level, at least—with a rasp of his silken tongue against hers. A heated ache throbbed between her legs and she finished unbuttoning his shirt enough to slide her hands inside. Mouths melding, breath mingling, the moment lingered as Carly enjoyed the crisp hair on his chest, the firm muscle. And while the kiss seared her to the core Hunter continued to hold her with nothing more than his hand at her jaw. Palms stroking his delicious torso, desperate for more, she pressed her hips to his, to the hard thighs...and other harder parts.

Firing her imagination. Leaving her knees shaky.

Hunter pulled his mouth away and without a word, his

piercing gaze on hers, rolled to his left, trapping her between his car and his unyielding length. Bringing new meaning to the term *lethal weapon*. His well-honed physique triggered all sorts of wicked fantasies. With the shift of position she'd expected, *hoped*, for more. But Hunter simply cupped her jaw with two palms instead of one, brought his mouth down, and began to kiss her with a reserve that left her shaking with frustration even as his tongue tasted hers. His grip on her face was self-controlled, yet sensual. Demanding, yet with a protective air that reminded her of being clasped to his side in the alley.

The sound of a car motor echoed along the concrete walls of the parking garage, growing closer, and Carly pulled her mouth away. She fisted her hands against his chest as she tried to catch her breath before it became humiliatingly obvious that he'd been so successful at reaching his goal.

He had everything to gain—her distraction—and she had everything to lose—like her objectivity about a possible story. Her pride. Her job. *Again*. Even potentially…her heart.

And that was something she'd never lost before.

The rough hair, warm skin and hard muscle beneath her fists were tempting, and she longed to spread her fingers to recapture as much of the sensation as she could.

She forced her hands down to her sides. "I guess I made a mistake."

The sound of the engine drew closer, and Hunter turned his back to the oncoming vehicle, casually leaning a shoulder against his car. "Your continued fixation on The Ditchinator?" he said, his gaze on her face as he fixed his buttons.

"No. I meant I suspect I'm the one that came unprepared. All your shooting range practice has come in handy." She pressed her lips together, tasting him, feeling the lingering heat of his kiss. "With your deadly aim I could really use that bulletproof vest."

A dark look flickered across his face. "Don't bother. It won't work," he said softly, his smile bordering on bitter as he reached the last button. "Some things cut worse than a bullet."

CHAPTER FIVE

"WELCOME back, Carly and Hunter," Brian O'Connor said.

The studio applause finally died as Hunter sank into the love seat next to Carly. Was he remembering wrong or was this a different leather couch? It felt smaller. Shorter. And his position next to Carly was close enough for him to smell her citrusy scent. His body still wound tight, he hummed with vibrant energy from their seductive encounter. A planned attack, actually. He hoped the effort to fluster Carly had worked. Unfortunately it had definitely distracted him as well.

"You two have become quite an item," the blond talk-show host said with a smile as he sat back at his desk. "I'll be the first to admit I enjoy a good debate."

Hunter bit back the urge to laugh and threw one arm across the back of the couch, mindful of Carly's nearly naked shoulder just inches from his fingertips. After tonight's kiss, "debate" was quite the understatement. He kept his eyes on Carly. "Ms. Wolfe is a worthy opponent."

"As is Mr. Philips," Carly said. With a hike of a brow, she shot the host one of her charming smiles before turning her loaded gaze back to Hunter. "I'm learning a lot about the art of war."

The message was hardly subtle, and the memory of their kiss twined its way around his libido and breathed it back to life. If it had ever died in the first place. When Carly had gone on the offensive during their encounter it had taken all he had to keep the moment in check. He should have known she'd fight back, but he shouldn't have enjoyed it so much.

"What have you learned?" Hunter said dryly. "That war is won in the attack tactics?"

"More like it's lost in a failure of the defensive," she said.

Was she referring to herself? Or him? Ironically, it applied to them both.

"If your offensive is strong enough," he said, "the defensive becomes irrelevant."

Her tone was a touch too silky for comfort. "You should know."

He eyed Carly levelly, struggling to maintain his composed demeanor, but his gaze was probably hotter than it should be. He sincerely hoped Carly was the only one to notice. "You're fairly skilled in aggressive tactics yourself."

Carly shifted in Hunter's direction, eyes twinkling with mischief as she crossed her long legs in his direction. Legs that screamed for verification that they were as smooth as they looked. So why hadn't he seized the opportunity when he'd had the chance? His gaze lingered a moment on her limbs before returning to hers, and the sparkle in Carly's eyes turned to delighted amusement mixed with a smoky awareness that was difficult to ignore. Hunter tried anyway.

"Aggressive tactics?" she echoed with an overly innocent smile. "Are you referring to my blog on Wednesday?"

She knew full well he wasn't.

"What else?" he said.

The sassy lady simply held his gaze and said nothing. But, much to Hunter's delight, her lips twitched—as if she was itching to laugh.

"Speaking of Carly's blog," Brian O'Connor said, interrupting Hunter's train of thought. "You did take a pretty good beating, Hunter."

Impatience swelled. He'd forgotten about the host. Hunter suppressed a frown, annoyed at his lack of concentration in the presence of this beautiful woman. And at the need to defend himself *again*. Not only that—this time he'd positioned himself within touching range of the sexy little troublemaker...

His insides coiled tight, the memory of kissing Carly barreling over his usual ability to remain calm. It had been hotter than he'd expected. More dangerous than he'd anticipated even after factoring in her looks and sultry ways.

The blond talk-show host grinned at Hunter. "Carly's Clan had some not so nice nicknames for you."

Despite everything, Hunter had to bite back a smile at the term. "'Carly's Clan' certainly did. And a good number of them can't be shared with your audience. Most of the commenters' choices of names aren't repeatable on TV." He turned his focus back to Carly. "But among the most creative ones I was called were reprobate—"

"Fitting," Carly interjected swiftly.

With a small smile, Hunter kept talking. "Degenerate—"

"Ditto," Carly went on.

"And a rake," Hunter finished.

"Rake?" Brian O'Connor said with a chuckle, beating Carly to the comment punch. "Who uses that word in this day and age?"

Carly's smile was genuine as the two stared at Hunter, making him feel as if he was on trial. "I don't know, Brian," she said. "But it doesn't quite suit the man, does it? Rake sounds far too..." She sent Hunter an *I'm-so-cute* smile and tipped her head. "Too romantic," she finished, and Hunter appreciated the playful look she flashed him as she went on. "I suspect Mr. Philips is a bit too cut and dried for the term."

The host chuckled and said, "You don't think he's a romantic?"

Carly rested her arm on the back of the couch. Their forearms were now lightly touching, the tips of their fingers each brushing the other's elbow—briefly breaking Hunter's focus. Carly's sparkling gaze remained on his.

"You mean beyond Mr. Philips's efficiently designed app? The one he uses to *gently* tell a woman it's over?" A murmur of amusement moved through the crowd. Despite the dig, Hunter's lips twitched. "I'm sure I have no idea," Carly finished.

But her eyes told him she did, and Hunter fought the smile that threatened.

"Speaking of The Ditchinator," Brian O'Connor said. "Today it moved to number five on the top sellers list. Carly has vowed to keep up the pressure until you discontinue the app. She's also mentioned she'd like to hear about the inspiration behind the idea. In fact all of Miami is interested." He leveled a pointed look at Hunter. "Care to share your thoughts?"

"Discontinuing the app isn't in my plans at this time," Hunter said truthfully, deliberately ignoring the mention of the story behind its creation. That was one truth he had no intention of sharing.

Clearly delighted, the host said, "Can I interest you in returning in a few weeks to discuss how you're holding up against Carly's campaign?"

Hunter glanced at Carly, who looked as if she wanted to laugh, and he could no longer restrain the smile. Since Carly Wolfe had entered his life tedium was certainly no longer a threat. In fact the excitement might very well do him in. But the thought of the two of them being through after tonight left him feeling disappointed.

"I'll accept the offer to return if Carly does." Hunter shot Carly a meaningful look. "Though I'm sure Ms. Wolfe will eventually tire of her game."

"Of course I accept." Her eyes on Hunter, Carly's tone was a heady mix of amusement, arousal...and a hint of resigned irritation. "And I guarantee I won't grow tired."

A slight pause ensued, and Hunter appreciated the mixture of emotions in her eyes—until the host interrupted.

"That's right," Brian O'Connor said with a chuckle. "Tenaciousness runs in the family genes. Carly's father is *the* William Wolfe, of Wolfe Broadcasting."

Even though they were barely touching, Hunter felt the instant tension in Carly at the host's words, and the light in her eyes dimmed a touch. As if she was preparing for the upcoming discussion to turn ugly. From his proximity, it was obvious the charming smile she was aiming at Brian was now forced.

"Just to be clear," Brian said, turning to address the audience, "there is no behind-the-scenes monkey business going on. Mr. Wolfe has never been involved in our decision to have Carly on the show." He held up his hands on display. "No screws have been applied to either mine or my producer's thumbs..." He hesitated with impeccable comedic timing. "Or to any other parts of our anatomy."

When the crowd's murmur of laughter faded Carly spoke, her smile bright, her tone light—but Hunter knew it wasn't genuine. "Anyone who's worked with my father is familiar with his strict business policy, Brian. He would never apply thumbscrews on anyone's behalf." She hesitated, her smile growing bigger, but the heart was gone. "Not even his daughter's."

Hunter's brow bunched in surprise. It was the second time

she'd said something to that effect, and he mulled over the development as the host chatted about William Wolfe's current media holdings with Carly. She remained outwardly relaxed, her demeanor easy, but the tension in her body was palpable. And though the host's comments were lighthearted, with every mention of her media magnate father her laughter grew more and more hollow. The audience was clearly oblivious, but the host *had* to sense her discomfort.

It grew worse when Brian said, "In his younger days as a newspaper reporter William Wolfe was famous for his dogged pursuit of a story. He was ruthless, even, in digging up the dirt on secret pasts and shady politicians. Your pitbull-like pursuit of Hunter, here, is reminiscent of your father."

Behind his arm, Hunter felt Carly's fingers grip the back of the couch tight even as he watched her face lose a trace of its color. "We are a lot alike," she said warily.

"I imagine your dad is pretty proud?" the host said, his smile not as warm as it should have been.

Clarity hit Hunter hard. Brian O'Connor clearly *knew* about Carly's dealings with State Senator Thomas Weaver. And the host was using that knowledge to his advantage— targeting Carly. Hunter's chest slowly constricted with anger even as he fought the emotion.

It's not your problem.

His mind scrolled through every reason he shouldn't get involved. She'd brought public scrutiny on herself, was targeting *him* using her popular blog. But the biggest reason by far? He'd traded in his need to be the good guy a long time ago. In the end his commitment to Truth, Honor and Justice— and all those other values worthy of capitalization—and his tendency to protect others...*none* of it had saved him.

"But the real question is..." Brian's grin radiated a double meaning for those close enough to see. "Just *how far* will Carly Wolfe go to get her story?"

The stunned look on Carly's face slammed Hunter in the gut.

Sonofabitch.

Carly stared at Brian O'Connor as her blood seeped lower, her chest clenched so tight it made breathing impossible. Damn, damn and double damn. The host had done some digging and learned about the Thomas Weaver Affair. Humiliation, regret and pain blended in her veins, concocting a potent mix that burned as it traveled.

Blinking back the emotion, she struggled for a light-hearted, suitably glib comment. But somehow she didn't think she could spin being accused of sleeping with a man for his story, or being fired from one of her father's newspapers, in a positive light.

She was good, but she wasn't *that* good.

Carly opened her mouth, struggling for something to say, but Hunter stopped her with a discreet touch of his fingers on her elbow. A protective, reassuring gesture. His posture remained relaxed, but the hint of coiled readiness always simmering beneath his demeanor was wound tighter than usual. It had been hard enough to calmly sit there after their kiss—wondering if he'd been affected at all, aware of him on every level. Now the icy blue eyes directed at their host were positively lethal, and a back-off attitude exuded from his every pore.

Hunter said, "What father wouldn't be proud of Carly, Brian?"

"My point exactly," the host replied, clearly refusing to back down. Both men were smiling, but the undercurrents were fierce. "She inherited the Wolfe tenacity. Wednesday's blog post proves that much. The uproar afterwards must have made you angry."

The host was clearly looking for more conflict—probably in an attempt to boost his ratings.

There was a brief pause before Hunter said, his voice smooth, "Not in the least."

Carly stared at Hunter. The fact she knew that to be a lie made the statement even more outrageous.

Brian O'Connor hesitated, momentarily looking stumped, and then he narrowed his eyes slightly at Hunter, as if sensing an opportunity. "Since it didn't bother you, perhaps you'd also be willing to share the story behind The Ditchinator?"

"Absolutely," Hunter said.

Carly's heart stumbled in her chest, and Brian O'Connor's eyes zeroed in on Hunter like a laser. The switch in his focus wasn't lost on Carly. Everything Hunter did was deliberate, and now was no exception. He'd purposefully placed himself between the host and Carly.

Protecting her…again.

The host's smile was clearly self-serving. "We'd all love to hear how your app got its start."

Hunter's ultra-cool demeanor and hard-edged alertness didn't diminish as he settled deeper into the couch, as if getting comfortable before beginning his tale. "It began where all good break-up apps begin, Brian." The secretive smile was back, and Hunter's control was firmly in place. "It started when I got dumped by the woman I loved."

Late Sunday evening, fingers curled around the leather rim of a newly purchased cowboy hat, Carly stood just inside the upscale boxing gym, empty save the two men in the ring. Hunter lightly bobbed and weaved in a circle around his opponent, his face obscured by protective headgear. His movements were light. Graceful. And the sheen of sweat on his naked torso only added to the moment of pure masculine beauty. His chest was nice to touch, but the visual was a sight she might never recover from.

She loved a well-dressed man, and Hunter knew how to play that card well. But he wore the silk shorts and athletic shoes with ease too. Hunter's sparring partner was heavier, but Hunter had the advantage of speed, agility and a calculatingly cunning patience. With every swing of his opponent's arm Hunter ducked, his reflexes lightning-quick. With a sharp jab, his fist snapped against his opponent's headgear. The two circled, ducked, successfully landed hits, and the dance continued. It was Hunter in his most elemental form. And it was magnificent.

Focus, Carly. Just focus.

She sucked in a breath, trying to concentrate on the task at hand. Since Hunter's startling on-air confession and his abrupt departure when the show was over she'd been struggling to make sense of it all. She felt stunned. Dazed. Never had she met a man with such a conflicting mass of mixed messages. When the going had gotten rough, her father had remained silent. Thomas, her boyfriend, had cut her loose to save himself. Yet Hunter, the man she was at odds with, had sacrificed his privacy to protect her.

In the ring, the two men finished, a double fist-bump signaling the end of a well-matched round. Hunter's opponent ducked between the ropes, hopped off the platform, and headed past her toward the front office, nodding on his way by. Seemingly oblivious to her presence, Hunter pulled off his headgear and picked up a towel draped in the corner, using it to wipe his face.

Gathering her courage, she took a deep breath, inhaling the smell of leather tinged with a hint of sweat. "I brought you a gift." White cowboy hat in hand, she approached the ring. Hunter slowly turned to face her, the hair on his forehead damp, sexily mussed from the headgear. As she drew closer, he leaned on the top rope, looking down at her.

"How did you find me?" he said.

"You told me the first day we met you belonged to a boxing gym. It wasn't hard to figure out which one." She held the hat in his direction. "This is for you."

He glanced at her offering. "You got the truth. You won the bet," he said. "No need to give me a consolation prize."

"It's not a consolation prize."

"Then what is it?"

"It's a simple thank-you gift." She stepped forward to the edge of the ring, the hat still extended up in his direction. "You asked me before if I believed you were falsely accused of leaking information. Now I can say unequivocally that I do." His expression was careful, his blue eyes cautious. He didn't respond, or take the hat, but behind his guarded look she saw the truth—even if he wouldn't confirm it out loud. She stared up at him and dropped her arm, asking the question that had been haunting her since his actions on the show. "Why did you do it?"

She knew the answer, but she wanted to hear it from Hunter. After all his talk about his business, his priorities, and the rest of the rubbish he'd said he believed in, his good deed proved otherwise.

"It seemed like a good way to get you off my back," he said simply.

Twenty-four hours ago she would have believed him. Now she shook her head. "Liar," she said. "That's not why you offered up your confession."

If you could call it that. His account of his break-up had been sweet and simple—laced with a no-nonsense attitude and summed up in a mere four words. He'd loved. He'd lost. But even as he'd coolly stated the facts Carly had sensed the part that he wasn't sharing. He'd fooled the audience, even the host, but Carly had seen in his eyes what the others hadn't. A part of him was *still* recovering, and the fact that he'd offered up the truth, all in the name of saving her, had been humbling.

When he didn't respond, she said, "You didn't give many details about your break-up, but it was good enough to distract the host." Several heartbeats passed, still with no reply, so she went on. "You did it to draw Brian O'Connor off my case, didn't you?"

The enigmatic smile returned. The ever-elusive look in his eyes was going to drive her to insanity—which, at this point, would essentially constitute circling the crazy block. Because she'd already arrived there courtesy of the lovely sight of a shirtless Hunter.

He bent over, stepped between the ropes and hopped down, landing in front of her. "Maybe," he said as he took the hat.

"Cut it out, Mystery Man." She propped a hand on her hip, doing her best to ignore the beautiful chest on display, the lean torso replete with muscle. "I'm getting you all figured out. You were falsely accused of leaking information and went on to start a company dedicated to helping people protect theirs. I think that's a great story. One that the public would be interested in hearing."

The look he shot her was sharp. "My life really isn't that interesting." And then, as if declaring an end to the issue, he turned and headed for the locker room.

Carly followed, heels clicking on the wood floor. "We obviously have different definitions of the word."

"Aren't you tired of me yet?"

"Not even close."

Hunter kept walking, his back to her. "Are you planning on joining me in the shower?"

"If I have to."

Hunter pivoted on his heel and Carly stopped short. For the first time his expression was a mix of curiosity, amusement, and a whole load of impatience. "Do you ever *stop* being the reporter?"

"No," she said, the answer easy. "I can't stop being who I am any more than you can." She crossed her arms, feeling the truth of her words. "I'm a journalist at heart. It's not just my nature, it's my *passion*. Just like being the white-hat-wearing protector is yours, despite the fact you quit the FBI." Even as she said the words she knew the truth. One way or another he must have felt he had no option. Carly dropped her voice an octave. "You were cleared, so why *did* you leave?"

A shadow crossed his face, and the silence that stretched between them was loud—until Hunter finally said, "That nosy nature of yours must have gotten you into a lot of trouble during your life."

"That's not an answer."

"It was simply time to move on."

Carly let her expression say it all. "I'd bet my brand-new Mini Cooper you didn't *want* to leave."

The moment lasted forever as he stared at her, and when he spoke his words surprised her. "The day before we were scheduled to take our first vacation together I came home and found Mandy had packed up her stuff and gone." He paused, as if letting her adjust to the change in topic. "I had an engagement ring in my pocket."

At the words *engagement ring* Carly's heart constricted so tight it was hard for it to keep pumping. It wasn't the answer to the question she'd asked, and his attempt to distract her was obvious, but she could no more change the subject back than she could stop asking questions. He'd cranked up her curiosity, exceeding her lifetime limit to the max.

Cowboy hat in hand, he leaned back against the door leading to the locker room. "After three months of living together it was to be our first trip, and I started with dinner plans at a restaurant she'd always wanted to try. It was too expensive for a government man on a government salary, but I figured it was worth it," he went on. "Because a guy only gets married once."

Once. The assumption brought the threat of tears, burning her eyes, surprising her. When Hunter Philips made a promise, he kept it.

"When I called Mandy from work to tell her where I was taking her she must have guessed what was coming." He shrugged his shoulders. "I suppose it was easier to say no by leaving than refuse me to my face."

She blinked back the sting in her eyes. No one should be dumped in a way so cowardly and cruel—especially when he'd been about to make the ultimate commitment. "What did you do?"

His voice was easy, smooth, but the words hit hard. "I got drunk and stayed that way."

It was hardly the response she'd expected.

He tipped his head, his cool eyes steadily holding hers. "After a week-long alcohol binge that probably should have killed me, Booker finally showed up, dragged me off the couch, and shoved me in a shower with my clothes on." Face composed, he folded his arms, hat dangling from his fingers. A faint smile of memory crossed his face. "It's all a little fuzzy, but I remember yelling at him to turn off the faucet." He cut her a dry look. "Unlike Florida, the middle of a Chicago winter means the water is frigid. But Booker just held me under the spray, and I was too drunk to push back."

The reedy stature and little-boy face of Hunter's friend made the whole thing hard to picture. Not with the physical state Hunter maintained. "I can't imagine your partner effectively fighting you back."

"Like I said," he said. "I was plastered out of my mind and my coordination was bad. Of course alcohol does have the advantage of being an excellent anesthetic as well." There was a slight pause, and he hiked a self-mocking brow. "The only problem was it kept wearing off."

Though his face was composed, his gaze calm, his tone said it all.

"What happened after the cold shower?" she said.

"I sobered up enough to get into dry clothes and sat shivering on the couch, yelling at Booker to get out. He wouldn't leave." He looked at Carly, his words matter-of-fact. But his face reflected a moment that was clearly seared in his memory, earning Pete Booker the title of faithful friend for life—till death did they part. "After about an hour of angry silence from me, Booker told me I needed to stop letting Mandy's defection get to me and start doing something productive, like fight back," he said, steadily holding her gaze.

The next step was easy to guess. "And that's when The Ditchinator was born."

"To keep me busy."

"And get back at Mandy?"

"An outlet for my frustrations." A rueful smile curled on his lips. "Booker helped me work on the program. It was originally designed for email. When vacation time was over and I had to go back to work he showed up at the end of each day and we kept adding features, making it more elaborate. We spent a month on the songs alone, each trying to outdo the other by finding the best tune to go with the message." The tension in his body eased a bit. "Every time I slipped back into my black funk Booker would find another song title that made me laugh. Soon we had so many we decided to list them all as options."

There was a long pause as Carly stared at him, sensing there was more to the story that he wasn't sharing.

"And now that the app is so popular you're laughing all the way to the bank."

"Trust me," he said wryly, a brief shadow crossing his face

"no laughing is involved." He cocked his head, his expression easing a touch. "But I'll take the money, nonetheless."

There was a long pause as they stared at each other. In some small way it must provide him with a satisfying sense of comeuppance. No wonder he refused to take it off the market. But this wasn't the time to discuss her thoughts on that subject again.

Hunter unfolded his arms, providing a better view of his delicious chest. "That's it, Carly." His eyebrow arced higher. "Now you know enough of the gritty details to satisfy even *your* inquisitive nature." He looked down at the white hat in his hand before lifting his gaze to hers, his tone reflecting that he was done with the conversation. "I appreciate the gift, but it's time to call it a night."

Though his expression was still coolly collected, his eyes sizzled with a teasing heat that set her heart racing as he went on. "Unless you're really going to follow me into the shower…" He paused, letting her fill in the blank, and then turned and pushed through the door.

And as it slowly closed in her face she stared at the sign. Men's Locker Room. Body on fire, she bit her lip with a frown. Damn him for being the action-hero defender, an honorable guy who was impossible not to like. Damn him for being so darkly guarded, inflaming her curiosity with his secretive air. And damn him for his well-honed chest paired with an unflappable composure—for provoking her with his teasing words and the sexy look in his eyes…and then walking away.

Heart pounding, she let a full minute tick by as she tried to decide what to do next.

Go home now, Carly. You're done.

But what would happen if she finally called his bluff? She longed to know what he'd do if she challenged him on his sizzling words paired with a frustrating reserve. If she pushed him, would he finally lose a little of that control?

Let it go, Carly. You're done.

She bit her lower lip, staring at the locker room sign, the distinct feeling of *un*doneness leaving her feet stuck to the floor, unwilling to leave. Several agonizing moments passed, but ultimately her curiosity was her undoing. Lips pressed in a determined line, the whisper of desire growing louder, Carly pushed open the door and stepped inside.

CHAPTER SIX

AT THE back of the locker room Hunter pulled out his duffel bag and shut the locker harder than he'd planned. The slam of the metal door echoed off the sea of pristine white tile. Mind churning, he set his bag on one of several long wooden benches, burning with a mix of emotions caused by reliving old memories. And by dealing with the beautiful, *determined* Carly Wolfe.

Annoyed with himself, he pulled out his towel and clean clothes, tossing them all on the bench. After shedding his clothes and shoes, he entered one of the shower stalls separated by chest-high tiled walls.

The sting of hot water felt good, easing his aching muscles and a bit of his tension as he shampooed his hair. He wished the soap could wash the troublesome journalist from his life as easily.

When the sound of footsteps came, Hunter glanced over the wall of the shower stall. Carly appeared, rounding the last row of lockers. Hunter's heart pumped hard and his hands stilled in his soapy hair.

As if she belonged in the male domain, she came closer and stopped on the other side of the low wall. The partition was just high enough to block her view of the lower part of his body. A part that was responding to her presence, her bold maneuver, and leaving his every cell crackling with electricity.

Which brought him to the main reason he'd agreed to go back on the show again. He couldn't lie to himself anymore. He'd duped himself into thinking it was all about his boredom with a job that left him unsatisfied. He could no longer deny the *biggest* reason he was unable to walk away from her—despite all the reasons he should.

Desire. Want. *Need.*

A longing so intense it was disturbing.

And he didn't want her here, testing his ability to keep the lessons of the past in mind. Proving that with every outrageous move by Carly Wolfe those lessons were getting harder and harder to remember.

Frustrated, Hunter stuck his head under the shower, rinsing out the rest of the shampoo. His gut tensed as he debated what to do with the woman who was driving him insane. Wishing she'd leave. Ignoring the small part of him that was hoping she wouldn't.

Finished, he turned his back to the spray, careful to keep his tone level. "Are you here just to watch or to seduce a story out of me?"

Her lips tightened at his slur. "As I recall, it was you who came on to me in the parking garage."

Despite everything, a wry smile crept up his face. He wasn't particularly proud of that moment, but it had certainly been memorable. And having her just a short wall away from his naked body wasn't making this conversation easy. His blood was enthusiastically lining up on its way to a part of him that was paying close attention. *Very* close attention. "I'm not even sure it was effective."

"Oh, it was effective." She propped her hand on her hip. "And if I turned the tables and tried the tactic on you? Would it work too?"

The question lit the fire that he'd fought so hard to keep banked. The sound of water hitting tile filled the room as he debated how to respond. For some reason he couldn't stop pushing her. Testing her. "Depends on how good you are." He nodded in the direction of the condom machine on the wall, multiple Kama Sutra pictures displayed on its front. "And how many of those positions you're familiar with."

Carly glanced at the dispenser, her eyelids flickering briefly in surprise at the images. It took a moment for her to respond. "I'm familiar with the first and the third." She turned to meet his gaze again, her tone dry. "Number five is physically impossible." After a pause, the sassy confidence was fully back in place and she stepped closer, folding her arms on the tile wall, eyes lit with challenge. "But I'm willing to try number four with you."

Heat surged, and he fought the smile. He knew what the little minx was up to, and he felt a punishing need to see if she would actually follow through. Almost as strong as the punishing need coursing through his body now. "Here?" He lifted a brow. "Now?"

For the first time her gaze dropped below his waist. "Why wait?"

If he got any harder he'd crack. "It's your call," he said, and counted out the pounding heartbeats.

Her pink tongue touched her lips, either in nerves or anticipation—or both—and her breaths came faster. "Got any quarters for the machine?"

"Side pocket of my gym bag."

Hunter waited, wanting to see just how far the bold woman would go. Knowing that this time pulling back would be impossible...

Heart thumping from their exchange and intense longing, Carly glanced at the condom dispenser again, conflicted.

She wasn't supposed to be here—not when she'd been trying to convince her boss to let her do a story on Hunter. She'd been refused each time, but sleeping with him now would still be stupid. Massively stupid. Yet, despite that knowledge, she was still torn between what she should do—which was retreat from the challenge—and what she wanted to do...

She cut her gaze to Hunter, forcing herself *not* to inspect the entire package again and risk a total meltdown. Arms crossed, water sluicing down his back, he regarded her with more than just desire in those slate-blue eyes. As always, there was a watchful waiting, an electric awareness that measured her every reaction. She'd never been involved with a man capable of exhibiting such restraint and self-control. And yet, even though he lived behind walls, the man had willingly stepped between her and a speeding emotional bullet.

The memory snagged at her heart, because it was something Thomas had never attempted to do. Instead, when his success had been threatened, he'd dumped her via the *Bricklin Daily Sentinel.* No warning. No phone call. Just her in her PJs, with a cup of coffee on a beautiful Sunday morning, and an article about what was next for the candidate running for California State Senate. Apparently her boyfriend's backup plan had been to feed her to the wolves—despite his vow to stick by her through the scandal.

And then, of course, there was her father's emotional desertion...

The painful memories robbed her of her breath even as the irony tightened her lips into a thin smile. How lame did it make her that she was so grateful that someone had finally stood up for her? Someone who wasn't even family or involved with her in a relationship. No, it was the guy she'd challenged to a very public duel.

What would it be like to make love to Hunter? She'd had her fair share of boyfriends, and was no stranger to sexual attraction, but she'd always been a little disappointed by how quickly it faded. How bored she became. Of course she'd never known anyone quite like the sexy, intense, white-hat-wearing Hunter Philips.

Don't do it, Carly. Don't do it! It's only lust.

But it wasn't really. It was much more complicated than that. And still, despite the fact she shouldn't, a part of her had to finish what she'd started.

Gathering her courage, she crossed to the gym bag, fished out some quarters and headed for the machine, not stopping to think about her plan any further. Fingers clumsy with desire—and a generous dose of nerves—she struggled with the mechanism but couldn't get the knob to twist. She smacked it in frustration.

Okay, so maybe the lust and nerves were a little stronger than usual.

"Let me." A wet hand rested on her left hip as an arm reached around her on the right, and a sensual longing swept through her so strong her knees almost gave way. Her mind froze, chanting out the change in circumstances.

Hunter. Naked. An embrace, of sorts, from behind. From Hunter.

Naked.

Breath fanning her temple, a damp heat emanating from his body, he turned the knob, his movements calm, collected. A condom dropped into the tray with a promising thunk. Carly turned her back to the wall beside the dispenser, examining his naked body. It was still a glorious sight, made much more devastating by his proximity. The lean, well-muscled chest peppered with dark hair. The taut abdomen and the long, powerful thighs. The straining erection.

Even now he seemed so sure of himself. So cool. Deliberate.

His eyes bored into hers. "Will we need more than one?"

With her body's current state of arousal she might not survive the first round. But there was no need to let him know how he affected her. Mouth dry, fingers shaky, she lifted her blouse over her head and tossed it aside. "It all hinges on your stamina."

He nodded at the machine and its display of graphic diagrams. "I choose the second go around."

Heart galloping nervously, she held his gaze as she removed her bra. "Just as long as it's not number five."

He inserted a second quarter into the machine. Eyes on hers, his gaze lit with a mix of humor, bone-melting desire and blatant challenge, he slowly twisted the knob. He *had* to know every crank was bringing her closer to the edge. "How about a modified version?" he said.

The mechanism caught, and a second thunk occurred.

Carly's insides twisted. Their relentless game of cat and mouse was leaving her coiled tight, never knowing which way was up. Or who had the upper hand. If either of them did.

"What if your sparring partner walks in on us?" she said.

His enigmatic smile returned as he pressed her against the wall. The tile was cold against her already over-heated skin. "Let's just hope he doesn't," he murmured as he lowered his head.

The moment his lips touched hers Carly responded eagerly. He pressed her mouth open, his tongue taking hers. The soul-drugging kiss pushed what little reason she had aside as his hands made quick work of her jeans and her panties, pushing them to the floor. Hunter sought the warm flesh between her legs, teasing her until she trembled, slick against his fingers. Her body's ready response was so quick it was almost embarrassing.

It's only lust, Carly.

Carly pulled her mouth a fraction from his, surprised her

voice was so unsteady. "I thought I was supposed to be seducing you."

His mouth moved to her neck, his fingers making her body sing, and he said, "You'll get your turn."

Hunter pressed well-placed, open-mouthed kisses on her shoulder, tasting her on his way to her breast. Her skin tingled in the wake.

Struggling to get the words out, she said, "Just remember—" His lips landed on a puckered tip, searing her nerves, and she arched against him. She closed her eyes and went on. "You promised two rounds."

One hand on her hip, the other between her legs, he drove her insane, his mouth traveling down her abdomen with intent. His words whispered across her belly. "When did I do that?"

"You bought a second condom." Her voice was weak. "That's an implied promise, isn't it?"

"Guess we'll find out."

She hoped they would, but she was too immersed in mind-bending pleasure to tell him.

Fire licked her veins, incinerating her every thought as his mouth crossed her hip on the way to her inner thigh. Carly instinctively spread her legs a little more, a welcoming gesture, and Hunter took full advantage of the invitation, replacing the teasing fingers with his mouth.

Her heart imploded, sensual forces gripping her hard. With a sharp hiss, Carly dropped her head back. His lips, teeth and tongue worked their spell on her body. So focused. His movements deliberate. Skilled. Strategically planned for maximum pleasure. Until Carly was shaking, the nape of her neck damp with sweat.

As his lips drove her closer to the sun, Hunter slid his hands up her belly to cup her breasts. His thumbs circled the tips, and solar touchdown became a near certainty. Back pressed against the cool tile, her body suffused with heat, Carly gripped his shoulders, her thighs trembling. Eyes closed, she gasped for breath. Flames of desire climbed higher, blinding her with white-hot light. Until Carly's body finally launched fully into the inferno. The orgasm consumed her, fanning out in a fireball of pleasure, and she called out Hunter's name.

As her cry echoed off the tile, Hunter stood and took in Carly's flushed face. Her eyes were closed, hair damp at her temples. The quiet was broken by the harsh sounds coming from Carly's throat, her chest heaving as she struggled to catch her breath.

The moment she'd entered the shower room, deep down he'd known where it would lead, despite his attempts to drive her away. And with the risk she posed to the peace he'd achieved with his past, thwarting her attempt to run the show had seemed necessary, her bold moves, her gutsy nature captivating him like no other.

Which was why pushing her up against the wall and taking charge had been so important.

Eyes still closed, her voice steady despite the breathless quality, Carly said, "Does that count as a round?"

"I was just getting you warmed up."

"Well done, you," she said softly. She lifted her lids, her gaze meeting his. "Now…" she slid her arms around his neck, her eyes dark with desire "…take me to the bench."

Hunter's heart thumped hard. Take-charge Carly was back, and need coiled tightly in his groin, choking off any hope of refusing her anything. Blocking all thoughts of the past. The beautifully outrageous, never-backs-down woman created fires within him he might never be able to extinguish.

The surge of alarm he felt at the thought wasn't enough

to change his mind, but it made his voice harsh. "Grab both condoms," he said, and she complied.

Hunter lifted her, and she wrapped her legs around his waist. As he carried her across the room the head of his shaft nudged the wet warmth between her legs, teasing him with its proximity. Taunting him with its readiness. Everything about her tested his restraint. She arched against him, pressing him closer, clearly wanting him inside. He straddled the wooden bench, one foot on either side, and sat on his towel with Carly on his lap, her legs draped around him. Gritting his teeth, fighting the need to thrust deep, he began to lean her back.

But was stopped by her hand on his chest.

Carly's voice was low, determined. "My turn. My choice." Gaze locked with his, she said, "So lie down, Mystery Man." His muscles tensed, but he let her press him back, coming to a stop when his elbows rested on the bench. Refusing to concede any more ground. She tipped her head seductively. "I want to see how long it takes for you to come unglued."

Hunter's lungs constricted as pleasure, anticipation and uneasiness wrapped around his chest, their position on the bench bringing reality home. Outside the frequency and duration of his relationships he hadn't noticed the subtle shift in his sexual life since he'd been played, like his tendency to gravitate toward women who were fairly passive.

Until right now, until Carly, he hadn't realized just how much he'd lost with his choices.

Heart pumping, agitated, Hunter stared up at her amber eyes. Her glossy brown hair fanned across her breasts, and he was incredibly turned on not only by her dominant posture as she straddled his lap but also by her aggressive moves. Despite his troubled thoughts, desire was the clear winner, made obvious by the fact he was so hot he was ready to burst. It all got worse when she cupped his face, lowered her head, and kissed him with a potency that seared him from the inside out, slanting her mouth across his.

Lips and tongues engaged in a duel, she dragged her nails down his chest, scraping the flat nipples, and a groan escaped him. In response, Carly gently began to move her hips, rubbing her slick center along his hard length. Sweat beaded at his temples as he fought the urge to take over. The sensual moment went on, lingering, driving him mad, until she tore her mouth away, sat up and opened a foil packet. When she grasped his erection his blood sang, and his every cell urged her to hurry as she rolled the condom on. With the look of a woman who knew what she wanted, she positioned herself over him and he arched up to meet her, going deep.

"Hunter," Carly groaned, her eyes flaring wide with shock and delight. And then her lids fluttered closed, as if the strength of her desire surprised her as much as his pleasure at her boldness did him.

But that hardly seemed possible.

She splayed her hands on his chest and began to rock her hips, nails digging into his flesh as she arched her back, angling to absorb more of him. He met her thrust for thrust. Eyes closed, cheeks flushed, her mouth parted, she—without hesitation or apology—slowly drove him higher. Pushed him further. Giving him what he craved. All the fire and sultry passion that had turned his head from day one was present in her movements.

Backing him closer to a line he didn't want to cross.

Rocking his hips in time with hers, bench hard against his elbows, he clenched his fists, slipping further under her spell with every painfully pleasurable moment. Her soft body, her citrusy scent and her relentless, no-holds-barred attitude gained more ground, stretching his reserve. Dragging him closer to the edge.

As if she sensed his waning restraint, Carly tunneled her

fingers into his hair and brought her mouth back down, devouring him. Desire shot through his veins, carrying the compelling need to the far reaches of his body. Drowning in the intensely disturbing feeling, he knew he should take over to preserve his sanity. The fact that he couldn't, *wouldn't*, made him angry with himself. Even as she consumed him, increasing the pace. Her mouth and hips greedy. Demanding he give up everything.

Carly dropped her hands to his buttocks and shifted, taking him deeper between her legs.

And he lost a little more of his hard-won control.

Carly lifted her lips a fraction, her gaze burning into his as she whispered wicked words that feathered across his mouth, her voice mesmerizing as she slowly pushed him back until he lay flat on the bench. She leaned over him, relentless as she made love to him from above. Her sweet smell, her softness and her seductive ways were threatening to undo him. His abdomen tensed. His sweat-slicked skin was damp against the wood bench as he fought the exquisite sensation of being immersed. Surrounded. Holding on by a thread.

Carly's moans grew more frequent. More urgent. And Hunter slid deeper, losing more of himself with every passing moment as Carly drew him closer to the flame. And then Carly cried out and her nails dug deep into his skin.

Like a bolt of lightning his control cracked, incinerating him in a blinding flash even as his mind went blank, engulfed by the terrible pleasure. He arched his neck and wrapped his arms around her waist, pumping his hips wildly. Bucking hard. His need desperate and dangerous. Almost destructive. With a harsh groan, Hunter clutched Carly closer as his muscles burned, tensed and coiled ever tighter. And when the pressure became so fierce he thought it would destroy him it snapped, releasing him with a force that shot him into oblivion.

CHAPTER SEVEN

"CARLY."

The lilting female voice cut through the murmur of guests in formal wear in the posh, expansive living room of William Wolfe's home. From the doorway leading to the back corridor—her only means of an easy escape—Carly spied the wife of the CFO of Wolfe Broadcasting approaching. Though she was pushing seventy, through the magic of expensive surgery Elaine Bennett's face had a mask-like look that defied designation.

For a moment Carly was a teensy bit jealous, because she felt as if she'd aged ten years in the week since she'd last seen Hunter, walking away from her at the gym.

Elaine Bennett's beaded black evening dress glittered in the light as she approached. "Your father must be so happy you're here."

Ignoring the urge to contradict her, Carly submitted to an air kiss from the woman. "Mrs. Bennett, you look lovely."

The woman eyed her with the critical affection of one who had known Carly since she was five, and when the lady lifted a perfectly plucked brow Carly knew it would be followed by a carefully targeted reproof. "Since you moved back to Miami we hardly see you. Your father isn't getting any younger, you know," Mrs. Bennett said, almost as if aging was a sin. "You shouldn't be such a stranger, Carly."

Nerves stretched tight, Carly murmured a noncommittal response and took a fortifying sip of her champagne as she watched Mrs. Bennett return to the other guests, dreading the thought of a run-in with her father. Their relationship had always been tenuous, at best, but since the Thomas Weaver Affair it had been as fragile as Abby's good humor.

She wouldn't have accepted her father's invitation—except *not* coming would suggest she was too ashamed to show. Or, worse, paint her as petulant. The elegant party was in honor of Brian O'Connor, not her—God forbid her father should ever celebrate his daughter. No, it was Brian O'Connor who had delivered a surge in ratings with the shocking history behind Hunter Philips's app—a scoop that had been avidly sought by others. The host had even secured a third show, which was now being hyped in the media as guaranteed to be a monumental success. And there was nothing William Wolfe admired more than success.

Hence his strained relationship with his disappointing failure of a daughter.

Carly gripped her champagne flute, refusing to let old emotions from her teenage years drag her down. She'd make her appearance, hold her head high and prove to her father she wasn't ashamed of her life, avoiding any one-on-one conversations. Because, after six sketchy nights of sleep, unable to keep her mind off of making love to Hunter, she didn't have the energy for a confrontation tonight.

She scanned the growing crowd, spying Brian O'Connor schmoozing with her father, and tension snaked between her shoulders. She longed for the appearance of a few naked actors, Harley-riders or drag queens—anything to liven up the party and get her mind off her current train of thought.

And then, as if the powers that be had heard her wish, Hunter entered the room, wearing a beautiful tuxedo. Her heart did a double take and her mind slipped back to the moment her world had collided with a new reality...

Stunned, Carly had clung to Hunter after they'd made love, pulse pounding, chest heaving. She wasn't quite sure what had happened, only that her body had been taken to heights that normally would require rocket fuel—and her ability to recover from the event had been greatly impaired by the knowledge of how aggressive she'd been. She'd wanted him, and had no regrets, but she'd all but hunted him down and backed him into a corner. So it had been hard to maintain that easy-breezy attitude when it was over. Especially when Hunter had retreated behind his wall.

He'd been coolly polite but decidedly detached as they'd spent an awkward few minutes getting dressed, the silence in the locker room consuming every available oxygen molecule. Carly had considered asking why he'd bothered obtaining a second condom, but her chance had ended when Hunter, ever the protector, had escorted her to her car and calmly walked away without a backward glance.

But right now he was headed in her direction.

Shoulder propped against the doorjamb, she gripped her clutch purse, smoothing a damp palm down the silk of her crimson spaghetti-strap dress. A dress that showed off way more leg than it should. At least she was appropriately attired.

Pushing aside the nerves, she said, "Mr. Philips—"

"Hunter."

His demeanor was *über*-cool, untouched, his gaze as sharply alert as ever—a far cry from the man who'd briefly come unhinged in her arms. He eyed her over his glass as he sipped his champagne, the absurdity of her use of his last name radiating from his gaze.

"Nice house," he said, nodding at the lavishly furnished living room, the moonless night obscuring its view of the Atlantic.

"Don't let it fool you." Her gaze swept across the imported tile and Brazilian cherrywood walls that gave off a warm, welcoming glow, carefully designed by an interior decorator with the blessing of her father. "It was decorated for effect," she went on dryly. "To create the illusion of warmth and comfort."

They spent a few tension-filled seconds staring at one another, until Hunter's gaze roamed down her body, lingering briefly on her legs, and a surge of remembered desire suffused her in heat. By the collected look on his face she knew it was a deliberate act.

His hint of a smile didn't quite reach his eyes. "Any number of things can be faked in this day and age."

His tone set her on edge, and she gripped the champagne flute hard. "For example?"

His eyes scanned the crowd of people and paused on Mrs. Bennett. "Youth."

Despite her amusement, the strained air prevented a smile. "Caring?" she said, forcing herself to hold his gaze. "Compassion?"

His words came out deceptively soft, his focus intense. "Or an orgasm."

The statement hit hard, leaving a trail of popping electrical energy as it settled deeper in her brain. She tried to decide which was worse: him thinking she was a reckless fool or that her participation had all been an act.

Stunned, she stared at him. What had started as a game that day in the alley had led to something that now felt deadly serious—a grave threat to her sanity, her peace of mind and her heart. And the tightrope of emotional peril she was crossing with Hunter was one she'd never attempted before. Toss in an intensely hot sexual experience and—well, a girl was bound to feel a little unnerved. Because there was nothing more beautiful than Hunter Philips coming unglued. Of course, getting him there had taken a Herculean effort. He'd resisted her to the bitter end. And as soon as it was over the wall had returned. So what did that say about his opinion of her?

Her stomach twisted, and she fought the urge to retreat down the hall to safety.

Keep it light, Carly. Keep it easy.

She cleared her throat, rallying her mojo. "I can't begin to tell you how crushed I'll be if you confess you faked your way through Sunday night."

The words briefly cut through the tension, easing the intensity in Hunter's eyes a touch. "That's where women hold a distinct advantage over men."

"Since that often isn't the case, I'll take it where I can."

His gaze dropped to her legs, his brow creased in humor. "I'm quite sure you will."

Struggling for her usual self-assurance, she leaned her back against the doorjamb. "You're just jealous I had visual confirmation you were very turned on." She sent him the best charming smile she could, given the circumstances. "Helped, of course, by the fact that you leave evidence behind when you fire off your...bullets."

He smiled. "You're not jealous of my weapon, are you?"

"No gun-envy here." She took a step closer and got a whiff of his cologne, bringing sensual memories of the locker room, and her tone turned huskier than she'd planned. "But you should teach me how to shoot yours."

His body grew still and heat flared in his eyes. His tone matched his gaze. "That could be arranged." His voice lowered to a rumble that was a mix of potent desire and distrust. "Would you approach that with pretend enthusiasm? Or would it be real?"

He clearly wasn't comfortable with her motivation in the locker room. But the truth was too painful, cut too close to her heart, to share. What was she supposed to say? That she'd never had anyone come to her rescue before? That she'd been the damsel in distress in the past, but no knight in shining armor had ever risked anything to ride to her defense? Her profound appreciation of his gesture of protection was so enormous it was pathetic. Almost needy.

And she was a confident woman. She shouldn't have been so desperate to conquer this man's reserve. It wasn't as if it proved he cared about her in any way. Or felt she was worthy of his on-air sacrifice…

Her breath hitched, but she pushed away the thought and steadily met his gaze. "Are you questioning the integrity of my responses?"

"Maybe."

She placed a hand on her hip. "Were my moans not authentic enough?"

"The moans seemed genuine."

"Were my groans lacking in honesty?"

"Your groans sounded sincere." He hesitated, and his tone grew heavy with meaning. "It was the shout at the end that I questioned."

The shout had been real, all right. She refused to look away. "I'm crushed you're second-guessing my enthusiasm."

His eyes held hers as the moments ticked by. When he spoke, there was suspicion and frustration in his tone. "I have no doubt your enthusiasm for your *job* is real."

Devastated by the insinuation, Carly could almost hear the creaking sound as his statement strained under the weighty load of meaning.

Outside of Thomas she'd never been involved with a man who'd hurt her when he'd walked away, as they all invariably did. Yet here she was, with a guy she wasn't even dating, wounded by his ability to take her in an explosion of hunger, calmly walk away, and with his next breath accuse her of dishonesty. Which meant he had a power over her no man had had ever before. Damn. The smile on her face grew tight, but she pushed back the need to pop the cork on her anger.

Don't go there. Don't let the emotion get the best of you.

But her aggravation was evident in her hardened tone. "I wonder if your doubt is a reflection of my past—" she moved closer, ignoring his wonderful scent and the hard physique encased in an elegant tuxedo "—or yours."

His gaze didn't waver, but a muscle in Hunter's cheek twitched. Four pounding heartbeats later he went on. "Before this conversation continues, I think a break is in order. I'll get us more champagne," he said as he took her empty glass, the heat smoldering in his eyes searing her to the bone, "but I'll be back."

She watched him head toward the bar and let out a breath, unaware she'd been holding it. But before she could relax another masculine voice spoke from behind.

"Hello, kitten."

At the sound of her childhood nickname her heart took an abrupt turn in her chest, speeding south. She briefly closed her eyes, preparing to face the man who doubted her more than most.

As Carly braced to face her father her stomach bunched into a knot. She was dreading his simmering judgment about her career, her life choices—and her *mistake*. She was used to the disapproving tone in his every comment. No matter how hard she tried, her efforts had never been good enough. But she was an adult now. She didn't need his praise. And she sure wouldn't beg him for approval.

Her moody, miserable, misunderstood teen years had been rough, and she'd constantly butted heads with her father. Unfortunately traces of that rebellious adolescent were reappearing more and more of late in his presence. She didn't like herself much when he was around. Which was the main reason she'd avoided him for the last six months.

Keep your cool, Carly. Keep it easy. And, whatever you do, don't let him see you cry.

Turning on her heel, she plastered a smile on her face. "Hello, Dad."

His hair now more gray than black, he was a striking figure of a man in his sixties. Tall. Fit. With his sharp features, he was imposing via the sheer volume of his eyebrows alone. And twenty-five years as head of a mega news corporation had honed his hard stare to a cutting edge.

"I assumed you wouldn't come," he said.

Good to see you too, Dad. I'm fine, thanks. How have you been?

She pushed aside the disappointment at his less than welcoming greeting. She knew better, and she really had to stop hoping for more. "Is that the only reason I was included on the guestlist?" she asked.

The muscles around his eyes tightened a touch. "If I didn't want you here I wouldn't have invited you."

Well," she said, trying to keep it light, "I suppose it would have looked bad if you'd invited everyone from the show except your own daughter."

His eyes grew wary and he frowned at her too-short dress, creating a flush of guilt-tinged resentment. Okay, so the hem length was a bit much. But she didn't need any more proof that he disapproved. Of course her father must have felt a sarcastic comment was in order.

"You've outdone even yourself tonight," he said. "Who's the poor guy this time?"

Her stomach balled tighter as she blinked back the pain. "I didn't bring a date." She tipped her head. "Disappointed?"

Her father's mouth went flat. "Can't say I'm eager to meet the latest good-for-nothing."

"Good-for-nothing?"

"Face it, Carly," he said, scanning the room before turning his gaze back to hers. "You should give your choice of men more thought before you hook up with them—or whatever you young folks call it these days."

Inhaling a calming breath, Carly straightened her shoulders, forcing an even tone. "Every guy I've *dated*," she said, mustering her patience, "has been a decent man."

"Every one of them has lacked ambition."

"I don't choose my dates based on the man's ambition for his job and his fat bank account." As a matter of fact, those attributes usually sent her screaming in the other direction. Hunter Philips was the single exception—for all the good it did her.

The displeasure in her father's eyes tunneled the hole deeper in her heart. "You set your standards too low, kitten."

"Maybe yours are set too high?" she countered.

The pause in the conversation was loaded as they regarded each other warily, and she wondered—*again*—why she'd bothered to come.

When her father went on, this time his tone was full of bewildered frustration. "The worst part is I don't think you care about your boyfriends that much. Instead you try on one fellow after another, and then wonder why they treat you so poorly in the end."

The words landed too close for comfort. "Is that what this party is really about?" Carly asked. "An excuse to get me here and harass me about my love-life?"

"It's a sad day when I have to throw a party just to see my own daughter." He let out the same long-suffering, resigned sigh he always did. The one that made her feel awful. "But as for your love-life," he went on, "you're an adult. Who you choose to run around with is your business."

"That's never stopped you from sharing your opinion."

"I'm more concerned about your professional choices."

Her heart withered a fraction as humiliation and shame came roaring back, and her patience slipped further from her grasp. "Come on, Dad. It's me. No need to sugar-coat your words." She stepped closer. "Why don't you just say you're worried I'll screw up again? Repeat past mistakes?" The frown on her father's face wasn't an answer, but it was all the response that Carly needed. "Well, there *is* good news. If I do muck it up a second time, at least it won't be on one of your newspapers. So you don't have to worry about that precious bottom line of yours."

Getting fired was her fault, not her dad's. But her sharp stab of doubt about his role in the debacle still cut deep.

She stared at her father, and for once the truth spilled out, free of sarcasm. "It's been three years, and I still can't decide if you were the one who ordered my dismissal or not."

Her dad's face flushed red, and he stepped closer. "Damn it, Carly," he said, the affectionate nickname long gone. "Your boss made that decision. Were you truly so naive as to think there wouldn't be repercussions?" He narrowed his eyes in disbelief, as if he still couldn't fathom how she could have been so stupid. "Just like you were naive enough to believe Thomas Weaver wasn't using you?"

"He *wasn't* using me. We didn't start dating until three months after my story ran." She lifted her chin, batting back the overwhelming emotion. "However I *was* naive enough to believe that the people who cared about me would stick around when things got ugly. But when the going got tough he turned his back on me to save himself. Just like you."

"What did you expect me to do, Carly?" he said. "Make excuses about my daughter's lack of judgment? Show a preference for my own flesh and blood? I run a tight ship, and business has to come first." His face shifted from anger and frustration—which she could handle—to the worst expression of all…disappointment. "I don't understand how you could have made such a rookie mistake."

She swallowed against a tight throat, her words thick. "I have a heart, Dad."

"Whether you choose to believe it or not, I do too."

"But I can't turn it on and off like you."

"As I've said…" His scowl grew deeper. "I couldn't step in on your behalf."

The pressure of budding tears burned her lids, and she tightened her grip on her purse. "Don't you get it, Daddy?" The name slipped out before she knew what she was saying. "I didn't *want* you to step in on my behalf," she said. She'd waited forever to hear her father say he believed in her. And here she was, three years later, still waiting in vain. "You have no faith in me at all, do you? I would *never* have asked you to show me that kind of favor." She fought to control the ferocious hurt. "But you didn't even trust me enough to give me the option of turning it down."

Though her dad's face broiled with anger, when Hunter appeared at her side with the champagne her father nodded in his direction and said, "Clearly *you're* too smart to fall prey to my daughter's charms."

Her heart convulsed, and Carly wasn't sure which was worse—the shame or the pain. She tried to respond, but her reply died when Hunter smoothly stepped closer to her side. A silent promise of protection.

His frigid, steel-like gaze focused on her father and he voiced an icy word of warning. "Careful."

But this was one encounter Hunter couldn't save her from. Wrestling with the need to cry, scream and lash out with her words, Carly blinked back the roiling anger. If she didn't leave now she'd make a fool of herself. After a last glance at her father's fuming face, she pivoted on her heel and headed out of the living room, leaving the murmur of happy chatter behind.

CHAPTER EIGHT

As WILLIAM WOLFE stomped off, Hunter watched Carly head down the hallway and wrestled with the intense urge to follow her, resisting the impulse. Despite the danger she posed, he'd shown up tonight because he couldn't seem to deny himself the pleasure of Carly Wolfe's company.

After they'd made love, his body completely spent, he'd realized the liberating release had been like none he'd experienced before. And he'd wanted her again. The moment the craving had hit he'd remembered exactly why she'd followed him into the shower room. Plagued by the disturbing thought she was using him, he'd had to bolt or risk losing himself in her a second time. And when he'd spied her sinfully sexy dress tonight, need had smashed him head-on. Angry at himself for being so susceptible, he'd provoked her. Insulted her...just like her father.

Regret churned in his gut. After the scene he'd just witnessed, he had a better understanding of the complex woman so full of softly rounded corners and sharp edges. Brashly forward, yet remarkably vulnerable. Driven at her job, yet oddly innocent at the same time. Hunter still wasn't entirely clear which side of the Carly equation *he* fell on—or, in the end, which side she would choose—but he was now convinced she was innocent of every accusation the press had thrown at her three years ago.

Fingers gripping the champagne flutes, he watched her turn into a room at the end of the hall feeling torn, grappling with the need not to be played for a fool again. But at least when he'd suffered his parents had supported him. Booker had stuck by him. But Carly...

When Carly had made her so-called mistake she'd been abandoned by the two people that had mattered most. The knowledge took a chink from his heart and burned in ways it shouldn't.

Jaw clenched, decision made, he left the party behind and strode down the long corridor, stopping in the open doorway at the end. Color high on her cheeks, mouth set, Carly paced the length of a masculine office done in forest-green, a bordering-on-indecent length of silky leg swishing back and forth beneath her red dress.

He hesitated, and debated changing his mind. Instead he said, "You want to tell me what just happened?"

She never broke her stride, and her tone matched the fury in her pace. "I want you to leave."

He was used to her charm-and-slash smile, the targeted sarcastic comments and the intentional flirting, but he'd never seen her so blatantly angry before. Not even when he'd insulted her.

Champagne in hand, he slowly entered the room. "I think you should talk about it."

"No," she bit out, looking close to either blowing her top or bursting into tears.

He set the glasses on a massive walnut desk. "You might feel better if you cried."

"No." Mid-stride, she heaved her purse onto the leather office chair. In a woman who normally brimmed with self-confidence the stark emotion, the seething vulnerability on her face, was hard to watch. "I promised myself I wouldn't cry about it again. Especially not *here*."

His heart twisted, but he ignored it. "Why not here?"

She reached the far wall and turned, heading back in his direction. "Right after the Weaver story blew up in my face and I got fired I came home, looking for support." Still pacing, she pointed in the direction of the desk, eyes burning with emotion. "And the moment I got back he sat me in this office and lectured me on a reporter's duty and the main goal of a paper...to make money. He went on and on about the importance of the financial bottom line." Her eyes looked suspiciously bright, but no tears welled. "He didn't give a *damn* how I felt."

It was the restraint that almost did him in.

She passed him, her scent trailing in her wake.

"Nothing I do is ever good enough. I've avoided him for six months." She fisted her hands. "Six *months*. And in less than two minutes he's making cracks about my love-life."

He watched her retrace her path across the room. "Has your relationship with your father always been difficult?"

"No," she said. "In some ways that would make it easier. Then I could just walk away. Instead I moved back to Miami." Her lips pressed in a thin line. "And like a moron I hang around, remembering how it used to be when I was younger..."

It was a dilemma he understood well. Lately he'd been spending a lot of time dealing with the past himself. He let out a long, slow breath. "It's hard to cut the good memories loose just to free yourself from the bad."

She stopped in the middle of the room and her gaze met his. "Exactly."

They studied one another for a moment. Several heartbeats passed and Hunter felt the pull, much as he had in the locker room. But this time it was so much more than sexual. Uncomfortable, he crossed his arms. "When did you two start having trouble?"

A shadow briefly flashed across her face, and she looked a little lost standing in the center of the room. "My mom died when I was a baby, so Dad's the only family I have. Things got rough when I hit my teens," she said, threading less than steady fingers through her hair. "Since then all he's done is berate me over every decision I make, all the way down to the clothes I choose to wear. Pretty soon, I just gave up." Her mouth twisted grimly, and she smoothed her hand down the silk covering her thighs. "I wore this dress tonight because I knew it would piss my father off." After a self-derisive scoff, she shook her head and turned to stare desolately out a night-blackened window. When she spoke it was almost as if to herself. "I don't know why I continue to antagonize him."

He knew. "Strike first before you get knocked out. It's a protective habit." He had a few of those himself.

She looked at him as if the idea was new to her. "Yeah," she said. "He's been known to throw a few fast punches. He once accused me of treating boyfriends like shoes from the sale rack." He lifted a brow in question, and she went on. "Tried on, adored for a few months, and then relegated to the back of the closet."

He leaned his shoulder against the wood-paneled wall. "Have there been a lot of men?"

"More than a few. Less than too many." She stared at him a moment before hiking her chin a touch. "Are you judging me?"

"No," he said truthfully. "It's not my place to judge. Why do these relationships end?"

"My fault, probably." With a self-conscious shrug, she sent him a small smile of defeat. "I get bored, and I suspect the guys can sense it."

Curious, he pushed off the wall and moved closer to Carly. "And what does the turnover rate provide you with?"

She let out a bark of laughter, as if the question was absurd. When he didn't return the humor she seemed to give the question some thought. "Mostly just a lot of embarrassing break-ups." She cocked her head. "Did you know there's a singing telegram service in town that specializes in break-up messages? I'm probably the only recipient in Miami whose address they know by heart." He bit back the smile as she went on dryly. "So the only thing the turnover rate provides me with is a lot of jokes in the office at my expense."

"And maybe another method of making your father angry?"

Her scowl was instantaneous. "No," she said, and then her expression softened to include a bit of uncertainty. "Maybe." She bit her lower lip, and then doubt replaced the frown completely. "I don't know," she said slowly, as if contemplating the possibility.

He stepped closer, looking down at her face. "Or maybe you don't want anyone around long enough to use you again. Like the senator did."

Denial surged, and her tone was adamant. "Thomas did *not* use me."

He studied her for a bit, wondering who she was trying to convince. Him...or herself.

"Are you sure?" He paused long enough to get her full attention. To hammer his point home. "That's hard to believe, seeing how when you finally became a hindrance instead of an asset he cut you loose."

"My story was already out. How was I an ass—?"

"With Wolfe Broadcasting in his pocket, winning elections would be a lot easier."

Carly closed her eyes, looking as if she'd been struck, and Hunter wanted to kick himself for being so blunt.

"Jeez." She paused, and then inhaled deeply as if to steady herself. "You're hell on a girl's ego, you know," she said softly. "I don't know what to believe anymore." She lifted her lids, and her gaze held an aching vulnerability that killed him. "All I know is…"

It seemed there was plenty she didn't *want* to know. "What?" he said quietly.

She scanned his gaze and her amber eyes lost a little of the gold as the brown intensified, growing darker. "All I know is that I want you again."

Heat and need socked him in the gut, setting off a sensual storm that promised to sweep away his resolve. This wasn't the reason he'd followed her here, but there was no flirtatious tone. No coy looks. No sassy challenge in her eyes. Just an open honesty that was clearly a cover for a painful defenselessness that made her scent, her soft skin and the desire in her eyes all the more difficult to resist.

His heart was pulling double duty, trying to keep the blood supporting his brain even as it drained to his groin. Outwardly he might appear calm, but Carly had to feel the earth quaking from the hammering in his chest. "Why?"

"Because you make me feel like nobody else ever has."

As he scrutinized her face, looking for the truth, he realized that making love to him in her father's house would be the perfect retribution for her.

Despite the need to pace, the restless urge to move, instead he said, "I should leave."

"Please stay."

His body now fully on board for anything she had planned, despite the fact his brain thought it a bad idea, he said, "It isn't fair, asking me while you're wearing that dress." His words were throatier than he would have liked. "I don't even think it's legal."

She tipped her head in that sexy way that slayed him. "Will you arrest me if it isn't?"

"I probably should," he muttered. He held her gaze, fiercely aroused and intensely troubled. Was he just another way for

Carly to get back at her father? Or an effective method for burying all those self-doubts?

For a brief moment he wondered if she wanted something more from him.

And what if she did?

Doubt battled desire, twisting his heart into impossible shapes, and he muttered his next thought out loud. "What other weapons do you have up your non-existent sleeves?"

She blinked several times and after a brief deliberation lifted her arms, placing her hands on her head in mock surrender. A position of submission. As if yielding all power to Hunter. "You can frisk me and look for more if you want," she said.

She steadily met his gaze…and he knew she was waiting for him to make his choice.

Gathering her courage, Carly waited, hating how much this man destroyed her usual confidence. He was hot, intriguing and dangerous, even when coming to her defense. And he never failed to step up on her behalf when it mattered most. She'd never fallen for a man before, and a part of her had always wondered why. With Hunter, she feared she was already more than halfway there…

Her heart skipped a beat and her stomach settled lower.

It's only lust, Carly.

She felt bare, exposed and defenseless as the seconds crawled by while he studied her, as if trying to decide what to do. Although the fire and focus in his eyes communicated he wanted her, it was obvious he questioned her motives.

But the unadorned truth was too hard to share: no matter how hard she worked, or how happy she tried to be, the sadness over her fractured relationship with her father made peace of mind impossible. Hunter's square-cut jaw, sensual lips and broad shoulders—and, more importantly, his protec-

tor mode she found so attractive—threatened to consume her
as well. And she was desperate for the latter to win. Even if
it was only for another sensually mind-boggling moment. It
wasn't a difficult choice, really. Who wouldn't choose feel-
good promise over dark disappointment?

Hope over despair?

Hands on her head, she stared at him, dying to know if he
was as good as she remembered. Maybe she'd just been pa-
thetically grateful for his on-air act of gallantry, sacrificing
himself for her? Maybe it had been how hard he'd fought her
in the locker room, and how utterly beautiful he'd been when
he'd taken the fall? Or maybe she was simply tired of guys
so laid-back they were just one step above dead?

"Frisk you?" he mused as he finally closed the last bit of
distance between them, his rumbling voice shimmying down
her spine. "I probably should." Meeting her gaze, he laid his
hands on her wrists, skimming his way down her bare arms.
The skin-on-skin feel left goosebumps in their wake. "Just to
be safe." He smoothed his palms down her sides, his thumbs
brushing the outer edges of her breasts in tantalizing promise before slowing to a crawl at her hips.

His gaze burned into hers, the warm hands scalding her
through thin silk. "What are you wearing underneath?" he
said.

"A thong."

His eyes turned darker as he slowly crouched. "Anything
else?" he said, smoothing his sizzling hands down her legs.

Anticipation reached critical levels, and her palms grew
hot against her head. "Nothing."

He looked up at her from his squatting position, hands
on her shins. "That means there aren't many hiding places
under this dress."

Her heart pounded at the memories of the last time he'd
knelt in front of her. "It depends on how thorough you are."

The mysterious smile was instantaneous. He smoothed his hands up over her knees, higher along her thighs, and stroked the sensitive nub between her legs. Awash in pleasure, heart battering her chest, Carly maintained his gaze even as her thong grew wet.

"I'm motivated to be very thorough," he murmured.

He lingered a moment, eyes so dark it was hard to remember them ever being cold. Her body was so hot and damp it was hard to be much more than a mass of needy nerve endings.

"Because you're a G-man following procedure?" she said, her voice breathless.

"Why else?" He stood, his hands smoothing up her belly, between her breasts, out and around both, before finally cupping the curves. "Technically I should check your back too." His thumbs skimmed her now taut nipples and pleasure surged, her body melting more. She fought to focus as he said, "But it's occurred to me you don't need any armaments beyond this."

His mouth claimed hers and she kissed him back with all the pent-up, conflicting emotions in her chest. Desire for Hunter, and fear of giving him too much power over her. Hunter simply took what he wanted, demanding everything, and Carly could do little more than comply.

Heat infused her every cell as his hands slid under her dress to clasp her buttocks, pulling her firmly against his hard length. She arched against him in agreement, their mouths engaged in a primal duel even as his thumbs smoothed soothing circles low on her back.

"We need to lock the door," she murmured between rough kisses.

"We need a condom," he said against her mouth.

"The second one from the dispenser is in my purse."

At her words, he pulled his head back, eyes still fiery with need, his brow creased in surprise. She had grabbed the condom on impulse, wanting a memento, and she wasn't sure if he found her charmingly funny or entirely too bold. For the first time in her life she didn't know where she stood with a man, and it was driving her insane.

After a split second, he said, "I'll get the door. You get the condom."

Fortunately neither endeavor took long. When they met back in the center of the room Hunter removed her dress and tossed it aside. "This time—" with a firm hand he gently pushed her down to the plush carpet and a thrill rushed through her "—I'm in charge." He kept pressing until she was lying back, and then he slipped off her thong.

Throat tight, body aching for him, she watched Hunter take off his tux, starting with the coat, bow tie, and then his shirt. The sight of the finely honed torso—the one he'd placed between her and her dad after her father's insult—left her dying to take control. The acute need to worship lean muscle, warm skin and the hard, protective planes of his chest was strong. But when he shed his pants, was naked, his erection visible in all its glory, her heart pumped so hard she feared it would break free from her chest and flop to the floor.

Maybe it was a good thing he was taking the lead.

He knelt and lifted her leg, kissing her ankle. He nipped his way higher, scraping his teeth across her skin, palms soothing the fire his mouth left behind. When he reached her inner thigh, with a quick dart of his tongue he licked the nub between her legs, and a sensual jolt shocked every cell.

Before she could catch her breath he moved his attention to the other leg, giving it equal time. As his teeth nipped up her second thigh she closed her eyes, body humming, nerves straining, and arched to meet him. His lips landed on her center again and lingered, sending hot pleasure rushing through her. She gripped the thick carpet, a moan escaping her lips and sweat dotting her temples.

Time hovered, her mind expanding even as her muscles contracted, focusing on the point where Hunter's lips, teeth and tongue brought her to an ecstasy that washed everything away. There was no yesterday to regret. No tomorrow to worry about. Only the beautiful way Hunter made her feel.

Mouth between her legs, he worked his sensual magic, pushing her closer to the brink, so close to climax her whole body tensed.

He drew back and, crushed, she let out a cry. *"Wait."*

"You'll have to," he said, and calmly rolled on the condom. And then, eyes on hers, he shifted up her body. Instinctively she welcomed him. He arched between her thighs, going deep. Relief shuddered through her and she shifted to absorb more of him, meeting him thrust for thrust. There was no doubt. No uncertainty or distrust. Just a desire strong enough, sure enough, to push aside all the worries.

Heart pumping in her chest, hair damp at her neck, she closed her eyes as their hips strained against each other, her release just moments away.

This time when he pulled out her eyes flew open and Carly clutched his shoulders, speechless as he began to kiss his way down her neck to her collarbone. She found her voice, frustrated and flabbergasted. "What are you do—?"

His mouth landed on a nipple, eliciting a sharp hiss, cutting off her words. He nipped and kissed, as if relishing her flavor, and the sounds of her soft cries filled the room. Gradually she grew louder, spurring him on as his lips traced a path down her abdomen. He licked the tiny dip at her navel, drawing out a groan from Carly before he continued down. When his lips landed back on the sensitive center between her legs she called out his name. He lingered, apparently taking delight in pushing her higher, until she was close again, so close to completion she almost felt it.

Once more, before she could peak, he swooped up her body and drove deep between her legs. Arching his hips, he took all he could, and this time her body's response bordered on frantic. She let out a sob, the pleasure and need so great she dug her nails into his back, her legs aiding his thrusts as their hips bucked in unison. Tears of frustration burned her lids. The intensity of his gaze and the dark, determined look on his face shoved her closer to the edge. She began to whimper. And his movements, though controlled, grew carnal. Rough. Primal.

Mind spinning, muscles straining, she marveled at his strength. At the hard body that pushed her to the brink, exposing her even as he held her close. The hips that drove her closer to a dangerous ledge, his arms providing security.

Laying her open even as he protected.

Until she burst through the barrier, crying out from the force of her orgasm. And clung to Hunter as he joined her, the quake shaking her body with a ferocity that rocked the very foundation of her world.

"Looks like that cloud is bringing rain," Abby said.

From the lounge chair beside her, Carly shaded her eyes from the glare. "I think we'll be fine," she said, staring at the single gray ball of fluff blotting the horizon.

The noontime sun sparkled in the brilliant blue Miami sky—clear except for the single offending cloud—and the lingering cold weather added a slight nip to the breeze. The utilitarian concrete rooftop of Carly's apartment building was strictly for maintenance access. It wasn't as nice as her multimillion-dollar childhood home overlooking the Atlantic. But Carly had added a few potted ferns, along with some used patio furniture, and with the city sprawled out in fron she considered it heaven. After about a week of wondering where she stood with Hunter Philips, right now she needed the tranquil haven.

"Pete Booker asked me to spend the weekend with him," Abby said.

Carly sent her a pleased grin. "And you said he wouldn't ask you out after the last date."

"Yeah, well…" Abby picked at her black leggings and smoothed her hand down the dark top with sleeves that flared at the wrists. "There's always a chance he'll change his mind."

Carly studied her friend, her tone soft. "Not every relationship ends in catastrophe, Abby."

"All mine have." She twisted to face Carly, her black hair in pigtails. "And unless you're holding out on me," she shot her a meaningful look, "so have yours." Carly resisted the urge to wince at the truth, and Abby went on. "Speaking of questionable relationships—have you heard from Hunter?"

Carly's heart took a tumble. "Not since my dad's party."

"You'd think by now he'd, like…you know…actually ask you out on a date."

Carly slunk down in her chair and pulled her sun visor lower, shading her eyes. Too bad she couldn't block her concerns as easily.

Confused, emotionally and physically exhausted from the evening, the moment she and Hunter had rejoined the party Carly had left. And she'd spent the last seven days wondering what Hunter would have done if she hadn't begged him to make love to her. No longer sidetracked by his disturbingly delicious presence, it was impossible not to scold herself for continuing to pursue a man who didn't trust her. Wasn't it enough to beat her head against the stubborn attitude of her father?

Must she continue to seek approval from those who doubted her the most?

After deliberating for hours, she'd decided it was time to cut her losses. Apparently self-control was impossible when it came to Hunter. She had no choice but to face him on the third show, but she could stay far, far away from him until then.

As plans went, it was all she had.

"And speaking of catastrophes," Abby said in a grim tone, as if she'd read her mind, "you put a lot of effort into getting approval to write a piece on Hunter Philips. Now that our boss has finally said yes what are you going to tell her?"

Carly stared at her friend, and tension flooded her faster than she could reason away her fears. The look on Abby's face reflected all the dark predictions she'd made from the beginning. For the first time Carly feared her friend wasn't so much a pessimist as a realist.

And then Hunter's voice came from behind. "Hello, Carly."

Carly's heart plunged to her stomach, and Abby shot from her chair, mumbling excuses about rain, getting wet, catching pneumonia, dying and burning in hell as she made a beeline for the exit. Gathering her courage, Carly twisted in her seat to watch Hunter approach, clad in a sleek leather jacket, pants and a dress shirt. He looked fresh and rested, but she hadn't slept well for a week, reliving every moment with Hunter in her father's house.

He sank into the lounge chair vacated by Abby. "Nice view," he said, nodding at the city.

She doubted he was here to take in the sights. "How did you find me?"

"I saw your car in the garage and asked your neighbor where you were."

They stared at each other, and silence fell. After her tumultuous family reunion, not to mention their sizzling interlude in the study, she was unable to play games or pretend to be polite—her nerves were too raw for her usual charm.

She needed peace—which meant she needed him to leave. "What do you want, Hunter?" she said bluntly.

His voice was low, sincere. His blue eyes warmer than normal, their usual frost…gone. "I have to attend a conference in Las Vegas this weekend." His gaze was steady. "I'd like you to come with me."

Stunned, Carly bit her lower lip, struggling to adjust to the development. A weekend together didn't exactly jive with her goal of avoiding the man. Unfortunately she loved how he made her feel, and it went well beyond what he did to her in bed—not that they'd technically made it to a bedroom yet. A part of her was tempted to risk a bigger piece of her heart just to spend more time with him. Another part was scared as hell.

She really should refuse.

Heart thumping with the force of a thousand bass drums, she tried to play it cool and keep it light. She hiked a teasing brow. "It won't make me go easy on you on the show."

"I'm not afraid," he said, his faint smile utterly seductive.

Her resolve slipped a bit. "I'm still going to challenge you to pull The Ditchinator."

"I can handle it."

Her heart thudded, and her attempt at keeping it light died. "My boss has accepted my request to do a story on you." If that didn't get him to bolt, nothing would. And, though his body didn't move, his whole demeanor tensed as her words hung in the air.

"And if I refuse?" he said.

"It doesn't matter. We've slept together. I can't write it now."

He cocked his head. "Have you told your boss?"

Ah, yes. There *was* that little hiccup to contend with. Carly briefly closed her eyes as panic threatened to overtake her, but she fought it back. After months of chasing Sue about potential story ideas, and having spent a considerable amount of time pointing out the advantages of a story on Hunter—including his current popularity with the local press—now she had to figure out a way to tell her boss no. Short of claiming the public's interest had waned, or sharing that she'd slept with the man, she was out of ideas. The first was an obvious lie. The second could get her fired. Again.

Swallowing past the boulder in her throat, she met his gaze. "I'll tell her soon."

She just had to figure out how. Sleeping with him hadn't been the smart thing to do. But the enigmatic Hunter Philips had captured her attention where every other man had barely registered a "huh." And now he was here offering her a whole weekend with him.

A gift that could eventually bite her in the backside.

Delay tactics were in order. "What kind of conference?" she said.

"The largest hacker convention in the US. Hackers, security experts, even law enforcement attend to keep up with the latest tricks. I've gone to Defcon every year since I was a teen."

"Did your dad take you?"

Hunter let out a laugh. Stunned, Carly watched amusement roll off the man. "No, my dad's not into technology—though he *is* retired FBI," he said. "His dad was a Fed too."

The news explained a lot. "It's in your blood?"

"Absolutely. But not in the same way. Dad is old school, and doesn't like reliance on computers, so we've had a few heated debates in our time," he said dryly, giving the impression he was understating the truth. And she knew a lot about heated family debates. "But..." His expression grew thoughtful as he looked out over the city. "Even when we disagreed about everything else," he said, and then turned to face her, "the law and justice were two subjects where we always saw eye to eye."

She tipped her head. "Fidelity. Bravery. Integrity..." she mused softly. Would that *her* family mantra was so noble. "You grew up living the FBI motto."

A dark look flitted across his face, and he shifted his gaze away. "Not exactly."

Surprised, Carly crossed her arms. "You mean you *haven't* always lived the life of a justice-seeking action hero?" Silence followed, and her teasing statement grew awkward as his expression remained serious, his eyes studying the skyline. Curiosity now at full throttle, Carly said, "Do tell."

Hunter didn't move, as if weighing his options, and it was a full minute before he finally spoke. "Booker and I grew up together," he said. "Being an eccentric genius works as an adult, but back then he was the target of every clique in school."

Given what she knew of Pete Booker, the news wasn't a surprise. She lifted her brows, waiting for him to go on. Instead she had to prompt him. "And...?"

"And until we became friends I never lifted a finger to stop them," he said bluntly, finally meeting her gaze, his eyes heavy with regret. "Our sophomore year, the wrestling team tossed him in a Dumpster while I stood by and did nothing." He let out a soft, self-derisive scoff. "That's just one of several instances Booker has never mentioned, though I'm sure he remembers." Hunter gazed out over the skyline, as if the memories were too distasteful to contemplate. "I know I do..."

Carly stared at his profile, remembering the teen years she'd spent clashing with her father. "Adolescents do stupid things," she said. "How did you two wind up friends?"

"When we were assigned a joint project in high school we discovered a mutual interest in computers. Booker invited me along to the Defcon conference with him and his dad." He smiled. "And I learned that, along with his bizarre and occasionally wicked sense of humor, he's a really good guy."

"I bet that changed things at school," she said softly.

He shot her a look with the remnants of a lethal intensity that had no doubt kept others in line. "After that I never stood by and did nothing again," he said. "No matter who was the target."

Carly's heart melted. Hunter was the most honorable man she'd ever met. With Carly he had put up the good fight, and probably still would. But when it came to push or shove the good guy inside of him always won out. Deep down, where it really counted, he *did* embody the FBI motto.

What would it be like to have a man like that in her life?

She blinked back the rushing rise of emotion, the last of her resolve slipping away. "So…" she said. "When do we leave for Vegas?"

Hunter's expression eased as he reached out and traced a line along her arm. The touch was simple. Warm. And clear in its intent. "Tomorrow night," he said, and he lifted his slate-blue gaze back to hers, sending a thrill skittering up her spine.

She wondered what the noise was, until she realized it was herself trying to breathe.

The light in his eyes made them breathtakingly beautiful as he said, "Right after I spend the day teaching you how to handle my gun."

CHAPTER NINE

JIM'S INDOOR FIRING RANGE was busy, but the shots fired by the patron in the adjacent booth were muted by the thick concrete walls and Hunter's headset. Fortunately the heavy earphones they were wearing had a built-in microphone system that allowed him to hear Carly's voice, including her sarcasm, albeit with a tinny sound.

"Is this how you dazzle the women you date?" she said.

His lips twitched as he reloaded the gun. "I wouldn't think you'd be so easily impressed."

"It's hard not to be. You handle that weapon like it's an extension of yourself." She nodded in the direction of the distant bullseye where Hunter's shots had been recorded electronically. "You hit dead center every time. I'm feeling inadequate already."

"You have other areas of expertise," he said, amused when she rolled her eyes.

Like holding a new firearm for the first time, it felt odd having her here—not necessarily wrong, just…different. And most likely that feeling would return when they boarded the plane for Las Vegas tonight. He'd never taken a woman to Defcon before—his days there were strictly his own. Mandy had wanted to come along once, but he'd talked her out of it, convinced she would have been bored. But this time he'd hated the idea of a weekend without seeing Carly. A disturbing trend it was best not to think too much about.

Concentrating on his current agenda was a better course of action.

Hunter attempted a serious tone as, with his nine-millimeter Glock 17 in hand, he stepped behind her. Both of them were facing the bullseye. "The safety is on, but remember to always treat a gun as if it's loaded and the safety is off." Mindful of her inexperience, he shifted closer, until he could feel the heat from her skin. Serious became harder to maintain. "Now, square your hips and shoulders with the target." He placed one hand on her hip, ignoring the delicious curve, and checked her alignment as he passed her the weapon.

Arms extended, she gripped the gun as he'd instructed earlier, and targeted the bullseye at the far end of the room. Her hip shifted beneath his hand, and her voice was almost… distracted. "Are you intentionally trying to mess me up?"

Biting back a smile, he said, "You're drifting down." He reached around her to lift her wrists—a pseudo-embrace from behind.

"Not. Helping."

"Just ignore me," he said, amused even as he tried to apply the advice to himself. Arms extended alongside hers, he leaned in to help her aim, his mouth at the level of her temple. The scent of citrus and the feel of her skin set his heart thumping dangerously. "Look down the barrel and square the sights with the target."

"I'm trying," she muttered. "And you'd think I'd get a few lessons *before* I learned to deal with distractions."

His lips quirked. "You're a quick study. I'm sure you'll have no problem. Now," he said, forcing the serious tone back to his voice. He lightly gripped her elbows. "Brace for the kickback. When you're ready, release the safety, check your alignment again, and slowly pull the trigger."

She did as told, and the gun fired with a loud bang. Carly didn't squeal, jump, or even flinch at the discharge. Instead she fired off two more shots in quick succession. When the echoing sound and the smell of gunpowder cleared, Carly finally spoke.

"Wow," she said with an awed tone. "The kickback is a shocker."

Maintaining her position, she turned her head to look at him curiously. Her lips close to his were heating his blood.

"Does the surprise ever go away?" she said.

"You get used to it," he said, doubting the same was true of touching Carly. He dropped his hands to her waist and shifted, his length now molded to hers from hip to thigh. Desire shot like bottle rockets, as forceful as any kickback from a gun. All parts of him tense and ready for action, he had to force his mind to focus. "You did a nice job."

"Purely a credit to your detailed instructions." She faced the bullseye. "You must spend a lot of time here."

"Every Friday morning before work."

After a pause, arms extended, gun aimed at the target, Carly fired off several mores shots before she turned her head again. Her bold gaze was mere inches from Hunter's. "You never did tell me why you still come."

He searched for an appropriate reply. In the end, a version of the truth seemed best. "I guess a part of me still misses my old job," he said, the understatement sitting uneasily in his gut.

After slipping the safety on the now empty Glock, Carly lowered her arms, twisting her shoulders to face him. "So why did you go into private business?"

The old resentment surged, and he stepped to the side and took his gun from her, careful to keep his tone even. "It was time to move on."

"It's a far cry from catching criminals."

"It's a living."

"So is writing columns about art gallery openings, night-clubs…" her lips quirked "…and trendy apps." A brief moment of amusement passed between them.

"Not your favorite kinds of assignments?" he said, holding her gaze.

"No." Her grin grew wistful. "I'm a nosy reporter that prefers people to facts."

"Who also has a tendency to get herself into trouble," he said dryly.

"I think that's why you've been following me around," she said. "I've decided I'm an outlet for your overdeveloped need to safeguard others. A need that hasn't been met since you left the FBI."

"That isn't the reason I joined the force."

Her eyes grew serious. "So what *did* you get out of it?"

He studied her for a moment, weighing his response carefully. But ultimately the unvarnished truth came out with more heat than he'd intended. "I got to catch the criminal bastards."

Either his tone or the words—or perhaps both—brought a smile of comprehension to Carly's lips. "You liked to out-maneuver them." Her grin grew bigger. "You liked the excitement of the chase."

The dull ache was back, and he clutched the handle of the Glock tight as she went on.

"Why don't you go back?" Her words were spoken innocently, as if it was that simple.

But innocence hadn't helped him much.

Gut churning, Hunter turned to the tables lining the wall, opening a gun case. There was a time when he'd been confident it would. When Truth, Honor and Justice—and all the other noble qualities he'd been raised to believe in—had meant something.

"That isn't my job anymore." He jettisoned the empty clip from the Glock, his back to Carly. "I have a business to run. Responsibilities. Commitments. And Booker hates the business end of things." Hunter reached for another magazine to load. "We should get on with the lesson."

He could sense her eyes on his back as she said, "You haven't told him how you feel?"

His jaw tensed, and he stared down at the second clip clutched tightly in his hand, struggling against the emotion that had been eating at him for months.

Instead, he said, "I owe him."

Her tone was skeptical. "Because of something that happened back when you were a kid?"

"No," he said firmly. "It's more than that." Because the friend who'd proved himself through thick and the worst of the thin deserved better. With a hard shove of his palm, he popped the clip into the Glock, loading the gun for another round. "When I told Booker I was leaving to start my own business I asked him if he wanted to quit his consulting work for the FBI and join me. He didn't hesitate."

"I'm sure he left because he wanted to."

"You're right. He isn't a martyr." Checking the safety, he set the gun on the table and turned to stare at her. "But he *is* a loyal friend who deserves better than getting dumped with an aspect of the job that he has no interest in."

"How do you know he's not interested?" she said.

"You've met him," he pointed out. "He isn't what you'd call a people person."

"Hiding behind his computer doesn't necessarily mean he doesn't want to branch out. Maybe he just needs a little encouragement. And if his interaction with Abby is anything to go by," she said, a wry grin forming, "he might not need much encouragement at all."

Unconvinced, he didn't respond, hoping if he said nothing they'd move on to the task at hand.

Instead, she said, "Look, Hunter. I know how loyal you are to Pete. And I know you feel some sort of obligation. But you need to be honest with him. You can't let a ridiculous sense of duty rule the rest of your life." She lowered her voice, but not its intensity. "Are you happy?"

He swore under his breath and turned to stare at Carly's electronic score. As was fitting for a first attempt, her aim was way off. In her assessment of him, unfortunately, she was unerringly accurate. "No," he said, blowing out a breath. "I'm not happy. I'm bored."

He'd never admitted to the feeling out loud—though he'd thought it, *felt* it acutely, every day.

"Talk to him," she said. "Tell him how you feel. Work something out. Establish a new set of rules for your band-of-brothers, bro-code mentality." She laid a hand on his arm. "A real friend will be able to handle the truth."

Torn, he nodded down at the gun on the table and lifted a brow. "Do you want to shoot another clip or not?"

She paused, pursing her lips and studying him for a moment. "Are you going to distract me again?"

His grin returned. "I'll do my best."

She smiled back. "Then count me in."

"In retrospect, the *Star Trek* convention tickets I sent you as a bribe weren't so wrong," Carly said with a teasing smile.

"This is where sci-fi meets reality." Hunter gazed around the crowded Las Vegas convention hall at the attendees of the Defcon conference—the annual pilgrimage destination for hackers. At a table in front of them participants with laptops were competing to see who could hack into the most servers in under an hour. So far Booker was in the lead, Abby cheering him on from behind.

Hunter nodded his head in the direction of his friend. "I never did tell you that Booker enjoyed the *Star Trek* convention in my place."

Carly shifted closer to Hunter's side, setting his body humming. "Which reminds me of something I wanted to discuss with you," she said. Her citrusy scent enveloped him, bringing back sensual memories of the past two days, and he hoped she was thinking what he was thinking. Carly said, "Have you talked to him yet?"

He sighed. Apparently her mind wasn't in sync with his. "I don't want to talk to my partner. He isn't nearly as pretty as you."

She narrowed her eyes in amused suspicion. "You're using delaying tactics."

"No." A grin hijacked his mouth, and he leaned closer. "I'm enjoying my weekend."

Which was true. He hadn't enjoyed himself this much since… He paused, trying to remember. Intellectually it should have been when he was with Mandy. But he was quite sure that he had never felt as alive in Mandy's presence as he did in Carly's. It wasn't just her smart, sassy ways, or that the sex was better—though that was a definite plus. Carly made the funny funnier and the interesting more interesting.

He would certainly never look at *Hamlet* the same way again.

"And, by the way, the next time you plan on sending a gift as a bribe," he went on, "I do have a list of preferences." He had several—and all of them involved a beautiful woman who had taken his life by storm. The timbre of his voice gave away the under-the-sheets direction of his thoughts. "Do you want me to share my favorites with you?"

Carly's quasi-serious expression melted into a welcoming one, and Hunter's body registered its approval. He loved her infectious enthusiasm. He loved how she'd embraced the playful side of the conference, cheering on the participants that succeeded at the annual "Spot the Fed" game.

As a teen, for him the conference had been about fun. As an FBI agent and then a security specialist Hunter had focused entirely on the business aspect. But Carly had convinced him to enter the "Crack the Code" competition. She'd even lured him away from a lecture for a lunchtime rendezvous in their room yesterday. And he hadn't been getting much sleep at night, either...

"You have a list of gifts that won't get sent back to me?" she said as she stepped closer, and he wondered if she could hear his heart thumping appreciatively in response. "This I'd like to hear," she went on. "Because I still have that secret decoder ring you returned."

"You kept it?"

"As a memento of our first show."

"I hope you still have the dress," he said in a low voice.

"I do," she said with a seductive smile. "And I brought it with me."

"Good. I can finally live out my fantasy of making love to you with it on."

"I don't think it will fit you," she said silkily.

Hunter laughed, and then leaned in to whisper in her ear, savoring her scent. "I'd give it a whirl in private, if that's what you wanted."

"Oh..." She pulled back until they were face to face, and her gaze turned decidedly warmer. "I definitely want."

The look seared him, frying the very marrow of his bones. But the heat in her eyes suggested her statement wasn't just about the dress, or even the ridiculous notion of him putting it on. It was almost as if she hoped for more, and it was shocking to realize they might have moved beyond desire and into something else.

It was easy to get lost in the sensual web she wove so

easily, because his body had begun to insist it was time for another noontime rendezvous. But still… "Do you want to know what I really want?" he said.

"Yeah." She lifted her chin, as if ready for anything—and she always was. "I do."

For a heart-pounding moment he tried to figure out the truth. What did he want? When the answer wouldn't come, he dropped his gaze to her legs, plenty exposed in the shorts she was wearing. "I want to know if they make shorts any shorter than that."

"Of course," she said breezily. "They're called bathing suits. But I don't think I'll be allowed in the convention hall wearing one."

"I don't think anyone would complain."

She looked at the crowd that consisted of people of all ages. Most were excited to meet like-minded people, engaged in conversations she probably couldn't understand. "I don't think anyone would *notice*."

His smile grew bigger. "Except me."

She smoothed a hand over his button-down shirt with a light in her eyes and the sassy self-assurance that set his soul on fire. "Your focus is one of the things I like about you."

Hunter gazed down at Carly, and beyond the intense desire that was growing by the second there was a sense of rightness, a light of possibility, that refused to go away. The feeling had been coming with greater regularity, and while he didn't necessarily trust it, the wholehearted, unwavering resistance that used to accompany the emotion was growing less acute. In truth…it was beginning to fade quite a bit.

Which in and of itself should have been concerning.

But right now he was simply going to enjoy himself. "And the other things you like about me?"

"I'm rather fond of your gun." Her grin grew bigger. "Your ability to remain cool under pressure. And I like how you wear that white hat." She glanced up at his hatless head and then returned his gaze. The teasing light in her eyes faded a trace as she grew more serious and dropped her hand from his chest. "Why haven't you talked to Pete yet?"

Hunter stifled a groan and turned to face the competitors at the table that included his partner, the guilt weighing him down. It would have been easier to ask for more time to pursue other interests—to break free of the stifling responsibility of keeping the business going—if it didn't feel like such a noose around his neck. But right now his life felt, if not perfect, as close to happy as he could remember. And he didn't want to ruin it with thoughts of his lingering dissatisfaction at work.

Hunter put an arm around Carly's waist and pulled her closer to him. "I'll discuss it with him when the time is right." His hand drifted lower, as if to hold her hip, but he kept right on going until his palm cupped the outside of her upper thigh. The feel of silky skin brought the desire back tenfold, not to mention some outstanding memories. "Currently I have other things on my mind. Like yesterday afternoon…" His thumb smoothed across her thigh, slipping under her shorts and tracing the edge of her panties at her hip. The crowd around them blocked most everyone's view of his hand.

Though she parted her lips, as if to catch her breath, her lids narrowed just enough to let him know she was trying to continue her discussion. The flush on her cheeks gave her difficulty in focusing away.

"I *could* go discuss business with my partner." He leaned in and spoke at her ear, pushing aside his frustration with the topic in favor of overwhelming desire. "Or we could go back to the hotel room and start working our way down my list…"

When she didn't move or speak, he straightened a touch to look down at her face, and the look of pure need in her eyes was his undoing. His fingers discreetly stroked her thigh, and the energy flowing between them could have lit the LED light display that covered the massive expanse of ceiling.

"Still susceptible to a pretty face, I see," a man said from behind.

The familiar voice from his FBI days plunged Hunter's heart headlong into blackness, snuffing out the light in his good mood, and his fingers gripped Carly's hip. In a blinding flash intense resentment flared. The sharp taste of bitterness. The bite of betrayal filling his heart.

Carly's wide-eyed look helped him regain his composure. Through sheer force of will Hunter transferred the pressure in his grasp on Carly's hip to the muscles in his jaw.

"Hello, Terry," Hunter said as he turned to face his old colleague.

Stunned, Carly took in the cold look that frosted Hunter's eyes—worse than any she'd seen to date—and a chill crept up her spine at the dark emotion exuding from his every cell. He dropped his hand from her hip and she instantly missed the heat.

Since they'd been in Las Vegas he'd been relaxed. Not coiled, tense, ready for trouble at a moment's notice. But now the reserve was back, and it was shocking how fast the old wall could so thoroughly, and so quickly, be thrown back up. She sensed the tension, the seething energy around the two men.

The redhead's buzz cut barely concealed his scalp, but it was the gleam of smug satisfaction in his eyes as he looked at Hunter that left her wary. Despite the chatter in the convention hall, the ominous silence between the two threatened to engulf them—until the newcomer decided to put an end to it.

The freckle-faced gentleman stuck out a hand at Carly. "Terry Smith," he said.

She mumbled her name and returned the shake out of courtesy, dropping his hand as soon as polite.

"Old FBI buddy of Hunter's, from his days with the Cyber Division," the man finished, though Carly doubted the word "buddy" was an accurate description. "Do you hack, or are you into security?"

"Neither," she said. "I'm a journalist."

The slight widening of Terry Smith's eyes registered just how much of a shock her profession was to him, vaulting her reporter's curiosity to lunar levels. But as he slid a sideways glance at Hunter, Terry's smirk grew bigger. Carly's heart flinched in preparation for what she sensed was about to become a worse situation.

"What is with your fascination for members of the press?" Terry's gaze touched back on Carly's. "Though who can blame you? She's hot too…"

Carly's heart tripped and fell, landing painfully on his use of the word "too." Hunter's face went glacier, rivaling the polar icecaps for frigid first place, and the menacing look that crossed his face robbed her of the ability to function. Hunter took a half-step forward and Terry's eyes briefly flickered with alarm. But whatever Hunter had intended was stopped by the sudden appearance of Pete at his side. His friend placed a restraining hand on his shoulder.

More mocking than holding real humor, Pete's boyish grin was aimed at Terry. "How ya handling that alcoholic habit of yours, Terry?"

The agent's face registered relief before he narrowed his eyes suspiciously at Pete. "Funny how it works every year at Defcon. My hotel room gets charged with another guest's consumption of alcohol." He paused and crossed his arms, the generic dark suit pulling tight across his narrow shoulders, his words thick with meaning. "Almost as if someone hacks the hotel computer and sends the bar bill from their room to mine."

Hunter's clenched jaw loosened a fraction, as if he was amused by the indirect accusation. "There are a lot of hackers at this conference with nothing better to do than stir up trouble."

Pete tipped his head in false sympathy. "Yeah, and you Fed boys will always be a target."

"It's a big bill too," Terry said, clearly finding little humor in the prank. "Hundreds of dollars."

"Pretty prohibitive with your salary," Hunter said.

"I guess whoever it is must be throwing a party," Pete added.

"Probably all in your honor," Hunter said. The FBI agent's lips tightened, and his grim look only got worse when Hunter went on, "Rumor has it every year the bill gets paid anonymously."

"Yeah," Terry said softly, his eyes glittering with accusation. "It doesn't undo the illegal act, though." He shifted his gaze between Hunter and Pete, as if looking for clues to the crime in their faces and trying to determine which one was doing the hacking and which one was paying the bill. "And if I ever catch the person doing it," Terry said, "I'm bringing him down."

"Lighten up, Terry," Pete said with a laugh and a playful slap of the agent's shoulder. "It's probably a couple of kids having fun at your expense." Pete's smile developed an edge. "Of course, with your poor skills, whoever it is should consider themselves safe from detection."

The insult hung in the air, and none of the three men made a move, as if each was waiting to see what his adversary would do next.

"A few of us are meeting up at the bar tonight." Terry's gaze swept back to Carly. "If any of you guys want to catch up, reminisce about old times…" his grin was positively derisive "…stop by." And, with that, he headed into the crowd.

Carly's mind twirled in the aftermath. It was too much information to be processed quickly, and as she watched the FBI agent walk away a million questions swirled in her head. Her curiosity was so sharp she couldn't decide where to start. With the reporter comment? With the history of the animosity between the three men? Or perhaps with who was hacking the hotel computer and stiffing Terry with the bar bill?

But when she turned to speak with Hunter…he was gone.

Hunter sat on a chair in the corner of his hotel room, thick curtains blocking all but a thin swath of the dying embers of the setting sun. After his aimless wander along the noisy chaos of the well-lit Vegas strip the dim light and silence of the hotel room was a relief. Out on the sidewalk he'd passed three Elvis impersonators, four superheroes, and a gold-painted human statue of Midas. Carly would have loved every one of them. He shouldn't have left her so abruptly, but he'd needed time to regain control of his anger.

Nursing the same bourbon he'd poured when he'd returned to the room an hour ago, Hunter stared across the posh penthouse suite. In his days as an FBI agent, a government employee on a limited budget, he'd been assigned one of the cheapest rooms on the bottom floor. Now he could afford the best of the best at the top. A massive room, lavish with plush furniture, thick carpeting, and a well-stocked bar that deserved someone who drank more than him. Since his drinking binge following Mandy's defection his taste for alcohol had waned.

Running into Terry had triggered an avalanche of troubled emotions Hunter had battled for eight years. At one time the salary slur he'd tossed at Terry would have left Hunter satisfied, knowing that he could buy and sell the man's life ter-times over and never pull a financial muscle. But in reality it was an empty win. Hunter hadn't minded the cheap rooms, the basic government-issue cars, or the limiting lifestyle of a G-man on a G-man's salary. The work, the satisfaction of his job had supplied him with all that he'd needed: a sense of purpose. A calling he believed in. And—the real chocolate frosting on the plain vanilla cake—the thrill of outwitting the crooks and beating them at their own game.

Until his integrity had been called into question.

The acrid memories of those dark days burned—the shame, frustration and humiliation of going to work while the agency's Office of Professional Responsibility had scrutinized his life. Being investigated like the criminals he'd been tracking for two years.

He clutched the cold tumbler in his hand, bitterness twining around his every cell, tightening its grip. Choking him. And twisting the knife still buried in his back.

A rustling came from the hall and Hunter tensed, not yet fit for human interaction. But the sound of a card swiping the outer lock was followed by the door opening, and a soft click as it closed.

Carly.

CHAPTER TEN

RELIEVED she'd finally found him, Carly paused, caught between her incessant need to know what had just transpired between Hunter and his old colleague and her intense longing to ease the expression on his face. She'd seen the Hope Diamond once, and his eyes resembled it now. Blue. Hard. Frozen. Though hope was hardly an apt description. There was such an underlying sense of…emptiness about him.

After the last few days with Hunter it was hard to adjust back to the elusiveness he'd exuded in the beginning. But the wall had returned, taller and stronger than ever, and his expression was sealed off—tighter than any super computer responsible for national secrets.

"After you left the convention hall," she said from across the room, "I came back here looking for you."

"I went for a walk."

She paused, refusing to be deterred by his less than approachable tone. "Agent Terry Smith is an ass."

"Yes, he is." He didn't even look at her when he went on. "He always has been."

"You two never got along?"

There was a pause before he spoke. "He considered me a rival at work."

Her eyes dropped to the glass in his hand, as she decided

how to proceed. "Is that bourbon you're drinking going on your hotel bill...or obnoxious Agent Smith's?"

The hardness in his expression lightened a touch, and the frosty look in his eyes thawed half a degree. "It's going on mine."

Encouraged, she crossed the last of the distance between them. "I figured as much," she said, tossing her purse on the bed as she passed by on her way to Hunter. "Pete's the one who's been hacking the hotel computer every year and switching the bar bills, isn't he? And you've been anonymously paying the tab." The scenario fit with everything she knew about the two. The eccentric mathematical genius and—ever the white-hat-sporting defender—his brilliant and fiercely loyal friend smoothing the way.

His brow crinkled in the faintest of amusement. "A little continued rivalry would be understandable, given our history. But hacking the hotel computer would be illegal," he said.

She came to a stop beside his chair, and something in the way he'd said the words, in his expression, made her question her assumption. "Are *you* the culprit?"

He finally looked up at her with a hint of a secretive smile on his face. "Why would I admit to a criminal act?"

Her heart untwisted and eased. She adored the look on his face and was relieved to see the barrier drop a fraction. But her curiosity climbed to heretofore unseen levels—and for her that was saying something.

"You're not going to tell me, are you?" she said.

"No," he said. "I'm not."

She fingered the strap of her dress, hesitating, but she had to ask. Although she suspected she knew the answer it was several seconds before she worked up the nerve. "Was your ex a reporter?"

Nothing changed in his demeanor, but his fingertips

blanched against his drink, as if crushing the glass. "Yes," he said. "She was."

The implications of the news were enormous. It explained a lot about his initial attitude toward her, and it opened up a slew of potential about what had happened between the couple. Was it more than just a girlfriend who had decided to move on? More than just a woman who'd changed her mind about a man she supposedly loved? Carly's thoughts spun with the possibilities.

She knew he wouldn't answer, but she tried anyway. "Were you ever going to tell me?"

The pause was lengthy. "Probably not."

His answer was more painful than she'd expected. "What happened?"

"It's not important," he said, his voice grim, and then he tossed back the last of his drink.

She blinked back the hurt and the growing sense of panic. Inviting her to the conference had seemed like a major step forward. Now she wasn't so sure. But there *had* to be hope, and the pain she sensed he'd buried for years currently outweighed her own. Her own need to heal his hurts, to tear down those barriers once and for all.

Exactly why she felt it so keenly wasn't a matter up for consideration. The last thing she wanted to do was examine just how much she needed to get back to the connection they'd shared the last few days. It had felt like a real relationship, not the over-him-in-forty-eight-hours kind. More like an in tense, never-will-recover, want-to-be-with-him-forever kind

The thought of this man walking away came perilously close to being frightening.

He carefully set his glass on a nearby table and looke up at her with an expression that squeezed her chest—utte bleakness, infused with a burning desire. A compelling com bination that made his tone gruff. "Did you put that outfit on for me?"

Heart now rapping hard, she glanced down at the leopard print slip dress she'd worn the night of their first TV show. She'd put it on earlier, with the thought of teasing him into a better mood when she found him, but now it seemed inappropriate. And very, very wrong. The light in his eyes was encouraging, but the fatigue, the sense of emptiness he kept buried beneath it all, was unmistakable.

"Hunter," she said, looking down at him. "It's been a difficult day, and you're tired."

"I'm fine."

"Have you eaten?"

Eyes on hers, he clasped her wrist, his grip firm. "I'm not hungry."

Pulse pounding harder, her resolve melted a touch. "You need to rest. You need to eat—"

"No." Gaze intense, fingers around her wrist, he reached up and cupped her neck, bringing her head closer as he murmured roughly, "I need *you*."

Her heart went wild in her chest as his mouth claimed hers from below. His lips and tongue held a desperation that was about more than just sexual need. It was intense, yes. Hot too. But the demand in his mouth was like that of a drowning man who seemed intent on taking her down with him.

She loved the way he made her feel. Special. Worthy of a sacrifice. But right now it was as if he needed her as much as she needed him...

Okay, Carly. This is obviously more than just lust.

The disturbing thoughts, the fear of wanting too much, were shoved aside when his hands raked up her thighs and over her hips. The despair and dogged determination in his touch set her skin on fire until she was sure her mostly naked body beneath the fabric would scorch her dress from the inside out.

With his mouth on hers, his palms consuming her body, her own need grew urgent. She began to unbutton his shirt, fingers clumsy with emotion, embarrassed at just how much this meant to her. This wasn't about control or dominance. It was about surrender—not to each other, but yielding to the intense need they shared. She unfastened his bottom button and smoothed her hand across his chest, craving the feel of crisp hair, warm skin and hard muscle. Meeting his mouth, kiss for kiss, she tried to absorb every sensation. Afraid it would be over too soon.

Dying to draw out the moment of being so desperately needed by this man—as if he could never walk away—she pulled her head back and knelt beside him. Her fingers fumbled as she tried to unfasten his pants, and she let out a small, self-conscious laugh. "I hope I don't hurt you."

"I'm not afraid."

Carly's hands stilled as she stared up at him, her heart pumping in her chest. Because he scared the hell out of her. But the frank desire in his eyes gave her courage, so she pulled out his erection and lowered her mouth to take a taste. Hunter's low groan drove her on, and she loved the way his hand threaded through her hair, cupping her head. Not with a sense of power or control, but one of almost vulnerability. A moment where his wall was at its lowest point. No reserve. No guard. Just his need in her hands.

Her mouth and her touch grew bolder, more demanding. Her hands, lips and tongue smoothed their way along the soft skin covering the hard shaft. Satin covering steel. The protector, the coolly controlled man, poised and ready at a moment's notice.

The desperation in his tone was her undoing, his voice ragged. "Carly..."

Hearing his plea, she stood and reached for the hem of her dress.

"No," he said, his eyes burning into hers, his voice tight with desire. "Leave it on."

Slick with need, throbbing from the force of the desire coursing through her veins, she slid her thong down, kicked it aside and fetched a condom from her purse. Fear, hope, and a feeling that came too close to love twined tightly in her heart. She concentrated on Hunter's almost desperate grip on her thighs as she straddled his legs, sitting on his lap as she sheathed him in latex.

Pulse doing double time, her breathing too fast, she said, "You seemed more amused than affected the first time I wore this dress."

His words came out a throaty rumble. "I was affected." He bunched her dress to her hips and positioned her over him, leaving her holding her breath. "*Very* affected."

Helpless in his arms, she arched her back as he began to slide inside.

"God help me," he groaned, filling her inch by delicious inch as he went on. "I still am."

Try as he might, Hunter couldn't hold back the moan of pleasure as he entered Carly. Her body was more than ready. Beyond welcoming. Wrapping him in a warmth that was less about heat and more about alleviating the years of ache within. Overcome by the sensation, he paused for a moment. With him embedded deep inside her, she cupped his face for a kiss that was part healing balm, part all-consuming need, and a very big part an emotion he refused to name. She pulled her lips back a fraction, hands on his cheeks, her warm amber gaze locked with his, and he began to move.

Their hips rocked in unison, slow yet sure, as they savored every sensation. And Carly let out a sigh, her eyes growing darker.

Somewhere along the way the teasing tones and the playful challenge had been left far behind. All that remained was his need to lose himself in Carly. The selfless way she matched his rhythm, held his face and looked into his eyes, mended the cracks he'd sworn were too massive to be repaired. The doubts and misgivings he'd clung to in order to preserve his sanity were slipping. His heart was now too large to be contained in a cynical box. The woman was a seductive mix of sassy strength and endearing vulnerability, but it was the caring in her gaze that drew him in. Called him to wade further, venture deeper.

Death by drowning didn't seem a bad way to go, so long as it was Carly he was submerged in.

Giving himself over to the sensation, he wrapped one arm around her waist, the other hand low on her back, and closed his eyes, burying his nose at her neck, immersing himself as he succumbed to the spell she cast. Turning himself over to the sensation, he basked in her citrus scent, her soft skin and the emotion she shared so readily. So freely. And so honestly.

The unequivocal return of passion in her hips as they met his urged him on. Every savoring thrust increased his greed. Wanting to claim it all, to absorb the very essence of this woman, he fisted his hands in her hair, raking his teeth across the pulse pounding at her neck. His breath turned ragged against her damp skin and she clung to him, each of them lost in the other. Although he maintained the unhurried pace, the slow, strong strokes of his shaft grew rough, rugged. And needy.

Until Carly let out a soft cry.

The brutally frank need built higher. Both frightening in its intensity and healing in its authenticity. Weakening him and strengthening him at the same time. And as her cries o surrender turned into a call of completion the start of her orgasm gave him a final push. He took the leap with her, following her off the cliff and plunging headlong toward the ocean. And then the pleasure hit hard and closed over his head.

Well, it wasn't quite what she'd envisioned, but there was no denying it now.

She was in love.

Carly's chest hitched on a painful breath as she lay next to a sleeping Hunter, staring up at the ceiling of the hotel room. For years she'd wondered how the emotion would feel—perhaps like double rainbows with pots of gold, or frolicking unicorns, or any other number of mythical, magical things she'd heard of through the years. It was supposed to leave her believing she could leap tall buildings in a single bound, not longing to hide out in a basement.

She'd expected to feel energized and ready to take on the world, not left flattened in its wake.

Carly squeezed her eyes shut, blocking out the fear and forcing her breaths to come at a more doable rate—one that didn't make her feel quite so dizzy or panicky. She turned her head to look at Hunter—which didn't help her lightheaded sense of anxiety either. The masculine edges of his face looked relaxed in sleep, as did the sensual lips that had minutes before consumed hers. This time had been different. He had made love to her as if all the barriers were gone. As if desperate to satisfy an emotional need via a physical one.

Or maybe that was her being naive again. Because sex was just sex, and with Hunter it had always been good, so what did it really mean?

Confused, she covered her eyes with her hand. Love hadn't brought the kind of harmony and feel-good vibes she'd always imagined. And how could she rely on a feeling of closeness in bed to mean anything? Perhaps, for Hunter, it really was all about the physical?

But she couldn't get beyond the feeling that facing his old colleague had brought all the old memories to the surface. That he had turned to her in a moment of pain—trusting her to see him through, having faith in the two of them.

And maybe pots of gold and frolicking unicorns were real and waiting for her right outside the hotel room.

With a subdued sigh, her doubts and fears too loud to be silenced, she rolled out of bed and quietly changed into jeans and a T-shirt. She combed her hair, slipped out of the room, and wandered down the hallway and into an elevator, pushing the button for the ground floor. As she descended Carly stared at her reflection in the mirrored wall, looking for the radiant glow that women in love were supposed to emit.

But where was the inner peace? The empowering sense of resolve? Or, for God's sake, at least her usual confidence? According to the generally accepted unwritten rules of romance she was now supposed to be an *über*-strong, formidable woman, endowed with the heroic ability to overcome all manner of obstacles simply with the power of the love in her heart.

All she felt was an overwhelming sense that she was no closer to breaching Hunter's mighty defenses than she had been *before* she knew she'd taken the emotional fall—but now failing to lure him out of his shell wasn't just about his happiness, but hers too.

Because, with those cool blue eyes, there was no way of being certain about anything.

The elevator doors opened and Carly made her way into the lobby, coming to a stop beside the marble fountain in the center. Feeling lost, she scanned the elegant scene. And then she spied obnoxious agent Terry Smith at the lobby bar.

A wave of discomfort settled deep in her belly. No surprise

that he lacked the imagination to seek out one of the many Las Vegas establishments that offered more than canned elevator music, hardwood floors, and an elegance so subdued it bordered on bland, generic posh.

She chewed on her lip, staring at the agent. He might lack imagination, but one thing he *did* have was knowledge about Hunter's past. All those tidbits Hunter hadn't shared…like the fact his former girlfriend had been a reporter.

Her heart and her brain crashed into one another again, leaving her struggling to adjust.

That little nugget of news about his ex had been relentlessly chugging around in circles in Carly's mind since she'd first learned the truth. Was there a link between Hunter's break with his girlfriend and his reasons for quitting the FBI? So far she had considered the events to be unrelated, but now she had a strong suspicion they weren't. With his ex being a reporter, it made the incidents a whole lot more likely to be connected.

And why hadn't he trusted her enough to tell her?

The ache returned, leaving her feeling vulnerable, and suddenly her need to know overwhelmed everything. She didn't require the nitty-gritty details, she didn't want a blow-by-blow account—though she would have gladly accepted both from Hunter if he'd suddenly decided to quit hiding behind unbreachable emotional barricades. She just wanted the answer to one question: had Hunter's girlfriend been involved with the leak that had led to him leaving the FBI?

And the only way to find out was to ask. She stared at the redhead, his scalp gleaming beneath the buzz cut.

Don't do it, Carly. Don't do it.

But, damn it, Hunter's past was about more than just *his* life now. It was about hers too. Love might not endow her with superpowers, but it did provide one indisputable truth—he held her future happiness in his hands.

Fear gripped her, more powerful than ever before. Retreating to what she did the best—seeking out answers, nosing out the truth—was the only way she knew how to take back a little of the massive control that had just been handed to Hunter. He now held her heart on a platter.

With a renewed sense of determination, she headed in the direction of the agent.

As the hotel elevator descended, Hunter cursed himself for conking out so fast. The late nights had caught up with him, and while Carly had slept in to make up for lost sleep Hunter had been up early, attending lectures at the conference. Still, the lost shut-eye had been a small price to pay for making love to Carly. Tonight, even after they were done, he'd pulled her close, wanting to stay awake and enjoy the sensation that had permeated every muscle in his body, making them slack. Loose. Unrestricted by the tension that had kept him bound tight for so long he couldn't remember the last time he'd felt so relaxed. The deep feeling of contentment, of *rightness*, came from holding Carly close. From making love to the woman who had wormed her way under his skin in a way that he'd never thought possible.

With her quirky love for the bizarre, her sense of humor, and her sexy, spirited love of fun, Carly had charged into his life and powered his way into his heart in a matter of weeks. Despite all his efforts he'd fallen so fast he was still struggling from the force of the impact. Life without her in it had become unthinkable. And the way she'd made love to him tonight suggested she felt the same way.

So why had he woken up alone?

Eager to be near her again, even if it was to inhale the fresh scent of her skin, to feel the warmth of her body sleeping next to his, he'd left the room with one purpose in mind: to tell Carly how he felt. That the stark emptiness that had threatened to swallow him whole was now filled with the smell of citrus…and the smile of a woman that filled gaps in places he hadn't known there were holes.

When the elevator doors parted on the ground floor Hunter exited and headed into the lobby. Pleasure hit when he spied Carly leaning against the counter at the bar. But the sense of well-being crashed when he spied who sat opposite her…

Special Agent Terry Smith.

The sucker punch to the gut almost dropped him to his knees. The emotional hit was so hard it knocked the air from his chest.

Heart pumping painfully, Hunter stood, frozen, staring at the two of them as the familiar, nauseating swell of betrayal set fire to his previous lighthearted thoughts, incinerating them in an instant. There was only one thing the two of them had in common. Him. And Hunter was one hundred percent certain he was the topic of conversation.

Instantly several memories flashed through his mind: Carly using her blog to rake him over the coals—subsequently making him the current subject of interest for the Miami press. Carly winning her boss's approval to do an in-depth piece on Hunter. And Carly making love to him—the first two times leaving him wondering what she had to gain.

Until tonight, when it had felt so different, so raw, it had lulled him into a sexually induced state of lethargy. Yet when he'd woken…she was gone.

Now she was talking to his former colleague. A man who knew every sordid detail about Hunter being duped by another woman. The duplicity, the slur on his good name, and the humiliatingly degrading days of being the subject of an inquiry by the department he'd sworn to serve.

Why was she talking to the FBI agent?

Hunter couldn't see beyond the most obvious answer. His story.

His vision tunneled and the edges grew gray, enveloping him in a black cloak that cut off every thought outside of confronting Carly Wolfe.

"Here you are," Hunter said from behind her, his voice encrusted with frost.

If she'd been a cat, his tone would have shaved several lives from Carly. She turned, and the look on Hunter's face left her frigid, chilling her to the core. Her heart thumped hard, forcing the blood through her frozen veins at an astronomical rate.

Terry Smith responded before her mouth could locate her tongue. "Hunter, come join our party. And just to prove there are no hard feelings—" the agent's smile was empty "—I'll buy you a drink."

Hunter's gaze remained fixed on Carly. "I'm not interested."

Carly's heart pumped harder and the strained atmosphere grew taut, the air dense from the tension. Was the anger on his face directed at his old coworker...or her? She had the horrible sinking feeling she was the cause.

The agent's grin lacked humor. "After you've paid my mixed-up hotel bar bill all these years, I owe you several hundred rounds at least."

"You don't owe me a thing," Hunter said.

His emphatic words about the yearly prank again left Carly with the impression that Hunter had done the hacking and Pete had done the paying.

"Not even one bourbon for old times' sake?" Terry said.

"I didn't want to drink with you back then," Hunter said his tone lethally even, "and I don't want to drink with you now."

The agent refused to shut up. "Come on, Hunter. All Carly's been doing is asking questions about you."

Hunter's face went dark, and Carly's heart sank like an anchor. She opened her mouth to refute Terry's exaggerated claim, but the agent went on.

"So it wasn't like I got to enjoy a nice chat with your girlfriend," he said, and the up-and-down perusal the man gave Carly came dangerously close to a leer.

Up until now he'd been almost pleasant, and certainly not inappropriate. Carly had the impression Terry's offensive look was more about making Hunter angry than anything else.

The agent's words as he went on confirmed her theory. "Tell me—is she worth it?" Terry said. "Maybe if I found the right angle she'd offer to sleep with *me* for a story too."

Before Carly could fully register the insult, Hunter's fist connected with the agent's chin with a loud snap. One moment Terry Smith was sitting on a barstool, and the next he was sprawled on the floor. The gasps from the guests were loud, and a waitress dropped her tray, shattering glasses on the hardwood floor. Silence followed. The whole room was shocked into momentary stillness.

The two bartenders rounded the bar and Hunter took a step back, hands raised in a non-threatening gesture. His gaze pivoted from Terry—still lying on the floor, rubbing his chin—back to Carly. "No need to remove me, gentlemen," Hunter said to the staff, his slate-blue gaze on hers, so empty the negative pressure threatened to suck the very life from Carly's soul. "I'm done here." And, with an air of finality, he swiveled on his heel, heading toward the lobby.

The murmurs of the guests at the bar returned as a bartender helped Terry to his feet. The agent was sullen as he angrily waved the help away. It took Carly all of eight seconds to recover fully from the incident before she took off across the lobby, chasing after Hunter's retreating form.

"What are you doing?" she said.

He didn't stop walking. "I'm leaving."

"Where are you going?"

He didn't slow his pace. "Home."

Her patience was rapidly growing slimmer. "What is your problem?"

"Apparently my ability to choose who I sleep with. Did you find out anything good?"

Frustrated, and more than a little annoyed, Carly struggled to keep up, her legs stretching to match the longer length of his. "I didn't get a chance to ask him much of anything. You barged in and dropped him with a lethal right hook before I got a chance."

"Sorry to ruin your interview."

Anger flared. "Damn it, Hunter," she said, grabbing his arm. But he was bigger and stronger and powered by a fury that was almost frightening. The momentum of his emotion and his strength carried them both forward as she clutched his arm and went on. "It wasn't an interview."

"Then why were you talking to him?"

She bit her lip, her steps still carried forward by her grip on his arm as he made his way to the elevator. Dismayed, she struggled for a way to explain.

Curiosity hadn't killed the cat, because death would have been too easy.

In the end, the truth was all she had. "I wanted to ask him a question."

He stopped to face her and shook off her arm, stepping closer. "What question?" His eyes were iced over, his face hard, and he looked so distant it was difficult to remember anything other than this coldly reserved Hunter.

"I wanted to know why you left the FBI," she said. He stared at her, as if sensing there was more. "And I wanted to know if your girlfriend had anything to do with it."

"You could have asked me."

"I *did* ask you, but you said it wasn't important."

"Sorry I wasn't cooperative enough for you. I didn't mean to ruin your plans. Or maybe this *was* your plan all along?"

Her patience lost so much weight it disappeared. "What the hell are you talking about?"

"Your plan to lull me into sleep with a good round of sex and then slip away to find Terry. Get the story you've wanted all along."

Carly was proud she didn't stomp her foot, and even more amazed she didn't slug him with her fist. But his jaw was so set, his expression so stony, she would have broken her hand while he would have hardly registered the tap to his face. Instead, hope died. Her heart burst. And her soul curled up in the corner and immediately began to lick its mortal wounds.

He'd made her feel worth protecting. But that was a reflection of him. That was who he was and what he did. It was no reflection of his belief in her. He'd faced down two supposed thugs because he would shield anyone who was threatened. He'd slugged a man because of a vile insult, but not because he considered *her* honorable. The need to defend and protect was simply hardwired into his being. He didn't trust her. Had absolutely no faith in her. And he never would.

The tears stung, but she'd had years of practice fighting them back. "You're not even going to give me a chance to explain."

The old feeling of helplessness, of abandonment, came rushing back. First Thomas, then her father. And now Hunter.

His face was so rigid she feared it would crack. "I came to find you because I missed you."

The stinging tears grew sharp, and her every breath felt heavy, as if she were breathing against a thick mask. "I came here to find some answers," she said, her voice thick with emotion. "Because I love yo—"

"Don't." He bit out the word so sharply it startled a nearby

guest, and he stepped closer, towering over her, his voice low. "Don't say it," he ground out.

Heart pounding, she froze, trying to find her voice again. "Hunter, I didn't learn a thing. I told you. I wanted to know the truth, and since you wouldn't tell me—"

"You want to hear what happened? Okay," he said, crossing his arms, his face hardly the picture of acceptance. "On the record, so you can use it to your heart's content and impress your boss with your in-depth knowledge."

Carly's soul curled up tighter, bled a little harder.

Hunter either didn't notice or didn't care. "I was used by a woman until she got what she wanted and left. I don't know if Mandy hooked up with me with that intention or not. I suspect my job simply pricked her interest and she decided to see where it led. But ultimately the story was more important than our relationship."

Despite her own pain, she hated the blank look on his face. "I'm sorry."

Hunter went on, ignoring her attempt at offering sympathy. "She wrote an article that revealed protected information about a cybercrime ring affiliated with the mob in Chicago. Information only our department knew. I'd been working on the case for two years, and I suspect she used a friend of mine from work—an FBI consultant—as her source. All I know is that it wasn't me," he said. Defeat joined forces with the anger in his voice and his lips twisted wryly, his bitter humor black. "But you can't prove a negative. And while a lack of evidence protects you from charges, it doesn't protect you from your colleagues' opinions." Hunter raked a hand through his hair, leaving it spiked on the top. "So I could have stayed and kept my job with restricted access, but I'd lost my zest for the work. Making money in a consulting business seemed the better option."

Her heart ached for him—the honorable man being accused. "I am not going to use the story," she said.

He continued as if she hadn't spoken. "Or maybe you need a little more blood and guts to really impact the reader?" He hiked a brow loaded with bitterness. "Like how devastating it was to be used by a woman I loved. How humiliating it was to be accused of putting the case I'd bled for at risk. The FBI was more than just a job. It was my life." He turned and headed for the bank of elevators.

Carly followed him. "I told you, I'm not printing a word."

Clearly unmoved by her words, he glanced down at her as he kept walking. "You forget I know how badly you want to prove to your father you've earned your stripes back." Reaching the elevators, he stepped inside one, turning to hold the doors open with his hands—blocking her entry. "So try this on for size, Carly," he said, looming over her. "You are a remarkable woman, but you should be less concerned about your father's opinion of you and more about your own. You can't earn your dad's respect until you grow up, act like an adult and develop a little respect for yourself." His gaze was relentless. "And that includes refraining from hopping from one loser's bed to the next."

Her hand connected with his cheek with a loud slap, but the sting in her palm was nothing compared to the pain in her heart. The words had landed too close to home. The last sliver of hope shriveled and died, and her words rasped out, heavy with furious sarcasm. "As opposed to someone like you," she said, holding his gaze. "Well, here's a newsflash for you, Mr. Philips. You don't hold a monopoly on fidelity, bravery or *integrity*." Livid, frustrated he was taking the wounds from his past out on her, she bit out, "One judgmental man in my life is enough, so you can take your paternalistic attitude and go to hell."

His expression didn't ease. "That's not a problem," he said. "Because I expect more from the woman I love."

Carly's heart soared even as the floor dropped out from beneath her stomach, the twin sensations leaving her sick. The sting in her eyes grew sharper, because the horrible part was she knew it was true. She'd felt the emotion when he'd clung to her in the hotel room. Hunter *did* love her. But she also realized why that news didn't bring the happiness she'd always dreamed it would.

Because there were all kinds of love. The unrequited kind, that often left one bitter. The kind that was reciprocated, sure and strong, which made a person feel invincible. And then there was the kind that was returned but wasn't mature enough to last, stunted by the shadows of the past.

And that was what she had with Hunter.

"I expected more from the man *I* love," she said. Hunter's expression remained walled up as she went on. "I need a man who'll stick by my side. Who has faith in me." She fisted her hands at her side. "I need someone who *believes* in me."

His voice was dangerously soft. "Unfortunately," he said as he straightened up to push the elevator button, "that man isn't me."

Stricken, Carly stared at Hunter's *over you* expression as the elevator door closed, cutting off the excruciating view.

CHAPTER ELEVEN

"LIFE sucks." Carly flopped back onto the plush comforter of the king size bed in the hotel room, staring up at the ceiling.

Abby shot her a sympathetic look. "I don't think Hunter meant the things that he said, Carly."

Carly dragged the back of her hand across her eyes, impatient with herself. She was tired of being madder than hell. And she was equally fatigued from feeling as if Hunter had whipped out a gun and blasted a shot at her chest at close range, leaving her bleeding in the wake of his retreat. Since he'd packed up and left, gallantly paying the bill for an extra day—as if she'd *want* to stay and gamble her money when she'd already lost her heart—she'd fought back the urge to hunt him down. To knock that dumb metaphorical white hat off of his head, stomping on it until it was good and flat.

The exhaustive flip-flopping of her emotions had left her wrung out and empty.

Abby sat on the bed beside Carly. "Look at it this way," Abby said. She placed a comforting hand on Carly's shoulder and crinkled her brow, the jet-black pigtails shifting in response. "He wouldn't have been so upset about finding you talking to his old colleague if he didn't really care about you."

Care? He'd *said* he loved her. For years she'd dreamed of hearing those words from someone she loved in return, but she'd never imagined that the moment could bring such agony.

"I don't know," Carly said. Which was true. She didn't know anything anymore.

"Well…" The doubt on her friend's face was hardly encouraging. "He decked that guy for the comment he made about you." Her overly bright smile looked forced, and it was painful to watch. "That has to mean something."

"It means he found an excuse to do what he's probably wanted to do for years, using *my* supposed honor as an excuse." Carly rolled onto her stomach and buried her face in her arms. Her voice was muffled, which made going on easier—because the next set of words were the hardest she'd ever formed. "Except he doesn't see me as honorable."

"You love him," Abby said softly.

Spoken out loud, the words doubled Carly's misery, and the weight of the monstrous entity was a burden that threatened to drown her.

Carly turned her head on her arms, looking up at Abby. "You said it yourself. These things rarely work out."

"Sometimes they do," Abby said. "You just have to believe that they will."

With monumental effort, Carly briefly pushed aside her pain and stared up at her friend. She wasn't sure which was harder: enduring the expected pessimism while lost in a mire of hopeless misery, or the bud of hope that was now emanating from her friend's face. "Since when have you been a love convert?"

Guilt flickered through Abby's eyes. "Since I got married."

The words lingered in the air and gradually seeped into Carly's consciousness, her eyelids slowly stretching wide as the news settled deeper. It took a moment for the rest of her body to respond. When it did, she shot up, kneeling on the bed. "Married?"

"Pete and I visited a chapel on the strip yesterday," she said with a smile. "Elvis officiated."

Blinking hard, Carly tried to reconcile the pessimistic, down-on-relationships woman she knew with the glowing, almost upbeat woman in front of her. Happiness for her deserving friend and sadness for herself combined to overwhelm her, and she leaned forward, gathering Abby in a fierce hug. "I'm so pleased for you," she said, her throat clogged with emotion. Carly closed her eyes, resisting the urge to burst into tears. This would hardly be the I'm-happy-for-you moment her friend must have envisioned.

Abby held her tight. "One day I'll return the sentiment."

Carly didn't have the heart to rain on her friend's newfound joy, so she said nothing. The words that wanted to form were all negative. She had no clue how to tell her boss the truth about Hunter without losing her job. She had no idea how to heal the rift with her father, especially now that she'd screwed up again. And, worse, she was sure she'd never recover from loving Hunter. Though the word "recover" was probably better suited to catastrophic events.

Well, as far as Carly was concerned, love ranked right up there with floods, hurricanes and other natural disasters.

Abby pulled back, holding Carly's arms. "What are you going to do now?"

Carly knew her colleague was referring to more than just Hunter, and she pressed her lips together, potential answers swirling in her brain. Run away? Leave everything behind and start all over again? It was tempting, but it hadn't helped her three years ago when she'd come limping back home. And it hardly seemed the best solution now.

Gathering her resolve, she met her newly married friend's gaze with as much confidence as she could muster. "I'm going back to fix what I can." She blew out a shaky breath. "Starting with my dad."

Carly turned into the long, oak-tree-lined driveway of her childhood home, half wishing it would extend forever and she could avoid what waited for her at the end. She could just drive on indefinitely, enjoying the sunshine and the song on the radio, pretending her life was okay. Moving toward the moment of truth, or one of them anyway, but without having to actually face her father.

Nice try, Carly.

She was exhausted from the trip home and missing Hunter like she'd never thought possible. No easy-breezy forty-eight hour recovery this time. Honestly, she wasn't sure forty-eight *years* would lessen the pain. But it was time to tell her father what had happened. She hadn't just screwed up again— would probably get fired *again*—this time she'd also lost the one man she'd ever loved in the process. So…not only had she managed to repeat past mistakes, she'd gone and topped her previous efforts.

What father wouldn't be proud of such an accomplishment?

Carly's lips twisted at the grim irony as she parked in the drive and stared up at the massive colonial house, hoping to find a little courage in the view. It hadn't always been associated with unpleasant memories. Her childhood had been as happy as it could be, given she'd been minus a mother and her tiny two-person family was all she'd ever known. They'd muddled through contentedly enough until she'd hit puberty. But she could no longer afford to be the resentful adolescent who'd felt inadequate and misunderstood, and it was time to let the hurt go. Time for her to stop stubbornly waiting for her father to apologize and take the first step toward reconciliation.

Because it was either forgive him for letting her down or give up on their relationship forever.

She briefly pressed her lids together, seeking a happier place, and then exited, closing the car door with a determined thunk—praying her resolve was strong enough to withstand the next few minutes. Losing her newfound sense of inner peace at the first test was hardly the new and improved, more mature Carly she was striving to be.

A few minutes later she found her father under the back brick portico, standing next to one of the giant pillars that faced the Atlantic. He looked as if he'd aged since last week. And, despite her obstinate refusal to move on, she wasn't getting any younger either.

"Dad," she said, and then hesitated, at a loss what to say next.

He turned, and she braced, waiting for one of the subtle sarcastic slurs he always tossed in her direction. Or maybe she was the one who fired first, in an effort to beat him to it. Perhaps they'd taken turns. She couldn't remember. Either way, it always ended with one of them, or both, too angry to continue the conversation.

Two stubborn people stuck in the same behavioral pattern for years. In retrospect, given all she'd lost, it seemed petty and pointless.

His face was closed off and hardly welcoming. "Hello, kitten."

The stupid tears that lived just a heartbeat away bubbled to the surface, but she blinked them back. If he noticed, he didn't say anything. He simply turned and leaned a shoulder against the column, staring out over the Atlantic, while Carly struggled to find the right words.

It was a full minute before he said, "I was just thinking about that time you disguised yourself as a waitress at a party I threw for the mayor." He turned to study her. "How old were you? Sixteen? Seventeen?"

It wasn't the conversation she'd planned on having, and she certainly didn't relish the thought of rehashing old arguments. Dealing with the current ones seemed ambitious enough.

"Fifteen," she said. "You were so angry you grounded me for a month."

He shot her a sharp look. "I didn't have much choice."

"A month is forever to a fifteen-year-old."

"The mayor complained that you were *stalking* him at the gala."

She chewed on her lower lip before responding. "That wasn't entirely accurate," she said, debating the wisdom of sharing the truth. Carly shifted on her feet. "I was actually trying to question his wife about his mistress."

Her father's heavy eyebrows shot up in surprise as he let out a faintly amused scoff. "You never told me that."

She gave a small shrug. "I thought it best you didn't know."

"No wonder the mayor was so livid," he mused.

A pause followed, and Carly wasn't sure if he was amused by her stunt, impressed with her teenage chutzpah or annoyed by the memories of raising a frustratingly independent adolescent. And the closer she'd grown to adulthood, the more her father had been unhappy with his daughter's choices. Now that she was grown up, it seemed nothing she ever did measured up in his eyes. It was a bitter pill that sat in her stomach, refusing to dissolve.

His brow dug deep furrows. "Why are you here, Carly?"

"I need—" Her throat clamped hard, blocking the rest of her words, but she forced her feet to carry her closer to her father. She scanned the turquoise waters of the Atlantic. The late afternoon sun was sparkling on the surface and the salty breeze was balmy. The cold weather that had arrived when she'd first met Hunter had finally passed and moved on. Much like Hunter himself. Pain pierced her. His absence was like an empty chair at a crowded table, a constant reminder he'd walked away. But he'd been right. It was past time to deal with her father as an adult.

"I don't want to fight with you anymore," she said. She drew in a breath. "I know raising me wasn't easy."

A small frown slipped up his face and he looked uncomfortable with the topic—or maybe he was simply suspicious of her intentions. It was several seconds before he responded. "I run a multi-billion dollar company with hundreds of people on the payroll," he said, his voice a mixture of exasperation and defeat. "But I never knew how to handle you."

"I'm not a staff member to be managed, Dad," she said. "I'm your daughter."

He sent her an aggravated look. "Employees are easier."

"Yes, because you can simply dictate what you want." Carly sighed and crossed her arms. "People in *real* relationships don't respond well to the method."

He stared at her for what felt like forever, and then shook his head, looking a hundred years older than he should. "I'm sure your mother would have done a better job," he said, his face haggard.

The sting of tears returned. "I'm sorry I was a difficult teen."

"It's just…" He blew out a breath and rubbed a hand across his forehead, leaving the wild eyebrows in even more disarray. He caught her gaze with an almost urgent intensity. "I won't be around forever," he said, his voice firm yet sincere. "And one of these days your choices are going to get you into *real* trouble."

A dull ache thumped, and Carly pressed her fingers to her temples, hoping to ease the sudden pounding. "Okay," she went on reluctantly. "You were right. Thomas was using me." She dropped her hands to her side. "But I didn't love him," she said. That fact had been made abundantly clear when she fell in love with Hunter.

The constant free-falling feeling returned and fear froze

her chest, making its work difficult. For a moment she could scarcely breathe.

Damn. Love didn't just hurt. It *paralyzed*.

"I know," he said.

Surprise drew her brows together in confusion, but her father went on with a small wave of his hand.

"Oh, I didn't believe that you'd slept with the senator for the story any more than I believed the rumor you'd fallen in love with him and let your emotions cloud your objectivity. I knew better. And in some ways..." he shook his head with a grim look "...I almost wished the latter was true."

Shocked, she stared at him, her mouth gaping as she tried to make sense of the words. "I don't understand."

He heaved out another heavy breath. "At least then you would have risked your career for something more than a fascination for a man just because he'd been labeled an individualist."

Carly held still, absorbing the words that were hard to hear even as her father went on, serving up more of the same.

"And since then you've been in and out of a number of relationships. Most of the men weren't worthy of your time, but I wouldn't have cared so much if you'd actually *loved* one of them."

She opened her mouth to speak, but there were no words of defense. And so far love had yet to provide her that warm, fuzzy feeling that got paired with the condition. Since the moment those elevator doors had closed in her face, with Hunter's words haunting her, she'd started to wonder if her relationships since Thomas had been about avoiding the big L. Because Hunter's accusations had left her raw, bleeding for the second time in her life—abandoned again, without the chance to explain herself. Her father hadn't wanted to hear her side three years ago, and Hunter didn't want to hear hers now.

But maybe her father was finally ready to listen.

"Thomas and I didn't start seeing one another until after the story was done," she said.

"I know that now." He paused, his frank expression brutally painful. "I wasn't as convinced back then."

It hurt to hear the truth and it seemed horribly unfair. But life wasn't fair, and maybe it was never meant to be. Regardless, it was up to her to handle herself, despite feeling she'd been wronged. And maybe that was the ultimate lesson.

The only control she had was over her own behavior.

"Carly," her father said, "when are you going to grow up and stop flitting from one guy to the next?"

Her heart wrenched, the pain stealing her breath. The time to come clean was now. Would he be happy to hear she'd finally fallen in love when he learned that in all probability her emotional development came at the cost of her job? Her boss had hired her despite her past, giving her the second chance that she'd just destroyed.

But the agony of losing Hunter put the threat in perspective.

"I've been asking my boss for approval to write a story on Hunter Philips." The tone in her voice must have held the warning that bad news was ahead, because her father looked as if he was bracing for the impact, and a little part of her heart died again. "She finally gave me the go-ahead, but…" Her voice stalled. She was too afraid to go on, dreading the look of disappointment in his face. Apparently her expression said it all.

"You've slept with him," he said, his face resigned.

Her heart clenched even as her stomach rolled. He eyed her steadily, and she wished she could read more beneath the weary acceptance.

"You can't do the story now," he said.

"I realize that."

"You have to tell your boss why."

"I realize that too."

Neither one of them spoke of the obvious.

Her throat so tight it was painful, she said, "I'm in love with him."

The expression on her face must have conveyed the massive ache in her heart, because her father didn't look happy for her. He looked like he was sharing her pain but wasn't sure what to do about it.

He took a hesitant step closer. "Carly…"

Letting the emotion wash through her, Carly crossed the last few feet, and he folded her awkwardly in his arms.

The hug was brief, but full of the familiar smell of the peppermints he loved, before he set her back. "I'm sorry he hurt you," her father said gruffly.

Conscious of his discomfort—her father would never be the touchy-feely sort—she tried to smile. She couldn't have her father thinking it was all Hunter's fault. She cleared her throat, clogged with unshed tears. "He's a good guy," she said. "An honorable one."

Too bad he couldn't believe she had the ability to be honorable too.

Her father raised a bushy eyebrow. "What are you going to tell your boss?"

She lifted her chin. "The truth," she said. And it was a good thing Hunter had pushed her to quit being stubborn about her dad, because she would need his support in the coming weeks. "I'm going to write the best damn profile piece I can on someone else and offer it as a replacement," she said, steadily meeting her father's gaze. "And then I'm going to go on Brian O'Connor's show, meet Hunter face to face, and finish what I started."

"Were you given a hard time when you backed out of tonight's Brian O'Connor show?" Booker asked.

Jaw clenched, eyes on the three-foot-long punching bag hanging in the well-stocked gym of his home, Hunter swung with his right arm. His fist connected with a satisfying thwack. "Not really," he said. He did his best to ignore the digital clock on the wall.

11:44 p.m.

A sickening feeling rose, burning his chest and his gut, as Hunter went on. "There isn't anything left to debate." Except maybe his sanity, considering he'd had to learn the same lesson all over again.

He landed another solid punch, forcing back the urge to pummel the bag in frustration, knowing Booker was waiting for him to say more. But Hunter was washed out, too tired from his workout—and the current state of his life—to engage in much conversation.

The week since he'd arrived home from Las Vegas had been busy, consumed by a job that at one time had seemed perfect. Hunter had managed to carve out some time to explore the idea he'd formulated after Carly had questioned his career priorities. But after all that had happened, dealing with Carly on live TV again went beyond his abilities. Surviving this evening, knowing she'd be on the air without him, was proving to be tough.

It would take a miracle to get through the next quarter of an hour without losing his mind, or his resolve *not* to watch the show. Hunter glanced at the clock.

11:45.

Hunter began to pummel the bag, the repeated thumps filling the silence until his friend spoke again.

"It's on in fifteen minutes," Booker said, as if every cell in Hunter's body wasn't acutely aware of that fact. "Are you gonna watch?"

Hunter's abdomen clenched as if hit. His chest and arm muscles burned from his intense workout, but in a way the pain was an improvement. Since his argument with Carly he'd moved through his days in a trancelike state. Numb. Anesthetized. Trying hard to forget the maddening sight of Carly talking with Terry.

And the devastated look on her face as the elevator doors had closed...

With a hard jab, Hunter's fist met the bag, jarring his left arm. But the sensation did nothing to ease the conflicting images in his head.

"Because I think you should tune in to see what she says," Booker went on.

"No." Hunter punctuated the word with a mighty slug. "I'm not watching the show."

Public curiosity had swelled since he'd backed out forty-eight hours ago. True to form, Carly hadn't canceled her commitment to appear. Whether she'd stuck with it for the publicity, or for some other reason, he wasn't sure. But he'd seen the advertisement announcing the replacement topic: the debut of Carly Wolfe's new series. A column spotlighting a different Miami resident every week. She'd finally reached her goal.

The question was, who had she chosen as her first subject?

The clock on the wall read 11:47, and bile rose in the back of his throat. His stomach churned at the thought of watching her discuss everything he'd vomited out in a fit of anger. Muscles coiled tight, he felt the dark potential twine its way around his limbs. He refused to watch as the woman he loved traded in all they'd shared to achieve the career goal she'd chased for three years.

The familiar feeling of betrayal, the boil of resentment, left him battering the stuffed leather bag with a one-two punch that jarred him all the way to his soul.

"I find this situation very interesting," Booker said. "I'm usually the one who sees a conspiracy at every turn."

Hunter raised a wry eyebrow at Booker. "Are you saying I'm being paranoid, like you?"

His shaggy brown hair was in need of a trim, and Booker's smile was wide as he brushed his bangs back. "Your suspicions don't involve whole nations and large governmental agencies. So, compared to me, you're small-time." His voice changed to a more serious note. "But you *are* skeptical of everything that moves, Hunt." He paused before going on. "And I think you're wrong about Carly."

Pushing aside the crushing doubt made worse by Booker's chastising expression, Hunter shot his partner a doubtful look. "Of course you'd say that. You married her best friend," Hunter said. He was still trying to adjust to *that* particular turn of events.

"Abby and I decided it would be better for our relationship if we didn't discuss you two."

"Smart move. Still, you might be biased."

"Or I might be right."

Hunter's chest clamped hard, squeezing with a grip so tight it made breathing and circulating his blood a mammoth chore. His heart still managed to pump the lingering fear to the far reaches of his body. Fear that he'd learn he'd screwed up the one good thing to happen to him in so long that he hadn't recognized it for what it was…

Real. Genuine. And built to last.

With a silent curse, Hunter closed his eyes. The last time he'd made love to Carly his heart had claimed it was legit. That she was on the up and up. But he'd taken one look at her talking to Terry and his heart had taken a sharp U-turn. All the old suspicions, the duplicities of the past, had come screaming back. The avalanche of anger, humiliation, the need for self-preservation had plowed into him with a force that had swept him up in its wake.

If Carly hadn't run the story he'd accused her of going after, what then?

He opened his eyes and began punching the bag again, the lingering question feeding the massive knot growing in his chest.

Hunter was saved from dwelling on the unbearable thought when his friend spoke.

"Is it back to business as usual, then?" Booker said.

Hunter stopped punching and turned to face his friend and business partner. Regardless of the outcome tonight, the status quo had changed. He couldn't continue to pretend his life was enjoyable. Actually, it wasn't even tolerable. Making money hand over clenched fist wasn't good enough anymore. It was time to come clean about his plans.

"I had a long talk with the special agent in charge of the Miami division of the FBI," Hunter said. With a look of surprise, Booker crossed his arms and leaned against the wall, clearly settling in to hear more. "They're very interested in help with their caseload," Hunter said, steadily meeting Booker's gaze as he went on. "I signed on to become a part-time consultant."

A few moments passed, and then a smile slowly crept up Booker's face. "Catching the criminals was always your specialty."

Relieved Booker understood, Hunter delivered the rest of his news as matter-of-factly as he could. "Which means I'm going to need more help in the day-to-day running of the business."

Booker didn't hesitate. "Not a problem."

Narrowing his eyes, he wondered if his friend understood exactly what he was asking. "I thought you hated dealing with the clients."

The pause lasted long enough for his partner's face to tak

on a guarded look. His words were cautious. "You set some pretty high standards, Hunt," Booker said.

Hunter stared at his friend, the implication of the statement washing over him as Booker swiped a hand through his shaggy hair again and went on.

"I hate feeling as if I'm not doing a good enough job."

Stunned, Hunter stared at his friend. "Did I give you that impression?"

"Not directly. But you're a hard act to follow," he said. "And you're fairly demanding when it comes to your expectations."

The possibility that Booker had been avoiding clients for a reason outside his social discomfort had never occurred to Hunter. Booker's voice dropped, and Hunter got a disturbing feeling the topic had widened to include more than just work.

"Sometimes you hold the people in your life to pretty impossible standards," Booker said.

Hunter's throat constricted so tight swallowing was impossible. He glanced at the clock on the wall.

11:55.

Booker picked up the remote control to the flatscreen TV mounted on the wall, holding it out to Hunter. "Do yourself a favor, Hunt," Booker said. "Watch the show."

Heart thudding loudly in his chest, Hunter removed his gloves and took the remote. Without another word, his friend headed for the exit.

Hunter stared at the black TV screen for a full four minutes, the digital numbers on the clock marking the passage of time, minute by agonizing minute. Either way, he had to know. He just wasn't sure which would be worse. Losing Carly as a result of her actions...or *his*.

Finally, unable to take the tension any longer, he pushed the "on" button and flipped to the right channel. His fifty-eight inch TV was filled with the image of Carly sitting on

Brian O'Connor's couch. Beautiful, of course, in a gauzy top
and skirt. But the sight of her lovely legs, glossy brunette hair,
and warm, amber-colored eyes was nothing compared to the
shock he got when the camera panned to the right. Sitting next
to her were two young adults in typical urban street clothes.
Thad and Marcus. The two graffiti artists she'd been interviewing that day in the alley. The first Miami residents to be
featured in her new series. Not him, after all, then.

Hell.

Nausea boiled, his chest burned, and Hunter gripped the
leather punching bag to steady himself, his mind churning
with memories. The vile words from his mouth. The stricken
expression on Carly's face. She'd said she needed a man who
trusted her. A man who had faith in her. Who *believed* in
her. He'd screwed up royally at the very moment he'd confessed he loved her.

So how could he ever convince her now?

CHAPTER TWELVE

DESPITE the ebony-colored tablecloths with their center-pieces consisting of dried dead roses, the ambiance on the restaurant's outdoor patio was festive. Carly was amazed that Pete and Abby had managed to find the perfect balance of Gothic and elegance to celebrate their recent marriage. Lit by candlelight that reflected off the blanket of fog covering the terrace floor, the evening was cast in an otherworldly glow. Waiters circulated, their platters laden with appetizers. Guests ordered drinks at two beautiful mahogany bars, crafted to resemble coffins. Or maybe they were real. If so, Carly hoped the caskets were new.

In jeans, sneakers and a black T-shirt, Pete Booker cast his wife of two weeks an adoring look, and Carly's heart tripped over a mix of envy and happiness.

Standing beside her, her father muttered, "This is the strangest wedding reception I've ever been to." He dubiously eyed a discreetly placed fog machine before turning his gaze to the bride's outfit.

Abby's black long-sleeved gloves were paired with a matching corset dress that flared into a full-length lace skirt, trailing to the floor with a Victorian flare and a Gothic attitude.

Carly's lips twitched in amusement. "Thanks for coming with me, Dad." She clutched the strap of her silver beaded evening purse, running a hand down her halter-top dress of midnight satin. It wasn't her usual choice, but all the guests had been requested to wear black. At least the color suited her mood. "I hated the thought of showing up alone."

"Yeah…" Her dad let out an awkward harrumph and shifted on his feet. "Well…" he went on uneasily, and Carly's mouth twitched harder.

"Don't worry," she said. "I won't start crying again."

Her dad sent her a look loaded with fear. "Please don't."

Carly almost laughed. She had rallied and poured on the charm for the final show, but when it was done she'd fallen apart—and her father had barely survived the onslaught of tears. She'd finally come to realize her dad did not handle a crying woman well—something she hadn't fully understood until now. He would never be the perfect parent, ready with an understanding hug, a reassuring smile and gentle words of wisdom. Then again, she was hardly the perfect daughter, either. But he was here tonight, supporting her in his own way. And for that she was inordinately grateful.

Because eventually Hunter would make an appearance.

Anxiety settled deep. If she ever decided to date again— like maybe a million years from now—she was going to give her choice more serious thought. Both for her sake and the man's. Hunter might have been protecting himself by throwing up walls, but outside of Carly at least he hadn't hurt anyone in the process. She, on the other hand, had left a trail of unhappy boyfriends in her wake.

All of them had deserved better than her pathetic attempts to stick with men who had no hope of capturing her heart.

When she spied Hunter heading in her direction, said heart sputtered to a stop, and she reached out to grasp the back of a nearby chair. After a few earth-shaking seconds she pushed away the budding, soul-sucking vortex of gloom.

Her father glanced at Hunter and then shot her a wor

ried look. "Do you want me to stay?" he asked, almost as if he hoped she'd say no. "Or do you want me to fetch you a drink?"

She was tempted to keep him around as a shield. But she'd made a pact with herself today that there would be no more wallowing.

She tried for a reassuring smile. "Drink, please," she said to her father. With a deep breath, she straightened her shoulders and met Hunter's gaze as he strode through the crowd in her direction. "I'm going to need it," she muttered.

Her dad headed for a casket lined with bottles, shooting Hunter a glare infused with a good bit of concern.

Hunter came to a stop a few feet from her. In an impeccably cut black suit, he looked as handsome and intimidating as ever—every muscle poised, prepared for battle. His cool slate-blue eyes were trained on her face. But this time his hair was spiked in front, as if he'd run an impatient hand through it multiple times. A brief flicker of uncertainty came and went, replaced with his usual determined gaze.

It took several moments and more than a few blinks of her eyelids to jumpstart her heart again. His presence had robbed her of her earlier confidence, so she'd just have to fake it until her mojo returned for real.

"I came to tell you I spoke with Booker and we're all square," he said carefully, his eyes probing, as if testing her response. "We've worked out a plan for me to put in some time doing consulting work for the FBI."

She refused to be swayed by the news. "Glad to hear it."

Neither mentioned their parting words at the elevator, but the ghost of their painful falling-out hung in the air, as if lurking in the fog-blanketed shadows. His eyes held hers, and the determined focus, the sense of purpose radiating from his face, made her heart work harder.

After a tension-filled pause, he said, "Congratulations on

your new series too. How did you get your boss to agree to your plans for your column?"

"I didn't sleep with her, if that's what you're suggesting."

A small smile appeared, more sad than amused. "It's not."

"I confessed everything, and then handed her a story on Thad and Marcus that blew her socks off."

His tone broadcast just how pleased he was. "Good for you."

"Yeah," she said. Just for good measure, she hiked her chin higher. "Go, me." Smart words, in retrospect. Because right about now leaving sounded like a wise plan. She'd missed him, had ached for him, but he also brought a host of sharp emotions along with the longing. Ultimately, it was the confusion and pain that drove her away. "Well…" She cleared her throat, the sound awkward. "I should find my dad." She turned on her heel.

He put his hand on her arm to stop her, his touch setting off all kinds of alarms. "I shouldn't haven't insulted you," he said, the regret in his eyes profound. "I'm sorry."

Ignoring the feel of his fingers on her skin, she took a deep breath, glad the initial icy tension was broken. His apology didn't make up for not believing in her, but it helped ease the ending. "I shouldn't have slapped you," she said with a tiny sheepish shrug. "It was an impulse reaction."

"I deserved it."

Oh, dear God, it was the agreeable Hunter from the first show. The one who was so hard to argue with. The one who knew how to work her to get just what he wanted, whether it be irritation, confessing her deepest doubts…or a sensual surrender.

The question was, what did he want now?

"Hunter," she said with a sigh, pulling her arm away. "I think we've said everything there is to say." Like he might love her, but didn't really know how. Not in the way she needed. The sharp ache resurfaced.

"I'm not finished," he said. "I wanted to tell you I spent the last week trying to perfect my new app."

She frowned, confused. "I don't care about—"

"Marry me," he said bluntly.

She sucked in a breath, feeling the hit, and her stomach clamped into a knot.

She shot him a look, trying to hide her weakening resolve. "You show up, after all this time, and just expect me to accept your proposal? It's been *seven days* since you left me high and dry on the TV show, and—"

"I had some work to do before I could face you."

She lifted an incredulous brow. "You confronted two men in a dangerous Miami alley, yet you couldn't deal with me face to face?"

"Not after the mistake that I'd made."

They'd both made several, and it was more than a few rapid heartbeats that passed before she was able to respond. When she did, the word came out soft. "Coward."

His lips twisted grimly. "In some things, yes."

Put an innocent in harm's way and he would bravely confront the most fearsome of opponents. But when faced with an emotional risk he cut and ran. It was a truth she needed to remember, despite the fact he was here now…looking wonderful…and her body was remembering the advantage of making love to a man with a fighter's muscles…her heart was remembering how the action-hero defender made her feel.

Protected. *Loved.*

Gathering her wits, she shifted her gaze away, blinking hard to maintain her composure. The guests were lining up at the unusual wedding cake: a six-tiered confection of white icing thick with a thorny trimming done in black. Carly tried to imagine taking the marital leap with Hunter, waiting for him to walk out…

"I can't marry you," she said. And with as much grace as she could muster, she headed for the bar and her father.

Halfway there her cellphone chirped, and she pulled it from her purse and opened the message. The soulful sounds of the song "Share My Life" crooned from her phone, and the screen filled with the words "Marry Me."

She gripped her cellular, her stomach settling on top of her toes. She hadn't recovered from the first proposal, and now he was sending a second. Another proposal that left her confused, doubting her resolve to be strong. Fingers shaky, she selected "No" and scrolled through the list of rejection songs to accompany her response. There were only ten. With feeling, she firmly jabbed the button next to "Love Stinks."

From behind her, the reedy sound of the song filled the air.

Carly whirled around to face Hunter, and his gaze held hers as he crossed closer, coming to a stop in front of her.

Now that she knew his plan, her whole body was filled with caution. "You *have* been busy."

"Designing the app is the easy part. Finding the right songs is hard." He eyed her levelly as he said, "I also discontinued The Ditchinator."

She gave him no leeway with her expression and she forced herself to maintain eye contact, desperately trying to calm her nerves. But she tipped her head, her voice reflecting her curiosity. "Why?"

His eyes held hers with conviction. "Because you wanted me to."

Feeling raw, Carly fought the urge to get misty-eyed. He'd done it to make her happy.

"I also decided you'd prefer something more positive," he said. "So I replaced The Ditchinator with The Hitchinator."

At the name, humor briefly overrode the angst, and he

mouth worked, biting back a smile. "Your new app needs a lot of work," she said, as lightly as she could, but all her doubts made it a tough sell. "The Hitchinator is a bit of a retreaded name, and the selection of music to accompany a refusal is pretty limited."

He tipped his head meaningfully. "But there are thirty ways to say yes."

"Do you think it will sell well?"

"I'm only worried about winning over one customer." His voice dropped a notch. "You."

Her heart pounded out its approval even as she struggled to remain strong.

"I didn't expect you to say yes...the first time," he said, taking a half-step closer.

She ignored the chaotic pumping in her chest, the surge of heat in her veins. The longing that went beyond the physical and traveled all the way to her soul. She forced herself to maintain his gaze, though her heart and her heated blood screamed *retreat*. To end the torture of continuing to tell him no.

"I should go find my father," she said, and turned and headed in the direction of her dad at the bar.

Ten feet from her intended destination, her safe haven, another chirp came from her cellphone. She stopped mid-step and glanced at her cellular with a powerful blend of dread... and hope. She pressed the button and the words "Marry Me" reappeared. The phone vibrated to the tune of Billy Idol's "White Wedding." Carly couldn't restrain the small bark of laughter. When the humor passed, again she pushed "No" and scrolled through the rejection choices, choosing one. But this time her fingers hovered hesitantly for several seconds. Biting her lip, she pushed "send."

Her selection of "Bad Romance" filled the air, coming from *directly* behind her, and Carly closed her eyes.

Don't let him charm you, Carly.

But her heart felt more vulnerable when she turned to face Hunter, standing just three feet from her. She gripped the strap of her purse. How could she survive this encounter when he was so close, looking and smelling wonderful and depriving her of her ability to breathe?

"Did you think Billy Idol's 'White Wedding' would endear me to your cause?" she said, knowing he knew it had.

"The first song was too obvious. And I know how much you love the unexpected," he said. "Besides…" He looked at a nearby table topped with an ornate haunted-house style candelabra, flickering in the night. "I've seen the video. 'White Wedding' seemed appropriate, given our current setting."

"Hunter—"

"I'm sorry I didn't believe you," he interrupted firmly, his eyes intense.

Her heart knocked faster, begging to be set free from its self-imposed cage, and panic squeezed Carly's chest. "Too little, too late," she said. "Before the last show I was hoping you'd turn up and say you'd changed your mind. That you trusted me and didn't need any proof beyond your belief in me." She stared at him, dwelling on those painful days. "An apology would have meant something *before* you had evidence I was telling the truth."

A host of emotions filtered across his face before landing on regret. "I know."

With a single finger he touched her hand, and her heart rattled the bars of its pen. But she fought the weakness and her growing doubts as he went on.

"I'm hoping you'll accept my apology anyway," he said. "And I'd be even more pleased if you'd agree to marry me."

Her throat ached as she fought back the tears and the overwhelming need to say *yes*. Good God, she was tired of crying. "Why should I?"

"Because I'd like a second chance." Her throat closed over completely, and when she didn't respond he continued. "I made a mistake," he said, his voice harsh with emotion. "But it doesn't mean I don't love you."

"I know you do," she said. "But Hunter—"

He opened his mouth to cut her off again, but Carly placed her fingers on his lips, stopping his words.

Shifting her gaze between two beautiful slate-blue eyes, she said in a low voice, "I can't live my life walking on eggshells, worrying that I might do or say something that shakes your trust in me again." She ignored the intense heat in his gaze and the feel of his lips, the unyielding softness that was oh, so uniquely Hunter. Her chest caught, and breathing became difficult. She dropped her arm, gathering the courage to continue. "All because you can't move on."

"I can," he fired off in a low voice. He shifted closer, towering over her, his tone softening. "Give me a second chance to prove it."

She still hadn't heard a good enough reason. "Why should I?" she repeated.

His words tumbled out. "Because I let my fear push you away," he said gruffly. Face frustrated, he raked a hand through his hair and looked across the crowded terrace. The pause felt like forever, but when he finally turned back, his expression was frank. Raw.

The last barrier was gone.

"I knew you loved me," he said, his words rough, heavy with the truth. "But I didn't trust the feeling and I was too scared to believe you. I don't deserve another chance. But I'm asking anyway," he said. "Because I'm tired of being unhappy and alone. All because I'm a gutless coward."

As if taking a moment to collect himself, he dropped his gaze to her bare shoulder and brushed her hair back, leaving a skitter of goosebumps. His hand settled between her shoulder blades, cupping her skin as if it planned to stay. He lifted his eyes to hers, and the brutal honesty stole what little composure she had left.

"And I think fear is driving your decisions now," he said.

Her mind balked at the idea and she hiked her chin, forcing the tears away with a watery sniff. "I am *not* scared."

The words sounded hollow even to her own ears.

Several seconds ticked by, and though his gaze was intense there was a touch of humor mixed with a hint of desperation. His voice, however, was pure daring conviction. "Then marrying me shouldn't be a problem."

As his warm palm cradled her back, Carly's heart thumped loudly in her chest, reinforcing the message that he could have called her a coward too, but hadn't. Or that he *could* have insisted he was right, which he was.

Despite everything, she sent him a suspicious look. "Are you *daring* me to marry you?"

"The woman I love never walks away from a challenge."

Her lips twisted into a self-directed frustrated frown. "Damn it," she said in a low tone. "I hate that you're right."

The happy sounds of chatter filled the air as his eyes continued to scan hers in a question, stripping her to the emotional bone. Until he said, "So, Carly Wolfe, which would you rather have?" Despite the words, in spite of the teasing light in his eyes, his tone was serious. "A life with me, learning how to do love right, or an endless succession of singing break-up telegrams?"

The question—and the skin-on-skin touch on her back—made breathing difficult. Which wasn't so good for formulating complicated responses. Fortunately the answer was simple. "You," she finally said. "I choose you."

Relief, joy and fire flashed in his eyes, and with a lightning-fast movement, Hunter hauled her against him. Her body collided with his and she sighed, her heart melting as she curled into his embrace.

His chest was hard. Protective.

The hand on her back was warm. And gentle.

Sandwiched between the perfect combination of unyielding strength and soothing comfort, she inhaled his familiar woodsy scent. The surge of happiness overwhelmed her and she buried her face against him, his soft jacket absorbing the embarrassing wet tracks on her cheek.

After a minute, Hunter said, "Just promise me something."

She slid her arms around his waist, blinked back the remaining tears and looked up at him. "Anything."

He glanced at the two coffin bars surrounded by guests dressed in black, their feet obscured by the mist from the fog machines. "No Elvis at the wedding," he said. "And no Goth-themed receptions."

Finally allowing herself to trust the joy, she let a smile creep up her face. "Can I ask the winner of the Pink Flamingo drag queen pageant to officiate?"

Hunter's eyes briefly flickered wider—but to his credit he said nothing.

She lifted an eyebrow. "Now who's afraid?"

"Good point," he said, his brow creased in humor, his fingers caressing her skin.

"So, tell me…" Her mojo firmly back in place, she flashed him her most charming smile and tipped her head curiously. "What kind of songs does The Hitchinator offer when I accept your proposal?"

A secretive smile spread across his face, and the light in his slate-blue eyes grew warmer. "I'll resend the message so you can hit 'Yes' and find out."

* * * * *

LET'S TALK
Romance

For exclusive extracts, competitions
and special offers, find us online: